ON THE RUN

Even as he spoke, he was running, with Julia dragging along behind, the red dust blowing up around their feet like smoke blazing a clear trail for their pursuers. Behind them came the howl of the Gwarulch, and a sound that Julia hadn't heard before—screaming and wild laughing, like that of an hysterical crowd. Mirran heard it too, and coughed out, "Glazed-Folk."

Julia grimaced, remembering the Glazed-Folk at the Namyr Gorge. She glanced behind to see if they were catching up, but there was nothing visible beyond the red dust. Then Mirran suddenly faltered, staggered for a few steps, and fell down. Julia stopped, and turned back, but he waved her on, gasping: "*Run*—run on! My legs are still too weak."

"No," said Julia firmly. "I won't leave you for them. I've still got my wand."

Mirran opened his mouth as if to say something, but only a rasping wheeze came out, and his head bent backwards toward the dust. Julia moved closer to him, the wand held ready in both hands.

THE RAGWITCH

GARTH NIX

TOR®

A TOM DOHERTY ASSOCIATES BOOK
NEW YORK

This is a work of fiction. All the characters and events portrayed in this book are fictitious, and any resemblance to real people or events is purely coincidental.

THE RAGWITCH

Cover art by Bryce Lee

A Tor Book
Published by Tom Doherty Associates, Inc.
175 Fifth Avenue
New York, N.Y. 10010

Tor® is a registered trademark of Tom Doherty Associates, Inc.

ISBN: 0-812-53506-5

First Tor edition: October 1994

Printed in the United States of America

0 9 8 7 6 5 4 3 2 1

To Shahnaz, my family, and friends.

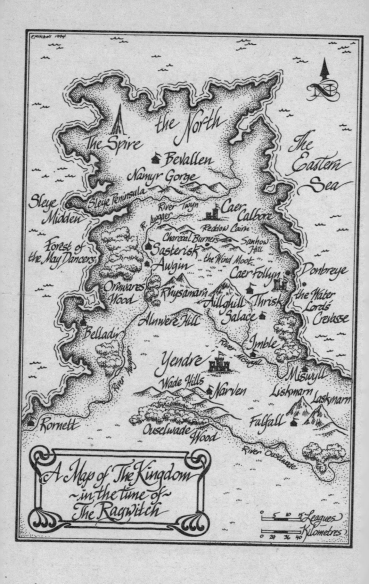

E. Mitchell 1994

the North

The Spire

Bevallen

Namyr Gorge

Sleye Peninsula

The Eastern Sea

Sleye Midden

River Twyn

R. Awgier

Caer Calbore

Redlow Cairn

Forest of the May Dancers

Charcoal Burners

Sasterisk

Sanhow Hill

Awgin

the Wind Moot

Caer Follyn

Donbreye

Ormwares Wood

Rhysamarn

Aillghill

Thrisk

the Water Lord's Crevasse

Alnwere Hill

Salace

Belladin

River Wanin

Ymble

Yendre

River Misuyll

Misuyll

Wade Hills

Narven

Liskmarn

Laskmarn

Rornett

Ouselwade Wood

Falfall

River Ouselwade

A Map of The Kingdom ~in the time of~ The Ragwitch

5 10 15 Leagues
Kilometres
0 24 36 40

CONTENTS

Contents

1

THE MIDDEN

C ome on, Paul!" shrieked Julia as she ran down
the dune, the sand sliding away under her bare
feet. Below her lay the beach, a white expanse
bordered by mounds of seaweed. Beyond the seaweed
lay the sea, a great mass of slow tumbling waves, each
solemnly dumping another load of the green-brown
kelp.

Julia didn't wait for an answer to her call—a brief
backward glance showed Paul atop the dune, staring
single-mindedly into the sea. She kept on running,
breaking into an erratic skip to avoid the stinging blue-
bottles cast ashore to die in the morning sun.

Entranced by the view, Paul slowly moved his gaze
along the beach, like a swivelling human telescope. He
looked mainly to the north, where grey rocks thrust out
into the sea, forming a spit, full of intricate pools and
dangerous channels.

Above the spit, a strange hill rose out of the sand, a

reddish hill, crowned with thousands of gleaming white fragments and shells. The hill dominated the shore, rising high above the lesser dunes that flanked it.

"Come on!" shouted Julia again. Paul looked down and saw that she was already walking towards the spit. He quickly switched from looking to walking mode, and took a diagonal path to meet her, half sliding down the face of the great dune.

"Isn't it fantastic?" burbled Julia, as Paul finally arrived at the spit, panting from his exertions. She spoke without looking at him, intent on the tiny fish that swirled about her toes in the rock pool.

"Yeah, great!" answered Paul enthusiastically. "Do you want to go out on the spit? We might see a dolphin from the end."

"Not now. Wouldn't you rather climb that?" asked Julia, pointing at the hill.

"What sort of hill is that?" asked Paul. "I've never seen a hill like that on a beach!"

"It's a midden. Daddy told me about it last night. You can just see it from the house."

"What's a midden?"

"An Aboriginal midden," explained Julia, "is sort of a really old garbage heap. It took thousands of years to build up, just by people dropping shells in the same place. That's what those white things are."

"But what about the red dirt?"

"Oh, that," whispered Julia, her eyes widening in mock fear. "The dirt is the remains of old, old bones."

"Maybe I don't want to go up there after all," said Paul, echoing Julia's tone of mock fear. Deep inside though, he was a little frightened. The Midden looked quite safe in the bright sunlight, but at night, it could easily be a different, more chilling place.

"Let's go then," shouted Julia, springing to her feet

and bounding up towards the Midden. Not quite so eager, Paul slowly got to his feet, and walked after her.

It took several minutes to climb to the top, as the shell fragments cut their bare feet, making it like walking across a field of broken glass. Still, it was possible to thread a precarious path through the shell patches by keeping to the sections of plain red earth.

On top of the Midden, the sea breeze was much stronger and the scent of salt was heavy in the air. From their vantage point, they could see clearly for kilometers, both to the north and south. With their newly extended horizon, an ocean-racing yacht had just become visible out to sea.

"The Sydney to Hobart race goes by here," said Paul, watching the yacht's spinnaker billow out to catch a sudden breeze. "We might see them go by if we stay long enough."

"Hey, I've found a nest!" cried Julia, who had started exploring the irregular bumps and hollows at the top of the Midden. Paul didn't come at once, so Julia reemerged from her hollow, and dragged him round to see her find.

The nest, if it was one, measured a good two meters in diameter, and was made of loosely woven sticks and dried mud. It was empty, save for a single ball of feathers about half a meter wide. Paul looked at it curiously, noticing that some of the feathers were longer than his arm, and very, very black.

"Julia, what sort of bird makes a nest like this?"

"Oh, some sort of sea eagle," replied Julia, who was poking at the ball of feathers. She found a scrap of brightly-colored cloth, and eagerly began to take the ball apart to find whatever might be inside.

"Sea eagles don't have black feathers," said Paul. "Anyway, this bird must be a lot bigger than a sea eagle."

"Must be a wedge-tailed eagle then. They're the biggest birds in Australia. Everyone knows that!"

"I think we ought to go," said Paul, a chill fear suddenly creeping up the back of his neck. As he spoke, the sun went behind a large black cloud that had sneaked in from the west. Almost instantly, the Midden was dark, the summer heat suddenly absent.

"I'll go when I find out what's in this," replied Julia, ripping feathers from the ball, "I think it's some sort of doll."

"Who cares?" shouted Paul. "This place isn't safe. Let's go!"

Julia ignored him, and continued to pull feathers from the ball. Already, she had uncovered a hand made from shiny pink cloth, and was pulling free a head.

In the twilight created by the cloud, a darker shadow swept across the nest, accompanied by a cawing shriek, horrifyingly loud. Instinctively, Paul looked up, and screamed. Hovering above them was a giant crow, its wings beating down a ferocious wind.

"Come on!" shouted Paul, holding a hand over his eyes to keep out the swirling dust. With the other, he grabbed Julia, and tried to pull her away from the nest.

"No!" cried Julia, pushing him away. "I've almost got it!"

Overhead the crow screamed and dropped like a stone, landing directly in front of Paul, who grabbed Julia. Both of them tumbled over backwards. The giant crow lunged forward as they fell, its vicious beak jabbing through the air, missing them by centimeters.

Lying on his back, Paul looked up into the crow's black eyes, glittering above the long, lethal beak. He saw the sudden spark of calculation as the crow decided who it was going to skewer.

The beak flashed through the air straight at Julia, but at the same instant, she pulled the rag doll free of the last remaining feathers. The crow disappeared in mid-lunge, leaving only an impotent shadow. Even that faded as the sunlight splashed onto the Midden, now no longer obscured by the black cloud.

"Look," said Julia, holding up the doll. "She's beautiful."

Paul looked at it, bemused, still half expecting the crow to come back. He saw an old rag doll in fairly good condition. It seemed unexceptional, save for the face, which to him looked malign and thoroughly evil. Its eyes were made of black-pupilled greenstone and seemed to follow him with an uncanny interest.

"It's evil!" exclaimed Paul, unable to believe his sister had become entranced by such an horrific thing. She hadn't even said anything about the giant crow, and now only had eyes for a grotesque doll.

"No, she isn't!" snapped Julia, clutching the doll to her and getting to her feet. "Her name is . . . her name is . . ."

"The Ragwitch," intoned a voice in Paul's mind, like the bass boom of a warning bell.

"Her name is Sylvie," said Julia, kissing it on the forehead. "Yes—I shall call her Sylvie."

As Julia kissed the rag doll, Paul thought he almost saw it curl a lip in satisfaction. He blinked—the doll's lips were unmoving, sewn into a perpetual smile.

Their walk back to the house felt strange to Paul. Normally, Julia skipped ahead, shouting at him to come and look at things, or just to catch up. Now she lagged behind, clutching the rag doll, hardly looking to left or right.

Crossing over from beach to grass, Paul felt more cheerful. They were almost at their house, and surely his parents would notice Julia's odd behavior; and they wouldn't approve of picking up a strange doll from the beach, particularly if he told them about the giant crow.

But he didn't. Within the first ten minutes, Paul knew that his mother couldn't see the rag doll. She'd even straightened Julia's shirt without paying any attention to the doll cradled in the girl's arms. If *she* couldn't see the doll, his businesslike father didn't have a hope. And Julia's behavior was put down to tiredness—normal after the first day's holiday at the beach.

"What about me?" Paul wanted to ask. "I'm not tired! Anyway, Julia never gets tired!"

But he knew that they wouldn't understand this simple logic. After all, they had a logic of their own. If Julia was tired, then Paul must be even more tired—so both of them would go to bed early.

Instead of going to bed and trying to forget his troubles, Paul went over to Julia's room. She was lying in bed, whispering to the doll. She didn't notice Paul until he spoke.

"Julia," Paul said anxiously. "Mum and Dad can't see your doll."

"I know," replied Julia smugly, looking up from the doll. "She told me that they wouldn't. You shouldn't be able to either, you know."

"Well, I *can* see it!" cried Paul angrily. "And I don't like it. It's evil and horrible, and it's making you go all strange!"

Julia was silent for a second, then she looked into the doll's black-pupilled eyes. They seemed to sparkle with their own dark flame, telling her what to do.

"Goodnight, Paul," Julia said, remotely. "Please turn the light off when you go."

"No," said Paul. "The doll told you to say that. You can see it in its eyes. Throw it away, Julia!"

Julia shivered, and Paul saw a tremor pass across her face. Slowly, she began to turn her head back to the Ragwitch, drawn to the black-glinting eyes. Horrified,

Paul dashed forward to grab it, to throw it away—anywhere away from Julia.

But when he touched the doll, it spat aloud and huddled closer to Julia, twining its three-fingered hands through her hair. And a chill voice burst into Paul's head, hurting the inside of his ears and somehow cutting at his mind.

"I am the Ragwitch!" screamed the voice in his head. "Your sister is nothing—she is only part of ME!"

With that "ME!," the Ragwitch screamed again, still inside Paul's head. He felt his arms stiffen, the muscles tensing, and suddenly he felt himself being hurled backwards, without control, to land sprawling against the door. Desperately, he tried to get his hands to obey him, but they crept up the door, towards the light-switch, and then, with a frenzied twitch, flicked off the lights.

In the darkness, the Ragwitch spoke again, but this time the voice was real—and it came from Julia. Low, and hissing, it crawled about Paul, sending shivers from his stomach out along his spine.

"Leave, boy. What can you do against my power? Your sister is mine, and MINE ALONE!"

Paul shuddered under the impact of the voice, and felt tears start in his eyes. The voice got into his head, and again his hands were moving, under Her control. Slowly, his hand turned the doorknob, and his legs began shuffling him out, away from Julia, out of the darkness and into the light.

"No," said Julia, in her normal, everyday voice. She sat up in bed, and looked straight at Paul. A shaft of light from the open door caught her face, and as their eyes met, Paul felt his muscles relax. Hesitantly, he tried to move, and found himself free of Her control.

"She wants to take me somewhere," whispered Julia, her face contorting under some great, unseen pressure. "Paul, you must . . . She wants to take me to . . ."

Looking into Julia's eyes, Paul saw them suddenly glow, and change color—a black wash floating out to cover the white. Slowly, the black coalesced around the pupil, and the white started to green over in exact duplication of the rag doll's evil eyes.

Paul felt himself becoming drowsy, looking into those gleaming, black-pupilled eyes. They seemed to get bigger, become like lanterns . . . lanterns illuminating a ground far below, as he fell towards them . . .

"Run!" screamed Julia—the real Julia. "Paul! Run!"

Shocked free from the mesmeric eyes, Paul turned and ran, slamming the door behind him.

Paul spent the rest of the night half-awake, with the light on and his door open. Every time a board creaked, he felt a start of fear—but the house was old, and prone to settling, and nothing stalked him through the night. His parents, normally guardians against fear, slept with an unnatural soundness, and could not be woken.

At last, towards dawn, fear became weaker than exhaustion, and Paul fell into a troubled sleep. He dreamt of giant black crows screaming in from the sky, only to turn into huge rag dolls, with black-pupilled eyes against green—eyes that grew larger and larger, and more menacing, filling the whole horizon with their glowing evil . . .

With a stifled scream, Paul fell out of bed, dragging the blankets with him. It took a few seconds for him to really wake up, and his heart to slow its pounding. Bright, cheery sunlight filtered in around the curtains. Sleepily, Paul looked at the radio clock next to his bed. It said six o"clock—at least an hour too early to get up. Paul yawned and climbed back into bed, rearranging the blankets with a few kicks and half-hearted dragging motions.

He was just rearranging the pillow, when he heard the front door close—the slight, snicking sound of someone easing the door shut as quietly as possible.

Paul knew it had to be Julia. His parents never woke up before eight. He felt an unpleasant butterfly in his stomach, remembering the events of the night before. And Julia's words: "She wants to take me somewhere."

"I'll have to save her," said Paul aloud, hoping the sound of his own voice would make him feel better. But it didn't—it only made everything seem even scarier than before. He just didn't know what to do. Julia was the one who knew what to do—Julia was the one who always knew, and now she was the problem.

Paul felt tears welling up in his eyes, and a terrible feeling of hopelessness swept over him. "What would Julia do, if it was me?" he suddenly thought—and there was the answer. Julia wouldn't abandon him, so he wouldn't abandon her. He quickly threw on his clothes, laced his sandshoes, and ran out of the house, not bothering to be quiet with the door.

There was no sign of Julia, but her tracks were easy to follow across the sand and down to the sea. Paul ran at first, but he soon slowed down. It was too tiring to run on sand.

But Julia hadn't stopped at the sea. Turning along the coast, she was heading for the rocky spit—or the Midden. Paul thought he knew which one it would be. Grimly, he began to run again, up towards the Midden, the hill of ancient bones.

As Paul expected, Julia was there, kneeling near the giant crow's nest, doing something with the sticks that it was made of. Paul could see no sign of the rag doll. Relieved, he sprinted up the last few meters, calling out, "Julia!"

Julia turned around—and Paul skidded to a stop in shock. He felt like he'd been winded, struck so hard he couldn't breathe at all. For the person in front of him wasn't Julia at all, but a hideous mixture of girl and doll: half flesh, half cloth, and the eyes and face had nothing of Julia left at all, only the evil features of the doll.

"Callach!" spat the Ragwitch, raising one three-fingered hand—and Paul was rooted to the spot: paralyzed, save for his eyes, which darted from side to side, looking for escape. He wanted to close them, to not see whatever was going to happen, but his eyelids refused to move.

The Ragwitch laughed, a chilling cackle that sent a spark of fear right through Paul. Then She turned back to the nest, and started to rearrange the sticks.

He had obviously been granted a slight reprieve. Paul watched the Ragwitch with some glimmerings of hope. She was taking the sticks out of the nest and making them into a sort of pyramid, breaking the tangled ring and giving it an ordered shape.

She worked quickly. In minutes the nest was no more and the pyramid was complete: a neat construction of sticks, as tall as Paul. He watched, fascinated, as the Ragwitch drew designs in the red earth around the pyramid—strange symbols that were all straight lines and nasty looking pictures, like some ancient form of writing.

She didn't look at Paul until the writing was complete. Then, She stood up, looming over him. Even in the short time since he'd first seen Her at the nest, She'd grown rapidly and was now at least two meters tall.

He noticed that She now had teeth as well—rows of thin, shark-like teeth, hideously out of place in that smiling, red-lipped doll's face.

She came closer, and Paul shuddered, watching the teeth as she leaned over him. But he made his eyes go out of focus—he wouldn't look into Her eyes, not after the night before. Her breath struck his face, cold, and somehow smelling of darkness and fear. Paul stared his eyes into even more of a blur, and waited to be killed.

Then the Ragwitch spoke, using Julia's voice—a voice changed and tainted but still recognizably Julia's.

"You will stand here forever, boy, as a monument to those who would keep me penned here. Alive, unmoving, and wishing you were dead. Much like your sister. Yes, she still lives . . . but only inside Me!"

The Ragwitch laughed again, and turned back to the pyramid of sticks. She extended her three-fingered hand, and began to chant: a rhythmic, dissonant series of words that rose and fell in a grating counterpoint, jarring Paul's ears.

As She continued the chant, sparks started to form about Her hand. The bright red flecks of light danced around, forming a globe of flickering light about her three fingers. Suddenly, the Ragwitch stopped chanting, and the globe of sparks flew forward into the pyramid of sticks, which exploded into flame. As the red flames flickered up, Paul felt a rush of cold bursting out from the fire, as though the fire itself were a giant, living icicle.

The Ragwitch bent over and drew another sign in the red soil. The flames licked still higher, and turned green at the tips, and a dull roaring filled the air, like a rushing wave. She stepped into the fire and turned to face Paul with her arms outstretched. Paul saw that She was laughing again, but he could only hear the roaring and the cold blasting at him from Her magical pyre.

Then the flames blew sideways, almost out to Paul's feet. Each tongue of flame was like the petal of a flower, with the Ragwitch in the middle, cupped like a dragonfly in a water lily. The flames flickered once, twice, and then snapped back in a blinding flash. The pyramid exploded, sending burning sticks flying into the air, some landing on Paul, to scar him with their icy flames.

There was no sign of the Ragwitch—and Paul found that he could move again. Numb from fear and disbelief, Paul's first thoughts were of anger.

"You were wrong," he shouted at the sky. "Your magic's no good. I'm going to find you and get Julia back! You won't get away from me!"

The shouting seemed to help a bit, and Paul felt strangely confident. Carefully, he began to gather the still-burning sticks, rearranging them into a rough copy of the Ragwitch's pyramid.

Together again, the sticks burnt heartily, washing Paul with cold. He looked at the red flames, had his second thoughts, and copied the last sign he'd seen the Ragwitch draw. The flames turned green at the tips, and the roaring sound began. Paul took a deep breath, screwed his eyes shut, and stepped into the icy heart of the fire.

2

THE FOREST OF THE MAY DANCERS/ THE SEA CAVES

A vagrant wind pushed leaves aside as it made an erratic progress through the forest, cooling the warm afternoon air. Birds called in the wind's wake, hawking after insects that the sudden breeze had carried with it.

Paul felt the wind against his face, refreshing after the stabbing cold of the fire. This was no sea air, he knew, for it was heavy with the dank, green smell of trees. The light that crept through his slowly opening eyes was different too: a cool, diffuse light, filtered through a thousand layers of leaves.

Eyes fully opened, Paul looked about cautiously, already afraid of what he'd done, and where he might be. All around him, great trees towered, their upper branches interlocking to block out the sky. Vines crept around their trunks, growing out amongst the lesser trees and bushes that struggled to survive in the shady half-light of the lower forest.

Something rustled in the undergrowth to Paul's side, a slight noise, no more than a falling branch. Even so, he leapt away with a sudden surge of fright-born energy. But the noise faded and was lost in the silence of the trees.

Gingerly, Paul began to pick his way through the spiky undergrowth. He thought about looking for Julia, but there was obviously no one about. Worse, he couldn't see the sun through the leafy canopy, though even if he could, he still wouldn't know which direction to take.

"You have to know where you are to know where to go," muttered Paul, mostly to hear his own voice. It sounded strange in the forest, a short break in the silence, soon gone and instantly forgotten. Did I even speak at all, wondered Paul, or just think loudly to myself?

After only a few meters, he came to a small clearing—a blanket-sized patch of grass and daisies, alone in the wilderness. Even that small distance had taken its toll. Shorts, while fine for the beach, were not the best clothing for thorn-laden undergrowth and spiked bushes. At least some of the scratches were from blackberries, Paul thought, comparing the purple stains on his fingers to the long red scratches on his legs. Starvation wouldn't be an immediate problem, though he was already bored with a diet of blackberries.

Beyond the clearing, the forest grew even thicker: darker, more impenetrable and daunting. Reluctant to enter that darkness, Paul sat down in the brightest patch of greenish sunlight and thought about his predicament.

First, he thought, I am all alone in a forest. I have no idea where it is, as I got here by walking through a fire. My sister has been taken over by a magical rag doll, and I have to do something about it.

But what? Julia was the one who had the ideas, and

knew what to do. Paul was a follower. He needed pro-
gramming for something like this—he needed someone
to give him instructions.

I wasn't meant to be in impossible situations, Paul
thought mournfully, eyeing the green walls that surrounded him.

"It's not fair!" he shouted at the forest. But the trees
absorbed the shout, and it was gone. No one will come,
said the darkness between the trees, you will wander the
forest, alone until you die.

"No, I won't," Paul whispered, brushing away the
morbid thoughts that swelled up from the back of his
head. "I'll find a path, and people, and Julia!" With this
whisper, Paul summoned up some reserve of determination, and got to his feet. Filled with resolve, he plunged
forward into the dim forest.

An hour later, much of the resolve and determination
had drained away. There was still no end to the forest,
and the light was getting dimmer. Cool breezes were no
longer refreshing—they were just cool, and becoming
cold. Worse, there were no more blackberries. Without
their refreshing juice, Paul was drying out, his stamina
fading as his throat parched.

But he could think of nothing else to do, so he kept
on, dragging his scratched legs through more bushes
and brambles, hoping to find another clearing or a path.
Gradually, the light slipped away, and the shadows
steadily merged shifting from grey to black.

The shadows at last became one, and the forest was in
true twilight, if only for a short time. Paul paused to look
at the darkening sky, and began to hear the noises of the
forest night. Still he kept on, stumbling over the roots and
vines he could no longer see. Panic was beginning to fill
his mind, and he could not think of stopping.

Suddenly, without notice, it was fully dark—a blackness so complete that Paul couldn't even see his hand in

front of his face. Exhausted, he slipped to the ground, shivering between the two cradling arms of a giant root.

Everywhere there were subtle sounds: leaves crunching, twigs snapping—each tiny noise magnified by the total blackness. Paul's heartbeat filled his ears, vibrating up through his cheekbones, a bass rhythm in counterpoint to the tenor sounds of something creeping through the night.

The noises became louder, and Paul stopped breathing, holding a hand over his mouth and nose. Whatever was making the noise was large, purposeful—and it was sniffing . . . searching . . . following his trail. Fear, sweat and blackberries, the scent of a hiding Paul.

The noise became footsteps, gentle, stalking footsteps, coming towards Paul. It knows I'm here, thought Paul desperately. It's coming quietly, hoping to catch me asleep, or unawares, it's . . .

Here! A sudden rush of footsteps, an abortive leap by Paul, and something cold and leathery wrapped around his legs. Ankles trapped, he crashed forward, face down onto the brown mulch of the forest floor.

More leathery tentacles wrapped around his wrists, and Paul's mind gave way to fear and exhaustion, screaming back into the impenetrable fortress of unconsciousness.

Paul awoke in sunlight, with the vague feeling that he was lucky to be awake at all. He felt strange, cramped, and in an unfamiliar bed. Then, fully awake, he remembered the events of the night before. In the daylight he saw that the leathery tentacles were just some sort of rope, and they were the reason for his cramped awakening.

He was lying on a wooden bed that was a little like a shallow baby's cot, with his hands and feet tied to the side-rails. Surrounding the bed were earth walls—he was obviously in some sort of hole. High above, the sun beamed down, harsh and bright without any leafy interference. On the far side of the hole, a rope ladder hung down from the surface, which was three meters or so above, at least by Paul's reckoning.

A prison-hole, thought Paul gloomily, just like in the film on T.V. the week before last. Only, in the film the bad guys ended up in the hole. But then, in the movies, heroes didn't go running around weird forests in shorts, sneakers and dirty white T-shirts. They also didn't worry about things like food and drink, Paul thought, acutely aware of his dry and cracking lips, and the dull, rumbling complaint of his stomach.

He tried licking his lips, but there was no moisture in his mouth. Even tears were beyond his dried-out body, and he found himself unable to cry. Closing his eyes, Paul thought he might as well die then and there, and save himself the trouble later on—when a few lumps of earth fell onto his chest.

"What were you doing in the forest?" a voice suddenly asked from somewhere above—behind Paul's head, so he couldn't see who it was. "And how did you get where you were?"

Paul's mind snapped back from his despairing thoughts, and he craned his neck back to see who was talking. But he couldn't raise his body from the bed, and so couldn't arch back far enough. He tried to answer, but only a dull croak came out.

"You wish for some water?" asked the voice, though not in a particularly compassionate tone. "Open your mouth."

Paul did so immediately, and a cascade of water splashed over his face, and up his nose. A little found his mouth. Despite being nearly drowned, it was a very welcome drink, revitalizing Paul's tiny store of determination, and lessening his feelings of despair.

"Now," said the stern, deep voice. "What were you doing in our forest?"

"I didn't mean anything," croaked Paul. "I was just looking for my sister, and then . . . I was just looking for people."

"People?" said the voice. "What sort of people were you looking for?"

Frightened by the voice, Paul didn't answer for a moment. It sounded odd, murky, and overlaid with rustling sounds, as if the speaker had to think before talking, and move his lips through a layer of leaves.

"I wanted to find someone. Anyone who could help me find Julia. A town, or a house, where I could find out where I was . . . where the forest is, I mean."

"Julia, towns, houses," muttered the voice, as if cataloguing items of interest. "You won't find any of them here. And you say you don't know where the forest is?"

"No, I don't . . . is it . . . is it very far away from Australia?"

"Australia?" repeated the voice, with an odd pronunciation of the name—all drawn and twisted. "Perhaps you are even further away than you can reckon. If it is of any use to you, this is the Forest of the May Dancers . . . I am a May Dancer," added the voice, suddenly closer. "At least, that is what your kind call us."

Paul felt a slight shudder go through his heart—a tremor of fear that passed through like a metal sliver. Footsteps crunched on the dirt above, and Paul looked up.

He had expected to see some sort of man. But the May Dancer who looked down on him had only the shape of a human. He was covered in shifting patterns of leaves, that rustled and moved about his body, revealing skin the texture and color of ancient bark. His head was also covered in leaves, which streamed behind him in a russet mane. And his eyes were those of an animal: the eyes of a cat carefully watching its prey.

Paul felt just like a mouse caught in the petrifying gaze of a hunter. Even the smallest movement might cause this strange creature to spring, to suddenly snap the tension.

"So," said the May Dancer, half closing his fearsome eyes. "You have not seen our kind before."

It was a statement rather than a question, Paul understood. Somehow, he had become the mouse that the cat couldn't be bothered chasing.

"You have never seen a May Dancer before," said the creature above, in a half-whisper, as if thinking aloud. "Therefore, you have never seen us dance on the borders of the forest. In fact, as you have never even heard of us, you cannot even be of this Kingdom. And you seek a . . . Julia."

Without warning, the May Dancer leapt across the hole, and was gone. Startled, Paul instinctively flexed his body to leap away—succeeding only in hurting his wrists and back, held by those leathery ropes.

The next few hours passed in a half-dream, marked by the slow drifting of clouds overhead. Faint sounds carried to him, the noises of the forest: strange birdcalls, and occasionally the heavier thumping of something larger passing nearby. From all this, Paul assumed that he was still in the forest, though the clear sky above indicated a large clearing.

By mid-afternoon, the sun was high above the hole. Paul lay beneath a layer of sunshine with only his feet in shadow, unable to look up because of the glare. The sun made him tired, despite his hunger, and he began to slowly drift off into a nightmarish sleep.

When he awoke, the hole was in darkness, though it was not cold. There were slight sounds all about the hole, sounds that might have been footsteps, or muffled

whispers . . . sounds that Paul almost heard, and then
wondered if he'd imagined them.

Then the May Dancer spoke again. "We have talked
of you amongst those of our people here, and you are to
say more. Questions will be asked, and you will answer
them. Do you understand?"

"Yes," said Paul. "Yes—anything you like."

Another Dancer, further from the hole, asked the first
question, in a softer, stranger voice than the original
May Dancer. The words seemed to be more of a wind
song than speech, and Paul couldn't understand it, being
mesmerized by the lilting tone, rather than listening.
The first May Dancer repeated the question: "How did
you come to be in the forest?"

"I was following my sister," replied Paul. He wasn't
sure how he'd come to the forest himself. "Her and that
horrible doll. They'd built a sort of fire—and then they
just disappeared. The fire was sort of scattered, but I re-
built it and jumped through—and I was in the forest. I
didn't mean to be there—I was just trying to find Julia."

"Enough," interrupted the May Dancer. Paul listened
to him talking to the others, whispers like wind in the
reeds, a tune played by the earth rather than by man. It
was rather eerie, he thought, listening to the long, sighing notes in the darkness. Only then did Paul notice that
there were no stars—none at all in the vast expanse of
black sky.

"Why did your sister build this fire?" asked the May
Dancer, his voice loud above the whisperings.

"I don't know," replied Paul, trying to make out the
May Dancer's form above him. "It wasn't really her. I
mean it was her building the fire, but she'd been taken
over. The doll had her under its control." Paul thought
back to the Midden, and the words Julia had spat at
him, in another voice. "The doll spoke to me before it

. . . they jumped in the fire. It talked of being imprisoned, and it called itself . . . the Ragwitch."

"The Ragwitch," echoed the May Dancer, the words twisting into a screaming wind, to be picked up by the other Dancers, and made into a raging shout. A shout of anger and hatred, but also a shout of ancient fear. The Dancers were moving as well, no longer silently gathered around the prison-hole. Branches snapped and crackled, the ground thudded with their heavy, stamping footsteps. Paul closed his eyes, and turned his head to the side, blocking the sound from at least one ear. The noise above was like a violent storm, filling the darkness with threats and danger—the sounds heard by people found crushed by falling trees, or struck by lightning during a thunderstorm.

Slowly, the noises died. The May Dancers crept back to the hole, drained of noise, if not the fear and anger. Paul listened to their whisperings again, tense, waiting for them to decide his fate. They seemed to be arguing in some fashion, for there were many interruptions, and changes of tone—but there was no foot-stamping anger, nor the sudden violence of their shouting.

A few stars appeared in the sky. Paul watched them spring into sight, and dimly saw the ragged edge of the long black cloud that had cloaked them. The cloud was blowing north, and more stars began to sparkle, lightening the sky.

The May Dancer leaned over to speak again, and Paul saw a dim silhouette, edged with starlight. Past him, Paul could vaguely make out "human" shapes, blacker than the darkness behind them. They moved slightly all the time, shifting positions to no apparent pattern or purpose.

"We have decided to release you," the May Dancer said flatly. "You will be taken to the edge of the forest, and from there you can go where you will—though you must not come here again."

Paul nodded dumbly, unable to speak. They were going to let him go, and the forest was the last place he'd ever go back to! But he was still wary of the May Dancers. They'd captured him and tied him up, and now they were going to let him go—just like that. But none of it made any sense! Why bother to tie him up, if they were going to let him go all along?

The May Dancer dropping into the hole made Paul start, then he relaxed as his bonds were untied. It was odd to see the leafy Dancer so close—the smell of him was like trees newly washed in a summer storm.

Blood rushed into Paul's hands and feet so quickly he yelped and bent to massage his ankles. A second later, a leafy hand covered his eyes, leaving behind two large green leaves which totally blocked his sight.

"Hey," exclaimed Paul, letting go of his ankles to feel his eyes. "What are you doing to my eyes?"

"It is a law," replied the May Dancer, picking up Paul, and easily hoisting him onto his shoulder. "No one of your kind is allowed to see us or the forest, save at our dances."

"But I've already seen you . . ." said Paul. "I mean, just briefly—I didn't really see anything . . ."

"You saw enough," said the Dancer. "But you are only a child, and our Laws are not strict for children of any folk. Also, there is the matter of your arrival, and your purpose . . . it is better that we do not interfere . . ."

The May Dancer stopped talking, and Paul felt himself tip sideways, as they climbed over the edge of the hole. He could dimly see the starlight through his leaf-blindfold, and when it suddenly became dark, he guessed they were deep in the forest—a guess made easier by the crackling of leaves and twigs underfoot.

An hour later, Paul was eagerly waiting for the leaves

and twigs to stop crackling and the May Dancer to stop his steady, stomach-bruising stride. Paul had an awfully cramped leg, and his position was several degrees from comfortable.

At last the May Dancer stopped and lowered Paul onto the ground—face down. The leaves fell from his eyes, and he rolled over to look up into the night. Ahead, the moon had just risen to illuminate the open lands beyond the forest.

* * *

Far to the north of the Forest of the May Dancers, the sea beat against the cliffs and dark waves foamed into deep caves—the Sea Caves, ancient home of many of the Ragwitch's evil-hearted minions.

In a black pool, far underground, the water seethed and bubbled, and the air above it grew suddenly chill. A red light filled the cave, banishing the darkness of centuries. The light grew brighter, and then the Ragwitch appeared in the pool, Her arms still outstretched, the eversmiling mouth still chanting. She had lost all trace of Julia's form, and was now only a gross parody of a rag doll. She was taller than a man, with huge bulging arms and legs that leaked straw. Her painted face appeared even more malign in its new proportions.

Floating easily in the pool, She looked around the cave and laughed—the chilling cackle that had scared Paul, and thousands of others over her grim past. Still cackling, She hauled herself up on a ledge, and took stock of Her surroundings.

Julia woke with a start, suddenly feeling that she was late for something. She sat up sleepily, opening her eyes—to see nothing but absolute blackness. Everything was black, totally black, and for a second Julia panicked, thinking she'd been struck blind. Then she remembered previous mornings, of waking up before dawn with the curtains tightly closed against any light that might be outside.

Giggling a little nervously, Julia reached down to throw off her blankets—and somersaulted. Just by reaching forward—but it was a slow somersault, like being underwater. Forgetting to be scared, Julia somersaulted again, and then did a few corkscrews ending with a flip. She seemed to be suspended in something like water, but it was stiffer, less fluid—like glue. And she could still breathe.

Then Julia remembered the Ragwitch.

"Oh, Paul," whispered Julia. "How could I be so stupid?"

A dull rumble, like distant laughter, punctuated her whisper, and at the same time, Julia caught sight of a small spark of light, like a candle in a distant window. As it was the only thing visible in the blackness, Julia headed for it, breaststroking through the strange atmosphere.

Slowly, the light became brighter, and Julia saw that it was some sort of globe. It seemed to produce the light itself, in irregular flashes—occasionally shifting through the spectrum, but always coming back to a clear white light.

Julia circled it, delighting in the light that made her new environment so clear and beautiful. She flipped end over end with ease, breaking into a swan dive to float slowly down past the globe. An eddy in the fluid pushed her close to the globe, and without thinking, she touched it.

Instantly, all was black again, and the fluid suddenly went cold. A voice came to her mind, chill and biting—the voice of the Ragwitch.

"Ah—you have found your way to the globe. But where do you think you are, little Julia?"

"I don't know," shouted Julia, half-angry, but afraid to show this to the awful creature who spoke into her mind.

"You are inside me," whispered the Ragwitch maliciously. "Your essence has been consumed. But I will let you live a little longer, for my amusement . . . and other things. Perhaps they will amuse you too, my little Julia, who loves her dolls. Look into the globe . . ."

Julia promptly somersaulted away, deciding not to do anything the Ragwitch wanted—though she felt more scared than ever. But even as she straightened out to swim away, a force gripped her, holding fiercely to the muscles in her arms and legs, twisting them back and forth, rippling them spastically under the skin. Then with a sudden wrench, her head twisted back towards the globe, and the rest of her body followed painfully.

Julia closed her eyes, but the thing inside pushed them open, making her look at the globe. Again, Julia forced them closed, only to have her own hands rise up to keep them prized open. Open—and looking directly into the swirling colors of the globe, colors that seemed to swarm out, enveloping her in a mist, suddenly going from rainbow-colored to a dull, choking grey.

It swept her up, and dashed her down into the globe. Falling, she felt her body become weightless—and then nonexistent. Without any physical sensations at all, Julia fell into darkness.

What might have been days or years later, Julia felt her senses returning. She could feel pain, and sense a glimmer of light emanating from somewhere. But her body felt strange and cumbersome, and her lips felt cold and leathery to her clumsy tongue.

Hesitantly, she opened her eyes, letting them adjust to the light. They hurt at first, but slowly came into focus.

She seemed to be in a rocky cave which was bathed in a dim reddish light. Eagerly, Julia looked around, hope welling up inside her. Escape from the Ragwitch?

Then she took a step forward and, looking down, saw her feet—long, leathery feet, that somehow seemed to be stitched, and were leaking a yellow, wet straw stuffing . . .

Julia's scream was the first and last time she had control of the Ragwitch's mouth. Even as it echoed, it was overlaid with a grim cackle, and Julia was paralyzed. She could still see, and hear, and feel, but could no longer move even the most insignificant muscle.

"For your amusement," said the Ragwitch out into the cave, though it was solely for Julia to hear. "For your amusement I will let you see through my eyes, hear through my ears, feel what I touch. But you will never inhabit your body again." Then the Ragwitch laughed, an obscene cackle, echoing out in the dark underground chamber. Still laughing, She began to run through the black tunnels, heading upwards towards the light.

3

AWGINN/THE SPIRE

After the May Dancer dumped him on the edge of the forest, Paul spent an uncomfortable few hours trying to sleep in a leaf-filled hollow, but he kept waking at the slightest noise, so he spent the remainder of the night awake and listening. Fortunately, dawn came before too long, promising something better than a cold hollow frequented by ants.

In the bright new sunlight, Paul saw that the lands ahead were clear, and obviously populated. Green fields stretched as far as he could see, gently climbing over small hills, or around the occasional small wood or copse—each full of trees quite different from those in the dark, crowded forest.

The forest lay quite high on the hill behind him, so Paul went straight down, delighting in the ability to run free of vines and clinging roots. Every now and then, a rough stone wall barred his progress—proof that these pleasant green hills were inhabited.

Then, as if further proof were needed, Paul spotted a flock of sheep and, more importantly, a shepherd. Eagerly, he ran towards them—before suddenly faltering. What if the shepherd were another creature, like the May Dancers, or possibly something worse? Paul quickly turned back to the nearest stone wall, and hid near where the shepherd and his flock should pass.

As they drew closer, his fear lessened. The shepherd wore a rough wool cloak, but the hood was pushed well back, revealing the cheerful, straggly-bearded face of an old man, who was whistling between his two front teeth—a pleasant tune, that sounded a little like "Greensleeves."

Paul needed no more, so he stood up and said, "Hello!"

The shepherd looked up, and stopped whistling. He looked dumbfounded by Paul's sudden appearance, and made no move to speak—or indeed, to do anything.

"Hello," said Paul, giving him a small wave. This seemed to puzzle the shepherd even more. He looked over his shoulder once, then looked past Paul, up to the forest, before answering, and his hand fell to the cudgel thrust through his belt.

"Hello," said the shepherd, warily. "What are you doing up here?"

"Nothing," replied Paul. "I just came down—out of the forest . . ."

"The forest!" interrupted the shepherd, quickly making a strange sign with thumb and forefinger against his head. "What were you doing in the forest? You didn't upset the May Dancers?"

"No . . ." said Paul hesitantly, somewhat taken aback by the old man's vehemence. "I don't think so. They let me go. One of them even carried me out of the forest—he dropped me just up there, at the top of the hill."

The shepherd appeared quite relieved at this, and

Paul noticed that he was no longer fingering the thick wooden cudgel at his side.

"That is well. The May Dancers are strange folk, best left undisturbed by the likes of us. Which village are you from, lad—and where did you get your strange garments?"

"I'm not from any village," Paul said, wishing that he was from somewhere nearby. He fingered the dirty hem of his T-shirt, and added, "And these are my normal clothes."

"Not from any village?" the shepherd asked, backing off and making the sign with his thumb and forefinger again. "Carried here by the May Dancers ..."

He began to back off still further, so Paul tried to put him at ease. "I'm only a boy—I was just looking for my sister. It's hard to explain ... but I'd never even heard of the May Dancers before last night. Honest!"

"Just a boy," repeated the shepherd, as if trying to convince himself this was true. "You're not ... a creature from the North?"

"No. I'm a normal boy. It's just that strange things have been happening ..." Paul looked back over his shoulder, up at the brooding forest. Suddenly, the full enormity of it all became too much. He was alone in a strange world populated by strange creatures and suspicious old men, and worst of all, there was no Julia to tell him what to do. Unable to help it, he sat down on the stone wall, and began to cry, brushing away the tears with the back of a dirty hand.

"Here, then," said the shepherd, somewhat surprised. "I meant no harm. Some strange folk sometimes cross near the forest—some of them might even take the shape of a young lad. But tears are beyond that sort ... I think." The shepherd looked at his flock for a second, and then at the sky, where the sun was just climbing up to its morning brilliance. "You'd best come with me, now. We'll start back down to the village. The sheep'll just have to eat as best they can on the way."

Paul looked up and, taking a deep breath, said (almost steadily), "Thank you. I'm sorry to make your sheep go hungry."

"Nay, lad," said the shepherd. "I've a bit of fodder for them at home, and they'll be up here tomorrow for a week. Here—you go over there, and we'll have 'em turned around before they knows it."

On the way down to the village, the shepherd told Paul that his name was Malgar, commonly known as Malgar the shepherd, as there were two other (unrelated) Malgars in the village of Awginn-on-Awgaer.

Paul listened carefully, and asked several questions about the village and the surrounding lands. Malgar answered easily, and gave no sign that he knew Paul was a stranger, not only to the village, but to the whole country.

He explained that Awginn lay in the Canton of Sasterisk, a large town to the northeast. This, with twelve other Cantons, made up the Kingdom of Yendre. It was more a loose collection of states than a Kingdom, except in times of war and trouble, of which the country had been free for many years. Malgar knew of no other lands, except for the wild country to the north, in which no people dwelt.

Paul had already guessed that he had been taken to another world by the Ragwitch's fire, and was now completely sure he wasn't anywhere on Earth. He had never heard of the places Malgar talked of, and the May Dancers were obviously not something he had dreamed up, since Malgar knew they lived in the forest. Paul felt sick at the thought that he was impossibly far from home. Running off to rescue Julia seemed like the dumbest thing he'd ever done.

It took several hours to walk down the gently sloping

fields, and through countless gates in the low stone fences. They saw a few other shepherds and their flocks, but Malgar took paths away from them, as if he didn't want Paul to meet them. And still they kept on walking, till Paul was staggering along behind, despairing of ever reaching the village, having a rest and getting something to eat beyond a piece of Malgar's bread and cheese. He was half dreaming of water beds and roast chicken, when Malgar stopped, and pointed out a stand of oaks ahead. Between them, and some distance away, Paul saw the dark blue strip of a river.

"The Awgaer," said Malgar. "Many boats pass along it, from Sasterisk down to the sea."

"It doesn't look wide enough for boats," said Paul in a small, worn-out voice. "It must only be ten meters wide at the most. You couldn't get much of a boat down that, surely?"

"This is one of the narrow sections, lad. It widens out before and after this point. But you are right. The river folk use special craft of narrow beam and shallow draught, which they pole along at a great pace. Strange people, but kindly enough. Come—the village is only a little way along the river."

In fact, Malgar's "little way" was still at least a kilometer. Despite his hunger pangs, Paul was half-asleep by the time they got there—so much so that he hardly looked at the neat, whitewashed stone cottages, with their yellow thatched roofs. It wasn't until they stood in the village square that he lifted his head to gaze about through eyes heavy with exhaustion.

In front of him, Malgar stood frowning, obviously in deep thought. Past Malgar stood a large building with a faded inn sign hanging above the door—a green head, garlanded with yellow flowers.

"Now we're here," said Malgar, "I don't rightly know what to do with you. I have to get these sheep home, but it's still half a league to my stead." He scratched his head again, and cast a slightly wistful glance at the inn, before deciding. "Well, best you come with me, lad. Can you still walk?"

Paul nodded, unenthusiastic about the prospect of walking further, and started to stand up, when a man stepped up from behind him, and laid a hand on Malgar's shoulder.

"Going where, Malgar Sheep-herder?"

Malgar turned to face the man, and inclined his head in a sort of half-bow. Paul wondered why he did that—the other man didn't look much different. He was dressed in much the same way as Malgar, except he had a short dagger hanging from his belt rather than a bog-oak cudgel. He was younger too, black-haired, with a long drooping moustache and sharp blue eyes.

"To tell you the truth, Sir Aleyne," said Malgar, with some relief, "I'm glad you're here." Rapidly, he outlined how he'd found Paul, and the small amount the boy had told him about the May Dancers, his lost sister and his home.

Aleyne listened carefully, occasionally glancing towards Paul. When Malgar had finished, he said, "Take your sheep home, Malgar. I will take the boy. To the inn, for rest—and then, I think, to Rhysamarn."

"Rhysamarn?" asked Malgar, obviously upset. "You really think the boy should go there?"

"I would say it is the only place for him," replied Aleyne. He looked down at Paul, who had fallen asleep against a large, conveniently resting sheep. Paul was much the worse the wear for his adventures, and Aleyne saw only a short, slightly plump boy of eleven or so, covered in dirt—a strange appearance for a visitor from other lands.

"He will sleep through this afternoon and night, I think," continued Aleyne. "And perhaps tomorrow. I shall take him to Rhysamarn myself, the day after. You have done well, Malgar."

Malgar looked down on the boy anxiously. "He seems a nice enough lad. He won't come to any . . . harm . . . on Rhysamarn?"

Aleyne smiled, and picked Paul up, easily cradling him in his strong arms. "It is the Mountain of the Wise, Malgar—not some cavern of the Ragwitch."

"The Ragwitch . . ." muttered Paul in his sleep. Aleyne looked down and saw Paul grimace as he spoke, teeth clenched and lips drawing back in a feral snarl.

"Yes," he said, as Malgar made the sign against evil magic, "Definitely, he must go to Rhysamarn."

* * *

As the night inked into the sky, the Ragwitch climbed out of the cave mouth and surveyed Her realm. Awe-stricken, Julia watched through the Ragwitch's eyes, as She surveyed the great crescent-shaped bay that curved around them. The Ragwitch stood on a slab of rock which thrust out high above the sea. Below this slab and right around the bay, other caves and holes stood out darkly against the grey stone. The sun lay low in the west, already beginning to set—and with the passing of the light, the caves became darker and the sea went from blue to deepest black. Down below, the pounding of the surf in the deep caves became an ominous drumbeat.

Then the Ragwitch screamed, a long, chilling scream that rose and fell with the rhythm of the surf. Deep inside the Ragwitch's mind, Julia felt what it was like to deliver that scream—the exultation of freedom, the flexing of power, and worst of all . . . the expectation of an answer.

At first, silence greeted the Ragwitch's scream, the silence of an audience just before the applause. But the answering calls were not long in coming: the dull rumblings of vast creatures, woken far beneath the earth, and the shrill whistlings of other beings closer at hand.

"You see, my little Julia," whispered the Ragwitch, Her leathery lips barely moving. "My servants remember My power well—even in this shape, they recognize Me! They still come when I call. You will like them."

"No," said Julia, defiantly. She was absolutely sure that the things that made those noises would not be likeable at all.

"Yes," murmured the Ragwitch. "You will like them. Eventually."

She turned to the cliff, and began to climb up towards the top. Julia noticed that there was some sort of path, or eroded staircase—whichever it was, the Ragwitch seemed to know every turn and rise, neatly avoiding places where the cliff had fallen away. Below them, the screams and cries diminished to be replaced by the sounds of movement: sounds of scraping claws, and footfalls that did not sound human.

Locked within the Ragwitch's mind, Julia kept trying to turn her head—a reflex to see those things behind her. But while she knew her head should turn, it could not: Julia's eyes were only those of the Ragwitch, and they were intent on the path ahead.

Eventually, the huge leathery form of the Ragwitch reached the top of the cliff, a flat expanse of low shrubs and grasses, ill-lit in the last red light of the sun. The Ragwitch set off purposefully, pausing only to thrust back some of the yellow stuffing that leaked from her side. Once again, She did not look back.

Crossing this flat, monotonous terrain seemed to take hours, and Julia dozed—asleep without closing her eyes, which were the Ragwitch's, and so, never shut. A dream-like pattern of images filled her mind: loping through this dull land, then hurrying towards a rocky spire, a tower of twisted, volcanic rock which sparkled even in the starlight. The Ragwitch went to the spire, and began to climb . . . tirelessly, hand over hand, up to the very pinnacle, up to the blackest part of the night sky.

Julia woke up in slow stages, as though she were swimming up from the bottom of a deep pool. The Ragwitch was now sitting on some sort of throne carved out of the glassy rock. Runes of red gold ran along the arms, disappearing down the front of the throne.

Then, the Ragwitch looked down—and Julia felt her mind twitch, trying to tell nonexistent hands to grab hold of something before she fell . . . for the throne was on the very peak of the spire she had thought was a waking dream. The throne rested hundreds of meters up, on the thin needle-point of the spire's peak, with nothing else about it, no flat place nor protective railing.

The Ragwitch looked up again, tilting Her head back, and Julia felt Her lips creaking back across the snail-flesh gums, the mouth opening to scream again. The Calling Scream, the Voice of Summoning, welled up from the recesses of the Ragwitch's dark power, high on Her ancient throne that men had called the Spire.

This time, Julia screamed as well, a thin, mental shriek that was swallowed up by the Ragwitch's own great roar. But it was there—a sign of Julia's resistance to her captor.

As the Calling Scream died away, the moon's first light crept across the ground. It slowly inched forward, crossing the sparkling rock of the Spire, to light up the ground before it: a sunken bowl of that same glassy, lifeless rock. But long ago the rock had been shaped into tiers of seats, which wound erratically around and around in a giant spiral, as though shaped by a drunken architect.

Then the Ragwitch's Calling Scream was answered

from the Terrace-Hole below by bellows and screams, mad hyena-like laughter and shrill whistlings.

"Now you see them," whispered the Ragwitch, Her thoughts battering at the silent Julia. "Do you like them?"

Julia didn't answer, horrified at the sight of the creatures that thronged in the moonlight below. The Ragwitch smiled again, and looked down at a particular group of followers.

Tall, sallow, humanoid in shape, they had patches of scale underlying their jaws and throats, and out-thrust upper jaws, with dog-like fangs made for rending flesh. Their arms were long and gibbon-like, ending in yellow-taloned hands. Their piggy, deep-set eyes looked up at the Ragwitch in adoration.

"The Gwarulch," muttered the Ragwitch. "Sneaking beasts—hungry for meat, but not too eager to fight for it. Except in My service."

Julia shuddered, feeling the Ragwitch's thoughts of blood and killing. And not just thoughts, but memories too. Stark, frightening images of past slaughters, the Ragwitch triumphant, feasting . . .

Julia screamed again, forcing the Ragwitch's memories away. But still, she could not close her eyes, and the Ragwitch looked down upon more of Her creatures, awaiting orders in the Terrace-Hole below.

"Angarling," She told Julia, mentally pointing out a group of huge, pale white stones, roughly-cut columns. Julia had taken them for statues, or part of the rock terraces. Through the Ragwitch's eyes and memory, she now saw that on each of the huge stones was the weathered carving of an ancient face—full of sorrow and torment, anger and evil, all etched into the white stone.

"Angarling!" shouted the Ragwitch, and the stones moved. Slowly at first, then more rapidly, they tramped to the base of the Spire. There they halted, and then came a great, welling boom which drowned out the cries of all the Ragwitch's lesser servants.

A dark shadow suddenly fell across the Ragwitch's face, and Julia quivered, though no reflex of the Ragwitch moved. Her huge leathery head slowly tilted back, greasy yellow locks of dank hair falling around Her shoulders. Up above, a creature fluttered, its wings casting a shadow right across the throne.

"The Meepers," whispered the Ragwitch.

It looks like a bat, thought Julia for an instant, but at the same time, she knew it did not. It had the wings and furry body of a bat, but the head was a fanged nightmare—a scaly mixture of piranha and serpent, with row upon row of gleaming teeth. And it was thirty times bigger than any bat, with wings that seemed wider than the sail on the yacht Julia had seen only the day before.

The Meeper straightened its wings, and dropped past the Spire, falling away to the right. Others followed it, and the Ragwitch laughed as they hissed and bit at each other for their place in the line.

Several hundred of the Meepers flew past in what seemed like several hours. Julia soon got more bored than frightened, and found that she could peer out of the corners of "her" eyes—perhaps even seeing things the Ragwitch could not. The creatures below disturbed her less now, and she began to count them—with a growing feeling of unease. She counted (or guessed at) over a thousand Gwarulch, at least a hundred of the statue-like Angarlings, and many hundreds of Meepers. And the thoughts of the Ragwitch were of fire and blood, death and destruction . . . Julia hastily tried to do sums in her head, barricading her mind against the memories— particularly the eating . . .

"Gwarulch, Angarling and Meepers!" shouted the Ragwitch, Her voice sharp and malevolent, echoed everywhere by the black stone. "But where is Oroch? Who is Oroch to disdain Me, when I stand upon My Spire?"

Down below, the Gwarulch shifted uneasily, muttering in their guttural language. Above, the Meepers flew in circles, angrily whistling at this Oroch who failed the Ragwitch. Only the Angarling were silent, white shapes impervious to any thoughts save the command of their Mistress.

"Again, I say," spat the Ragwitch, "Oroch! Your Mistress calls!"

Inside the Spire, a rock cracked—and then another. Through the Ragwitch's straw-stuffed feet, Julia felt the Spire shiver, and for a giddy second, was certain She would fall—that they would fall.

Then the Spire steadied, and a single block of stone fell from halfway up, to smash unnoticed among the ranks of the silent Angarling. Julia watched, transfixed, as a hand emerged from the hole—a barely recognizable hand, wrapped in what looked like tar-cloth, or linen soaked in treacle.

It was followed by another hand, and then a head, a faceless, cloth-wrapped head, that tilted back and forth like a broken toy. Then it steadied, and opened its mouth, a red, wet maw, stark and toothless against the black cloth.

"Oroch was trapped, Mistress," the thing moaned. "Locked in the Spire I built for you. But their work could not keep me when You called."

"Oroch," said the Ragwitch with satisfaction. "Come to me."

The Ragwitch held out a single, three-fingered hand, in gross parody of a handshake. She flexed her fingers, and Julia felt a thrill run through them, a spark of sudden power. Quick as that spark, Oroch was there, holding Her fingers with both his tar-black, bandaged hands. His legs scrabbled for a second, then he relaxed, swinging slightly from side to side. Julia marveled at the Ragwitch's strength, for Oroch was at least two meters tall, though thin and spindly.

"Your power is not diminished, oh Mistress," gasped Oroch, his red maw panting.

"It is increased!" shouted the Ragwitch, suddenly throwing Oroch in the air and catching him as he hurtled back down. "Now that I have a body of undying cloth, it is *increased!*"

4

GWARULCH BY NIGHT/THE RAGWITCH LOOKS TO THE SOUTH

The Awe-guh-ay-er," Paul said once again, trying to match Aleyne's pronunciation. The two of them sat at the prow of the *River Daughter*, which was rapidly making progress down that difficultly-named river, aided by the current and the poling of Ennan and Amos, the brothers who owned the narrowboat.

As Aleyne had expected, Paul had slept through two nights and a day, waking only that morning, rested if no less anxious. They had immediately embarked on the *River Daughter*, and the pair had spent the morning talking. Paul had spoken of his "adventures," and of Julia and the Ragwitch; he'd also learnt that Aleyne was in fact Sir Aleyne, a Knight of the Court at Yendre— though from Aleyne's description of what he did, he sounded more like a cross between a policeman and a park ranger, and he didn't look at all like the knights in books or films. Aleyne had a particular love of the river

Awgaer, and spent much of his time on its waters, or in the villages that shared the river banks with the wild-fowl and water rats.

"Perhaps you should just call it 'the river,'" said Aleyne, laughing at Paul's eighth attempt. "I hope you can do better with Rhysamarn—the Wise might refuse to see you if you can't pronounce the name of their favorite mountain."

"Really?" asked Paul, who was often taken in by Julia's jokes, but Aleyne was already laughing, his black moustache quivering with each chuckle.

"No, lad—just my joke! But the Wise are strange, it's true, and Rhysamarn is a strange mountain—or so they say."

"You've never been there?"

"Well, I have almost been there," replied Aleyne. "But I didn't see the Wise. It was some years ago, when I was more foolish and rather vain. I thought to ask the Wise . . . well, I thought to gain some insight into pro-curing the love of a certain lady—a passing fancy, noth-ing more."

"What happened?" asked Paul eagerly, hoping that Aleyne (who was looking rather sheepish) wouldn't avoid the question and trail off into a completely differ-ent story.

"To tell the truth," continued Aleyne, "I was halfway up the mountain when my horse brushed a tree and knocked down a wasps' nest. The wasps chased me all the way down to the water trough at the Ascendant's Inn, and my face was so stung I couldn't go to Court for weeks—or see the lady."

"Perhaps you did see the Wise after all," laughed Amos, who had been listening at the stern. Ennan laughed too, till both had to pole hard to keep the narrowboat straight within the current.

"Maybe I did," said Aleyne, "The lady in question

did turn out to be rather different from what I had thought . . ."

"Yes, but why are you taking me to this Rhysamarn place?" asked Paul. "Will the Wise find my sister, and take both of us back where we belong?"

"As to the first," answered Aleyne, "only the Wise could possibly know what has become of your sister— especially if she has become mixed up with . . . the One from the North."

Paul noticed that while Aleyne didn't make the sign against witchcraft as often as old Malgar the Shepherd, he still did it occasionally—and he didn't like using the Ragwitch's name, now that he suspected She really did exist. "The One from the North" was the phrase he used to speak of the Ragwitch, or "Her," with a hissing, audible capital "H."

"And for the second," Aleyne continued, "I have never heard of such a place as yours, with its . . . carz and magics, so I suspect that if it does exist—and I believe you—the Wise will know of some way to get you back there."

"I hope so," replied Paul sadly. Relaxing in this boat was all very well, and safely exciting, but it was still the world of the May Dancers, their forest . . . and the Ragwitch. Paul wished the Ragwitch had taken him, rather than Julia, so his sister would be the one who had to look for him. Still, from what Aleyne had hinted at, being with the Ragwitch wouldn't be very nice at all— maybe even scarier than the forest . . .

Paul slowly drifted off to sleep, one hand trailing over the side, occasionally brushing the water. Aleyne watched him, as he turned and mumbled about his sister Julia, and how life just wasn't fair.

When Paul awoke, it was early evening. The *River Daughter* was rocking gently, tied up against a jetty of old, greenish logs. Sitting up, Paul saw that the river was no longer narrow, but had widened into a majestic, slow-moving stretch of water at least a hundred meters wide. On either bank, open woodland sloped away from the river. To the west, yellow sunlight filtered down through the trees, the evening sun dipping down behind the upper parts of the wood. Paul watched sleepily as a bird flew up from the trees, crying plaintively as it rose higher into the greying sky.

"Ornware's Wood," said Aleyne, who had been sitting on the wharf. "Not as old as the May Dancer's forest, but much more pleasant. And the only creatures you should find here are hedge-pigs, deer, squirrels and suchlike."

"No kangaroos?" asked Paul, half-heartedly. From the sound of it, they were going to have to walk through this wood, and it was still much like the May Dancer's forest, no matter what Aleyne said.

"Kangaroos," mused Aleyne (after Paul had described them), "No, I think there are none of those in Ornware's Wood. But I have heard of animals like you describe, far to the south. Anyway, we must be going. There's still an hour left of this half-light, and we will camp not too far away."

"O.K.," replied Paul. "But where's Ennan and Amos?"

Aleyne looked at the empty boat for a second, then answered, "They've gone to pay their respects to a . . . man . . . who holds power over the next stretch of the river."

Paul wondered about Aleyne's hesitation in describing the person the boatmen had gone to see. But Aleyne had already grabbed his pack, and the smaller one he'd made up for Paul—though it seemed heavy enough to its bearer.

Half an hour later, it seemed even heavier, although the going was easy, and the wood pleasantly cool. Paul was glad when Aleyne finally stopped, and dropped his

pack against a gnarled old oak. Paul thankfully followed suit, and sat down next to his temporarily-eased
burden.

"We shall camp here," said Aleyne. "There's a small
stream beyond that clump of trees. It drains into the
river, and its water is clear and fresh. This will do very
well; and from here it is a little less than a day to the
Ascendant's Inn at the foot of Rhysamarn."

Paul looked glumly around the camp site. He didn't
like camping, particularly when there was no shower
and toilet building nearby, nor a caravan in case it
rained. Julia, of course, loved camping, though she normally didn't get the chance if Paul had anything to do
with it.

"Where's our tent?" he asked Aleyne, as the latter
opened up his pack, and took out a small iron pot.

"Tent?" replied Aleyne, holding up the pot to the setting sun to look inside. "I have no tent—nor indeed, a
horse to carry such a heavy thing, all poles and cloth!
I've a wool cloak, same as you'll find in your pack.
Good greasy wool will keep the weather out."

"Oh," said Paul, who hated the feel of wool, and
didn't like the sound of "greasy" wool. "Do you think
it will rain?"

Aleyne cast an eye up at the darkening sky, and said,
"No clouds up there tonight. It might be cold, but it
won't rain."

Paul looked up, noticing how dark the sky was becoming. Night seemed very close—and of a threatening
blackness. Paul shivered, and hastily opened his pack to
find the wool cloak. Aleyne smiled, and putting the pot
aside, began to gather sticks from a dead branch that
had fallen nearby.

A few hours later Paul sat by the crackling fire,
drinking soup that Aleyne had made in the pot, from
salt-dried beef and herbs he'd gathered in the forest.

Paul dreamily watched the sparks creeping up the side of the little pot to suddenly launch themselves into the air with a snap and crackle. Warm and content, he wrapped himself in his woollen cloak, and fell asleep.

Across the fire, Aleyne suddenly started, as if disturbed by a sudden thought. He stood up, listened, then rapidly doused the fire, smothering it in dirt. With the fire gone, the night was once again complete. Aleyne listened in the darkness for a while, then lay down between the roots of the old oak. He didn't wrap himself in his cloak and kept his dagger close at hand. As he fell into a wary sleep, an old memory crept into Aleyne's mind of a picture in his father's house: a picture of a distant ancestor, standing fully armed and armored upon a battlefield, a dead North-Creature at his feet. Aleyne had always wondered why the artist had made him look more than a little afraid . . .

Paul awoke in darkness to find Aleyne crouched at his side, barely visible in the starlight. He opened his mouth, but Aleyne quickly put his hand over it, before leaning forward to whisper, "Do not speak normally. We must be quiet."

Paul nodded. "Why?"

"There are creatures in the forest. I heard them earlier, in the distance, but now they are nearby. I think they are . . . dangerous, and they seem to be hunting. Get up—we must leave now, before light."

Paul nodded again, and began to crawl towards his pack. Aleyne stopped him again, and gestured to leave it. Taking the boy's hand, he began to creep away, leaving his pack as well. Paul stumbled after him, still too sleepy to argue.

Several hundred meters and many scratches and bumps later, Paul felt Aleyne suddenly stop and kneel down, dragging Paul with him. Aleyne pointed to his ear, and then back the way they had come. At first Paul heard nothing, then he caught a sort of snorting sound—and the jangle of metal. The old iron pot, realized Paul, probably being thrown against a tree. Whatever it was back there obviously had a bad temper.

Paul started to get up again, but Aleyne didn't move, so he knelt back down. The snorting sounds were louder, and butterflies started in Paul's stomach as he realized they were getting nearer. Then the snorts suddenly stopped, to be replaced by a long, high-pitched howl. With a sudden jerk, Aleyne leapt to his feet, dragging Paul with him.

"They've found our trail!" he shouted, careless of the noise. "Run!"

But Paul was already running, almost as Aleyne spoke. He knew this forest would turn out just as bad as the other one, and had no desire to meet anything that howled like the thing behind them. Crashing through branches and stumbling over the uneven ground, Paul was unaware of Aleyne behind him, till he touched his shoulder, directing him to the right.

"This way," shouted Aleyne, "It's our only chance!"

"Can't you fight them?" panted Paul, narrowly ducking an overhanging branch, a dim outline seen at the last moment.

"I don't even know what they are," replied Aleyne, stumbling behind him. "But if they're what I think they are—No!"

"What do you think—ow!—they are?" asked Paul, panting for air. But Aleyne didn't answer, only pushing him on from behind. The ground was rising steeply in front of them, and the trees were becoming thicker, so Paul often had to use both hands to fend off branches. Oddly enough, the trees seemed to be in rows after a while, and the way became easier, almost like an over-grown road—though Paul was so short of breath he hardly noticed.

Then the howling began again, closer behind them, and Paul forgot about breathing. All his thoughts went into his legs, and into watching the way ahead in the dim pre- dawn starlight. But no matter how fast he ran, the howling drew closer and closer, until Paul felt he had to look behind. A low branch chose this precise moment to get in the way of his foot, and Paul went flying over into the leaf-littered ground. Aleyne checked in mid-stride, and turned to face their pursuers, his pitiful dagger at the ready.

Paul quickly rolled over and looked back to see Aleyne silhouetted above him, the starlight reflecting on his blade. And there, in front of him, loomed a larger shadow, over two meters tall, with grossly overlong arms, and talons as long as knives, that seemed to crawl with shadows.

"Ornware!" shouted Aleyne, drawing his dagger across his thumb, and then plunging it into the trunk of the nearest tree. "Ornware! Blood of mine, and Blood of Tree, on Ornware's Road to Summon Thee!"

Nothing happened, and their pursuer loped forward, making small grunting sounds. Aleyne stepped back before it, aware that it could kill him whenever it chose. Paul kept his eyes on the creature, and started to slip back under the trees.

"Gwarulch," whispered Aleyne, as the monster crept forward, stalking its prey.

As he spoke, the Gwarulch struck, an arm swinging across at throat level, talons extended for a killing slash. But Aleyne saw it coming. Ducking under the blow, he threw himself sideways under Paul's tree, as the Gwarulch leapt forward.

"You should have thrown the dagger at it!" shouted Paul, stumbling away as the Gwarulch burst through the branches. Aleyne didn't answer, for the creature struck at him again—this time successfully, tearing open the front of his tunic and shallowly slicing his chest. He tried to dodge again, but the Gwarulch was too quick, backhanding him across the head. With the crack of branches, Aleyne fell to the forest floor, in front of Paul's horrified gaze.

The Gwarulch looked at Paul with deep-set, piggy eyes—and pounced, talons extended. But his small size was to his advantage amongst the thick foliage; he slid between two large branches, and the talons raked bark instead of flesh.

Despite this, Paul knew the Gwarulch would get him eventually. He desperately looked around for a branch or a stone, or any sort of weapon—and then, he saw Aleyne's dagger, still protruding from the tree. He leapt for it, as the Gwarulch leapt at him.

Paul's hand fastened around the hilt, and he half-turned, to draw and throw it, as the Gwarulch emerged from under the tree. Out of the tree-shadow, it was a hideous sight. Vaguely ape-like, its upper jaw protruded to show ripping fangs, and its eyes were piggy and lit with an evil intelligence. It eyed Paul with something like amusement, and licked its lips in a very human gesture.

Paul vainly tugged at the dagger as the Gwarulch advanced, still licking its lips with a bluish, forked tongue. It reached out a taloned hand, and gripping Paul's hand in its own, pulled the dagger out of the tree.

With his free hand, Paul punched the Gwarulch in the stomach, almost breaking his fingers on the thick, leathery flesh. It hurt him so much, he thought it couldn't possibly have harmed the huge creature—when it gave a surprised sort of yelp, and sank to its knees. Dragged down with it, Paul looked into its fading eyes as it toppled over, letting go of his hand.

Then he saw what had really killed it. A wooden spear-shaft projected from its back, a thick spear of dark wood, engraved with runes that seemed to dance along its length.

In between the trees, Paul saw another silhouette. Instinctively, he knew it was the thrower of the wooden spear. Although man-like, the figure's head seemed strange, and Paul had to look twice before he saw that the man, if man it was, had a full set of antlers.

"Who calls Ornware?" said the antlered man, "When Gwarulch walk among his trees?"

Paul gulped, and tried to sit up. Aleyne had called out to Ornware, but Aleyne was lying over by a tree, unconscious, if not . . . dead.

"We did," he whispered, not daring to look up. Dawn was closer now, and the first cast of light was just allowing real shadows to creep out from the pale star-lit imitations. And the shadows that lay across Paul were of antlers.

Paul heard an amused snuffle above him, and risked a glance upwards. The antlered creature was still there, but it had moved closer to the dead Gwarulch, and was pulling out the spear. It came out easily enough, surprising Paul—the spear had almost gone through the other side, and he knew no normal man could have removed it. But then normal men didn't have antlers.

The creature twirled the spear, then approached Paul, driving the butt of the spear into the ground near the boy's feet. Paul looked up—straight at that antlered head, meeting the creature's eyes: deep yellow eyes, the color of daisies, with thin, bar-like pupils of darkest green. They held power, those eyes, and violence lay beneath the placid daisy-yellow.

"I am Ornware," said the eyes to Paul, communicating a sense of power, like the overhanging branches of a huge oak. "I am Ornware of Ornware's Wood, as the trees are Ornware, the earth, the birds, the animals. All are Ornware."

"Aleyne called you," said Paul, his voice quavering, eyes still locked into Ornware's—lost in those deep yellow pools.

Then a few hundred meters away, a Gwarulch howled—their tracking sound. Paul flinched and blinked, breaking his gaze away from Ornware's.

Ornware's antlered head turned to face the direction of the howling, and he twirled the spear again, bringing the bloodied point close to his mouth. Paul watched, horrified, as a wide, crimson-red tongue lashed out, cleansing the point with one swift motion. Then Ornware was gone, leaping into the trees like a stag, towards the approaching Gwarulch.

"The Gwarulch will bother us no more today," said a cracked voice behind Paul. Aleyne was sitting up, fingering his head. His unruly hair was caked in drying blood. "But I am glad Ornware has other foe to hunt, else he might have turned against us."

"But I thought you called him?" asked Paul, going over to help Aleyne up.

"You may call him," replied Aleyne, looking back down the path. "But only in dire need. Ornware is the walking dream of the forest, only woken at its need, or by a call such as mine. But he is a dream of the forest's fear and anger, and knows little more than blood. Worse, being a creature of raw passions, he likes nothing but the hunt and the kill. He is like a summer storm that saves you by dousing a fire, only to strike with lightning moments later."

A howl further in the distance punctuated Aleyne's words, and he answered Paul's unspoken question with a finger drawn across his throat. Obviously the rune-carved spear had found another Gwarulch heart.

"Come on," said Aleyne, leaning on Paul. "There

should be a stream on the other side of this hill, where I can wash these cuts, and try to get us halfway clean for Rhysamarn and its Wise Men. With such an early start, we should be there by mid-afternoon."

* * *

The Gwarulch had not been idle in reaching as far south as Ornware's Forest so soon after the Ragwitch's ordering of Her War. While the settled folk to the south were unaware of it, the Gwarulch had long lived near, or even within, the northern border, and the Meepers had been quick to fly to isolated bands with orders to waylay travellers and other isolated folk.

Julia had not been idle either. When the Ragwitch was busy, she found it was possible to wrench her mind away. When she did this, she only ended up back "inside" the Ragwitch, near the globe, but at least she got her own body back—despite the Ragwitch's past assurances that Julia would never feel her own body again. The Ragwitch even seemed amused by her efforts to escape, and never punished the girl—apart from forcing her mind back to attach itself to the Ragwitch's senses.

"What lies between us and the Old Border, Oroch?" asked the Ragwitch, as Her lieutenant alighted from the back of a large, leather-winged Meeper. She had taken up residence (if you could call it that, for She never slept), at the base of the Spire, where she received the reports of the Meepers, and gave orders to Her army.

"A new town, Mistress," replied Oroch, in his mewing, high-pitched tone. "Bevallan, they call it. A small place, without walls or castle. Only a tower, and that is of no great size. They have discovered peace in your absence, Mistress."

"It will not be a discovery they enjoy much longer," spat the Ragwitch. "But what of their Magic: their famous Magi, all cluttered up with Staves and Rings and

Talismans; those Wizards, whose flesh is foul and blood rancid?"

"None, Mistress," chuckled Oroch, bandages whipping in the breeze as he laughed. "The Art is forgotten, as *You* were . . ." He stopped in mid-sentence, dropping to his knees as the Ragwitch towered above him to encircle his puny, bandaged neck with one of Her hands.

"Forgotten?" hissed the Ragwitch, spit bubbling between the rows of Her needle-teeth. "Then I shall remind them, will I not, Oroch, my Architect? I shall remind them, and myself remember the sweetness of their flesh."

Behind Her, the stone shapes of the Angarling boomed, feeling their Mistress' anger. The Gwarulch moved about uneasily, careful to avoid the rocking, moving Angarling, as they drew closer to the Spire. The Meepers, high above, twirled and dove about the Spire, revelling in the prospect of bloodshed.

Watching through the Ragwitch's eyes, Julia shuddered, and once again started to do sums in her head. Even the thirteen times table was preferable to the Ragwitch's memories, presented to Julia as they were with every nuance of sight, hearing, feeling . . . and taste.

"Assemble the Gwarulch chieftains and the Old Meeper," the Ragwitch instructed Oroch. "I will . . . talk . . . to the Angarling."

Julia breathed a mental sigh of relief as the memories of pillage and feasting faded, to be replaced by a strong memory of the Angarling, still as stone, being woken by a young, human Witch, on her first small steps to power . . . Surely not the Ragwitch, thought Julia, as she felt her host clumsily lumbering towards the Angarling, those straw-stuffed legs straight and never bending, the puffy three-fingered hand outstretched to caress her oldest allies—the Stone Knights of Drowned Angarling.

"Tomorrow," She said, touching the white stone of the nearest Angarling, caressing the lines of the frozen face. "Tomorrow shall be death and ruin, and the sun will sink all bloody in a sky as red as fire."

* * *

"The sun is high, my stomach grumbles, and I think it's lunchtime," said Aleyne, pausing to let Paul catch up to him. They were climbing up a hill again, where the forest grew less thickly, but Paul was always slow uphill.

"I also think Rhysamarn is only a little way away, and at its foot, there is the Ascendant's Inn. And since . . ."

"We lost our packs," interrupted Paul, "we might as well go on because there's nothing for lunch anyway."

"Exactly," smiled Aleyne, who hadn't missed Paul's bad temper, or the slight quiver of his lower lip. "How are your feet?"

"Sore," grumbled Paul, who was now well over the night's dangers, and more concerned with his various discomforts. Trust Julia to get kidnapped to a place without buses, he thought sourly, as Aleyne set off again, trying to pick the easiest way up the hill. And every "adventure" I have is always without food, and in forests full of prickles and thorns . . .

Paul was still thinking about thistles, because they were the most immediate nuisance, when Aleyne suddenly stopped ahead of him. Paul looked up from the ground, and saw that the trees no longer rose up to the sky, and only a few meters further on lay the top of the hill—the real top, and not just another tantalizing close ridge.

"Well," said Aleyne. "We're there—or near enough."

Paul rushed up the last few meters, onto the flat rock

where Aleyne gazed to the east. They were truly on top of the hill, for below them the forest thinned out to nothing, to be replaced by green fields which stretched down to a narrow river spanned by a wooden bridge.

On the other side of the river, the land stretched up again, turning from lush farmland to yellow heather, which grew up and up, along the slopes of a mountain that disappeared into mist.

"Rhysamarn," said Aleyne, in a sort of deep, polite tone. Just like he was talking about a church, thought Paul, who was busy looking for the inn. Then he saw it—a large, yellow house, with several red-brick chimneys, the whole place nestled in the folds of the heather, just a little way up the Mountain of the Wise.

"Let's go," said Aleyne, looking back from the mountain to see the boy several meters below him. Aleyne noted with amusement that Paul was not slow going down hills—at least those with the prospect of food and shelter at the end. But then, neither was Sir Aleyne, sometime Knight, and watcher of events on the River Awgaer.

5

RHYSAMARN/THE MOUNTAIN
OF THE WISE

Three days later, Paul was looking down on the
Ascendant's Inn again, but this time he was
standing amidst luxuriant yellow heather, headed
for the secret heights of Rhysamarn. And this time he
was alone.

The Ascendant's Inn had provided a very welcome
rest. The innkeeper, Master Aran, had welcomed them
with foaming pints of a heady beer, of which half a pint
was sufficient to stun Paul. Then they enjoyed three
days of idling around the fire, fishing in the river
Rhysamarn, and best of all, sleeping on the goose-
feather beds under heavy eiderdowns.

Then on the morning of the fourth day, Master Aran
had said that Paul should go up—alone. How he knew,
he didn't say, but Aleyne said that this was the normal
practice, and Paul must go if Aran said so.

It's all very well for him, thought Paul crossly, looking down at the distant figure of Aleyne, standing out-

side the inn. He doesn't have to struggle up this mountain where it's all cold and damp.

It *was* cold and damp, but to tell the truth Paul hadn't really been bothered by it. Aleyne had bought him good woollen clothes from Aran, and roughly cut them down to size. With a sheepskin coat, soft doeskin boots, and a broad-brimmed hat, Paul didn't feel the cold at all.

All I need is a sword, thought Paul, or a short-sword anyway. He practiced a few film-style lunges and slashes, and thought swashbuckling thoughts, till it occurred to him that he might really need a sword—and if he were attacked by things like the Gwarulch it wouldn't make much difference anyway.

"Just let me find Julia," he whispered up at the mountain. "And get us back to where it's safe."

Suddenly, the mountain looked like less of an obstacle, compared to the problems he might have to overcome to get home—the Ragwitch, and all her powers, for one. Setting his hat firmly on his small head, Paul set off, up into the mist that shrouded the Mountain of the Wise.

There was a sort of path up through the heather, which wound its way between the large rocky outcrops that occasionally loomed up out of the mist. Paul took care to follow the path—the mist had become much thicker, and he knew that getting lost here would mean certain death, as no rescue teams or helicopters would be around to find him.

The mountain grew steeper, and the rocky parts more numerous, and Paul was forced to use his hands to scramble up. The path became less distinct among the rocks, and he had to stop and look for it several times. Hours passed in this stop-start way, and Paul began to feel less confident. Suddenly climbing a mountain all by himself seemed incredibly stupid. He wouldn't have done it at home, after all. And looking for "the Wise" didn't seem very sensible—he didn't even know what they looked like!

Aleyne had said to keep to the path, and not to stop for too long, thought Paul. He started up the mountain again, then he suddenly remembered Aleyne first telling him about the Wise, and his journey up the mountain. Aleyne had said "I rode my horse"—but the path was too steep and narrow for a horse.

I must have gone the wrong way! thought Paul, angry at all his wasted climbing. He thought of all that effort, and considered going on. But it was obviously the wrong path . . .

"Down it is," said Paul aloud, turning back down the path. But even as he took the first, easy downhill steps, the path seemed to fade away, melting into the yellow heather, or the green-grey mottled stone.

He took a few more steps, but the path disappeared, leaving no sign of its prior existence. He quickly looked around, and the path uphill was going too—though it was contracting, racing up the hill, rather than fading.

With a strangled yelp, Paul jumped after it, taking great bounding steps up the slope. The heather brushed against his legs as he crashed through it, chasing the path that retreated just a little faster than he could run.

Then, without warning, both the path and the boy burst out of the mist, into yellow sunlight. The path suddenly stopped, and Paul jumped on it, taking great satisfaction in seeing his boot-prints on the open dirt. He took a few steps along it, to give himself a head start, in case it started to race away again, and looked around.

Downhill, a thick wall of mist obscured any view, but uphill, the sun was shining, its warmth already touching Paul's mist-wet clothes and face. A little further along, the heather started to fall back, and above this border of heather loomed the grey shale peak that was the top of Rhysamarn.

But it was what lay in between that attracted Paul's attention. Just above the heather, but before the grey stone, lay a field of dark brown earth. It was larger than a suburban garden, but not really a decent market garden size. And in the middle of it, an old man was planting something that looked very like cabbages.

Hesitantly, Paul walked over to the field. Aleyne had told him that the Wise appeared in different guises, but he hadn't expected an old man planting (or transplanting) baby cabbages.

"Hello," said Paul, upon reaching the edge of the field. "I'm Paul. I'm looking for the Wise."

The old man looked up from the cabbages, revealing a lined face, rosy cheeks and a reddish nose. His white hair and moustache threatened to weave a mask around his face, but he parted the long locks with a dirty hand. The bright eyes that looked at Paul were in no way obscured or dimmed by his bushy, walrus-like eyebrows, which quivered as he spoke.

"The Wise, eh? Well, you've come to the right place. Rhysamarn—the Mountain of the Wise. Or literally, Place of Wisdom, Mountain."

"Yes," said Paul, doubtfully. This wasn't the reception he'd been expecting, particularly since the old man hadn't stopped transplanting cabbages. He had hundreds of them, it seemed, in a wooden box that he dragged along between the rows.

"Well, come and help, boy," snapped the old man. "Part of being wise is knowing the value of things. And advice got for nothing is often worthless. In your case, I would say you need counseling to the value of . . . about eighty transplanted cabbages."

"Uh," said Paul, who'd avoided even doing the

weeding in his father's garden. But he knelt down next to the box of cabbages, and asked, "What do I do?"

The old man told him, demonstrating how to make a suitable hole, with a clenched fist pushed into the soil, and twisted several times. Paul soon learnt the knack of it, but even so, he lagged behind the old man. Closer to, this potential sage looked even more unsuitable for the role of one of the Wise. He was dressed in a simple robe of what looked like sackcloth, and wore wooden sandals that clattered as he crawled forward on his knees. And having been in the cabbage field all day, he was covered in dirt.

The sun rose higher above the cabbage planters, and then began its slow decline into the west. As the shadows lengthened, Paul kept looking at the old man, hoping that he was about to call it quits. The cabbage planting business had seemed easy enough at first, but it soon became tiring, and his back was stiff from being bent over all day.

Failing the signal to stop work, Paul would have welcomed some conversation, or at least some questions regarding why he was there. But the old man was silent as he planted the cabbages with a monotonous regularity; left fist in to make the hole, right hand to pick up the cabbage and place it carefully, left hand to smooth the dirt around it. Over and over again.

Eventually, the sun sank low enough to send the distant clouds red, and Paul had had enough. He stuffed his current cabbage in a hole, smoothed it over, and stood up, his back creaking.

"I've had enough," he said, a trace of self-righteousness creeping into his voice. "I've been planting cabbages nearly all day—a lot more than eighty cabbages!"

"One hundred and thirty-two, by my count," said the old man cheerfully. "I was wondering when you'd realize." He got up, straightening his back with the help of both hands thrust against his backbone. "Well, I suppose for that number of cabbages, I can give you supper as well."

The old man bent down again, and pulled a thick, oil-cloth covering over the box with the remaining cabbages.

"What do I call you then?" he asked Paul, "Boy? Cabbage-Planter?"

"My name is Paul," said Paul. "What shall I call you?"

"Old Man?" suggested the sage, rolling it off his tongue as if to see how it sounded. "Cabbage-Planter? Tanboule? Tanboule is the name of my house—so you may call me that. Tanboule the house and Tanboule the old man. And one shall go to the other for a supper of cabbage and bacon, bread and tea. Eh, Paul?"

"Err . . . that sounds very nice," said Paul, who was thinking Tanboule didn't seem so much wise as mad. Still, he did seem to be on Rhysamarn mountain . . .

Obviously encouraged by the mention of supper, Tanboule took off up the slope at once, easily outpacing Paul with his long strides. Unlike Aleyne, he didn't stop for Paul to catch up with him, and was soon a dark speck against the grey shale. Paul struggled on angrily, slipping on the wet slabs of stone and wishing he'd never even seen the stupid old man and his cabbages.

Then he looked up, and even the dark speck had gone. Tanboule was nowhere to be seen, and there was no sign of a house up on the rocky peak, or even a cave mouth. Paul hesitated and looked back down the mountain, but the mist was as thick as ever. And he could clearly see the cabbage-field—a little square of dirt on which he'd spent considerable labor.

"At least I deserve to eat some cabbage," muttered Paul, "And I'm going to get some, like it or not!" And with that promise, he started back up the shale, using his hands when the rockface became too steep or broken.

Twenty minutes later, he reached the approximate spot where Tanboule had vanished—and the mystery of his sudden disappearance was explained. Paul had been climbing a peak that he thought was the very pinnacle of Rhysamarn, but it was only a lesser projection from the high mountain that lay before him. Down below Paul, there lay a saddle between the two peaks: a tiny valley of yellow heather, nestled between the greater and lesser peaks of grey shale.

In the center of this valley, halfway between each peak, there was a house. Or at least, Paul thought it was a house. It was obviously wooden, but each end was curved up, to touch the red-tiled roof and its iron chimneys (of which there were three). Even stranger, it didn't appear to have a door, and the only windows were high up on the sides, and round like portholes. In fact, it looked like a particularly fat houseboat, stranded in the heather at least six hundred meters above sea-level, and over two hundred kilometers from the nearest coast. A bird flew from its roof, a black shape silhouetted against the orange sky, triggering memories of old pictures showing an ark atop a mountain, and an old man sending out a dove.

But it was still a long way down, and the air was chilling as the sun set, so Paul steeled himself, and carefully began to make his way down the treacherous slate.

When Paul at last arrived at Tanboule's peculiar house, the sun had finally given in to the night. But the house was lit up inside, with cheerful yellow light flickering through the porthole-windows, and smoke billowing from at least two chimneys, carrying with it the smell of frying bacon and cabbage.

But Paul couldn't find a door. He walked around the

whole building twice, and even felt the wooden planks, but there was definitely no doorknob, handle or bell.

"Hello in there!" shouted Paul, after his third circum-navigation. "Mister Tanboule! It's me, Paul! Can I come in?"

"Of course, lad," came the reply, in Tanboule's voice—but Paul couldn't see him till a rattling sound attracted him to the other end of the house. There, a rope ladder was dangling down the side, leading up to what looked like the tiled roof. However, by shielding his eyes from the lantern light, Paul saw that there was a space between the eaves of the roof and the top of the wall—and that was the door.

Tanboule was waiting at the top as Paul climbed in through the hatch. "Welcome aboard, Paul," he said, standing aside to let Paul drop down from the roof-door.

But Paul was staring at the interior of the house through the hatch, and wasn't moving.

Immediately below him, Tanboule was standing on a raised platform next to a shining binnacle, complete with a huge bronze compass. Next to that stood a ship's wheel, with a note tacked to it, which read *Rudder temporarily disconnected, T.*

A ladder led down from the first platform to another which extended for most of the length of the house, ending in another ladder going to a forward platform and down through an open hatch. In between the two higher platforms were casks and bags, chests and rugs, all piled haphazardly around some old wooden furniture, and three cast iron stoves, one of which had a frying pan hissing away on it. On the floor next to the cooking stove, a cat was playing with what looked like a piece of dried haddock.

"So it is a boat!" exclaimed Paul, jumping down to admire the binnacle. "I suppose you ended up here when the floods went down?"

Tanboule shook his head sadly. "I built it here. Forty years I studied with the stars, calculating the advent and time of a Great Flood. Then ten years building this craft, high up on the mountain."

"To save all the animals?" asked Paul, looking around. It didn't really look big enough for two of everything, not with all the junk.

"To save myself!" declared Tanboule. "I never did like animals much. But it was all a mistake. The Flood never came!"

"Why?" asked Paul. "Were the stars wrong?"

"They weren't wrong," snapped Tanboule. "The stars don't lie—but they can be mischievous. There's nothing they like better than a joke, particularly if it's a long one, played on someone who deserves it."

"Why did you deserve it?" asked Paul, as they descended to the long platform, which Paul already thought of as the "main deck."

"I deserved it because I was wise and selfish," sighed Tanboule, flicking a tear from a white-browed eye. "Now, I am wiser (I hope), and less selfish. Which reminds me—why are you here?"

"Well . . ." began Paul, but Tanboule interrupted him, crying out: "Cabbage! The cabbage is burning! Come on, lad—save the cabbage. You can tell me your story over dinner!"

Over a dinner of slightly burnt cabbage, bacon, tea, and thick, crusty bread, Paul explained his troubles to Tanboule. At first, the old man hadn't seemed terribly interested, but he soon became more serious, and asked Paul many questions, particularly about Julia, and the pyramid of flaming sticks that had transported Paul from his world to that of Tanboule (as he put it).

"So," said Paul, when he had told all he could remember. "Will you help me?"

Tanboule sighed, and rubbed his great white eyebrows with the back of a gnarled hand. "We will help you, Paul—but I fear that more than good advice is needed here. For your story is but a little part of a bigger story, one in which many people have played their parts, for better or for worse or for no effect at all."

"What do you mean?" asked Paul, who thought his troubles were complicated enough already. The fact that they might be like one tiny part of a huge puzzle was both terrifying and hard to understand.

"It is partly your story," said Tanboule, taking a great swig of his tea, "because it is the story of the Ragwitch. A long, and sadly true tale which has yet to find a happy ending. Since it will undoubtedly have some bearing on your troubles, I suppose I'd better tell it to you—though this particular tale is worth far more than the planting of one hundred and thirty-two cabbages. Fetch me another cup of tea, Paul, while I compose my voice."

Composing his voice seemed to entail Tanboule eating more bread, so Paul poured himself some more tea as well, while he was waiting. Not that the drink was exactly what he'd call tea—it was sweeter, and scented with lemon and raspberry, but it was made from similar leaves and boiling water.

At last Tanboule finished eating and, stretching himself back, began, without introduction, his rambling tale— part history, part legend, but mostly a true account of an ancient evil.

"Quite a few centuries ago, this Kingdom was a less settled place than it is now," began Tanboule. "There were no northern towns or castles, and fell creatures held sway over the lands north of the river Twyn and regularly came south to raid the smaller towns and villages.

"These raids, by such creatures as the Gwarulch,

were an accepted part of life, albeit an unsavory part. But, as such acceptance is wont to do, it merely prolonged the crisis that was to arrive.

"In this case, the raids became worse, and after a few years, the creatures were no longer merely raiding, but actually conquering the northern marches of the Kingdom.

"The King in those times was a lazy fellow, addicted to the quiet contemplation of dragonflies on mirror-smooth lakes. In fact, he even had a mechanical dragonfly that flew over a pool of the stillest mercury. Without his active control, the Canton Lords each tried to deal with the problem individually—but they failed to check the hordes of North-Creatures that were pouring over the Twyn. At last, the creatures came to the inner cantons of Salace and Thrisk—and the King was forced to do something.

"Fortunately, he did the right thing, which was to abdicate in favor of his son, who became King Mirran the Ninth. He was the total opposite of the old, dragonfly-watching King, and he gathered his army and attacked the North-Creatures, driving them back across the Twyn and into the far North.

"This took several years, of course, and during that time, the nature of the war changed. And sadly, it was King Mirran who was responsible for the changes, and the destruction that was to come of them.

"You see, all through this long war, magic had played no part. There were more Sorcerers, Wizards, Witches and even mere dabblers about in those days, but the Patchwork King would not allow them the use of Magic for war."

"The Patchwork King?" asked Paul. "Who was he?"

"He ruled, and as far as I know still rules, in the land of Dreams and Shadows, where everything that could be is and isn't at the same time—and if you can understand that, you're Wiser than all of us here at Rhysa-marn. But it is from this land that all Magic stems, and it is to this land that all Magic-Workers must go, though now I doubt if any more than a handful know the way.

"This was not always so, for there were tales and legends of an Age of Magic, when wars were fought with all manner of Magic. Yet no true records survived from this Age, and it became no more than a legend known only to a few who sought after ancient lore.

"One such person was a young Witch, who worked as a healer with the King's Army, for the Patchwork King allowed Magic for this purpose . . ."

"A Witch?" interrupted Paul. "I thought they were always evil?"

"Whatever gave you that idea?" asked Tanboule. "They're like everybody else—good, bad, or middling. Anyway, she sought greater powers, and when not actively working, she researched ancient lore, talked among the stars, and learnt spells that had been lost for many centuries.

"It was this learning that she took to the King. For somewhere she had learnt of the Angarling: ancient warriors turned to stone, and submerged beneath the sea in the shallow waters off the Sleye peninsula. These warriors, she told the King, had sworn to serve against Evil, but had been taken unawares by an enemy Sorcerer, and turned to stone. The existence of these Angarling proved that the ancient wars of Magic had occurred, and that there had been a time when the Patchwork King did not rule all Magic.

"Obviously, these Angarling knights were from this time, before the Patchwork King, so he would not be able to forbid their use. Furthermore, the spells required to wake them and make them serve were also from a time outside the reign of the Patchwork King—and the

Magic the spells contained did not come from his land of Dreams and Shadows.

"Anxious for any help, the King agreed to let the Witch do her work. Foolishly, he did not consider one obvious fact: that if this waking Magic did not come from the Patchwork King, it could only belong to that other, Nameless Realm, so long closed to mankind—a place of death and witless violence, nightmares and fear, ruled by no one and composed only of a raw, ungovernable power . . . a power wishing the destruction of all life that did not worship it.

"Indeed, the Witch had already gone too far in her researches, and had been tainted by the lure of this power. With the King's permission, she continued, and opened one forgotten door too many. She walked within the dark void beyond, and exchanged her heart for power, and her love became a lust for slaughter and dominion over every living thing.

"She danced the steps of Seven Wakenings, and the Angarling made their heavy way out of the sea at Sleye. But not to join the King. She cast another spell, and the once-noble Knights were perverted to her cause. With the Stone Knights' help, she joined the North-Creatures, and became their Queen."

Tanboule paused to move the cat from where it had started to play with his empty plate, and took it up to lie in his lap. The cat purred happily, as Tanboule stroked it, and resumed telling the story.

"The war went badly for us then, with retreat after retreat, each following a great victory of the North-Creatures. For the Patchwork King still allowed no use of Magic, and the North-Queen used all the dark powers of the Nameless Realm.

"At last, our armies were defeated, broken and dispersed. All save a tattered remnant, besieged within the shattered walls of Yendre, once the bright capital of a cheerful, wealthy land. The King was there too, a wreck of a man, who took all the blame for the Kingdom's destruction upon himself.

"The North-Queen's creatures attacked the castle at dusk, and after a fierce battle, carried the day. King Mirran was slain, as were all the defenders in that last, hopeless stand."

"What happened then?" asked Paul, as Tanboule faltered and stared into space, gently running his old hands over the cat's ears.

"What happened then . . ." said Tanboule softly, "what happened then should have no part in any tale. It is enough to say that . . . for several years after that, the North-Queen ruled from the Spire—a grim edifice raised for Her by a renegade Wizard, and pupil of her foul Magic—and Her creatures roamed the Kingdom, carrying out Her will. They slew every living thing they could find, destroyed forests, fouled rivers and salted fields—and in the doing of it, turned much of the Kingdom into a desert, a desert that grew with every passing day.

"All this time, the Magi, the Magic-workers who might have been able to oppose the North-Queen, were being hunted down and slain. For the Patchwork King still would not allow the use of Magic. Till, one day, the Magi began to gather at Alnwere Hill—where the standing stones climb up to the Pool of Alnwere, all ringed about with a hedge of rowan trees, themselves older than the stones.

"By this time, there were few of the Magi left alive. But they gathered together, and bided their time, hidden beneath the protection of stone and tree. Midwinter was their goal, when the icicles hang all a-silver from the trees, and the white of snow removes all color from the land. Midwinter—the time when man and woman, child and beast, curl up and dream of warmth and light and colors richer than those of any worldly spring.

"At such a time, the land of Dreams and Shadows is close to that of ours, and this greatly augmented the Magi's powers. They lit the great Midwinter Fire, and at the striking of the midnight bell, they cast the first of their great spells against the North-Queen, where She held state atop Her Spire, hundreds of leagues to the north.

"In some ways the battle of Magic that was fought between North-Queen and Magi was worse than the original destruction wrought by the North-Creatures. Her spells spread ruin across the land, and the Magi were themselves forced to turn to similar destructive Magic.

"In the end, She would have won. The Magi's Magic was never one of destruction, and they could not match Her power. Alnwere Pool lay dark, and showed no vision, and the great Midwinter Fire lay in ashes. The Magi lay about it: Wizard and Witch, Sorcerer and Enchanter—all too weak to resist as the North-Queen's dark Magic overwhelmed them."

Tanboule paused, and Paul looked away from his face for the first time. He'd been so intent on listening, he hadn't noticed the room growing cold. The nearer fire had burnt down to ashes, and the stove was no longer glowing a cheerful cherry red. Tanboule sighed, and indicated to Paul to stoke up the fire and put in a few pieces of the heavy wood that lay stacked at its side. Paul quickly did so, eager to regain the cosy warmth in which Tanboule had begun his tale—though from the sound of it, a blazing fire would be small comfort for the horrors Tanboule was about to reveal.

"The Magi were beaten . . ." hinted Paul, when the fire was burning brightly again, and Tanboule seemed ready to resume.

"Yes . . ." said the old man. "They *seemed* beaten,

when from a most unexpected quarter came help for the dying Magi. Help from Ornware and his kind, the wild spirits of forest and lake, wood and stream. And with them rose the Wild Magic, that untamed power of Nature, in all its uncontrollable passion.

"No one knows what happened in the last wild hour, in the darkest part of the night. Who called the Wild Magic (if anyone did) no one knows, and whether it served them or itself is also a mystery. But in the morning, the North-Queen was gone, and all the Magi were dead, their Magic broken. Alnwere Pool was dry, the standing stones fallen. Only the rowans remained, bent over as if from a great wind.

"Later, a few Hedge-Wizards and minor adepts learned a little of what had occurred. And they discovered one important fact: the North-Queen had not been killed. She had been thrown out of this world—an act which should have killed Her. But even at the end, and amidst the bitter cold of the transfer, She had great power. She conjured a body for Herself, one that would be unsleeping, tireless, with no bones to break, or blood to bleed, or heart to stop."

Tanboule paused, and watched Paul's face. Paul saw Her in his mind, all bloated limbs and leaking straw, and said, "A rag doll . . ."

"Yes. A rag doll. And Her spirit passed into that body, and She went from being North-Queen to being Ragwitch. Oh, She was banished to another world—a simple world, where the people understood Magic and that it should be left alone. And wards and guards were set upon Her (for that was the nest, and the crow), but She was still alive. As were Her creatures, though they scattered to the north, and most of Her major servants vanished with Her, being either slain or banished on that grim Midwinter Night.

"Here, Her fate became a thing for tales and stories,

songs and legend. Genuine fear of the North-Queen became a sort of tame uneasiness about the Ragwitch, and She became the common blame for all household misfortunes or petty ills.

"Yet even this has faded with time, and now the Ragwitch is thought of only as a name, as the common conception of evil and all that's 'not right.' Her North-Creatures have kept to the Sea Caves and other such remote corners of the land, and are rarely seen near even the most northerly settlements. Till now, of course. Gwarulch roam a-hunting, and worse things are to follow. It is a pity your folk lacked the wisdom of the people who made the Hill of Bones—but perhaps the Ragwitch already had Julia under Her control. In any case, because of your sister, She is back—and make no mistake, She is still North-Queen, as well as Ragwitch. And She will destroy this Kingdom if She can . . . and everyone in it."

6

TANBOULE'S ADVICE/
THE SACK OF BEVALLAN

Paul sat stunned, a half-empty cup of cold tea in front of him. He knew Julia was in trouble, but not that much trouble! And everything was suddenly becoming very complicated—it was getting worse than math homework, or writing a report on some stupid play. Except here, failure meant much worse than a bad report.

"So where is Julia?" he asked Tanboule, who was sitting open-mouthed, staring at the tiny red glow of the fire between the bars of the stove. "How can I get her back?"

"Where is Julia?" repeated Tanboule, dreamily. "Where indeed, but in a place far stranger than any you or I have trod. She has been consumed, and any part of her mind that still exists will be within the Ragwitch."

"So how do I get her back?" said Paul, a little more urgently. Tanboule seemed to be drifting off into a daze, just staring into the fire.

"I do not know," replied Tanboule slowly, his eyes unfocused and dreamy, and his voice all heavy with sleep. "Yet I feel that it can be done, and that it will serve the Ragwitch ill."

"Can't you tell me anything?" asked Paul, leaning over to grab the old man's arms and shake him. "You have to tell me where to start, what to do . . . I don't know anything about this place!"

Tanboule's head slowly tilted forward onto his chest, and Paul felt the muscles in the old man's arms slacken, as if he had fallen into a momentary sleep. Then, suddenly Tanboule spoke again, his voice booming, filling every nook and cranny of the boat, echoing out into the night beyond.

"You must seek the Wild Magic that cast the Ragwitch away. Search out Air, Earth, Fire and Water, and bind them to your aid! For the Magi are dead, and the way to the Patchwork King long forgotten. Only the ancient powers of the Beginning can help you now!"

"Oh," said Paul. He sat down again and absentmindedly drank his cold tea. Across from him, Tanboule fell into a deeper sleep, while Paul fought a sudden temptation to ask him how he could get back home—alone, without Julia. But the moment passed, and Paul went over to a pile of rugs and cushions, kicked them a few times to vent his frustrations, lay down, and fell asleep.

Tanboule already had breakfast cooked when Paul woke up. It was cabbage and bacon, bread and tea again, but Paul ate heartily, after a cursory wash.

Tanboule was strangely silent over breakfast, so Paul refrained from asking any of the questions he had stored up. Fortunately, fried cabbage seemed to have a good effect on the old man, and both his humor and his tongue gained a little life over breakfast. But neither of them mentioned the Ragwitch, or the tale Tanboule had told the night before.

Then breakfast was over, and Tanboule pushed the plates together, picked up the frying pan, and threw the lot into a bowl of water.

"Washing up later," he said, taking Paul by the arm and leading him to the hatch. "First, we must talk again, about the Ragwitch and what you must do. The early morning air is good for talking."

With that remark, he climbed up the ladder and disappeared through the hatch. Paul sighed and climbed after him. As he had suspected, the morning air was more cold than thought-provoking, for the sun had barely risen over the higher peak of Rhysamarn, and Tanboule's house still lay in shadow.

"Last night," said Paul, "You told me to seek the . . . Wild Magic . . . Air, Earth, Water and Fire—or it might have been Fire and Water—but those four anyway. And something about them being the Beginning powers, and the only things that can help now."

"I said that?" asked Tanboule, surprised. "I wasn't . . . asleep . . . by any chance, was I?"

"Yes," replied Paul unhappily. "Does that mean it isn't true?"

"No," said Tanboule. "It means it is most certainly true. For I was half-asleep and half-awake and half-dreaming. Perhaps I have given better advice than you or I can know."

"But what does it mean?" asked Paul.

Tanboule sighed. He picked up a stick and broke it in two, giving Paul one half, and throwing the other away.

"Knowledge is like that broken stick, Paul. I can give you half of it, but the other part is lost. You would be a long time seeking amongst the heather for the broken stick, and it is the same with the knowledge you need. I have told you all I know, and now you must search for the rest. But remember: here, Air, Earth, Fire, Water all refer to magical beings, not the everyday forms with which you are familiar. Just as Ornware the Antlered Man is a physical aspect of his forest, so too, other powers are represented by physical beings. The May Dancers, for example, are but aspects of that ancient forest. There are many of them, because the Magic of the forest is very strong.

"You must seek out the Elementals, and gain from them the knowledge that you need to get Julia back. But remember that the Elementals are part of Nature's work, and are thus of the Wild Magic. They may not desire to help you, and indeed, may put troubles in your way. But I think the Wild Magic has its uses for you, and so you will be used. And if luck and your actions bend the Wild Magic a little way to your needs, then all might yet end well."

"That's all very well to say," said Paul. "But where do I begin? I mean, where can I find these Air and Earth thingies, for example?"

"The Master of Air and the Earth Lady," corrected Tanboule. "And the Fire Queen and Water Lord. As to their location, I do not know."

"Oh, great," said Paul sulkily, thinking of all the cabbage planting and the dangers in getting to Rhysamarn, only to get a lot of information that he couldn't use. He wasn't Sherlock Holmes, after all! More like Watson, he thought glumly.

"However," added Tanboule. "There are many people who remember the tiniest fragments of lost tales: a verse from some ancient song, or even a snatch of some childish rhyme—and all of these have some knowledge in them. I suspect you might meet someone who knows such a tune or two if you leave the mountain now."

"Back to the Ascendant's Inn?" asked Paul, brightening at the prospect of seeing Aleyne again. He'd know what to do, and it wouldn't be left totally up to Paul. If Tanboule was so wise he ought to know that Paul didn't like having to work out things for himself.

But Tanboule was shaking his head. "No, not back to the Ascendant's Inn. A different track, and one that does not have an end as definite or as cosy as the inn."

"Can't I go back and see Aleyne first?" asked Paul, looking about him, at the yellow heather stretching out, and the grey shale, stark and alone against the sky. It all seemed forbidding and threatening again, and he dreaded having to set forth alone.

"No," said Tanboule. "Your friend is no longer at the inn. He also sought the Wise, and he has duties he must attend to—which include alerting the King to the Ragwitch's presence."

"Probably no one will believe him anyway," muttered Paul. "If they think She's just an old story."

"They will believe," said Tanboule sadly. "For by then, She will have provided proof, and they will have heard the news from the North."

Paul looked at the old man—for a second he was about to ask him more, and what the news might be. Then Tanboule sighed again, and turned away, saying: "Come on, Paul. Get up the ladder, and fetch your things. I must set you on your path before the sun is much higher in the sky. And I still have many cabbages to plant."

* * *

A black cloud of smoke hung heavily over Bevallan, half- lit by the huge fires that flickered yellow and or- ange, down in the middle of the town. Off to one side, shapes moved back and forth amongst the smoke, surreal figures accompanied by the clash of weapons, screams of fear, and the vicious cries of hunting Gwarulch.

Julia looked out of the corners of the Ragwitch's eyes

at the silent ranks of the Angarling. They ringed the Ragwitch, high on the small hill that overlooked what had once been the town of Bevallan. The Angarling had carried out their task, and now stood, stolidly awaiting new orders.

The Ragwitch stirred, and lumbered further down the hill, and Julia shuddered as the Angarling grew closer. For they were no longer gleaming white, but smeared with reddish stains, of which there could only be one origin.

They had led the attack upon Bevallan. Great, crushing stones that lumbered on regardless of the blows rained down upon them. And there had been few of those anyway, thought Julia, remembering the panicked people in those half-dark minutes before dawn.

Only a few of the townsfolk had tried to fight the attackers—they were the ones still fighting in the western part of the town, where the houses and huts were close together and the greater numbers of the Gwarulch couldn't get at them.

Everyone else had just tried to flee—running, screaming, from the crushing stones and the lip-licking Gwarulch that came bounding in after the invincible Angarling. Some had made it out towards the southern edge of the town, clutching valuables and children, pets and precious livestock. But the Meepers were aloft, waiting for just such a target, too cowardly to join in the real fighting.

Julia took a firm grip on her thoughts, and tried to detach herself from the Ragwitch's senses, to hide away deep in Her mind, around that white-lit globe. But the Ragwitch wasn't as distracted as Julia had thought, and before she had got halfway, Julia was snapped back, Her thoughts filling up her mind.

"Escape, Julia? From such entertainments as I offer?" sneered the Ragwitch, biting into Julia's mind, sending images of the morning's slaughter.

"I won't watch!" screamed Julia, deep within the Ragwitch. But she knew that there was no alternative—the Ragwitch was too strong, and even the short moments when Julia returned to the globe were allowed by the Ragwitch, probably to make returning to Her foul thoughts and senses even worse.

"Watch, and learn," whispered the Ragwitch aloud, letting Julia feel Her wormlike tongue writhing in a cloth-dry mouth. "Watch as we walk among my new subjects, in this place they once called their town."

With a wave of a cumbersome hand, the Ragwitch began to descend into the smoke-clouded ruin, the Angarling crushing a way before Her, with a guard of Gwarulch pacing needlessly behind and to the sides.

Up close, the destruction was even worse than Julia had first thought—and there were many dead, crushed by the Angarling, or ripped by the teeth and talons of the Gwarulch. Here and there, a Gwarulch corpse bared its fangs in a rigor nothing would release; often, the dead Gwarulch were lying wrapped around a man or woman—victims who had taken their murderers with them in those few frenzied seconds of mortal combat.

After the first few minutes, shock captured Julia as the Ragwitch lumbered through the wreckage, pausing occasionally for closer inspections of rubble or corpses. Julia felt it was like some awful slide-show, where the images flashed up on the screen so quickly they were like a continuous picture, but you could never quite get to fully see each individual scene.

And the noise was eerie too—or rather, the lack of it. The screaming and sounds of fighting had faded out, and through the Ragwitch's ears Julia could only hear the hiss and crackle of flames, the rasping of stone on stone of the moving Angarling and the panting of the nearer Gwarulch with their smoke-rasped breaths. And, of course, the rustle of the Ragwitch dragging Her cloth feet along what had once been Bevallan's main road. All of it seemed to build up into a rhythm of unreality in Julia's head, and she hardly noticed the Ragwitch's constant stopping and starting—just the hypnotic swaying motion of the Angarling and the high-pitched wheezing of the Gwarulch, in and out to the beat of the walking stones.

Then the Ragwitch spoke, a high, screeching series of words that broke into Julia's semi-conscious state, sent the Gwarulch scuttling for cover, and caused the Angarling to shift clumsily back to their Mistress, forming a haphazard ring of stone around Her.

Angry thoughts swarmed through the Ragwitch's mind, lightly touching Julia as they swarmed past like molten butterflies. Each carried memories of pain and hatred, and an intense, biting cold. Then they were gone, and the Ragwitch's private thoughts once again drew back, away from the small section of Her mind that Julia shared.

A few minutes passed while the Ragwitch stood completely still within the ring of Angarling. A few of the guard Gwarulch sneaked back, but they took care to keep still and silent, echoing their Mistress' mood. Julia took the opportunity to peer about, but she could see very little through the gaps between each Angarling, and there was still a lot of smoke. They seemed to be in some sort of square bordered by houses, most of which were either blackened ruins, or were still burning. All except one house, a timber, two-storey building of green panels between exposed black beams. It stood unharmed, between two other burning houses—and it wasn't even singed.

The Ragwitch moved Her head, and Julia had the uncomfortable feeling of having her eyeballs move involuntarily—except they weren't really hers, she thought sadly, so it was only an imaginary discomfort.

At first, Julia couldn't see what the Ragwitch had turned to look at, then Oroch emerged from the smoke. He was still wrapped in tar-black bandages, but now he wore a blue silk shirt, still bloodied from its previous owner. Six Gwarulch formed a ring around him, peering into the smoke with their harsh red eyes, looking for anyone foolish enough to attack the Ragwitch's most trusted servant.

"So, Oroch!" snapped the Ragwitch, before he was even past the Angarling. "The Art is dead and forgotten in Bevallan! Then how do you explain that?"

Oroch followed Her outstretched arm, and saw the green house standing intact amidst blackened ruin. His wet, red mouth gaped several times, and then he squeaked, "Perhaps just luck, Mistress? A simple coincidence, to have avoided the fire . . ."

The Ragwitch hissed, exposing her shark-like teeth, and Oroch fell silent, cringing. She towered over him, and slowly reached out a puffy, three-fingered hand. Clumsily, She gripped the end of one of Oroch's bandages.

"Three failures I allow you, Oroch," She whispered, Her voice full of menace. "And then we shall see what lies beneath these bandages I placed upon you so long ago. That house is protected by the Rune of Lys, and the Rune of Yrsal, and the Rune of Carral. And they are fresh-painted, Oroch, and that is your first failure. Two more, and . . ." Cruelly, She started to draw the end of the bandage off. Oroch whimpered, and She let go, turning towards the black-beamed house of green. "Lys, Yrsal and Carral," whispered the Ragwitch, her worm-like tongue flicking out with each word. "But that is only three of four, and none to keep out Me!"

She laughed at that, and Oroch chuckled. The Gwarulch picked up Her mood, and grinned, exposing their yellow, dog-like canines thrusting out of white-flecked gums. Julia listened to Her cackling, and felt a sudden bond with whoever might be in the green and black house. I hope they get away, she thought, with an urgency she hadn't felt before, even for herself. Oh please, let them get away!

"Forward," said the Ragwitch, and the Angarling tromped ahead, carven faces set towards the house. The Ragwitch let them advance until they stood just outside the lower windows, and then halted them with a wave of Her puffy arm. Inside the house, a shutter banged, and the Ragwitch laughed again, striding forward to the heavy, oaken door. She reached out to the handle, and the iron flared like a giant sparkler at a fireworks display. Inside, a clear, high voice said, "Lys!," a woman's voice, or perhaps a girl's, with a note of command and urgency.

The handle spat white sparks even higher as the woman inside spoke, but the Ragwitch merely reached forward, and the light dimmed and the sparks went out. With a slight flick, the Ragwitch forced the door open, and compressing Her limp body through the doorway, stepped inside.

"Yrsal," said the voice, more urgently, this time, and both Julia and the Ragwitch instantly saw the speaker. Just past the front door, she stood in the hallway. Tall and slight, her white hair hung down past her waist, over a green robe. Julia saw her face, old and kind, with sea green eyes that somehow saw Julia, and not just the Ragwitch.

But the Ragwitch saw only the old woman's meager trappings of power; a silver knife, a stalk of rowan, and knowledge of only three scant runes.

"Yrsal," said the old woman again, in a commanding tone, holding the silver knife up against her chest. A little light ran along the blade, but the Ragwitch raised an arm, and the blade dimmed, and tarnished, turning black before the woman's eyes.

"Carral," said the woman, softly, dropping the knife, and drawing the sprig of rowan. "Carral," she said again, blowing gently on the sprig, and placing it on the floor. It lay there for a second, then shivered, and began to throw out green shoots. Julia watched amazed at the sprig's sudden growth and the Ragwitch's inaction.

Inside a minute, the sprig was a full-grown rowan tree, and the old woman seemed to relax behind its protection. The Ragwitch watched, unmoved, as the old woman stepped back and admired her handiwork.

"Pass that, if you can, monster!" called out the woman cheerfully. "You might have got everyone else, but Rowan will fix you!"

The Ragwitch bowed Her head, and for a fragment of a second, Julia thought She might be beaten. Then, Julia felt the Ragwitch laughing inside, as She reached forward and touched the rowan tree.

"On the contrary," hissed the Ragwitch, suddenly snapping up to her full height. "I shall have you, Half-Witch!"

The rowan tree shriveled at Her touch, and the old woman screamed as the Ragwitch loomed above her, and slammed her down onto the floor. She tried to squirm away, but the Ragwitch bent down, pinning her with one outstretched hand, as her toothy maw bent closer and closer towards the helpless victim.

As she fainted, Julia caught the partial image of the old woman's left hand reaching up to touch a tiny silver acorn to the Ragwitch's side. Then it and everything else vanished into a panicked blackness.

7

A Friend of Beasts/Lyssa

Paul looked back up at Rhysamarn again, unsure of how he'd gone so far in such a short time. He'd only left Tanboule a few hours ago, but he was already past the grey shale and the heather, and was once more looking down on green fields neatly separated by low stone walls. Directly below him, a road stretched from right to left, cut into the broken ground where the foothills of Rhysamarn flattened out into the valley.

There were quite a few sheep about (they were black and scrawny, unlike the merinos Paul was used to), but there was no sign of any people—or of any kind of house or village. The valley grew wider to the east (or what Paul thought was east), so he cut across in that direction, walking easily down the hill to the road.

Upon closer inspection, it wasn't really a road, but more of a well-travelled track. Paul noticed wheel-marks in the yellow clay, and for an instant, thought of cars. But the tracks were treadless, and very narrow.

Still, they were tracks, and a sign of other people, so Paul kept heading east, feeling reasonably cheerful. Tanboule had said nothing to ease his mind, but at least he now had a definite purpose, even if it did sound a little bit mad.

Paul laughed to himself, imagining asking a passerby for the Earth Lady's address, or directions to the Water Lord's house. He was still giggling a little when a voice suddenly addressed him from behind.

"Hey! Boy! Have you seen a hare go past?"

Paul turned around slowly, expecting to see whoever had spoken, but the road was empty, and there was no one over in the fields, or up on the hill.

"I said, have you seen a hare?" asked the voice again, from the sound of it, not too far away. At the same time, a dark shadow fell across Paul, and he shivered, instinctively looking up to face whatever new horror might be there.

"Well, have you seen a hare?" asked the voice, a little angrily—and this time, Paul could see the speaker. About ten meters above, a huge balloon drifted silently along, the bright yellow lozenges painted on its sides brilliant in the sunlight.

A wicker basket swung below it, suspended by a complicated tracery of ropes and wires. In the basket, a rather short man was hanging over the side, calling to Paul. "Have . . . you . . . seen . . . a . . . *hare*!" shouted the man. "You know, like a rabbit, but with longer ears!"

Paul looked around quickly, but couldn't see anything. "No, I haven't seen a hare!" he shouted. "Where's it supposed to be?"

"She!" shouted the man. "It's a she! And she's supposed to be . . . oh, never mind! I'll come down."

Paul watched as the man leaned back into the basket and vanished from sight. He was expecting a loud hiss of escaping air or gas to make the balloon sink, but there wasn't a sound. Instead, the balloon silently rose up several meters, and started to steadily climb into the sky, accompanied by a loud outbreak of what sounded like the man cursing and swearing.

The balloon started to head east, so Paul followed it, since it was heading in his direction anyway. It went up and down rather erratically, before finally coming down to land, several hundreds meters up the road. The short man immediately got out, and began fastening ropes to the stone wall, an ancient stump and anything else nearby that looked solid. Obviously, he'd had to land like this before, as the balloon started to rise again, till the anchor ropes were at full stretch, and the basket was a meter or so above the ground.

Closer to, Paul saw that the short man was in fact, more of an older boy than a man—though muscular and solidly built, he was rather short, though still taller than Paul. He wore an odd assortment of clothing, including several brilliantly colored shirts, all of which seemed in bad repair. A mulberry-colored hat rested shapelessly on top of his windswept, sandy-colored hair, and he looked and acted like the most disorganized person Paul had ever met.

"Hello!" he cried, as Paul ran over to help him with an escaping rope. He favored Paul with an uneven smile before letting out a cry of dismay, and rushing over to yet another anchor-rope that had somehow come undone.

"Know anything about knots?" he called out to Paul, who was quietly retying the nearest rope, which had just pulled out of the most complicated and useless knot he'd ever seen.

"I know a couple," replied Paul, dashing over to help retie the main anchor-line, which had suddenly relinquished its hold on the old stump. The balloonist rushed past to tie up another rope, and Paul took a closer look at him. He seemed human enough, and Tanboule had said that he would meet someone who could help him. But Tanboule had also said that there would always be some humans who would serve Her . . .

Then the balloonist tripped, and fell swearing amidst a tangled skein of ropes. Paul looked at him vainly trying to free himself, and decided that anyone who could swear with such color and variety must be all right.

"I'm Paul," he said quietly, helping untangle the other boy. He felt a slight qualm in doing so—the balloonist was at least two or three years older than Paul, and at school, if a younger kid helped an older one after an accident, the younger often ended up with a belt around the head—after all, someone had to be blamed for the accident. But the balloonist merely dusted himself off, and said, "Thank you. Allow me to introduce myself. I am Quigin, a Friend of Beasts."

He made an elaborate sort of bow, complete with many waves of his hat, but this was lost on Paul, who was looking around for some beasts. He half expected to see a griffon wheeling in from the sun, or perhaps a pair of wolves loping through the fields—but the sky was a clear, vacant blue, and there was nothing in the fields, save sheep.

"A Friend of Beasts?" asked Paul, hesitantly, "I'm not quite sure . . ."

"Well, Friend of a Beast, at the moment," interrupted Quigin. "Leasel. She's a hare. But I have almost finished my apprenticeship, and then I'll have more time to make friends . . . with beasts."

"What are you an apprentice of?" asked Paul, thinking of electricians and plumbers—or whatever equivalents they might have in this rather backward kingdom.

"I told you," replied Quigin, surprised. "I'm an Apprentice Friend of Beasts. Don't you believe me?"

Paul started to say that he did believe him, but

Quigin just kept on talking. "Look—I'll just find Leasel, and that'll prove it!"

"Fine," replied Paul. He was starting to think that this strange boy probably couldn't help him anyway, but after cabbage-planting wise men, he wasn't so sure. In any case, Quigin ignored him, and started walking along beside the nearest stone wall, calling out, "Leasel! Leasel!"

After he'd called several times to no effect, Quigin came back and sat down on the wall. Paul sat down next to him, and said, "Excuse me . . . but . . . what was your hare doing down here, while you were up in the balloon?"

"Having lunch," replied Quigin, rather sharply. Then he sighed, and added, "I still haven't quite got the knack of that balloon thing yet. So instead of landing, I lowered Leasel on a piece of rope, so she could get something to eat. But the first thing she chewed was the rope, and then she just ran off into the weeds, somewhere along this wall."

"Well, surely she'll come back," said Paul.

"Yes. I suppose so," said Quigin. "Master Cagael's Friends never run off!"

"Are they hares too?" asked Paul, just to be polite. But Quigin didn't seem too pleased with this question, only grunting before reluctantly answering. "No. He's got eagles and dogs and otters and all manner of beasts. I'm the only Friend of Beasts whose Friend is a stupid hare."

He looked at Paul with an angry glare, and then suddenly jumped to his feet. Paul leapt back nervously, but Quigin ran off down the wall to dive at something that was lurking in the weeds. There was a scuffle for a second, then he stood up with a silver-grey hare, held securely by its two long, aristocratic ears.

"Leasel?" asked Paul.

The other boy nodded, but didn't answer. Instead, he held the hare up to his eyes, until their noses were almost touching. The hare seemed to be trying to look away, but slowly her eyes focused on Quigin's, and he began to whisper in a voice so low Paul couldn't even catch the language, let alone the words.

After a few seconds, Quigin put the hare down, and released her ears. Paul expected her to dash off like any disturbed animal, but she quietly began nibbling on a large, nasty-looking weed.

"She was sorry for being troublesome," said Quigin. "So she'll probably behave for a few hours with any luck. Now, with Leasel out of the way, all I have to do is get back to Sasterisk. You wouldn't know anything about balloons would you?"

"No," said Paul, surprised that anyone would ask him if he knew anything about balloons. Mostly people just assumed that he didn't know anything about anything.

"Never mind," said Quigin, cheerfully. He sat down on the wall, and started to scratch Leasel behind the ears, while Paul wondered if he should continue walking along the road. He was just about to get up and go, when Quigin jumped up again, and slapped himself on the side of the head.

"Paul! You said your name's Paul!"

"Yes," replied Paul, wondering why Quigin was looking at him in such a strange way—almost as if he was trying to remember where he'd seen him last.

"You're certain your name is Paul?" asked Quigin again, almost fearfully. When Paul nodded, he sighed, and sat down again, scratching his head.

"Is my name important?" asked Paul anxiously. He'd read stories where people had their heads chopped off because the natives hadn't liked their names. But that was always when they spoke different languages . . .

"Paul," said Quigin, out into the air, as if he was talking to himself. "He was very exact. He said Paul several times, and even spelled it out for me. Paul as in 'shawl,' except with a 'p.' "

"Who said this?" asked Paul, rather nervously. "What are you talking about?"

"The man who lent me the balloon," replied Quigin, vaguely pointing towards the great yellow-lozenged balloon and the wicker basket below it. "Master Thruan. He's a friend of my Master, and a great traveller and storyteller."

"But what did he say about me?" asked Paul.

"Well," said Quigin slowly. "I didn't believe him at the time, but he told me that I could borrow his balloon. I'd always wanted to ride in a balloon, so I jumped at the chance . . . and Master Cagael didn't mind giving me the day off . . ."

"Yes, yes," interrupted Paul. "But what did this Thruan tell you about me? Did he mention the Elementals?"

"No," replied Quigin. "He said that if I should meet a boy named Paul, I was to take him wherever he wanted in the balloon—no matter how long it might take! And Master Cagael agreed! But I thought it was only a joke . . ."

"This Master Thruan," said Paul. "What does he do?"

"He doesn't do anything that I know of," said Quigin. "Leastwise, he doesn't work like normal folk. He travels mostly—though not always by balloon."

"Oh," replied Paul, disappointed. "He's not a Wizard then?"

Quigin raised one eyebrow, and paused, before replying. "I didn't say that," he said. "Though there's few enough of that sort round these days. Mind you, my old Gran always said there was something a bit sorcerous about Master Thruan. And if he weren't up to his ears in Magic, how would he know I'd meet you?"

"Well," said Paul hesitantly. "If he said you were to take me anywhere, I'd like to go and see this Master Thruan."

"That's one place I can't take you," said Quigin. "He's gone—and he never tells anyone when he'll be back, or where he's going. I suppose we could try looking for him . . ."

"I suppose so," answered Paul, doubtfully. Master Thruan seemed like a good person to talk to about the Elementals, and where Paul might find them. But if it took too long to find Thruan, it might be too late for Julia—and everyone.

"Anyway, we really have to go where the wind blows us," said Quigin cheerfully. "Normally, a bit of a southerly comes up about dusk, and that will take us to Sasterisk, at least. Now, what are you doing wandering about all by yourself? And why are you looking for Wizards?"

Paul started to reply, intending to tell Quigin only that he was looking for his sister. But Quigin kept losing the thread of the story, and Paul kept on starting again, and telling him a bit more, so that after a while Paul found that without really meaning to, he'd told Quigin the whole story.

Strangely enough, Quigin didn't seem too concerned when Paul mentioned the Ragwitch, or retold Tanboule's story about the North-Queen. He just nodded his head, and chewed thoughtfully on a long blade of grass, before asking questions like: "How many points did Ornware's antlers have?" or "Did the May Dancers leave trails of leaves when they walked?"

Paul was getting a bit annoyed at all these irrelevant questions, when Quigin spat out his blade of grass, and said, "Let's get going then!"

"What?" asked Paul, bewildered by this sudden action after so many laconic questions. "I thought we had to wait till dusk, when the southerly comes up—to take us to . . . um . . . Sasterisk?"

"But we aren't going to Sasterisk," said Quigin, as if that explained everything. "Come on, Leasel!"

Paul looked down as the hare sat up, her bright eyes meeting Paul's for a second. Then she put her head back down, and placidly resumed nibbling at the weeds, almost as if to say, "I'm not going anywhere."

"Come on, Leasel! Paul!" said Quigin again, taking several steps, and then turning back to make hurrying gestures. "We have to get aloft before the wind changes!"

"But where are we going?" asked Paul.

"To the Master of Air, of course," said Quigin, in an exasperated tone. "That's where you want to go isn't it? And Master Thruan said to take you where you want to go."

Paul looked at him, feeling slightly dazed at the speed at which Quigin had solved his problem. If he *had* solved the problem. "You know where to find the Master of Air?"

"Not exactly," said Quigin. "But I do know where we can find out."

"And we need to go by balloon?" asked Paul, looking at the frail wicker basket, and the slender network of ropes and wires that connected it to the balloon.

"Yes, yes," said Quigin, impatiently. He pointed to the east, towards a distant mountain, itself only a tiny lump on the horizon, half obscured by long lines of wispy cloud. "It's over there."

"On the mountain?" asked Paul, hoping it wasn't. He didn't like mountains much any more, ranking them after forests as places to avoid.

"No," said Quigin. "Above the mountain. In the air. Or as the birds would say . . ."

He drew a deep breath, and let out a shrill whistle,

which rose and fell, echoing harshly across the fields. At the sound of the whistle, Leasel froze, and then bolted away, streaking through the weeds like an over-charged toy train.

"Wort!" swore Quigin. "You'd think she could tell the difference between me hawk-whistling and a hawk hawk-whistling!"

Paul watched him run after the hare, nearly falling over with every step. He seemed to be all loose-limbed and very clumsy—but he was also very fast. Somehow, he seemed to have the movements of a tall, gangly person, mistakenly wrapped up in a stocky, muscular body.

I hope he can work the balloon all right, thought Paul anxiously, watching the older boy catch Leasel by falling on her. For a second Paul thought of Aleyne, and wished he were there instead of Quigin. But at least the Friend of Beasts seemed a cheerful person—he had hardly quivered at the terrors Paul had described.

And he did know how to find the Master of Air. Or at least, he said he did.

* * *

Julia hesitantly opened one eye, half expecting to still be tied into the Ragwitch's senses. And she was very much afraid of what she might see, if they were still inside the green-panelled house with the old lady. Or whatever the Ragwitch might have left of her . . .

Slowly her eyelid crept open, and Julia sighed as the comforting white light of the globe splashed onto her face. It might only be a temporary refuge, but at least she was back in her own body, floating in the strange fluid deep in the Ragwitch's mind.

Relieved, she opened her other eye, and blinked to make sure she was seeing straight. Then she arched her back, spreading her arms and legs like a starfish, rejoicing in the feel and movement of her own body—so different from the ghastly, leaden motions of the Rag-witch's straw-stuffed limbs.

But even the slightest movement took more effort than usual, and Julia shuddered, realizing that she must be getting more and more used to feeling the Rag-witch's body, so that she could hardly remember how to work her own. And if Her body was becoming familiar, perhaps in time, Her mind might do the same thing . . . and Julia would be totally consumed.

Julia shivered at the thought, deliberately intensifying the feeling, wriggling her backbone to let the shiver climb all the way up the back of her neck to make her hair stand on end. The Ragwitch never shivered. And Her hair was flat and rancid, caked to the sides of that evil face—nothing could make it stand on end.

"Shivering?" said a voice behind Julia. "But then, you cannot be cold here."

The voice was not the Ragwitch's. It was a kind voice, full of warmth, totally unlike the chilling, biting feel of Her voice, or the thoughts She sent to retrieve Julia from her refuge. It was a human voice, the voice of the woman from the green-panelled, black-beamed house of Bevallan.

Julia turned around joyfully, expecting to see the green- robed woman, her white hair floating above her, like Julia's own. There was no one there—but in the distance, a yellow light flickered where there had never been one before. It was like the light of the globe, but softer and weaker, and far smaller.

Eagerly, Julia began to swim towards it, praying that this wasn't some sadistic trick of the Ragwitch to raise within her a hope that couldn't exist.

Close by, the yellow light came from an unsteady fire which flickered, occasionally flaring, only to die down into a dull yellow glow, and then grow back to a rea-sonably constant flame.

But Julia had no eyes for the light. For around it, in a circle about three meters wide, was a ring of holly, each sprig cleverly woven together, the red berries outermost. Within the ring, there was green grass, shorn close enough to make the finest croquet lawn or golfing green. And next to the flame was a rowan tree. A springtime tree, all covered with white flowers. As Julia watched, the tree shook slightly, and the flowers trembled as if touched by a light-fingered breeze. The flame flickered too, and Julia blinked as it flared back after the sudden wind.

Then, instead of a rowan, the green-gowned lady was there, sitting cross-legged on the turf. She smiled at Julia and gestured for her to step over the holly and into the ring.

"Now we can talk freely," said the old lady, as Julia carefully stepped onto the springy turf. "Sit down, child."

Julia sat down obediently, relishing the feel of the soft turf. She pushed her hand into the soft dirt beneath, squishing it between her fingers—before realizing what she was doing.

"Oh, I'm sorry," she said, hastily wiping her hand on the turf. "I wasn't thinking . . ."

"Don't worry," the lady said calmly. "Feeling it will make it stronger—will make *you* stronger, and better able to resist the Ragwitch."

Julia shivered at the mention of Her name, and instinctively looked about, fearing the sudden intrusion of Her thoughts, and the destruction of this small green circle and the old woman. Like She had destroyed Bevallan, and . . .

"But you were in the house," began Julia. "And She broke the rowan tree, and . . . She called you a Half-Witch . . ."

"She can make mistakes, you know," said the old

lady. "I may look and act like a Half-Witch, but I am both more and less than that. And very, very different. That body the Ragwitch killed out there was not me—though I could be easily slain if She perceived my true nature."

"Then, when she bent over you . . . your body . . ." said Julia, shivering again, despite the cosy warmth of the fire. "You weren't really there . . ."

"Didn't feel a thing!" declared the old woman cheerfully. "But enough of this! We have not yet exchanged names, as I am told all prisoners do upon sharing a cell."

"I'm Julia," said Julia.

"And I am Lyssa," replied the old woman. "I came here with eyes wide-open, hoping to find the truth behind this . . . thing . . . that had risen in the North. And I find that it is far, far worse than I expected. And I also found you—to add mystery to peril. But a brief mystery, I hope—if you can tell me how you came to this place."

"I'm not sure I should talk here . . ." said Julia, nervously. She felt sure the Ragwitch's thoughts would touch upon her soon, and speaking Her name would somehow bring them closer. Lyssa seemed to feel her anxiety, for she gestured to the holly ring, and began to sing, in a high, clear voice:

Rowan to guard, leaf and tree
Holly to hide, thee and me
Sun-fire and greensward sing
To ward us here within the ring . . .

"An old rhyme but true enough," continued Lyssa, though Julia felt that she had left part of the song unsung. "If you know the way of it. The Ragwitch cannot see or hear us inside the braided holly. But you cannot stay too long, or She will notice your absence, and break my wards with Her dark thoughts."

Julia looked back out into the fluid that seemed to stretch endlessly away. In the distance, the globe pulsated, its white light now seeming harsh and cruel compared to the comforting yellow flame. Across from her, Lyssa smiled, and Julia wondered how anyone could smile, lost within the strange prison of the Ragwitch's mind.

"I smile because that is all I can do," said Lyssa, and Julia realized she must have spoken aloud.

"You should smile too," continued Lyssa, reaching out to touch the corner of Julia's mouth with her smooth, warm fingers. "We are both still alive, and that is more than many can say, after Bevallan."

Julia sat silent, not answering. She was indirectly responsible for all those poor people—and any others that might get in the way of the Ragwitch's dark designs. Which was probably everybody in the whole country—or at least, all the good people, and anything that wasn't cruel and monstrous like the Ragwitch Herself.

"I wish," whispered Julia. "I just wish I had never . . ."

"Sssh!" interrupted Lyssa, suddenly getting to her feet. "Look at the globe!"

Julia snapped her head round to look, and saw the globe suddenly flash brighter than it ever had before. Dark, sickly-looking purples and greens clouded its surface before vanishing in a flash of light, only to re-form again in an instant.

"What's happening?" asked Julia, automatically looking at Lyssa and expecting an answer. But Lyssa was no longer standing next to her—she had crouched down, and was mumbling to herself. As Julia watched, Lyssa seemed to fall inwards on herself, her skin crackling and folding, her arms thinning out and stretching—and then, there was only a white-flowered rowan next to the yellow flame. But Lyssa's voice lingered in the air, like the last, fading notes of a chance-struck harp.

"The Ragwitch is being attacked, Julia. You must see what is happening . . ."

"But I can't!" wailed Julia. "She always takes me back! I can't do it by myself!"

"Touch the globe . . ." whispered the leaves of the rowan. "Touch the globe . . ."

And then there was silence in the ring of woven holly, save for the merest whisper of the yellow flame. Off in the fluid, Julia swam towards the globe—eager to see, yet at the same time dreading what might be there.

8

A GUIDE/THE NAMYR STEPS

Paul shivered as the balloon hit another freezing downdraft. He wasn't really cold in his heavy cloak, but every time they hit cold air, the balloon dropped at least thirty meters—and the mountains were very close underneath.

The balloon dropped again, and Paul felt his stomach lurch—obviously it felt like staying up while the rest of his body went down. It was like a particularly fast lift— but much more disturbing. After all, the balloon wasn't held up by cables and huge winches. In fact, Paul didn't know what was holding it up. At first, he'd assumed it was a hot-air balloon, but it didn't have a burner to keep the hot air going into the gas-bag. If the gas-bag was a gas-bag . . . every time Paul looked up, he thought he could see dim shapes moving about behind the yellow silk.

"Quigin . . ." said Paul, once the balloon settled again. "What keeps this balloon up?"

"Things—creatures," said Quigin. "I've got some more in a jar somewhere, in case we lose some through a rip or tear. They're quite interesting, close up."

Paul shuddered, looking down at the interior of the basket. All along the sides, various leather bags were attached to the wicker framework, each one labelled with a small picture, representing its contents. Leasel the hare sat in one corner, chewing on a pile of dandelions, and ignoring the sudden rises and falls of the balloon. Every time they hit a particularly nasty crosswind, she just fastened her teeth into the leather bands that bound the wicker basket together.

"We'll be there by midnight," said Quigin, cheerfully. "And the moon is three-quarters full tonight—so they will be flying."

"Who will be flying?" asked Paul anxiously, suddenly thinking about moons, bats and horror movies. "And is midnight a good time to arrive?"

"It's as good as any other, isn't it?" said Quigin. "It'll be bright with the moon, so we can . . . *look out!*"

Suddenly, the balloon dropped again, the basket swinging madly from side to side. Paul fell to the left and then to the right, barely managing to grab a side-rope, to avoid being tumbled over the side. Quigin fell past him, but Paul managed to grab him for a few seconds, just long enough for the Friend of Beasts to catch hold of the edge of the basket.

"Thanks," gasped Quigin, immediately wedging himself between two of the leather bags to lick his rope-burned hands. "Mind you, I wouldn't have fallen far. That last drop's put us right over the top of Aillghill mountain. If you look now, you can see Aillghill Force—the waterfall."

Paul reluctantly got to his feet, being careful to hang on with both hands, and wedge his feet under the bags. Then, taking a deep breath, he looked down.

Quigin was right—he would have only dropped about ten meters. Directly below, a rather flat-topped mountain reached up to meet them. Clad in ice and snow, it flashed under the light of the evening sun, so bright, Paul had to half-close his eyes to see the beginning of the waterfall.

A few hundred meters below, a great spume of ice burst out from the mountain. Made up of thousands of frozen strands, it sparkled like the most delicate glasswork. High up, only a little water trickled down this icy tracery, but as each tiny rivulet combined, the fall grew stronger. Thousands of meters below, the waters finally crashed together in full flood, raising a vast and impenetrable mist.

"The mist," said Quigin, pointing dangerously over the side, "only goes away about once every hundred years when there is a particularly bad winter, and *all* of the waterfall freezes, not just the top part. They say there's caves full of treasure down there, under it all."

Paul stared after Quigin's pointing hand, and thought momentarily of treasure, sunken in the mist. Then he looked back up at the clear sky and the setting sun. Another night in this strange world, thought Paul, shivering—and where might Julia be, awaiting nightfall and the three-quarter moon?

"What do we do now?" he asked, forgetting about the treasure. "Does the Master of Air come here?"

"He may," replied Quigin, still staring into the mist. He waved his arm vaguely about the sky. "There's certainly enough air around."

"What do you mean—he may?" asked Paul, who was beginning to wonder whether Quigin really did know anything about the Master of Air. He obviously knew little enough about ballooning.

"He may," replied Quigin, standing up to look at the sky. "But what I had in mind is to follow a guide."

"A guide?"

"Yes," replied Quigin. "And there's the first of them now."

Paul followed his gaze, looking into the sky. At first, all he could see was a brown speck a little below them and at least a kilometer away. But it was closing rapidly, easily climbing, spiralling up with the change of a single wing tip. A hawk, or an eagle, thought Paul, though not a very big one.

"I'll have to screech and whistle," said Quigin, apologetically. "I've told Leasel, but you'll probably have to hold her."

"Sure," said Paul, kneeling down next to the dandelion-chewing hare. He stroked her ears, feeling the soft grey fur, then took hold of her securely around the neck, as Quigin took a very, very deep breath.

The resulting series of hawk-cries scared Paul almost more than Leasel. The hare started as Quigin began each sequence, but Paul's hands seemed to calm her. Paul kept expecting Quigin to run out of breath, but the Friend of Beasts kept up the calls for what seemed like several minutes.

Then a hawk was perched on the rope-rail, folding its wings, its golden-brown eyes peering hungrily into the basket. Quigin chirruped at it, a strange sort of half-clucking—and it turned to face him.

Squatting on the floor of the basket, Paul couldn't quite see the hawk, but Quigin seemed to be staring at it and it was meeting his gaze. Then, like he'd done with Leasel, Quigin began to talk in that soft tone that was like the whisper of a whisper. Occasionally, the hawk made a slight whistling noise, but Paul felt certain that the bird was talking to Quigin through its eyes alone. Finally Quigin glanced away, and the hawk half-lidded its eyes, and stretched its wings a little.

"Well," said Quigin. "She'll take us to the Wind Moot, and there the Master of Air may receive us."

"What else did she talk about?" asked Paul.

"Mice and sparrows," replied Quigin. "But at least I managed to find out where they hold the Wind Moot—and get us invited there."

"But what is the Wind Moot?" asked Paul.

"It's a sort of meeting place for birds," replied Quigin. "I think I can remember how Cagael described it, from *The Book of Beasts*, 'High above certain mountains, where the currents of air run both cold and warm, to climb or fall through the clouds; the Birds of the Claw travel the way from East to West, and under Sun, or Light of Moon, the Wind Moot meets . . .' "

"The Birds of the Claw?"

"Oh, falcons, hawks, eagles," explained Quigin. "Some of the larger owls, if the Moot is under moonlight. Sometimes other birds are called, ravens, swifts and suchlike. But it's mostly for the hunters."

"What do they do there?" asked Paul, thinking of a great cloud of birds, circling around, high in the air, for no apparent reason.

"They talk," replied Quigin. "Or so I've been told. I've never been to one myself."

"Oh," said Paul, looking at the hawk's cruel, curved beak, and remembering the giant crow that had attacked him on the midden so many days ago and a world away. "How big do these birds get? I mean . . . will it be safe?"

"I don't know," said Quigin cheerfully. "But it's bound to be interesting!"

The hawk seemed to agree with Quigin, because it whistled briefly, and flew up, circling the basket before slowly flying off towards the setting sun. It flew slowly, and circled back several times—obviously waiting to guide them.

Quigin whistled again, and the hawk started climbing, up towards the first of the evening stars. The Friend of Beasts watched the bird's effortless flight, and then addressed the balloon above, making some ritual gestures with his fingers and hands.

Paul watched, entranced, as the shadowy figures inside the gas-bag swelled and assumed a slightly orange hue. The balloon rose steadily in silence, following the hawk up into the night sky.

"I think I've finally got this balloon sorted out," said Quigin, happily. "Look, there's another hawk—and there, some sort of eagle . . . "

* * *

Julia screamed as she joined the Ragwitch's senses, a long, inward cry of pain. Normally, it just felt unnatural and somehow unclean, but this time, pain lanced through her and she could see only blurred, cloudy visions through the Ragwitch's eyes.

Slowly, the pain eased and the mist cleared from her sight. Julia felt the now familiar bloated limbs and dulled senses of the Ragwitch, and then Her thoughts burst into her mind, cold and biting.

"Pain, Julia? But it is not I that cause you pain. I am not unkind to those that serve me well. As you have begun to do."

Julia didn't answer, letting the dull ache in her head fade away, so she could see properly. Dimly, she felt that the Ragwitch was pleased with her, a prospect that was terrifying. What could she have done that helped the Ragwitch?

Gradually, Julia's sight cleared, and she saw that they stood upon a road, a thin, gravelled road, bordered on each side by lightly-wooded fields that looked as if they might once have been open farmland. Ahead, the road wound up through a clear expanse of short, greyish bushes towards a great cleft in the hills beyond, a jagged gorge of off-white rock, dripping with greenish water.

The Ragwitch gazed towards the gorge, and so, of course, did Julia. But they could see only a little way into the dark passage, where the road dipped down past the white stone bluffs.

Only then did Julia realize it was night. Instead of the sun, a huge three-quarter moon hung low over the gorge—almost directly above it, but not quite in the right place to light up the depths below.

The Ragwitch moved Her head, straw spilling from the rounded folds at Her neck, and Julia saw that She stood on the road alone—but under the shadow of the trees, the Gwarulch lurked, and the Angarling stood as silent as the stillest trees. And there was another shape, black in the blackest shadow. The Ragwitch beckoned, and it stepped forward into the moonlight. Julia recognized Oroch, and hoped this was not another of his failures—she didn't want to even begin to see what lay under those tar-black bandages.

"Oroch," hissed the Ragwitch. "Have the Gwarulch returned?"

"No, Mistress," said Oroch, squirming. "First two and twenty, and then four and forty went down to the Steps. But none have returned. And the Meepers have lost fifteen of their number, and now they will not fly."

"Order them aloft, or twice that number will burn!" spat the Ragwitch, menacingly. She leaned over Oroch, and he stepped back, slipping on the thick gravel.

"That which holds the Namyr Steps is not for them," continued the Ragwitch, spittle dripping from Her red-painted lips. "I have been attacked, Oroch—they have dared to attack Me! And now, they will answer for it!"

Oroch nodded fearfully, hesitantly squeaking out, "But what is it, oh Mistress? Is it . . . dangerous?"

Julia felt a strange amusement ripple through the Ragwitch, before She answered. "It has already cast a spell against Me, Oroch. But it is only one, and not of the First Rank. And what of spells, when all that strike Me first strike the child?"

As She spoke, Julia felt the Ragwitch's amusement increase, and then, She was cackling aloud, while Oroch giggled, and the Gwarulch in the trees snorted their agreement at whatever She enjoyed.

And inside, She whispered to Julia under the cackling, "And so, my rescuer, you are curse and spell-trap, chantward and shield. And those who may strive against Me, will wound and pierce a child. And you will feel the pain of every spell against Me. You will feel the pain . . . "

The Ragwitch stopped cackling, and slowly began to move down towards the gorge called the Namyr Steps. Behind Her, Oroch capered, still giggling; the Angarling lumbered after Her, and the Gwarulch streamed through the trees on either side, pausing only to rend any small beast or nocturnal bird that fled too late. Above, Meepers flew as far back as they dared, fearing to go on, but obedient to their Mistress, who was their greatest fear.

"She's coming," said Thruan, holding out his thumbs which were twitching, seemingly without his control. "We had best leave while we still can."

The woman who had come up beside him shook her head. "That's what I came up to tell you—we can't get out. There is a Black Veil across the last of the Steps. Lyalbec touched it, and it withered his arm." She grimaced, showing an old white scar that ran from the corner of her mouth to one of the face-bars of her helmet. "Fortunately, Lyalbec is left-handed. He can still use a sword. If that will do us any good . . . ?"

She phrased the last part as a question, and Thruan hesitated a second before answering, black eyebrows meeting above his wide nose, a frown of puzzlement rather than deep thought.

"I think swords and arrows will play a little part, before the night is done. But only a little, and it will not be enough for us. I am now sure that it is the Ragwitch we are facing—once North-Queen and Witch—for there is a great and evil power there. And yet . . . my first spell against Her was not countered, nor exactly turned . . . "

A whistle higher up the gorge interrupted him, and the woman picked up her bow, and loosened the basket-hilted sword at her side.

"I'll go up now," she said. "If whatever comes down the Steps is flesh and blood, we'll stop it. If not—well, at least Aenle got through before the Black Veil formed. Caer Calbore will not go unwarned."

"My thanks, Captain," said Master Thruan. "I will do what I can."

She nodded and said, "It is well we met you going north. If one must fight, and on a stricken field, it is easier to bear in company. Farewell."

Thruan watched her climbing up the limestone steps that gave the Namyr gorge its name. On either side of the passage, men and women rose up from their brief rest, buckling on breastplates over buff coats, or strapping on their helmets with the three-barred visors. Higher up, Gwarulch corpses grinned, either feathered with arrows or slain by Thruan's Magic, more chilling to them than the sharpest steel.

Thruan watched, counting, till all thirty of the survivors were spread out below the topmost step, readying their bows, laying out blue-feathered arrows for a last stand. Then he looked to the pool of water on the seventy-seventh step and bent his mind to the south-east. He hoped to have one last look at his balloon, and perhaps learn more of the significance of this . . . Paul.

Slowly, the water began to cloud, and Thruan saw a field of stars behind some scudding wisps of cloud. Birds of prey wheeled across the sky, hundreds of them, circling a yellow-lozenged balloon. Two figures stood within the basket: one, Cagael's apprentice, Quigin, and the other, presumably, Paul . . .

Another whistle came from above, and the vision faded. Thruan turned from the pool, and began to climb the steps, readying his scant powers. Already bow-strings twanged above, and Gwarulch screams echoed in the gorge. But the Gwarulch were not alone, and Thruan's thumbs twitched in dire warning as the Ragwitch reached the topmost step, death and darkness rolling like a cloud before Her.

9

THE WIND MOOT/GLAZED-FOLK

This is fantastic!" shouted Paul—he had to shout, over the shrill cries and whistles of all the birds that surrounded the balloon. Everywhere he looked, there were fierce-eyed hawks and falcons, wheeling and screeching like a flock of some strange, sharp-taloned seagulls.

The balloon, like the birds, was riding on a warm up-draft. Looking up, it seemed to Paul that he was falling, falling towards the brilliant, three-quarter moon, and the clear, steady twinkling of the stars, riding in their strange constellations with even stranger names.

Paul had never thought that so many birds of prey would gather in such a small space—from tiniest hawk to the largest eagle, spiralling upwards to some airy and mystical location.

Quigin loved it, of course. Paul had been unable to get him to listen to anything—he was too intent on the roar of bird-calls. Every now and then, he nodded his head, and mumbled, "Of course . . . but I knew that . . . well, at least a bit . . ." Then he would screech in return, and even more birds would gather around the balloon. One old eagle (it had a bald head) even went so far as to hitch a ride, gripping the rim of the basket with talons the size of Paul's fingers. It watched him with an unblinking eye, then turned its attention back to the sky, either not noticing or ignoring the terrified Leasel, who lurked in the darkest corner of the basket, surrounded by the solid leather bags.

Suddenly, the balloon lurched, falling off the updraft. The birds stopped climbing too, and fell silent, until the only noise was the rush of air from thousands of wings, and the rasp of Paul's and Quigin's breath, hot and steaming in the high, cold air.

Paul sneaked a glance over the side of the basket, shivering as he realized how high up they were. Aillghill mountain was just a tiny white speck below, brilliant in the moonlight. The world seemed to curve away forever on every side, and for the first time in his life Paul knew the world was really round.

Still looking down, Paul felt his head become light and somehow disconnected, and for an instant, he felt like jumping off, to float above the enormous world below. But the basket lurched again, and he looked back up, grabbed the railing, and took a deep breath to regain normality.

"High up, aren't we?" said Quigin unnecessarily. "I've never been up this high before. Or at night. And the birds . . . I've learnt more in the last hour than in the last three months . . . why, Master Cagael will be . . ."

"Quigin," interrupted Paul, in a small, rather shaky voice. "Do you think that might be the Master of Air?"

Quigin stopped in mid-sentence, and looked where Paul was pointing with a hand that seemed to shiver with something more than cold. Paul was pointing to-

wards the moon, and at first Quigin couldn't see anything. Then something passed between him and the
moonlight. Something swift and dark that blotted out
most of the moon's three-quarter disc.

Quigin nodded in answer to Paul's question, but Paul
wasn't watching. He was thinking, if that is the Master
of Air, what am I supposed to do? And he remembered
Tanboule's words, a dim and hardly remembered warning: ". . . and indeed, they may put troubles in your
way . . ."

The dark shape grew closer and closer, still following
a line directly in front of the moon. Squinting against
the light, Paul could vaguely make out the thing's
shape, a shape that became more clearly defined as it
drew even closer with each beat of its vast wings.

The birds started calling again as it approached—
softly, in time to the beat of the larger eagle's wings. It
was obviously a most respectful welcome.

Then the dark shape was level with them. It was no
longer blocking out the moonlight, but shining in it: an
enormous eagle, with sky-blue feathers that ruffled in
its wake; beak and talons as silver as the moon, and
eyes as black as coal.

Paul stared at it, thinking its body alone was bigger
than his school bus, and the wings were longer than his
uncle's glider. His throat dried up, and he felt a pulse of
fear, much like when Ornware had stood above him
with his bloody, rune-carved spear. Then he had lain in
the shadow of antlers, but now he faced the far greater
shadow of the eagle's wings and an awesome, more elemental power.

The great bird circled the basket, watching, while
Paul opened and shut his mouth several times, and
Quigin stood gaping. Then, Paul caught a glint in the
eagle's eye, a spark of silent laughter, and he suddenly
felt everything would be all right.

"Hello!" shouted Paul across the winds. The eagle checked its motion, and began to hover in place, with a constant beat of wings. It seemed to consider Paul for a moment, and then . . . dissolved. Slowly, each blue feather became transparent, as though the color were being drained from a stained-glass window, leaving only tracery behind. And then even the vague outline of an eagle vanished, pieces tumbling towards the balloon like chaff in a breeze.

"Slugweed," whispered Quigin, in a tone of vast amazement. "Wort and Sheepsbane."

Paul just stared at the empty space where the eagle had been. Already, the last fading feathers were gone, but in their place, Paul could just see something taking shape, like mist rising from the ground.

"What should I do?" whispered Paul to Quigin, as the shape opposite them began taking on a more substantial form. It was starting to look like an enormous human head, at least twenty meters high, with flowing hair and a beard that trailed below, blowing back into the space normally occupied by a neck.

"You could say hello again," whispered Quigin. "I mean, when you said it last time, the eagle fell apart . . ."

"But I want its help," Paul whispered back, controlling a strong urge to join Leasel in the dark corner, and close his eyes. The head was getting features now, and they didn't look particularly nice.

"I could try hawk-whistling at it," said Quigin doubtfully. He looked around at the column of birds, which were silent again, after their greeting cries. They seemed undisturbed by the appearance of the head.

"I suppose you . . ." began Paul, when the head suddenly moved. Its nose (which had only just appeared) began to twitch, and the mouth began to yaw open, revealing a cavernous, mist-walled void, complete with tongue and tonsils.

"It's going to sneeze!" shouted Paul, ducking down into the basket, with Quigin close behind. Great gusts of wind sucked into the mouth, the ropes and wrappings of the basket whipping about in the sudden vacuum. Paul and Quigin shut their eyes, held onto the basket, and waited for the mammoth explosion of a twenty-meter-high head's sneeze. But at the last moment, it held the sneeze in, and gave a gentle sigh instead.

The air was suddenly calm, and the basket still. A great voice boomed out with a gentle rush of warm air:

"I am the North Wind and the South Wind, the Wind from West and East. I am the still air, the fiercest zephyr, the dusty wind from a tomb. I am the bearer of birds, and the carrier of clouds. I am the Master of Air."

Paul gulped twice, and slowly stood up, unconsciously bending his knees so he didn't have to show anything but his eyes and mouth above the rim of the basket.

"Hi!" he shouted nervously. "I'm Paul . . . Your . . . um . . . Mastership. Tanboule sent me to you . . . at least he said . . ."

"What did he say?" boomed the Master of Air, or at least his physical manifestation, the Head. Paul noticed it had no teeth—but it had the yellow, predatory eyes of an eagle.

"He said you could help me," shouted Paul, wishing he knew what to say. "He said that you could help me get Julia back from the Ragwitch."

The Head's eyes widened at this, the lids pulling back and then closing again, as the Master of Air narrowed his eyes, and considered the tiny speck of a boy before him.

"Why should I help you?" asked the Head, in a less booming, and slower tone.

Paul bit his lip, and looked at Quigin for advice. But Quigin just smiled, and shrugged. Not for the first time, Paul wished Aleyne was there to help him. Or Julia . . . but then, if Julia was here . . . he wouldn't be . . . .

"Well?" said the Head, in the slightly impatient tone of a teacher asking a very easy question. "Well?"

"Well, just . . ." began Paul, trying to think of a reason the Air itself would help him. But what could possibly influence the Master of Air?

"You should help," he continued, "you should help . . . just . . . *because*!"

Even as he shouted "because!," Paul felt a terrible sense of failure. I've come all this way, he thought, through all sorts of terrible things, and when I get the first chance to really help Julia, I blow it! "Because"— what sort of answer is that?

"Because?" rumbled the Head, gusts of warm air rolling out with every syllable. The gusts became stronger, and the Head repeated Paul's answer several times, each time stretching the word over several breaths, till it was a series of unrecognizable coughs.

Then Paul realized the Master of Air was laughing.

"You don't have to laugh at me!" shouted Paul, suddenly angry at this vast head, and the smallness of himself and his answer. "You could just say it was no good! You don't have to laugh!"

The Head slowly stopped laughing, and the huge yellow eyes once again gazed at Paul.

"Your answer is sufficient," said the Master of Air, his great mouth spreading with every word. " 'Because' is as vast as the Air itself, and like the Air, it covers all else. I like it. And . . . because . . . of that, I will help you. Cup your hands, Paul."

Paul stared back at the Head, wondering if he'd heard right. It was like guessing every question in a multiple choice exam, and getting ten out of ten. Slowly, he cupped his hands.

At first, nothing happened, save for a tickling sensation in his palms. The tickling grew, and became a breeze, contained within his hands alone. And then it became an icy gale that forced his arms back and forth, with the strength of it in his grasp. But he didn't let go, and when the gale blew away to nothing, he opened his cupped hands. Inside was a single sky-blue feather as light as the air.

"That," whispered the Head, "is the Breath. Guard it well, and use it at your need."

"But what will it do for Julia?" asked Paul anxiously, tucking the feather into his belt-pouch. "And what do you mean by the Breath?"

The Head only smiled, and the birds began to take voice again, screeching and whistling. But there was no answer from the balloon, none of the enthusiastic shrieks of Quigin, trying to master his trade. In fact, as Paul looked around, there was no sign of Quigin at all. At some time while Paul was talking to the Master of Air, the Friend of Beasts must have fallen from the basket.

Then Paul heard Quigin's voice, high above his head, just like when they'd first met. Looking up, Paul saw that Quigin lay directly under the balloon, and was looking intently through one of the yellow silk panels.

"What are you doing?" asked Paul. "I thought you'd fallen out. I wish you wouldn't—"

"Paul," interrupted Quigin, sounding very puzzled. "I think that Master Thruan's dead."

"What?" asked Paul.

"I think that Master Thruan's dead," replied Quigin, frowning. "All the lifting spirits are leaving the balloon, and they couldn't do that if Master Thruan was alive

. . . though now I come to think about it, he did say not to fly too high . . ."

"You mean we're going to crash?" shouted Paul. "Can't you stop the spirits leaving?" Already he could see orange shapes drifting out through the silken panels—and the balloon did seem to be dropping.

"No, I can't," said Quigin. "Still, at least we got to see the Wind Moot!"

"Can't you get the birds to hold us up or something?" shouted Paul. The balloon was definitely falling, and so many of the spirits were leaving the balloon it was starting to collapse into itself. And to make matters worse, the Master of Air's Head sounded like it was going to sneeze again!

"They're not listening!" shouted Quigin, after a series of frantic whistles. "They're arguing about the right to ride the Northwest Winds!"

"Try again!" Paul shouted back, anxiously looking between the balloon and the Head. Although they were dropping rapidly, the Head was keeping level with them—and it kept sucking the balloon closer with every intake of breath, the mouth gaping open wider and wider.

"It's going to sneeze!" shouted Paul, as the balloon swung up against the Head, the basket tickling its nose.

"Uh . . . uh . . . uh," gasped the Head, and then it sneezed, an enormous explosion of air and sound that deafened Paul and Quigin, and picked up the balloon, throwing it through the air, faster than the swiftest hawk, out over the eastern sea, across two hundred kilometers or more.

* * *

"His name was Thruan," said Julia, shivering. She dug her hands into the comforting turf, adding, "He was the last one that She got. She just . . . She just looked at him, and said his name, and he . . . he was dead."

Lyssa nodded, and rested a cool hand on Julia's forehead. It felt odd, but somehow comforting, like the pleasant shade of a tree on a warm summer's day.

"Lie still, Julia," said Lyssa, bringing up her other hand to push Julia carefully onto the turf. "Lie still. Nothing can harm you here, behind the braided holly."

Julia closed her eyes and relaxed, feeling Lyssa's hand stroking her forehead, across and up to the right, and then across and up to the left, like a longways cross. Then, Lyssa began to sing, a gentle lullaby of ships and the sea and the rolling of the grey-green waves. She began to count the waves, and Julia tried to follow, but was asleep before the count reached twenty.

When Julia awoke, Lyssa was standing next to her, watching the globe. She was singing to herself again, but it was a song that echoed power, and was not at all a lullaby.

"Good morning," said Lyssa, breaking off her song as she noticed Julia's open, if sleepy eyes. "If it is morning in the outside world."

"I think so," mumbled Julia. "How long have I been asleep?"

Lyssa smiled, and said, "I do not think Time runs true here, Julia. But perhaps, half a day."

Julia nodded, wondering at how rested she felt after such a relatively short sleep. Then she remembered that it was her first real sleep since before she found the Ragwitch—since then, she had only managed brief naps riddled with waking nightmares. She felt hungry for the first time too, but this passed quickly, and soon she felt the familiar dulled appetite of her strange life— neither hungry nor content, but something unpleasantly in between.

"Now you are awake," said Lyssa, "I think you should tell me how you come to be here."

"Yes, I suppose so," said Julia, hesitantly. "In a way, this is all my fault."

Slowly, she began to tell Lyssa about the midden, and finding the rag doll encased in the ball of feathers. Lyssa stopped her every now and then, to ask quite difficult questions, and she was especially interested in the midden, saying, "Even in her banishment, She contrived to be close to some power. A Hill of Bones would be such a place—particularly without its human guardians. Under certain stars and a sea wind, Her prison would be weak, and She could attract . . . you . . ."

"It's funny," said Julia, "But I don't really remember finding the doll. I mean, I know I did, but I can't remember anything properly, until I woke up here inside Her . . ."

Julia continued telling her story without faltering, until she got right up to the events of the night before, with the moon hanging low over the Namyr Steps, and the people who had tried to hold the gorge.

"What happened then?" prompted Lyssa, as Julia hesitated after describing the entrance to the Steps, and the beginning of their slow descent into the gorge.

"She just killed them," whispered Julia, tears starting in the corners of her eyes. "The Gwarulch and the Angarling didn't have to do a thing. She just walked down saying their names and pointing . . . and they died."

"You're sure She said their names?" asked Lyssa. "And they died?"

"Yes," sobbed Julia, now openly crying. "But they didn't stay dead! She called them again, and they got up—but their faces were all white and sunken, and they moved like Her! And their eyes didn't move at all— they just stared ahead, all red and empty!"

"So," said Lyssa, grimly. "I have heard of such. They are not really dead, but their minds are sleeping. She has Glazed them, and they are now Glazed-Folk, to serve Her till their bodies fail. But tell me—how was She attacked?"

"A . . . Wizard," mumbled Julia, through her tears. "Thruan—the one who almost got away. And, Lyssa— every spell he cast against Her only hurt me!"

Lyssa frowned, and said reluctantly, "That is an old spell, and one I thought forgotten. But here, dry your tears."

She gave Julia a large handkerchief, pulled out from one sleeve of her dress. It smelled faintly of fresh green leaves, and absorbed tears far better than mere cloth. Julia dabbed at her eyes for a while, and then whispered, "She told me that I was Her curse-ward, and spell-shield, and that every spell against Her would hurt me instead. And they did . . ."

"Well, we shall have to put a stop to that," said Lyssa cheerfully, taking back her handkerchief to mop up a few missed tears. "I have been thinking, while you were asleep, and there is something we can do against Her. It will be very dangerous, but . . ."

"I don't mind!" interrupted Julia, "I wish I could kill Her!"

Lyssa smiled sadly, and said, "I doubt it anyone could do that now. But perhaps we can trouble Her, in our way . . ."

It was still cold on the lowest of the Namyr Steps. The Ragwitch lay sprawled against it, as if upon a throne. Behind Her, the Angarling stood, one every two or three steps, looking like natural projections from the rock. Around them, Gwarulch were still looting the dead, or beginning to build campfires for their grisly luncheon.

In front of the Ragwitch, the Glazed-Folk stood, their

faces already shining with the pale hue of the dead, their eyes red-washed and inhuman. Thruan stood a little way in front of them, his mouth gaping open.

"This Paul," hissed the Ragwitch. "Describe him."

Thruan's mouth opened and closed several times, but no sound came forth. The Ragwitch hissed again, and Thruan began to speak, his voice rasping and slow, devoid of all emotion.

"He . . . he . . . he . . . ten, eleven . . . brown hair . . . he walks slowly . . . and worries . . . about his . . . sister Jul . . ."

"Enough!" spat the Ragwitch, climbing ponderously to Her feet, swaying slightly on the wet limestone of the Step. "Oroch!"

Oroch came quickly, running nimbly down the steps, his black form like a shadow leaping across the white steps, dodging between the Angarling.

"Yes, my Mistress?" he asked, red maw panting.

"Send any Meepers we can spare to the east," ordered the Ragwitch. "To Aillghill and beyond. They are to find a yellow balloon—and capture those in it."

Oroch bent his head, and started back up the Steps, but the Ragwitch laid Her hand across his head, one bloated finger at each temple, and Her middle finger across his black-wrapped head.

"And send messengers to My Gwarulch in the east."

"With what message, Mistress?" whispered Oroch, trembling beneath Her grip. "What are they to do?"

"Tell them," She said, lips arching back to show the rows of teeth. "Tell them to hunt. Tell them to hunt . . . a boy who travels in a yellow balloon."

10

THE MEMORY/A VILLAGE BY THE SEA

We must go further into the Ragwitch's mind," said Lyssa. "This small area around the white globe is only a tiny part of Her consciousness—a prison, separate from the rest of Her mind."

"I've tried getting out," said Julia, still sniffing back a few tears. "I swam for ages and ages, and I still ended up back here at the globe."

"Ah, but you didn't have a prisoner's friend, did you?" said Lyssa, smiling. "Remember, I am not a prisoner here—and if I can escape, so can you."

"But won't She just call me back?" asked Julia. "It doesn't matter what I do, I have to go when She calls—or part of me anyway. Does my body stay here when I'm with Her?"

"No," said Lyssa. "We don't really have bodies here. And this place doesn't really exist—not like the real world, with good earth, and trees, and flowers."

"Except for the turf," said Julia. "And you ... the rowan tree."

"That's just a reflection of the real tree," said Lyssa. "But it's your way out of here ... and She will never know. Look!"

With a sudden flick, she drew a single hair from Julia's head, quickly transferring it to her left hand. In her right hand, she held a rowan twig, with a holly berry stuck on the end, and a long blade of grass tied lengthways across it.

"Ean, Tall, Yither, Wuin," sang Lyssa, as she wound the hair around the twig. Then, with a clap of her hands, she threw the whole thing into the yellow flame, crying, "Tan!"

And there were two Julias.

"I won't!" cried the Julia that had just appeared, stamping her foot. "I'll never like your monsters! And I don't care if I get hit by spells!"

"That's me!" exclaimed the original Julia. She'd always wondered what she looked like rightways round, instead of same-side backwards like in a mirror.

"I hate you," said the second Julia, out into the darkness. She stamped her foot again, stepped out of the ring of holly, and swam off towards the globe. Julia watched, fascinated, finally understanding what she did wrong with her left leg when she was swimming.

"The twig-maid will deceive Her for some time," said Lyssa. "But, like all things of Nature, she will not be able to endure so close to her. And then, the Ragwitch will know I am here ... so, we had best begin our journey now."

Julia smiled and nodded, happy at being saved from being drawn back into Her senses. Even if it was only for a few days, the relief from not feeling those bloated limbs was like a second Christmas. Better still, she wouldn't have to endure Her thoughts, or see the results of Her actions.

"Julia," said Lyssa, for the second time in a slightly louder voice. "Please—you must listen to this. We are going to enter the main part of the Ragwitch's memory, and there are things that you must, and must not do.

"Firstly, the place we are going to will seem to be real. I mean, it will seem to us like there are real trees, and plants, and birds, and people. But you must remember that it is not. What you see might change its form and nature in a second—and there will be many things you cannot see.

"I can only give you this to use against them." Turning aside from Julia, Lyssa seemed to reach her hand into the yellow flame. Golden sparks rose briefly from her fingers, showering outwards like a brilliant firework. And then the sparks and flame were gone, and the green turf was suddenly blue in the harsh light of the distant globe. And in her hand Lyssa held a wand of yellowed wood that held the hint of golden sparks and the bright and cheerful flame.

"Touch that to anything that threatens you, or anything that you are unsure of," said Lyssa, giving the wand to Julia. "Not only will it drive dangerous creatures back, it will also reveal the true nature of things."

"What sort of creatures could be in Her mind?" asked Julia, reluctantly taking the wand. "And aren't you coming with me?"

"In answer to your first question," replied Lyssa, "you will encounter Her memories. The part of Her mind to which we will travel is Her distant memory, and it is populated with all the creatures, landscapes and people of Her grim past. And, yes, I will be going with you. But only to the very beginning of the memory."

"But why?" exclaimed Julia, close to tears again. "I thought . . ."

"Here," interrupted Lyssa, "I am as I choose to be—just like the outside world. But in Her memory, I already exist. I am very old, Julia. Older than the Ragwitch—I was ancient when She was North-Queen. But She remembers me, how I was when She walked in human form. And inside Her memory, that remembrance will rule my shape and form."

"But why does that mean you can't come all the way?" asked Julia.

"Because," said Lyssa, smiling sadly, "She remembers me only as a Rowan. In Her memory, I will stand with my sisters on Alnwere Hill, roots drinking from the deep waters of the Pool."

Julia bit her lip hard, ashamed to be crying again, but upset at losing her only companion so soon. Lyssa smiled again, and took her hand, saying, "Come—we must go, before the twig-maid joins her consciousness."

"But where?" asked Julia, looking around at the blackness and the single white globe.

"Why, into the globe," replied Lyssa, pushing off into the darkness. "But I shall guide you along a different path."

* * *

The first, hesitant rays of sunlight were just striking the sea as Paul, Quigin and Leasel crawled onto the soft sand of the beach. A few hundred meters behind them, out past a long sandbank, the wicker basket bobbed on the waves, securely anchored by the yellow-panelled balloon which was now full of water.

Paul coughed again as the last little rush of a wave pushed up against his nose and throat. He knew he should go a little further up the beach, but it was so easy just to sink into the sand.

The Master of Air's sneeze had carried them just out past the land, and Quigin had used the reserve bottle of lifting spirits to slow their landing—or crash, as it turned out to be. Paul had only just had time to kick off his boots, before they were plunged into the sea, last-minute gulps of air knocked from their lungs, and nothing but choking water all around them.

Another wave washed past, more foam than water, but it was enough to make Paul crawl a little further, before he collapsed again.

"Just a little rest, Julia," he muttered, feeling fingers pulling at the back of his neck. I only want a little rest, thought Paul dimly. Julia can swim all day with her friends, but I'm tired. I don't like the pool . . .

Paul coughed again, and made a feeble effort to crawl a little further, and then collapsed, waves foaming at his ankles.

I've drowned, thought Paul, as he felt consciousness returning. He seemed to be a long way underwater, and the surface was only a dull, rippling light above. He kicked desperately upwards, and the light seemed to get closer and closer, but he absolutely had to take a breath . . . and then the light somehow changed, and hardened, turning into the smiling face of Quigin.

"Quigin!" said Paul, waking up, and focusing on his friend's face. "You've got a black eye!"

"I think you kicked it when we fell," said Quigin, lightly touching the bruise. "It could have been worse."

"Yeah," said Paul, propping up on one elbow to have a look around. He still felt fuzzy in the head, but that was a lot better than feeling drowned. He saw that he was lying on a straw-stuffed pallet that was leaking in one corner—though that might be due to Leasel, who was sitting near his feet, looking guilty. Quigin sat on an upturned cask that smelled rather strongly of fish.

In fact, the whole room smelt of fish, thought Paul, after taking a few tentative sniffs. It was obviously some sort of fisherman's store—a single-roomed hut, constructed from driftwood, with only a single door that doubled as a window. Around the straw pallet, there were piles of nets and ropes, and odd-looking tools— mostly of sea-rusted iron.

"Where are we?" asked Paul, and then, suddenly feeling the absence of his pouch, "And where's my pouch? Is the Breath safe?"

"Oh, everything's here," said Quigin, holding up a loosely tied bag of sailcloth, with pieces of Paul's clothing trailing out of it.

"We even got your boots back," he added, holding up a salt-encrusted pair. "That is, one of the shell-fishers did. They're the best swimmers, because they dive for shells, and everyone else fishes from boats . . ."

"But where are we?" interrupted Paul.

"A village," answered Quigin, as if stating the obvious. "Somewhere on the eastern coast. The people here are Trazel-fishers, and dive for Raunshells. I think the place is called Domebreye."

"That's Donbreye," said a voice from the door, a slow, bass voice, that cast a pall of tobacco smoke over the fish smell.

Coughing, Paul sat up higher, to get a good look at the man in the door, and was surprised by the size of him. He could barely stand within the door, and that only by bending his head. And he was as thin as an oar, with a sea-worn face that somehow seemed even thinner, probably because the rest of him was encased in a heavy wool coat, trousers of a sort of dull tartan, and what looked like shark-skin boots.

"I am Deamus," said the man (pronouncing it Day-mouse), folding himself over a little more, so he could fit into the hut. "And you are Paul."

"Yes," said Paul, almost adding a "sir." Except for

his height, Deamus looked just like the Headmaster at Paul's school—though he was perhaps a little younger.

"Your friend Quigin has told us you are searching for your sister," said Deamus, ponderously. "And he had tales of great enchantment and ancient evil. Many of our folk will not believe it . . . but I wonder . . . there have been creatures in the sky these past nights, and . . ."

He paused for a moment to take a puff on a long, loose- rolled cigar of green tobacco that shed half-burnt flakes every time it went from hand to mouth. Through the cloud of smoke, Deamus fixed Paul with a thoughtful gaze.

"Is it true," he asked, "that you have seen the Ragwitch? And that She really is the North-Queen, who once despoiled the Kingdom?"

"I haven't seen Her here," said Paul, hesitantly. "But I did see Her in my own . . . country, and Tanboule the Wise said She was the North-Queen in a different form, and that She was already . . . fighting in the north."

"Slaying more than fighting, I'll warrant," said Deamus. "But if the Wise know She is back . . . has word been sent to the King at Yendre?"

"Yes, I think so," answered Paul. "Aleyne . . . that is, Sir Aleyne was sent by the Wise. But that was only yesterday—when I first met Quigin . . ."

"Four days ago, you mean," interrupted Quigin, who had been absently stroking Leasel. "You've been lying here like a stunned fish for the last three days."

"Four days," muttered Deamus. "I was worried why we had not heard. But four days is not enough for the message to go to Yendre, and for the Storm Boy to come from there to us."

"The Storm Boy?" asked Paul, wondering at the way Deamus had said it—as if it were something dread, but somehow expected.

"It is a statue," replied Deamus, somberly. "The mark of our fealty to the King. A prime Trazel-fish we send at Midsummer, to the Court, and the King sends back a brandy pudding of the same weight as the fish. But the Storm Boy, now he's an older thing altogether. For the Storm Boy is the call to War, and that we have not seen since my far ancestors' time."

Silence followed Deamus' explanation, until the fisherman blew another cloud of smoke, making Paul cough.

"Ah, I'm sorry lad," said Deamus, making some attempt to clear the smoke with his hand. "We all puff away here—it's good for the lungs, to clear the sea damp from them."

Paul nodded, biting back a comment about cancer and all the other diseases associated with smoking. Still, maybe they didn't have those here—and it was marginally better than the smell of fish . . .

"We've some nice Trazel cooking down at home," said Deamus, mistaking Paul's expression for one of hunger. "Why don't you come down and have some? It'll do you better than that fish oil this lad's been feeding you."

"Fish oil?" asked Paul, glaring at Quigin as he felt the gorge rising in his throat.

"Fish oil, molasses and some herbs," replied Quigin, holding up an earthenware bottle. "Do you want some more?"

Paul didn't answer; he just struggled to his feet and weakly made his way to the door. Deamus stepped back out, steadying Paul as his legs buckled under him.

"Easy, lad," he murmured, as Paul gulped at the fresh sea air. "You were nearly drowned, and your strength is all watered down."

Paul didn't reply, thankful to be out of the fish and

tobacco smell, and away from the helpful Quigin and
his fish oil cocktail.

After a few deep gulps of air, Paul looked around and
saw that the hut lay on a rocky ridge. To the north, he
could just see the beach where they'd crashed. To the
south, and much closer, there was a harbor, crowded
with small boats sheltering behind the breakwater.
Around the harbor, and climbing up to the ridge, there
were forty or fifty wooden houses, with roofs of greyish slate, and yellow-brick chimneys shining in the
sun.

There were lots of people about too, small figures, all
clustered around the harbor wall, intent on some great
business. From a distance, Paul could hear shouts and
laughter, and the faintest touch of some cheery song.

"It is a Festival day," said Deamus behind him. "A
day for the sea, when we give thanks for its bounty. I'll
not tell them your news today, young Paul. Tomorrow
will be soon enough to prepare ourselves for the Storm
Boy."

"Will many of you have to go?" asked Quigin, who
had come up behind. Turning back, Paul noticed that
even while talking, Quigin was watching an albatross
cruise effortlessly above, and other birds as they dived
about the rocks.

"All who can bear pike and sword, and march five
leagues," replied Deamus, still watching the festive
preparations below. "Perhaps thirty of the men, and a
score of the women."

"The women too?" asked Paul. "Is that normal?"

Deamus looked back at him, puzzled, and said, "We
have never answered the Storm Boy before. But the
women practice on King's Days, as do the men. I do not
think the North-Creatures are particular as to their
prey—so it is best if all can fight, if they must."

"You've never fought against other people, then?" asked Paul, rather doubtfully.

"Other people!" said Deamus, shocked. "We could not!"

"Not even if you were attacked?" asked Paul. "If others wanted your land or something?"

"We have our place," replied Deamus sternly. "We are bound here to earth and sea—it would not answer to others. And their places would not answer to us. Only the North-Creatures know no home, and so seek to take ours from us, even if it will avail them nothing."

"I see," said Paul, for the first time really understanding what the Ragwitch meant to this peaceful Kingdom. She brought war and destruction, and many people would die to stop Her—if they could. He suddenly remembered Malgar the Shepherd in his village to the northwest. Maybe, even now, his people were fighting the Ragwitch—and from what Tanboule had said, probably losing. Instinctively, he reached for the blue feather in his pouch, the Breath—and realized he was dressed in nothing but a wool undershirt that hung down to his knees.

"I'll just get dressed," said Paul, tottering back inside.

"Aye, and then we'll join the festival," said Deamus. "Though I don't think Paul will be dancing."

Quigin nodded absently, watching Leasel bound off into the dune grass that grew a little way up from the beach. There were sand lizards there, and he wanted to learn how they spoke.

"I'll come down to the village later," he said, poking his head into the door, before heading off after Leasel, making lizard calls deep in his throat.

* * *

The transition through the globe was different with Lyssa leading the way: slow, and gentle, with none of the numbing loss of senses that normally accompanied Julia's passage. But the light was very bright, and Julia was forced to close her eyes.

When she opened them, it was to gentle sunlight, and she breathed cool, clean air. Lyssa stood at her side, silver hair flowing in the breeze.

To Julia, it seemed that every aspect of the land about them was like some long-forgotten pleasure. They stood on a green hill which overlooked a small, but very blue, lake. From its shores, broad-leafed trees marched up to the bottom of the hill. Birds flew in the distance, and there was no hint of any cloud.

"Remember, Julia," said Lyssa. "None of this is real. It is a memory of the Ragwitch—an early one, for the land is clean, and not despoiled. But Her memories shift, and overlap; you must be prepared for any change . . ."

Lyssa's voice faltered, and her body shimmered for an instant, like a fleeting mirage. Then, she firmed again, and continued, "Quickly—I am called to my tree! You must look for Anhyvar, a woman, with long red hair, who wears a silver star upon her breast. She will be near the sea . . ."

"But what do I do when I find her?" asked Julia, clutching Lyssa's hand. "Oh, please don't go!"

Lyssa wavered again, and her hand became insubstantial, passing through Julia's like mist. Then Lyssa plucked something from her hair, thrust it into Julia's other hand—and vanished, her voice drifting across the hill.

"Send it to the wind when you find Anhyvar . . . and I will come . . ."

Julia listened carefully, and looked at the small russet

leaf she held in her palm, before tucking it neatly into her shirt pocket.

"Near the sea . . ." she muttered to herself, looking down at the lake. A kilometer or two away, on the other side of the lake, she could just make out a river. And rivers flowed into the sea.

Drawing the yellow-gold wand, she held it before her and strode boldly down the hill.

An hour later, Julia began to notice changes to the north. A great mass of black cloud was rolling in—a solid wall of darkness, with lightning striking before it, and thunder rolling behind.

Julia eyed it suspiciously and quickened her pace. She had no desire to be caught out in the open.

Then, without warning, the whole sky was black—though the cloud wall couldn't possibly have reached the river. Lightning danced a jagged dance down the hill behind Julia, and thunder crashed against her ears, dry, booming thunder, without any hint of rain.

She started to run, the lightning following her, forking down in great strokes, flashes of light making the landscape flicker and move as if lit by a gigantic strobe. Amidst the shrieking storm, Julia ran blindly, her hands pressed to her ears, and her feet stumbling over the madly lit ground.

Then the clouds were gone, and the sky was blue and silent, as if the thunder and lightning had never been.

But the land around Julia was not the same. The river was gone: a dry ravine wound where the water had once run deep. There were no broad-leafed trees, and the grassy hills were yellow and cracked like overbaked scones.

A memory change, thought Julia, looking around at the wasteland. Lyssa had said that at the height of Her power, the Ragwitch had turned much of the kingdom into a desert. Obviously, the land about Julia was a memory from this time—so Her North-Creatures were bound to be about.

Julia looked back at the hills again, before continuing along the path of the dried-up river . . . not noticing the dark silhouette of something crouched just behind the crest of one of the closer hills.

11

THE SEA FESTIVAL

The sounds of happy preparations grew stronger as Paul walked slowly down towards the harbor, with Deamus half supporting him. It was a rather slow and frustrating progress for Paul, as his legs kept going rubbery and giving way. And there always seemed to be just one more house to walk around before they reached the sea.

Then there were no more houses, and they stood on the slate-tiled harborside, a broad expanse that stretched from the breakwater to the boatsheds a hundred meters away. Because of the Festival, trestle tables lined the quay, covered with food, ranging from fish to lobster, with all kinds of shellfish and edible seaweed in between. Only the barrels of wine and beer (of which there seemed an awful lot) hadn't come from the sea.

Around these tables, scores of cheerful men, women and children, were all fearfully busy (or pretending to be), either putting out food, rearranging it, tuning musical instruments, practicing dances or just getting in the way.

No one paid any attention to Paul and Deamus, so Paul sat down on an upturned keg on the fringe of all the activity, and waited for Deamus to decide what to do next.

"This is the Sea Festival," explained Deamus, waving his long arms about like a sort of daddy-longlegs. "A holiday for us, and a time to give our thanks to the sea."

Paul nodded, his attention wandering to the water's edge, where a woman stood staring out at the sea. Unlike the rest of the revellers, she wore no bright colors or jewelry—just a simple black dress. As Paul watched, she cast something into the sea at her feet and turned away, disappearing into the crowd.

Deamus followed Paul's gaze, and added quietly, "We thank the sea for our livelihoods, but it knows cruelty as well as kindness. Avelle's husband and only son were lost in a great storm just a few weeks gone. Today is also a time to grieve for those who have been taken by the sea. But come—I would like you to meet my own wife and children. I have a daughter much the same age as you."

"Couldn't I just rest here for a bit longer?" asked Paul anxiously. He was always nervous about meeting people—especially girls. Julia's friends often made fun of him when she wasn't around to protect him. And who knows where Julia is now, thought Paul, miserably. And his parents had probably given them both up for dead—if they'd taken the time to notice.

"Rest all you like," said Deamus, noticing Paul's eyes begin to go a little teary at the corners. "Come across when you're ready. No one will disturb you till then."

Paul watched him walk across to one of the further tables, towards a tall, black-haired woman who was almost as thin as Deamus. No one else could be Deamus' wife, thought Paul. A few seconds later Deamus kissed her on the forehead, confirming Paul's opinion. Next to the woman was a small, dark-haired shadow of herself, again, obviously their daughter. She saw him looking, and returned his gaze with a calm disinterest that made him quickly look away—straight at Quigin, who had just appeared, red-faced and panting, with Leasel close at his heels. The Friend of Beasts staggered, and bent over, his mulberry-colored hat falling at his feet.

"What is it?" asked Paul. He got up himself, with the vague expectation of having to run somewhere too.

"Ran . . . all the way . . . from the dunes . . ." puffed Quigin. "Couldn't find . . . sand lizards . . . but there are creatures . . . gathering behind the dunes."

"Creatures?" snapped a voice behind him. "What sort of creatures?"

Paul looked up from Quigin, and saw a tough-looking man clutching a still-writhing lobster with considerable dexterity. Paul thought the lobster was very unlucky to be held by such a hard-faced person—anyone else would have let go. Quigin gasped out, "Gwarulch! I think they're Gwarulch! And coming this way!"

The hard-faced man looked carefully at Quigin, as if the possibility of encountering Gwarulch in the sand dunes was as unlikely as finding a ring around the sun. Then, in a voice that cracked through the festive chatter like a slamming door, he bellowed, "Deamus!"

Deamus looked up at once, and hurried over. So did most of the other fisherfolk, leaving their tasks, music and chatter behind.

"Deamus," said the man, passing his lobster to a woman at the front of the crowd (who passed it on when it snapped at her), "This boy says there are Gwarulch beyond the dunes. You brought the boys here. What do you know of this?"

"I know nothing of Gwarulch," replied Deamus slowly. "But Paul, here, brings tidings of a great and ancient evil. I had hoped we need not speak of it till the morrow. But it seems we must . . ."

Around him, the fisherfolk muttered and fidgeted, many making the sign against evil with their thumb and forefinger. Deamus cleared his throat, and said bluntly, "Paul has told me that the Ragwitch has come to the North. And She is no tale for the children, but the North-Queen come again, in a different shape and form."

No one spoke for a moment, but Paul felt everyone looking at him, and saw in their eyes a kind of dread, reserved only for bearers of evil news.

"Is this true?" asked the hard-faced man, looking from Deamus to Paul, who shivered under his gaze.

"Yes," said Paul, slowly getting to his feet. "I have been to see the Wise, and Tanboule said She had returned. And Gwarulch chased me and Aleyne through the forest . . ."

Paul's voice trailed off as he remembered that night in the forest, running through the blackness between the trees, the Gwarulch howling a few steps behind . . . and then the one that had trapped him, standing over him and licking its lips. He shivered at the memory, and then shivered again as a chilling scream sounded far off in the dunes. A Gwarulch had found Quigin's trail—and was summoning the hunt.

Only the hard-faced man seemed unaffected by the scream. The rest of the villagers had gone as still as an old, brown-toned photograph, the color fading from their ruddy cheeks. Paul watched their throats moving, as they compulsively swallowed to keep from crying out. And they all seemed to be looking at him.

Then the hard-faced man spoke, and Paul realized that it was he the villagers were really looking at. "I am

Sir Rellen," said the man to Paul. "And I have fought Gwarulch far to the north. They can be killed."

His words seemed to unfreeze the fisherfolk, and a wave of sound and action leapt out of the stillness. Deamus was the first to react, his long arms flapping as he leapt onto a keg, and cried, "You've heard Sir Rellen. Gwarulch can be killed! And we are warriors—at least on King's Days! Go—fetch your weapons and armor, and we'll show these monsters how the fisherfolk of Donbreye fight!"

Everyone paused for a second at his words, as if the whole thing couldn't really be happening, and then ran towards their houses. Some bellowed as they ran, as though somehow the sound could inflate their courage. But most were grimly quiet. Sir Rellen walked, and whistled a melancholy little tune. Paul watched him for a second, and thought of Aleyne—the two knights were very alike, at least in their attitude to danger. Paul tried to whistle himself, but his lips were dry, and he soon gave up.

Deamus also watched Sir Rellen, and then turned to his wife. "You'd better get ready, Oel," he said. "Take the better helmet, and please bring my armor and sword. Sevaun can help you, but be quick. I want to talk to Paul for a moment."

Oel nodded, and turned away without a word. As they walked, Sevaun slipped her hand into her mother's, her shorter legs striding further to match Oel's quickening stride. Paul felt a pang of something like jealousy, as once again he thought of Julia, and wished she were there to hold his hand.

"Do you think you can beat the Gwarulch?" he said to Deamus, looking back up to the fisherman. "I've only seen one, but it was very strong . . ."

"I don't know," replied Deamus. "But we can probably hold them off long enough for you to escape."

"Me?" asked Paul, surprised. He hadn't really thought of escaping. At least, not without everybody else. There seemed to be safety in numbers—or he hoped there was. "You're going to fight so I can get away?"

"Yes," replied Deamus. "You and Quigin. From what he told me, the Wise think you can somehow harm the Ragwitch . . . so we must get you away."

"Why doesn't everyone run . . ." Paul began to say, when the Gwarulch howled again, drowning out his voice. They were closer now, near the hut on the ridge. And there were answering howls from both north and south, along the rocky shore.

The howls subsided a little, as if the Gwarulch were drawing breath, and the silence was filled with the clatter of armor and the thud of heavy boots—the sound of the fisherfolk returning to the harborside.

They made an odd company. Some wore buff coats overlaid with back and breastplates, others just the coat, or a buff jerkin and perhaps an armored gauntlet. Most had open-faced steel helmets, shining with fish oil which had been applied to ward off the rust. Only Sir Rellen wore a full suit of armor; blue enamelled back and breastplates, with flexible plates covering his thighs, and gauntlets of layered steel and ringmail. He wore a helmet with a three-barred visor and a back shaped like a lobster's tail that hung over his neck.

The fisherfolk's weapons were almost as varied as their armor. Some had long pikes, others halberds, or even tridents. Most had a sword or a long knife as well. Again, Sir Rellen was different. He carried a poleaxe, that hung from his wrist by a worn leather strap.

The Gwarulch had stopped howling altogether, and Paul imagined them slinking down the hill, running from hut to hut like cats on the scent of mice.

"It's me they're after," he said suddenly, touching the

feather of the Breath in the pouch at his side. "The Ragwitch knows I'm going to get Julia back."

Deamus looked at the boy's face, and saw the fear that lay just under the appearance of determination. "Yes," he said, putting his hand on Paul's shoulder. "That's why they're slow in coming. They're surrounding the village, so none may escape—at least over land."

"The boats, then," said Quigin. "I've got a fair idea how to sail. At least, a sailor once told me how it was done."

Deamus shook his head, and pointed at the sky. "You wouldn't get far on the sea either. Look up."

Both Paul and Quigin looked up at once. At first Paul couldn't see anything, then Quigin pointed out a patch of sky. There, circling with a lazy watchfulness were nine or ten large, black shapes. Too big even for the largest eagles ...

"What are they?" asked Paul, thinking back to Tanboule telling him about "things worse than Gwarulch." The thought of things worse than Gwarulch was not a pleasant one, and Paul felt his pulse begin to beat faster, throbbing behind his ears.

"I think they are Her creatures, though I do not know a name for them," said Deamus. "They have been in the sky overhead for three nights. Yesterday, they circled over your balloon—and today, the Gwarulch have come."

"And so has your armor," said Oel, stepping between two pikemen. Paul stared at her for a second. The thin fisherwoman was gone—and in her place was a new Oel, bulky in a buff coat, with a steel helmet framing her face, and a basket-hilted sword at her side. She carried Deamus' buff coat, a metal gauntlet, and a rather tarnished helmet, with bronze-rimmed cheek pieces that clattered as she passed it over.

Sevaun was different too. She was still her thin, dark self, but now wore a green cloak shot with silver lines, and carried a wand of ivory which was inlaid with shells. She had a very serious expression for a girl who couldn't be more than ten years old.

"As I was saying," said Deamus, as Oel helped him put on his heavy buff coat, "you wouldn't get far on top of the sea. But you should have no trouble underneath it."

"I don't think I can hold my breath very long," said Paul, thinking about those terrible few minutes when he'd almost drowned escaping from the balloon. "I'd rather not try . . ."

"You won't have to hold your breath," interrupted Deamus. "Sevaun is a Waterwitch, and her Magic is very strong on this Day of the Sea. She should be able to cast a spell that lets you all breathe water like air—and you can walk out onto the sea floor!"

"Can you really do that?" asked Paul, rather doubtfully. "I mean, breathe water and everything?"

"Yes," said Sevaun solemnly. "But only today, because it's the sea's special day."

"From here, you should walk south, staying underwater as long as possible. We will meet you ten leagues or so south of here."

"You won't try to defend the village?" asked Quigin, who'd just sent a most unenthusiastic Leasel to spy on the Gwarulch.

"No," replied Deamus heavily. "We are too far north to last any real trouble. We'll fight our way south, and join the King. One day we will return here again."

He almost said something else, but stopped and adjusted his sword belt instead. Paul thought he knew what he had almost said—that not everyone would return. Maybe not anybody. The people around him were preparing their weapons, or just talking quietly, and, looking at them, Paul felt homesick for his own, un-eventful life at home. Despite the warmth of the sun, he shivered, and wondered why he wasn't brave like the people in films—and the battle hadn't even started . . .

Then, even as Paul shivered, Rellen pointed with his poleaxe towards the hill, the sunlight flashing on his gauntlet. "They are moving again. Deamus, we must prepare to break out."

"Yes," sighed Deamus. "Would you shape us as you see fit, Rellen, and lead us when the time comes?"

"I hoped not to fight again," said Rellen somberly. "But it seems I must."

Deamus turned back to Paul, and behind him, Rellen started moving the people of Donbreye into a diamond-shaped "hedgehog" of pikes and swords, with the un-armed people in the middle. Paul and Quigin watched silently for a moment, taking comfort in the sudden bustle of movement, and Rellen's sure, confident voice.

The hedgehog had just begun to really look the part, all bristling with pikes, when Leasel returned, her long ears laid flat in fear of the Gwarulch. Quigin touched noses with her briefly, and relayed her message—true to their nature, the Gwarulch were sneaking closer rather than charging down for an all-out attack.

"Paul, Quigin—you must go," said Deamus. "And Sevaun, you must go with them."

The girl wrinkled her forehead, and said, "Oh, do I have to?"

Deamus looked at her sternly, much more sternly than his father ever could, thought Paul, and Sevaun nodded reluctantly, without speaking.

"Come on then," she said to Paul and Quigin. "Go down to the harbor steps while I say goodbye to Mother."

"Goodbye, Paul," said Deamus. "Goodbye, Quigin—and Leasel."

Paul started to answer, when a shout filled the air, and a fisherman reeled out of a nearby house, clutching his neck. A loud, hissing shriek followed his scream, and Gwarulch poured out of the doorway—huge, vicious shapes that towered over the fisherfolk, who fell back before their sweeping talons and snapping fangs. Then Rellen was charging at them, shouting, "To me Donbreye!"

At once, or so it seemed to Paul, there were charging people everywhere, and the village resounded with roaring war cries, Gwarulch howls and the sharp screech of talons meeting steel.

"Go! Go!" shouted Deamus, before he was swallowed up in the fighting, his lanky form taller than all but the Gwarulch, and his sword out and stabbing fiercely.

Paul took one last look, and then ran for the harbor steps, heart pounding at the thought of a Gwarulch leaping on his back. Running behind him, Quigin almost fell over Leasel, and his hat tumbled off, only to be snatched up by the faithful hare. Sevaun ran some way behind, and kept pausing to look back.

"Hold hands and close your eyes," she shouted at them over the noise of the battle, "and hold your hare, you!"

The boys did as they were told, though both were afraid to shut their eyes. Sevaun watched them for a second, and then began to dance, her wooden clogs clattering on the steps in a rhythmic pattern. As she danced, the sounds of fighting seemed to fade, until the boys could only hear her footsteps, and a sort of gurgling, watery chant Sevaun sang in a very high voice. Then Paul felt her wand touch his nose and mouth—and all at once he was choking, and coughing, just like when he had drowned before.

"Quickly, jump in the water!" shouted Sevaun, and as Paul opened his eyes and goggled at her stupidly, trying desperately to breathe, she raised one small heavily-clogged foot and knocked him sideways off the steps and into the water.

Quigin looked at her, threw a protesting Leasel in, and jumped straight after. Sevaun took one last look behind her before touching the wand to her own face and dropping into the water below.

In that brief instant, she saw Rellen vainly trying to stem the tide of Gwarulch, as more and more of the vile creatures pushed against the fisherfolk and their wall of pikes. They had already broken their way through in several places, and the hedgehog was disintegrating into one vast, swirling mass of hand-to-hand fighting.

As the waters closed over her head, she heard Rellen's voice, dim and far away: "Break south! Anyone who can, break south!"

12

THE BEAST/TO THE WATER LORD

E very living thing must have left this area or died, thought Julia, as she walked past the piles of bones and long-dead bushes that lined the dried-up stream—but she still stopped every now and then to look ahead, particularly when the husks of trees clustered together, making a perfect place for something to hide.

The yellowed hills were long behind her now, and she felt that it was time for a drink, if there was a clean-looking water hole somewhere. The stream had cut a deep gully into the dried earth, so Julia had to climb down the crumbling banks, to the squelchy mud that lined the bottom of the stream. A very thin trickle of water ran murkily through the mud. Julia eyed it distastefully, and decided to keep walking.

After another hour, Julia was having second thoughts about drinking from the dirty trickle. There'd been a few pools of water along the stream, but all of them were full of yellowish mud and small insects. They also smelled like compost.

Julia looked at the latest dirty pool and its swimming insects, and then up at the sky, hoping to see signs of a memory change. If everything went back to green fields and clear streams she thought, life would be much easier.

She was starting to laugh at the idea that anything could be easy while you were trapped inside an evil Witch's mind, when there was a faint splash somewhere behind her—as if something had disturbed one of the pools further back along the winding gully. Quickly, Julia held out her wand, ready to touch whatever was approaching.

For a few seconds, everything was completely still. Julia held her breath and listened more intently—and caught the slight sound of metal clinking and the sucking noise of footsteps in the mud.

Gripping the wand so hard her knuckles shone white, Julia took a few hesitant steps towards the last corner of the gully, her mind flashing through pictures of all the terrible creatures she'd seen through the Ragwitch's eyes—or that She had shown Julia from Her memory. And now, Julia was in that memory . . .

But the thing that rounded the corner was like nothing she'd seen before, a shambling man-sized monster, caked in mud and dried blood, with black and silver rags hanging from its twisted shape in a fall of tatters. Rusted iron rings clinked under the cloth as it shambled along like a broken mechanical monkey, all hunched over, its arms trailing along in front. The beast stopped in front of Julia and slowly, almost as if it had forgotten how, it straightened its back—and looked at Julia through clear blue eyes set in a face curled back in a bestial grimace.

With a shock, Julia realized that it was a man—somehow twisted and altered, but definitely human. It looked at her for a second, and she felt the tiredness and the horror in it, even as its mouth opened to snarl, and the bandied legs bent for the killing spring.

Screaming, Julia thrust the wand out, striking the beast's chest as it sprang. It knocked her down into the stream where, half-blinded with mud, she scrabbled fearfully for the wand, expecting to feel ripping teeth and claws within seconds. Then she felt the familiar golden warmth of the wand under her hand, and having hold of it once again, she sat up, wiping cold mud from her face. Eyes clear, she looked around—but there was no sign of the creature.

Still trembling with shock, Julia got to her feet, the wand held ready against attack. The creature was lying on its back in the mud, a few meters upstream. Golden sparks trailed up and down its body, and a yellow light flickered all around. Very faintly, Julia could hear Lyssa singing, and the distant hum of harp strings lightly struck.

She watched entranced as the sparks stripped away the bestial features and straightened out the body of the creature, though they didn't remove the mud and dried blood. As Lyssa had said, the wand was revealing the creature's true form. No longer a twisted monster, it was a man of thirty or so, with long red-brown hair and a worried face, lined with cares and trouble.

Despite this welcome change of appearance, Julia kept the wand ready. Lyssa had told her that it would reveal something's true nature . . . and it had, but the man might still be a servant of the Ragwitch. Or rather, the memory of one. Julia looked at the sky again, hoping for a memory change that would remove this person before he woke up. But the sky remained blue and calm, with the sun beating down on the arid fields and the dried-out stream— and the man was waking up, and muttering. Curious, Julia edged a little closer to see what he was saying.

"Torches . . . more torches," he mumbled, eyelids flickering. "The barricades . . . will they stop the Stone Knights? Bring more to the . . ."

"Stone Knights . . ." whispered Julia to herself. "He must have been fighting the Angarling . . ."

She hesitantly reached out and shook him, careful to keep the wand ready in her left hand.

"Were you at Bevallan . . . or the Namyr Gorge?" asked Julia. She could think of no other place where he would have fought Angarling. But if he was just a memory, surely he should be in a place that was the memory of Bevallan?

I wish Lyssa were here to explain it all, thought Julia, as she struggled with the idea of being in the Ragwitch's memory, and how this man-beast could belong to Her recollection of parched hills and dried-out streams.

She shook the man again, slightly harder, and he stopped mumbling to himself and his eyes began to open. Julia moved back a couple of steps as he raised himself up on one elbow and looked blearily around.

He frowned when he saw Julia, but not in anger. More as if he were puzzled, and couldn't understand what was going on. Julia noticed that his hand automatically crept to his side, as if seeking a sword.

The man looked around the stream-bed again, and then back at Julia. He made no move to get up, but Julia stepped back, for there was still something dangerous in his look.

"Where are we, girl?" asked the man. "How far are we from Yendre?"

Julia stepped back, and didn't answer. How could they be close to or far from anything, trapped inside the Ragwitch's mind?

"Speak . . . I mean you no harm—unless you are one of Her servants."

Julia looked back at him for a moment, and saw that behind all the mud, dried blood and danger, there was something human and kind in the man, something Her creatures never had.

"No," said Julia. "I am an enemy of the Ragwitch."

"The Ragwitch?" said the man, clumsily getting up onto his knees. "I know nothing of a rag . . . witch. I am speaking of the North-Queen, as She now calls Herself."

"The North-Queen . . ." said Julia, thinking back to what Lyssa had told her. "But the Ragwitch is the North-Queen . . . She has come back in a different form." Then she remembered that she was effectively in the past. Here, in Her memory, it still was the time of the North-Queen. But how was she going to explain that?

The man was silent for a moment, his breath wheezing as he stood up and steadied himself against the side of the gully. "You speak in riddles, girl. But I admit my mind lies heavy in my head, and I misremember . . . we were retreating to Yendre, and the Gwarulch were close behind, and She not far behind them . . ."

He paused to wipe his eyes, his hands shaking with the effort. Without thinking, she got out her handkerchief, and wiped the mud from his eyes. He looked at her as she cleaned off the mud, but his eyes were far away.

"My thanks," he said. "My body seems weaker than my mind. For now that I remember, it was the Citadel at Yendre I last saw, with the great gate borne down by the Stone Knights, and the red flicker of Gwarulch eyes in the moonlight. My guards . . . my friends . . . fell about my feet as we were driven down into the very cellars of the keep. My sword shattered on an Angarling back, and then She was standing above me . . . with Gwarulch pinning me to the floor. I begged Her to slay me, but there was nothing human left in that beautiful shell . . . She just looked, and said nothing. Then there was a strange room, of air like water, and a globe of white light . . . a prison cell, where She spoke to me and showed the wasteland that was once my Kingdom. And then . . . the cold and darkness, and vague unformed memories—for a long, long time. And now at last, I have woken, though it be in some desert wasteland."

"The white globe . . ." whispered Julia. "Then you're not a memory either . . ."

"A memory?" asked the man, trying to smile. "What do you mean?"

"This isn't a desert," began Julia slowly. "It's worse than that . . ."

"Worse?" asked the man, managing a brief smile. "It could be no worse than the prison of the white globe."

"But it's the same!" cried Julia. "We're in Her memory—this is just a memory of a place, and the place with the white globe is just another part of Her horrible mind!"

As soon as she'd said it, Julia wished she'd told him in a nicer way. He seemed even weaker, leaning against the side of the gully, his breath coming in long, wheezing gasps—but he seemed to understand. When he finally spoke, he talked into the side of the gully, and didn't look at Julia.

"You called Her the Ragwitch . . . and said She was the same North-Queen, that She had come back. Where did She come back from? How was She made to go? And what has happened to the Kingdom?"

"I'm not really sure," said Julia. "I'm not from your Kingdom . . . but I know that when She was the North-Queen she beat everyone, and ruled the Kingdom, destroying it with Her creatures and Magic—these dried-up lands must be a memory from that time. But then the Magi and the Wild Magic attacked Her, and everyone thought that was the end of the North-Queen.

But She wasn't dead— just trapped in a different world—and She had to make herself a new body, so she became the Ragwitch. And for hundreds of years the Kingdom was all right, till . . . till She managed to get back. And now She wants to destroy everything!"

Julia trembled a bit on the last few words, but the man didn't seem to notice. He didn't look at her, for his eyes were full of tears, and he whispered, "I am King Mirran, and it was I who let a young Witch cast the spells that took her to the Nameless Realm, and the lure of evil. And it was I who could have stopped her in the early days of her power, when the Angarling made their slow way up from the sea. And still, there is no end . . . no end."

He paused and took a ragged breath before turning to Julia.

"Now, tell me—what is your part in this?"

Julia trembled at the idea of telling this King that she was the one who'd helped the Ragwitch return, and for a second she almost ran away. But he looked so grim and terrible and sad that she slowly knelt down in the mud, and he sat beside her and listened: about how she found the Ragwitch, and what had followed after, at the Spire, and Bevallan and the Namyr Gorge.

"You have been led to help a great force of evil," said Mirran, when she had finished. "But unwittingly so. I have done far greater wrong, with greater knowledge. You should not be ashamed."

Julia bit her lip a little, and nodded, afraid that she would burst into tears if she said anything. She still felt awful for freeing the Ragwitch, but it wasn't as if she'd done it on purpose, and it didn't compare with King Mirran, who had suffered for so long. She briefly wondered why he hadn't stopped the Witch all those years ago. She thought he was probably wondering too, sitting in the mud and brooding.

"Come on," said Julia. "There is still hope. We can fight Her by doing what Lyssa said—go to Her memory of the sea."

"And what then?"

"Then," she answered, "we find Anhyvar."

"Anhyvar!" exclaimed Mirran, staggering to his feet. "Anhyvar! Don't you know who she is?"

"No," said Julia, surprised at his reaction. "Lyssa said she is a memory of the Ragwitch we have to find. A woman with long red hair, who wears a silver star . . ."

"Anhyvar," interrupted Mirran bleakly, "is the Witch who became the North-Queen. Lyssa has sent you to find the Ragwitch's memory of Her former human self."

* * *

It was quiet under the water after the noise and tumult of the battle at Donbreye. Only the swish of bubbles as they moved disturbed the tranquility of the water. High above, a yellow-green glow marked the surface, quite different from the dim green light where Paul, Quigin, Sevaun and Leasel walked on the bottom of the sea.

Almost as soon as they'd all arrived on the seabed (Paul upside down and struggling), Sevaun had led them south at a brisk pace. At first she had been in danger of leaving them behind, as the boys and the hare floundered along, trying to walk normally. But they soon learned to half-swim, just using their feet to push off from the bottom every few meters—except Leasel, who gave up and was now being carried in the front of Quigin's shirt.

Paul was still the slowest, because he couldn't really believe he was under the sea and still breathing. It was like a dream, but far more solid—in fact, *too* real, and after the first few minutes of worrying about drowning, Paul forgot about the strangeness in his efforts to keep up with the others.

Their half-swimming, half-walking progress was a lot of fun in the beginning, but after an hour or so, Paul was very tired. And the underwater world wasn't half as interesting as the films he'd seen of tropical reefs and brightly colored fish. It was all green and weedy instead, and he'd only seen a couple of very drab fish— probably Trazel.

"Can we stop for a while?" he asked Sevaun. Surprisingly, the words were quite clear, and no bubbles came out of his mouth. All part of the spell, thought Paul, whose opinion of Sevaun was rather higher than his regard for most girls, partly because he was a bit frightened of anyone who could do real Magic . . .

Sevaun looked back as he spoke, and said, "I suppose so. But we should try and get a long way south, like . . . like Father said."

Paul nodded, thinking back to Deamus and the fisherfolk . . . and the Gwarulch. He hoped they would all get away, but deep down, he knew that maybe none of them would escape, and even if they did, Donbreye would never again be the same quiet fishing village. Sevaun was obviously thinking about them too; seeing her red eyes, Paul thought that she was probably crying, though the tears just mixed with water, and were washed away by the sea.

"They'll be all right," he said clumsily, wishing Julia were there to look after Sevaun as well as him. "We'll meet up . . ."

"Sevaun," interrupted Quigin, pointing over her shoulder. "Do you know what those things are?"

Both Paul and Sevaun leapt around at once, creating a swirl of bubbles that made it impossible to see anything. Then, as the bubbles cleared, they saw three dark, finned shapes hurtling through the water towards them.

"Sharks!" cried Paul, fearfully, but Sevaun laughed

and stepped forward, saying, "They're dolphins, silly! Dolphins are friendly!"

"Dolphins!" exclaimed Quigin. "I've read about dolphins. But I haven't got up to underwater animals yet. How do you say hello in dolphin?"

Quigin found out almost immediately, as the dolphins arrived, turned in a foaming circle around the children, and back-arched through the water, their bottle-noses split with cheery smiles. Paul smiled too, mostly with relief that they weren't sharks.

After the first excited meeting was over, the dolphins seemed eager to make Paul and his friends do something. Eventually, with quite a bit of gentle prodding from the dolphins, Quigin said, "I think they want us to hang onto them. Perhaps they're going to take us south."

"Maybe," said Sevaun. "Dolphins are the special servants of the Water Lord. Perhaps he sent them to help us. After all, it is the Festival Day."

"The Water Lord," whispered Paul, and then more loudly, "I need to see the Water Lord. I hope they take us to him."

"I don't," said Sevaun. "The Water Lord can be very nasty in person. Even Waterwitches don't go and see him . . ."

"But I have to," said Paul, trying to convince himself that he did. "I have to," he said again, going over to the nearest dolphin. Gripping it tightly around the fin, his cheek pressed against the smooth grey skin, he whispered, "Take me to the Water Lord, please, Dolphin."

The dolphin rolled its clever, kind eyes back towards Paul, clapped its long mouth together a couple of times, and took off.

Quigin looked after the departing dolphin, tucked Leasel in, held onto his own dolphin, and was following within seconds. Sevaun hesitated, looking back towards the land, her small face set in a frown that was holding back tears. Then she climbed astride the last dolphin, hung onto the fin like a saddlebow, and was away after the others. Away from the shallow coastal waters, and into the deeper, darker sea.

After an hour of speeding through, and sometimes above, the water (where the children had to hold their breath and the dolphins took in air), Paul's dolphin arrived above a great, dark hole in the ocean floor, and slowly began to circle.

Looking down, Paul saw that the seabed had cracked apart to make a huge canyon, its edges lined with waving green weed. What little light was left from the surface went only a short distance into this great black trench in the sea. But as Paul watched, he saw a single spark of light approaching from below, like someone carrying a torch up a flight of darkened stairs. It took a very long time to get closer, and only then did Paul realize the canyon must be hundreds of meters deep.

Quigin and Sevaun arrived while the light was still coming up, but no one said anything. They all just looked at the tiny speck of brilliance emerging from the vast expanse of darkness.

Then, quite suddenly, there was a shape around the light, a shape that made Paul shudder. For the light was on a stem that grew out of a fantastically ugly fish, fat and bloated, with blunted spikes sticking out all around it, and two huge goggly eyes that shifted back and forth on stems. And it was coming straight for Paul.

Close up, it was even nastier than it looked approaching, and it had an out-thrust lower jaw that kept grinding forward and back very unpleasantly. It stopped a few meters away from Paul, who had crept around to the other side of his dolphin.

Then the dolphin gave a little flip, and Paul lost his hold. For a second of absolute panic, he thought he was going to sink into the great hole below and be lost forever. Then his madly threshing hands caught hold of something, and he grasped it like a drowning man grabbing a life jacket—and realized he had grabbed the light-stalk fish. It clapped its jaws once, and started to swim strongly downwards. Too frightened to let go, Paul went with it.

Looking back, he saw his friends being whisked away by the dolphins. Quigin pushed away from his, and tried to swim down towards Paul, but his dolphin came back and nudged him upwards again. The last Paul saw of Quigin was his favorite mulberry hat, sinking down ahead of him and being lost in the blackness; Paul almost expected to see Leasel going after it, as the hare had done so many times before.

But within a few short minutes, he couldn't even see his friends—just the faint glow of the surface, far above. Around him, the fish's lantern cast a dull light for about an arm's length, and within that small area, Paul could see quite clearly, though there was a total absence of color. Beyond that, there was just an enormity of blackness.

13

GOLDEN FIRE/
THE WATER LORD'S CATCH

Mirran was still weak after the golden wand's transformation, so he and Julia walked slowly along the gully. He told her a little more about the North-Queen, and the war that followed, but avoided saying any more about Anhyvar—except to say that the Magic she had hoped to find to end the war had only made it fiercer and more horrible, by making her into the North-Queen.

In return, Julia told him all she could remember of what Lyssa had said about the end of the North-Queen's reign—how the Magi and the Wild Magic had cast Her out, and She had taken the form of a rag doll to survive. And over many hundreds of years, the Kingdom had recovered, and forgotten the North-Queen, and what had been learned of the Ragwitch became a thing for scary tales and a blame for bad luck.

Mirran had listened carefully, particularly to what Julia knew about affairs after his defeat in Yendre, and supposed death. Then he asked her about the Ragwitch, and what She had done since Her return.

The color faded from Julia's face, and she leaned against the side of the gully as she thought of the answer. She didn't want to remember the people of Bevallan, fleeing from the Gwarulch and unstoppable Angarling, only to meet the Meepers swooping in from the sky. Or the Glazed men and women, "survivors" of the Namyr Gorge, all pale as death, with their halting movements. But she told Mirran, and he listened as if such things were no surprise to him—and in fact, he had seen far worse, when the North-Queen was at the height of Her power.

"You have endured great evil," said Mirran, when Julia had finished. "Few would have the courage to keep going. Many grown men and women would have given up before now."

"To be completely absorbed by Her?" asked Julia, shuddering. She could think of nothing worse than being a part of that loathsome leathery monster, and Her vicious, ugly thoughts. "And I had . . . have Lyssa to help me."

"Yes," said Mirran thoughtfully. "The aid of one of Alnwere's rowans is worth a great deal."

They walked in silence after that, for an hour or more, till the stream suddenly dried up altogether, and the gully led out into an open plain of red and blowing dust. The sun hung low in the sky, and its red glare made the land ahead look like a sea of drying blood. Mirran stared in horror, and mumbled something Julia didn't hear.

She turned to ask him what he'd said when her question was drowned by a chilling howl that burst out behind them, echoing down the gully and onto the plain. It was a sound Julia knew well, though she had only heard it through the dulled ears of the Ragwitch. A hunting Gwarulch had found their trail—and Gwarulch never hunted alone.

"Gwarulch!" cried Mirran. "And I am unarmed. But if they are just memories . . ."

"Lyssa said they'd be real to me," said Julia, fighting back the urge to run, screaming. "Real and dangerous."

"Then," answered Mirran, taking her hand, "we must run!"

Even as he spoke, he was running, with Julia dragging along behind, the red dust blowing up around their feet like smoke blazing a clear trail for their pursuers. Behind them came the howl of the Gwarulch, and a sound that Julia hadn't heard before—screaming and wild laughing, like that of an hysterical crowd. Mirran heard it too, and coughed out, "Glazed-Folk."

Julia grimaced, remembering the Glazed-Folk at the Namyr Gorge. She glanced behind to see if they were catching up, but there was nothing visible beyond the red dust. Then Mirran suddenly faltered, staggered for a few steps, and fell down. Julia stopped, and turned back, but he waved her on, gasping: "*Run*—run on! My legs are still too weak."

"No," said Julia firmly. "I won't leave you for them. I've still got my wand."

Mirran opened his mouth as if to say something, but only a rasping wheeze came out, and his head bent backwards toward the dust. Julia moved closer to him, the wand held ready in both hands.

Just like softball, she thought for a second, as she realized she was holding the wand like a bat. She swung it a few times, and tried to imagine the Gwarulch as a softball she was going to hit for a home run.

The baying and screaming was much louder, but even so, Julia was unprepared when the Gwarulch and Glazed-Men burst through the veil of red dust. There were six or seven Gwarulch, loping along easily, all looking much larger and more vicious than they did through the eyes of the Ragwitch. And the Glazed-Folk were more inhuman, with their red-rimmed eyes and gibbering, laughing, loose-jawed mouths. Their hands gripped weapons of rusted steel, and they were staring at Julia. The Gwarulch licked their lips.

Julia looked back at them, hefted her wand, and tried to think of them like the Ragwitch did—as rather weak and puny servants, useful, but not particularly valuable nor trustworthy. Julia found it surprisingly easy to think like the Ragwitch, and vicious amusement rose in her like an exhilarating wave. These were her creatures, for Julia to treat as she pleased. Without thinking, Julia straightened up to her full height, and hissed, "How dare you come against me?"

Her voice had the sinister, powerful tone of the Ragwitch. Shocked at herself, Julia almost apologized to the approaching horde of monsters. But they had stopped, suddenly unsure of themselves. Who was this girl with a wand, who spoke like their Mistress, the North-Queen?

Cowardly at the best of times, they were afraid to approach further. Once again, Julia felt a triumphant, sneering sort of voice rise up in her. Kill one or two, it whispered, and rule the others. You will find Anhyvar more easily, with servants to help you. Slash them with the wand, burn them with golden fire . . .

"No!" shrieked Julia, in her own, distressed voice—breaking the spell of fear that had held the Gwarulch. They sprang forward, talons grasping and teeth bared, with the Glazed-Folk close behind.

Julia met the first one with a full swing of the wand, and golden sparks flung the Gwarulch back, blackened and burning with golden flames, while the sound of drums thrummed in the air above Julia's head. The next Gwarulch, too slow to twist aside, met the same fate, but not before a talon-edge had ripped a tear down Julia's arm.

Then, within another second, it was all over. Without warning, the sky ripped with lightning for a second, turned black, and filled the stars and scudding clouds. A new moon hung on the horizon, and there was no sign of the Gwarulch or Glazed-Men. Julia could only see five or ten meters in the moonlight, but the whole area seemed to be different. A memory change had struck again.

With an inaudible sigh, Julia collapsed onto the ground, holding up her bleeding arm. She felt sick, and for a few seconds her stomach churned and bile burned the back of her throat. Then she remembered Mirran— had he been lost in the memory change?

But there was coughing coming from somewhere on her right, and she could just see Mirran sitting up in the moonlight, not far away. With a hand clasped over the cut in her arm, she crawled over to his side.

He stood up, coughing a little, and cleaned Julia's cut with one of her socks, and bound it with the other, while she sobbed with the pain and horror of it all. When the bandaging was finished, Julia took a few deep, short breaths and said, "I thought you'd gone with the memory change."

"No," said Mirran quietly. "I am a prisoner, not one of Her memories—though I came close to being slain by them. You were very brave, child. I . . . I hoped for a daughter once. Perhaps she would have been like you."

Julia didn't answer, and when Mirran looked closely, he saw that she was asleep or unconscious. But her breathing was steady, and pulse strong, so he gently folded her hands under her head, before getting up to walk around. He could smell salt and that meant they were near the sea. Perhaps near Sleye, where Anhyvar had lost whatever made her human, and called the Angarling from the sea.

He looked back at Julia, a small dim shape on the ground, and wondered that she could sleep, cut and all. But then he had always been able to sleep when he was a boy, despite cuts, cares and bruises. There had been no nightmares then, he thought wistfully—awake or asleep. Still thinking of his childhood, he also lay down, and fell into a kind of half-sleep to dream of better days.

* * *

Deeper and deeper went the light-stalk fish, as Paul hung on with a grip of deathly fear. He was afraid of where the fish was going, but even more afraid to let go, in case he sank all the way to the bottom. If there *was* a bottom to the endless abyss of black, all-enclosing water.

Vaguely he knew that he was far deeper than scuba divers ever went, and that he should have been crushed by water pressure or got the bends (whatever they were). But the water-breathing spell seemed to take care of that—at least Paul didn't feel any different, except that there were dull booming sounds in his ears, like the echo of far-away drums.

Then he realized that he actually could hear drums, or at least some bass vibrations through the water. And there was a dim shape looming ahead of him, just a touch lighter than the dark water.

The fish clapped its jaws again, and wriggled a little to change direction—towards the lighter shape. As they approached, Paul realized that the water was no longer dark and the shape ahead was some sort of vast door-way in the canyon wall—a doorway closed with great strands of weed, with a bright light shining out between the little gaps and holes in the curtain of weed.

Seeing the light, Paul's fears lessened, and he remembered how the Master of Air had really been quite kind, despite his awesome presence. Perhaps the Water Lord would be the same ... He closed his eyes for a minute to reinforce that hope. For some reason life seemed a little more hopeful when Paul closed his eyes and counted up to sixty.

He'd just reached forty-five when the first weed brushed past his face, a cold, slimy shock that made his eyes snap open. The fish was going straight through the curtain of weed, and great slimy tendrils kept brushing over Paul, leaving dark-brown stains and pieces of rotten vegetation behind.

The only good thing about it, thought Paul, removing some slime from his face, was that it was getting lighter and lighter. Obviously there was some sort of enormous lantern beyond the weeds—something like an underwater lighthouse.

But it was far more spectacular than that. As the fish burst through the last layer of weed, Paul cried out and covered his eyes with weed-slimed hands. For they had emerged into an enormous underground cavern of shining emerald-green water. And it was lit, not by a single light, but by thousands of luminescent fishes, octopi, squids, strange creatures, and glowing weed—a swimming galaxy of brilliant stars.

As Paul's eyes slowly adjusted, he realized that the light-stalk fish was taking him to the very center of the cavern, where the most luminous creatures of all shed their light around a sphere of black and troubled water— the only dark part of the entire amazing cavern.

As Paul approached, he felt his fish begin to shudder, and soon he was shuddering too. A deep vibration of sheer power seemed to emanate from the sphere of black water, a power that beat at Paul's temples, scaring him, and at the same time, filling him with some of its strength. He felt like he didn't know whether to laugh or cry, and just bit his lip instead.

It was only when the salty tang of blood trickled into his mouth that Paul realized he really had bitten his lip—quite deeply. And with pain came the realization that the fish he was hanging onto was a dead weight in the water. It was no longer swimming. And that the black watery sphere before them had begun to slowly spin, green water foaming into it like an unblocked drain. A whirlpool that was going to suck the light-stalk fish in . . . and Paul with it.

Immediately, Paul pushed away from the fish, and tried to swim out of the vortex of the whirlpool. Arms and legs thrashing wildly, he forgot every aspect of the swimming style he'd learnt over so many cold mornings at the pool. He was still floundering when the main swirl of the whirlpool caught his legs, twirled him about, and swept him into darkness.

It was almost instantly calm within the black sphere, and as the currents became still, so did Paul. He trod water steadily, just to keep his place, and looked around.

It wasn't as dark as the abyss outside the cavern—obviously some of the sea-creatures' light filtered in. It was more a sort of grey, thought Paul, like on a moonlit night. That reminded him of the Master of Air, and the great bird that had been so fearsome at first sight. Perhaps this black whirlpool was just the Water Lord being fearsome to start off with. Paul hoped so.

Thinking that it might only be some sort of test made Paul feel a little better, so he started to swim about. He trusted the dolphins, at any rate, and was sure they wouldn't have brought him to the abyss if it was going to be really horrible.

Then he saw something coming down towards him, a rope of luminous weed being let down from somewhere

far out of sight above. It stopped a meter or so above
Paul's head, and he noticed a loop in the end like a
handhold, just the right size for him to grab.

Paul hesitated for a second, then reached out to grab
the loop. It was instantly snatched out of his hand, and
the rope flicked up about five meters. Puzzled, Paul
watched it go, then swam after it. He didn't have to go
far, because the rope came back down, stopping about
the same distance away from him as before.

Once again, Paul grabbed the loop, only to have it
snatched away. This happened several times. Finally,
Paul swam up to it very slowly, got very close, and
lunged at it with both hands.

With a triumphant cry, he got a firm hold on it, only
to find himself suddenly bound tight, as folds of rope
fell down from above and wrapped themselves around
him. The rope snapped tight, and started dragging Paul
upwards at high speed, the water foaming past him like
the jet from a tap.

Seconds later, Paul burst from the black depths into
green-lit brilliance, and was pulled sideways by the
ropes, zig-zagging across the cavern to a cave carved
out of the wall, lined with the gleaming sides of cowrie
shells, all green and mottled in colors never seen above
the sea. In the middle of this cowrie-paved cave, his
legs firmly planted on the back of a giant turtle, a man-
like figure was pulling in the rope hand over hand. Paul
stared at him, but couldn't quite make sense of what he
saw.

The figure was man-like, but seemed to be made of
constantly swirling sea-patterns. He shimmered fluidly,
and small waves moved back and forth across his burly
chest, while different colored currents swirled up and
down his arms. And when Paul looked at his face, all
he could see was the deep, blue-black expanse of the
open sea.

Obviously, Paul had been caught by the Water Lord— fished up from the black waters. He hoped the Water Lord wasn't going to do to him what fishermen did to fish.

"So," boomed the Water Lord, deep vibrations buzzing in the bones behind Paul's ears. "You are Paul."

"Yes," whispered Paul, puzzled as to where the sound was coming from. The Water Lord's face was still featureless, and the sound seemed to come from all around.

"Why have you come here?" asked the Water Lord. He leaned towards Paul, and the boy felt the terrible force in him; the waves and currents that roiled his surface hinted at a vast energy within like some huge coiled spring.

"I came to ask for your help," said Paul slowly. He was really uncertain now. The Water Lord's lack of a face was strange, inhuman, and far more threatening than the giant, bearded visage of the Master of Air.

"My help . . . against the Ragwitch . . ." boomed the voice again. It was so low and loud it was starting to give Paul a headache, and made it hard for him to concentrate.

"Yes . . . against the Ragwitch," answered Paul. He struggled to think of a reason for the Water Lord to help him. "She will try to destroy the streams and rivers . . . all the fish and things in the water . . ."

"Yes," came the Water Lord's reply, a flat agreement that she would try these things.

"The Wise said that I could harm her—stop her," said Paul. "If you and the other Elementals help me."

The Water Lord said nothing to this, but more waves broke on his surface, and Paul felt as if he were watching some sort of inner struggle between the conflicting natures of the Water Lord—between the sea which provides, and the sea which destroys. Then the waves quietened, and the Water Lord stood completely still. As Paul watched nervously, a bright blue tear welled out where his left eye should have been. It hung from his face for a brief second, was caught by a current, and spun off into the water towards Paul. Without even thinking, he caught it in his outstretched hand.

It was surprisingly solid, almost like jelly, and warm as well—even hot. Paul flipped it from hand to hand, like a hot biscuit, while it cooled. Strangely, with the teardrop in his hand, he'd almost forgotten where he was—if only for a second.

The booming voice reminded him quickly, with a sharp stabbing pain in his head, as the Water Lord said: "That is The Blood. Keep it with you always. Now— *leave here!*"

The vibrations from the last words were so severe that Paul was stunned for a moment. Disoriented, he floundered about, looking for the light-stalk fish, a dolphin, or any guide to get out.

But none of the light-fish came any closer, and as Paul looked back, he saw black waves rising across the surface of the Water Lord. Each wave seemed to disrupt his man-like form, and his whole shape was becoming fuzzy at the edges, as if it were about to mold itself into something else—and whatever the Water Lord was going to become, the process was very disturbing.

Paul started to swim away, The Blood safely stowed with The Breath in his leather pouch, but he couldn't help slowing to look back again, which was a big mistake. For the Water Lord had completely lost his human shape, and was now a whirling mass of black and writhing water—another whirlpool that was growing with every second. Paul didn't need another look, and struck out and up, swimming furiously. Thoughts raced through his mind, of the fisherman's shack at Donbreye, and Deamus saying "the sea . . . knows cruelty as well as kindness . . ."

The phrase was still running through his head when the black waters reached him, caught him, and once more swirled him down to the darkest waters of the Water Lord's deep crevasse.

14

SLEYE MIDDEN/SHARKS

High on a narrow headland which thrust out into the sea, the setting sun cast long red lines of light across the branches of the trees like trails of fire. Julia leaned against one of the sun-fired trees, and looked out through a break in the forest to the sea beyond. The scent of salt was very strong, and if she closed her eyes she could almost feel that it was her family's favorite stretch of coast, and she was standing near the front of a rented beach house on the first day of the holidays.

But when she opened her eyes, there was the great red setting sun, the trees bright as flames, and it was Mirran sitting nearby—not Paul. With a start, Julia realized that what with all her own troubles, she hadn't thought of Paul for ages. The last time she'd seen him was when the Ragwitch had been taking her over—and he'd run out of the bedroom. With a pang, she hoped he was all right. Paul would miss her dreadfully, and worry too. Julia realized that she missed Paul as well—his comforting, loyal presence, always ready for whatever they were going to do next. She wished he was there with her, and then wished that she was with him. Safe . . . back at home.

Mirran interrupted her thoughts by getting to his feet, mail-shirt clinking. "We must move on," he said wearily. "If Anhyvar is anywhere, she will be here. I am certain that this is the headland to the north of Sleye . . . though . . . it doesn't seem quite right."

"Even She can't remember exactly," said Julia, "so I suppose it isn't exactly the same. You know, how you think that somewhere is just as it is in your head, and when you go there, it's not?"

"Yes," muttered Mirran. "I believe you have it. Now, we had better not talk as we walk. These trees could hide Gwarulch or other of Her creatures—and I'd rather surprise them than be surprised."

Julia nodded, and drew her wand, just to be on the safe side. Mirran hefted the stick he'd torn from one of the trees, and moved off. Julia followed, noticing how quietly he could move, despite the odd clink from his mail-shirt.

Nearer the end of the headland, the trees thinned out, and a wind rose up from the sea, cold and moisture-laden. Small bushes replaced the trees, and jagged rocks thrust up from the ground in clumps. The headland rose up too, and as Julia climbed, she noticed the earth was red beneath her feet. A few yards on, white shells and broken shards confirmed her fears.

The hill on the headland was another midden.

And at the top of the midden, Julia suddenly knew, would be Anhyvar, the woman Lyssa had told her to find. But Mirran said that Anhyvar was the woman who became North-Queen, and then Ragwitch. What if this was all the wrong memory, and it was the Ragwitch at the top of the midden—somehow herself inside herself? She might be up there now, the doll's everpresent smile split to show the shark-like teeth, and pudgy three-fingered hands reaching out to pull Julia into her evil embrace forever . . .

Without realizing it, Julia slowed at these thoughts, and with the last one, she stopped altogether. For the first time in her life, she couldn't go on, and something snapped deep inside her. Dropping onto her heels, she grabbed herself around the knees and tried to curl into the smallest ball she could.

The next thing she knew was Mirran's voice somewhere near her left ear.

"What's wrong, child?" he asked, concern in his voice. "Are you hurt?"

Julia didn't want to answer, but she heard her own voice babbling about the midden, and the Ragwitch waiting. But she felt that she was really drawing away, to some far-off place. Mirran kept talking to her, but the words couldn't travel the distance.

For what seemed like forever, Julia's head whirled with all the images of her time with the Ragwitch: from their emergence in the Sea Caves, the trip to the Spire, Oroch's unearthing, to the slaughter of Bevallan and the poor Glazed men and women of the Namyr Gorge. But most of all, her thoughts went back to that single second in the Midden, when she'd first seen that scrap of cloth sticking out of the unearthly nest.

But Mirran kept talking, and gradually Julia began to listen to what he was saying, and her sobbing ceased, and she became aware that Mirran was talking about Anhyvar.

"She was so eager to find new Magic," he said. "At first, only for healing, as the Patchwork King had decreed there would be no other Magic used in the war. But her enthusiasm went further, and she threw herself into her researches. She so desperately wanted to end the war, to put a stop to all the pain and hurt of so many people.

"For many years while the war dragged on, she spent the summer with the army, as a healer for the wounded and sick. In winter, she prowled the libraries of Yendre, talked with others of the Magi, and consulted with the Stars.

"Then one day, she came to me at Caer Calbore, where the army was resting after a hard-fought month of clearing the North-Creatures from the lands around the Awgaer upspring. She was happy, excited, more enthusiastic than ever. She told me that there had been an Age of Magic before the Patchwork King gathered all the reigns of Magic to himself—and that she had uncovered the secret to its hiding, and would be able to unleash it at her will. Furthermore, she spoke of the Stone Knights of the Angarling, waiting under the sea at Sleye. They would be the perfect means of bringing the war to a rapid end.

"I asked if she had talked of this to the Wise, or any other of the Magi, and she answered no—she was afraid they might take the path to the Patchwork King to warn him. And jealous of other powers, he might forbid her.

"Foolishly, I accepted this—but later, when I realized exactly what Magic Anhyvar had found, I knew that, even then, the first cold tendrils of that evil power had begun to warp her nature, and wrap around her heart.

"So, she left for Sleye, with a small escort of soldiers, and my blessings and hope."

Mirran paused and looked at Julia. She raised her head, and uncurled a little, before nodding at him to go on.

"I never saw her again after that, save at the fall of the Citadel in Yendre, when it was only her shape that remained. I heard what happened at Sleye from one of her escort—the only one who escaped. He was sore wounded, and raving, but he spoke of her conjurings, on the headland above Sleye. He said that she had cast her spells, and was waiting, when a vast black door appeared, that shook and rumbled as it opened. Anhyvar was drawn within, screaming and fighting, and the door swung shut and disappeared with a rolling clap of thunder.

"They were good soldiers, and despite their fear, they waited and searched about the place.

"Anhyvar returned in the dark of early morning. The soldier who told me the tale said she came upon the camp without warning, and struck them with a spell that held them fast. He was on watch, a little way from the camp, and so escaped—after he saw that she was no longer the kindly Healer-Witch they had escorted. For she Glazed those soldiers into mindless servants, and laughed as she worked. It was the laugh that made the soldier run.

"And the rest, I think, you know. She woke the Angarling, and perverted them to the service of evil, during which time I did not move against her, much to my later sorrow. Then, she went north, subjected the Gwarulch Elders and Meepers to her rule, and declared herself to be the North-Queen.

"So, if it is Anhyvar we shall find atop this Hill of Bones, it should be a human woman, whose major failing was a blindness to the faults of anything that could bring an end to the war."

"She doesn't sound too scary," whispered Julia, wiping her nose with a muddy handkerchief. "I hope you're right."

"I hope so too," said Mirran. "My memories of Anhyvar were befouled and tainted by what she became and my own bitterness. I would like to see even a memory of her true self again."

He paused, and helped Julia up, before adding, in a voice so soft it almost passed Julia by, "We were to be married—when there was peace. We both wanted the war to end too much . . . and not just for the people . . ."

* * *

Paul trod water again, his tired arms feebly moving beside him. His whole body felt strained and stretched from his efforts to swim up and out of the black depths.

But no matter how far he swam, and how far up, there seemed no end to the awful darkness. Paul had begun to think that it moved with him, and he could swim a thousand kilometers and it would still be there.

Worse, every time he could swim no further and even treading water was too much, he sank down for what seemed an eternity. It was rather a nice feeling, slowly sinking. It made Paul sleepy, and it would be very easy for him to give up and go to sleep.

He would have too, except for one thing: the water-breathing spell. Paul couldn't remember exactly what Sevaun had said, but he thought the spell would only last for the Festival day—and that day must be nearly over.

Drifting ever downwards, Paul asked himself what Julia would do, or Aleyne . . . or even Quigin. But it was no use. He was sure that they would find some way out, but he couldn't think of what they might do. After all, he was up against Magic, as well as being on the very bottom of the sea.

Magic . . . thought Paul suddenly. I've got Magic too . . .

He carefully opened his pouch, thrusting in a hand to make sure nothing would fall and be whisked away by currents. The Blood, still a ball of warmish jelly, met his fingers first, but he pushed it aside to grab the feather that was the Breath. It was of the Air—perhaps it could help him get back to the surface.

From the moment it left his pouch, Paul knew it was a good idea. The feather radiated a soft blue light that relieved the darkness of much of its terror. And it felt buoyant, and seemed somehow to be bigger than it used to be.

In fact, it *was* bigger, Paul realized—and growing—stretching out tremendously, and with every surge of growth, Paul felt it rising up, carrying him with it. Within a few minutes, it was a meter long, and speeding up like a bubble in a glass of soft drink, Paul hanging on with all his remaining strength.

Seconds later, they burst out into the cavern of the light-fishes, but the feather didn't stop. For an awful moment, Paul thought they were going to rise to the roof of the cavern and be trapped there like a real bubble, but the feather changed direction, and sped for the weed-strewn gateway.

Then, like a giant's shout, a voice boomed through the water, its rage and anger shaking Paul right through to his bones. Looking back, he saw the black whirlpool spinning and whirling at great speed—and out of it came finned shapes, all over ten meters long, with skins of dusty white. Paul knew at once that those were no dolphins, but great white sharks.

The sharks snapped at the light-fish, and wove back and forth like hounds sniffing out a scent. Then they swung their long heads towards Paul, and he imagined their hungry, single-minded eyes focusing on him—for in unison, they all curved around to charge directly at the racing feather and the boy.

"Come on! Come on!" shrieked Paul, as he felt the feather slowing to negotiate the weeds. He swarmed further up the feather, and started urging it along as if it were a horse. Behind him, the sharks didn't even try to avoid the weed-barriers. They just ploughed right through, and seemed hardly slowed at all. Then the feather was out of the weed, and in the blackness of the trench. It seemed to pick up speed again, but Paul could no longer see the sharks. He kept looking back, and thinking he saw a flash of white in the feather's bluish glow, and every time his heart beat even faster, till he felt that it was shivering a thousand times a second, and not really beating at all.

Those few minutes in the total blackness of the abyss, never knowing when a shark would catch up, were among the worst in Paul's life—but there was also an exhilarating, exciting feeling in the sheer speed of the jetting feather; and Paul felt less afraid when he saw the first smattering of light above, and no white shapes behind.

They broke the surface like a flying fish, Paul holding his breath as they hurtled over ten meters into the air, and then back into the water again. In that arcing flight, Paul had caught sight of two things: land, and fins breaking the water. Both were about five hundred meters away, though the fins were getting closer every second.

As they sank below the surface again, Paul felt confident of continuing to outdistance his pursuers—until the feather began to shrink in his grasp, and he had to start kicking to keep from sinking. In a few seconds, the Breath had shrunk to its normal size, and Paul was swimming at his own slow pace. He frantically struck out towards the shore, occasionally sticking his head out of the water to check the direction—and finding he still couldn't breathe the air. He didn't look back—he knew the danger of slowing, even for a second. Besides, it was better not to know, he thought—better just to be taken without warning.

Just then, something did touch his foot, and he

screamed and looked back—straight at a dolphin's snout.

Relief flooded into him as the dolphin surged alongside. Without needing to be prompted, Paul grabbed the dolphin's fin, and it accelerated away towards the shore—very directly, without the high-spirited jinking and leaping the dolphins had displayed before. Obviously it knew about the sharks.

Relieved of the effort of swimming, Paul took a long look behind—and there they were. Four long, fearsome shapes bearing down towards him, minds set on eating. They seemed very fast.

Paul clutched the dolphin even tighter, closed his eyes, and pressed his cheek against the dolphin's comforting side—so he missed seeing its prodigious leap out of the water and onto a long green wave that was curling into the beach.

He opened his eyes when he felt the extra burst of speed, and the foam rushing past his face, as dolphin and boy surfed onto the beach and slid three meters up the wet sand, straight to the feet of Quigin and Sevaun.

Paul goggled at them stupidly, and made sucking fish-like motions with his mouth, choking on the air— till Sevaun touched his nose and mouth with her seashell wand, and he could breathe again, sob with relief, and lie in the sand next to the beached dolphin.

Since Paul was obviously incapable of explaining what had happened since they parted, Quigin lay face-to-face with the dolphin, and seemed to have a lengthy and interesting conversation—obviously Quigin had learned dolphin-talk very quickly.

Sevaun stood silently, watching the fins of the sharks circle out beyond the surf. When they left, and headed for the open water, she helped Quigin push the dolphin into deeper water, and drag Paul further up the beach.

"I seem to do a lot of this," said Quigin amiably. "I mean, dragging you out of the water."

"Thanks," mumbled Paul. "You won't have to any more. I'm never going for another swim in my life."

"Don't be silly," said Sevaun. "Of course you will."

"And I'll drag you out if you need it," added Quigin. "By the way, did you see anything interesting down that crevasse?"

"Um, yes," replied Paul, rather surprised to think of it like that. "I suppose I did."

"Let's hear about it then," said Quigin impatiently. "What sort of things live down there?"

"Can't I have a rest first?" asked Paul. "And shouldn't we find Deamus and the others?"

"Father's at the castle, with . . . with most of the others," said Sevaun, in a rather trembly voice. "We only came back to look for you a little while ago—and then the dolphin said you were on the way."

"The castle?" asked Paul. His brain felt as sodden with water as the rest of him, and he was having trouble working out just what was going on, and where it was going on at.

"Caer Follyn," answered Quigin, pointing inland. "And a very good castle it is too. The towers are full of owls, and there're dune mice in the kitchens."

"Oh good," said Paul faintly, though he didn't quite see how the presence of owls and dune mice improved a castle. "Can we go there—and get something to eat?"

"Of course," said Quigin, helping him up. "You can tell us what happened on the way."

"And you can tell me what happened to Deamus and Sir Rellen and . . ." Paul began to say, when he noticed Sevaun was crying, and Quigin rubbing at his nose.

"Ah," said Quigin, for once rather somber and quiet. "Sir Rellen . . . Sir Rellen . . ."

"The Gwarulch killed him," whispered Sevaun. "Sir Rellen, Tannas and Fayle, Sedreth and Horvarth . . ."

She stopped talking, and sniffed back the tears, as Quigin added, "Sir Rellen stayed behind to help the wounded get away."

All three were silent after that, and Paul thought of Sir Rellen when he'd first seen him, calmly handling a lobster—and those other names, of people he'd never known, but had probably seen, all laughing and smiling at the Sea Festival of Donbreye. Now he could never see them again.

Paul slid his hand into his pouch, and felt the feather of the Breath and the teardrop of the Blood, and swore fiercely to himself that he'd find out how to use them, and stop the Ragwitch and all her creatures—to rescue Julia, and to help all the people whose lives the Ragwitch would take or ruin.

"Come on," he said firmly. "Let's go up to the castle."

15

ANHYVAR/ALEYNE

Julia felt strangely calm as they approached the top of the midden. Having made the decision to go on, she felt a sort of acceptance of her fate—whatever it was to be.

There'd been another memory change about fifty meters from the top of the midden—but only a small one. The sun had suddenly blinked into night, and it had become very cold and windy. But within a minute, it was dawn, and warm again. And the land hadn't changed at all.

Perhaps, thought Julia, there could only be very small memory shifts this close to the midden. After all, it had to be one of Her most powerful memories.

Ahead of Julia, Mirran suddenly stopped and stared ahead. Julia moved up the last few meters, and stood level with him—and looked out onto the shell-strewn top of the midden, gleaming white in the morning sunshine.

In the very center, a ring of blue flames danced and flickered slowly, too slowly to be real flames. They were cold, too: Julia felt their chill, despite the warming sun.

In the middle of the ring, she could just see a woman lying among the shells, her long red hair trailing out to one side. She wore a plain black dress, stark against the whiteness of the shells, and the silver star upon her breast sparkled with the blue light of the flames.

"That is Anhyvar," said Mirran quietly.

"What do we do now?" asked Julia, as she tried to get a really good look through the circling flames. As she spoke, she shivered from the cold of the flames. The fire seemed to drain all the heat out of the air, and her breath came out like fog on a frosty night.

"We must wake her," replied Mirran. He hadn't taken his eyes from Anhyvar, and now he stepped forward towards the icy flames, arms outstretched.

"Don't!" cried Julia, grabbing at his arm. "You'll freeze!"

"What?" he asked, gently prising her grip loose. "Freeze? Why should I freeze?"

"The flames ... they're ice-cold ... can't you feel it?"

"No ..." replied Mirran thoughtfully. "What do *you* see ... and feel?"

Julia hesitated for a second, then looked hard at the flames, and felt the cold beating against her face.

"I can see Anhyvar sleeping," she answered, "in a ring of cold fire. The blue flames are sort of slow—and they're very, very cold."

Mirran shook his head slowly, and narrowed his eyes, as if to concentrate his sight. Then he said, "I see Anhyvar sleeping, but no ring of fire. She sleeps inside a crystal coffin ..."

"What?" asked Julia, unexpectedly giggling. "A what?"

"A crystal coffin . . ." replied Mirran, with a smile starting on his face as well. "Yes . . . that does seem unlikely. My mother used to tell me a story about a princess in a crystal coffin . . ."

"Things aren't always what they seem here," said Julia, remembering Lyssa's warning. "The wand shows me things as they really are."

"Yes . . ." murmured Mirran. Gingerly, he walked towards Anhyvar, one hand stretched out in front, as if he were playing blind man's bluff.

He was saying, "I still can't feel anything," when the very tip of his finger touched the ice-fire. It sparked out a cascade of icicles that jetted across his hands, and Mirran jumped back, cursing.

"My thanks again, Julia," he said as he retreated from the ring of flames, cradling his frozen fingers under his arms to try to recover some warmth.

They stood in silence for a few moments, with Mirran looking at Anhyvar, and Julia staring at the flames, trying to make a decision. She thought of calling Lyssa, but somehow she knew that pointing to Anhyvar inside a ring of cold fire was not what Lyssa had meant when she'd said "when you have found Anhyvar."

"I'll try," she said, finally. "The wand should protect me . . ."

The flames were like dancing icicles up close, radiating a bitter, biting cold. Julia shivered with both cold and fear, and reached out with one hand, into the outermost flame—and snatched it back, as the flames bit into her like some sort of needle-toothed beast, cold chilling deep into her bones. But the wand sent answering surges of warmth to help her; and within the ring,

Anhyvar stirred and muttered, as if rising up from the deepest dream.

For a second or two, Julia stood next to the flames, shaking and half sobbing, hands held tightly around the warmth of the golden wand. Fleetingly, she thought of turning back, but there was nothing to turn back to—except the Ragwitch, and becoming part of Her.

"Haaaah!" Julia screamed, and leapt forward, throwing her entire body into, and through, the freezing flames. She fell onto the sharp shells on the inside of the ring, but couldn't even feel the cuts in her cold-numbed hands. There was no sunlight here—only the cold blueness, dancing to the crackle of the icy fire.

White and shivering, Julia went straight to Anhyvar, grasped her by the shoulders and yelled, "Wake up! Wake up! I'm so cold . . . please . . ."

But Anhyvar only stirred slightly, and muttered into the pillow of her hair. Julia sobbed, and shook her again.

"Wake up! Please wake up! I'm so cold . . . please . . ."

Julia shook her again and again, and then began to cry, her tears falling and freezing as they dropped. Tears of ice fell like hail upon Anhyvar, and glistened against the black of her dress like diamonds. One tear fell on her face, and unlike the others, began to melt. Julia watched it turn back to water, and trickle down the side of Anhyvar's face, and then into the corner of her mouth.

And as the tear disappeared, Anhyvar's eyes flashed open. Unfocused for a moment, she seemed hardly alive. Then she shook her head, her eyes cleared, and she looked straight at Julia, who was still shaking her and crying. Without saying a word, the red-haired Witch sat up, and brought Julia close into a warming embrace. Only her silver star was cold, where it pressed against Julia's cheek.

Anhyvar slowly stroked Julia's hair, and she felt the cold ebb from her limbs to be replaced by a warm, glowing feeling. But still Anhyvar said nothing, so Julia looked up at her face.

She was staring out at the flames, and Julia saw that she was looking at Mirran, and somehow beyond him as well, and there was a great sadness in her face. Out over Julia's head, she whispered, "So much pain . . ."

Then, after a long, sighing breath, she said, "I have slept overlong it seems. And much has been done while I slept that should never have been done."

"Then you know," whispered Julia. "You know that you're not . . . well . . . not really . . ."

"Alive?" replied Anhyvar. "Since that day at Sleye I have been a prisoner within myself, and my body has become, in turn, both North-Queen and Ragwitch, while my true self slept. I would rather have truly died than these things should happen. But you have woken me at last, Julia . . ."

"You know my name?" asked Julia, surprised. It felt rather good to hear her name from this woman who'd taken away the deathly cold.

"Now I am awake," said Anhyvar, "I know all the Ragwitch knows—for I am Her, and She is me."

Julia stiffened at her words, and broke free from Anhyvar's embrace. But Anhyvar said quickly, "Oh, I mean we are like two different parts of the same person. I am the good part, and she is wholly evil, and far more powerful—even now that I am no longer sleeping. But let us quell these flames . . . and . . . let us go to Mirran."

* * *

Despite his good intentions, Paul had collapsed from shock and exhaustion before he'd made it to Caer Follyn. The uncomplaining Quigin had hoisted Paul up across his shoulders and carried him the last few hundred meters, up the hill, through the bailey of the castle (now the camping ground for the fisherfolk of Donbreye) and round and round a circling stair to a soft feather bed in one of the towers, just below the friendly owls.

There, eight hours later, Paul woke up with the unpleasant feeling of not knowing where he was. It was dark, too, but as the sleep cleared from his eyes, he saw there was a lit candle by the door. In the dim pool of golden candlelight, he saw the glint of armor, and heard the soft thk-thk of a sword being burnished.

As his eyes totally cleared, he followed the burnisher's arm from the light up to a face in the shadows—and a familiar voice said, "Can you say Awgaer yet, Paul?"

"Aleyne!" cried Paul happily, sitting up in his bed like a jack-in-the-box. "What are you doing here?"

"Looking for you," replied Aleyne drily. "What else would I be doing?"

"Were you really looking for me?" asked Paul. He thought that would be unlikely—he didn't feel important enough to have someone like Aleyne looking for him. Then he remembered the Breath and the Blood. They were important . . . but then, Aleyne couldn't have known about them . . .

"Yes," replied Aleyne, breaking into Paul's rather sleepy train of thought. "I was looking for you. When I spoke to Maghaul at Rhysamarn, she . . ."

"Maghaul? Not Tanboule?" interrupted Paul.

"The Wise are many, and Rhysamarn is a big mountain," replied Aleyne. "Though I've heard tell that they are all different parts of just the one. Anyway, I spoke to Maghaul, and was told to warn the King, and then to find you—and to look on the eastern coast. So I rode like a dervish to Yendre, raising the hue and cry as I went. Yet when I arrived at the Citadel, the news had gone before me. Messenger birds had flown from Caer Calbore, telling of a great murder at Bevallan, and a battle at the Namyr Gorge, where a company of borderers and some sort of Wizard tried to hold Her at the Steps. So the King had already called the folk to war, and the muster tokens had gone forth."

"The Storm Boy . . ." muttered Paul, thinking back to the fish-stinking hut, and Deamus's explanations.

"Yes. The Storm Boy is such a token. In fact, I was bringing that one myself. I have carried such tokens to several of the coast villages over the last two days. It seemed sensible, since I had to come this way in search of you. Then, this morning as my company and I rode north, we had the good fortune to rescue the folk of Donbreye from a band of Gwarulch."

"But not everyone, and not Sir Rellen," said Paul sadly.

"No," answered Aleyne, looking down to the sword he burnished, and blowing gently, his breath fogging the steel. "He fell earlier, trying to hold the Gwarulch in the village—he helped many of the fisherfolk to escape. He was a famous Knight, and friend of the present King's father. He fought on the borders for many years to keep such folk as those of Donbreye safe—whatever he was facing, be it fire, flood or foes. I hope that I will look after the people of the Awgaer as well as Sir Rellen, who watched the coast."

He again looked up from his sword, and said, "Now you must rest again, Paul. There will be many things to do, come the morning."

"Yes," answered Paul, quietly. "I'm glad you found me."

"I'm glad too," said Aleyne. "Though you do seem to attract a great deal of trouble."

"I don't mean to," replied Paul. Somewhere above his head, an owl let out a melancholy hoot, and he added sleepily, "Have you met my friends Quigin and Sevaun?"

"Yes," laughed Aleyne. "In fact, I think that was Quigin hooting. And I've met Deamus and Oel as well. Everyone has told me a great deal about what you've been doing."

"I'll tell you again, tomorrow," mumbled Paul. "Most of it was horrible . . . and tiring . . ."

"Goodnight," said Aleyne. He reached over to snuff out the candle, but saw that Paul was already asleep, so he picked up his scouring cloth again and turned his attention to the blade across his knees. There had been Meepers above the tower earlier in the night, watching for any lone sentry that might fall asleep, or perhaps a chance to get at Paul—for Aleyne was certain they were after the boy. And the Gwarulch hadn't retreated far, and were bound to be slinking back under the cover of darkness.

The morning seemed to dawn immediately after his conversation with Aleyne, and Paul awoke with the expectation that it had all been a dream. But there was Aleyne, half asleep on the stool by the door, his sword by his side. He raised his head as Paul got out of bed, and said, "Good morning! Are you ready for a hard day's travelling?"

"Travelling?" asked Paul, half-heartedly. He felt like curling up in front of a fire all day, steaming the water out of his bones. After all, he had been underwater for almost a whole day!

He was just about to voice these protests, when Aleyne smiled, and said, "Because if you do feel like travelling, forget it! The muster won't be complete for a day at least. Then we travel."

"Where to?" asked Paul. "I have to find the Earth Lady or the Fire Queen."

"They may be found upon our path, I hope," said Aleyne. "At least as well as anywhere else. And it is certainly no longer safe for you to be travelling alone, or in a small group. It is too much of a coincidence that the Gwarulch attacked Donbreye so soon after your arrival—for there are many villages further north that are still untouched."

"You mean She sent them to get me?" asked Paul. "They know where I am?"

"Perhaps," answered Aleyne, then, seeing Paul's dismay, added, "but you are quite safe here. I have a company of borderers with me—they've often fought Gwarulch on the northern border. And there are a lot of villagers—as well as the hardy fighters of Donbreye."

"Oh well," said Paul, nervously checking his pouch to make sure the Breath and the Blood were safe. "I don't know what else I could do. And the Wise did tell you to look for me, so it must be the best thing to do. Where are we going?"

"Why, to join the King's army, of course," replied Aleyne. "I thought I told you . . . the King is marching north to relieve the siege of Caer Calbore, which has been holding out against the Ragwitch and Her horde of North-Creatures."

"Are you sure that's the best thing to do?" asked Paul, thinking that a horde of North-Creatures sounded worse than anything—and to actually go towards Her and a horde . . .

"I am sure it will be . . ." replied Aleyne. But secretly, he wondered. He'd read a little about the North-Queen while he'd been in Yendre. She had defeated all the Kingdom once—a Kingdom that was far more warlike and prepared than at present. Now that She had come again in the form of the Ragwitch, marching to do battle with Her might be the most dangerous thing anyone could do. But the Wise had told the King to give battle . . . and to find Paul. Aleyne hoped this wasn't one of the rare times that the Wise were hopelessly wrong.

* * *

Two hundred kilometers to the north of Caer Follyn, Caer Calbore's defenders were hard pressed. Already the inner and outer baileys had fallen—no wall or gate could stand against the Angarling, and where they smashed an opening, the Gwarulch and Glazed-Folk followed. Now, only the Great Keep still held out, and the Gwarulch were filling the ditch before it with logs and stones, bodies and earth, to make a causeway for the Angarling to cross and break the gate. Standing high on the wreckage of Caer Calbore's outer walls, the Ragwitch watched Her servants work.

When the causeway was complete, She raised one hand to signal the attack—and then suddenly, She swayed, with Her fat, three-fingered hand clasped to the side of Her head. Around Her, the Angarling let out a great boom of noise, their deep-carved faces screwed up in mortal pain. Then the Ragwitch screamed, a scream of rage and hate that shattered the broken stones before Her, and sprayed the backs of the attacking Gwarulch with lethal splinters. She screamed on and on, and the rock splinters flew with deadly purpose among the ranks of the Gwarulch, who howled and ran aside, abandoning the attack. Only the Glazed-Folk kept throwing themselves forward, cackling and screaming—to be feathered with arrows, or pushed back from the ramparts, their ladders breaking on the rocks below the keep.

Within a minute of Her scream, a tide of Gwarulch flowed away from their Mistress as She stood among the troubled Angarling, oblivious to the battle before Her. Only Oroch moved against the tide, the Gwarulch parting before him, despite their haste to slip away from Her awful scream.

When Oroch finally reached Her, the Ragwitch fell silent. He bowed, and squeaked fearfully, "What ails you, Mistress?"

The Ragwitch didn't look at him, but Her mouth moved slightly, and Oroch thought he heard a voice long forgotten—the voice of a human Witch, in the times before either She or Oroch himself had entered the service of evil. And that voice said, soft in anguish, "So much pain . . ."

Then the Ragwitch looked at him, and She bared Her mouth still more, showing her shark-teeth in anger. "Why is the attack slowing?" She hissed, raising one puffy arm. "Why do the Gwarulch slink away?"

"You . . . you screamed," began Oroch, but She cuffed him to the ground, spittle blowing as She spat, "Bring them back. I will lead the next attack Myself!"

She watched his black-bandaged form scamper across the rubble to the Gwarulch chieftains, and wondered at the feelings that had so briefly tormented Her, feelings from the past She thought she had buried completely in the service of evil and the Nameless Realm. For a moment, She wondered if the girl had something to do with it. But Julia was there, tied to Her senses, silently watching the battle, and slowly fading into the Ragwitch's grim mind.

Casting Her thoughts back to the attack, the Ragwitch raised an arm, and a black fog drifted from Her hand. Twirling it like a rope, She flicked it at a nearby Gwarulch. He yelped once, and slowly fell to the ground, life ebbing till he was no more than a wind-blown husk. Satisfied, She curled the fog back into Her hand in readiness, and, fixing Her gaze on the main gate of the keep, lumbered forward, the Angarling forming their protective ring around Her.

Watching through Her eyes, the twig-maid shook and shivered. She was already crumbling, becoming less of Julia, and more of a flame and rowan. Soon the Ragwitch might discover the true nature of the twig-maid, and then . . . She would look deep inside Herself for Julia.

* * *

As the Ragwitch screamed and the Gwarulch and Glazed-Folk attack on the castle faltered, the Castellan of Caer Calbore wearily made his way up the long stairs of the highest tower at the southern corner of the Keep. Atop this tower, the castle's Friend of Beasts spoke to his swiftest falcon, and the Castellan hurriedly scrawled the message she would carry.

"Send the falcon when the upper gate falls," he said to the Friend of Beasts. "I hope she can outfly the Meepers."

"She is sure of it," said the Friend of Beasts, but the Castellan was already clanking back down the stairs, to prepare for what would certainly be the enemy's last and successful attack. The Friend of Beasts watched the Castellan's blood-streaked helmet disappear around the corner, then read the message before he tied it on. It said only, "Caer Calbore has fallen to the Ragwitch."

Down below, he heard the hunting howls of the Gwarulch start again, and the thunder of Angarling against the gate—then the dreadful screaming of metal and wood, as the great steel-bound doors gave way, and the howling changed to a note of triumph above the clash and screech of weapons and the fading shouts of the defenders.

He gazed deep into the falcon's eyes, giving her his last instructions—then he threw her into the sky with a flick of his wrist and watched her speed southwards for a moment, before he picked up his sword and started down, down towards the tumult of battle.

16

A PICNIC WITH LYSSA/
MASTER CAGAEL & FRIENDS

Julia looked away embarrassed when Mirran greeted Anhyvar but they didn't fall into each other's arms as she'd thought they would. Instead it was a formal greeting: Mirran took her hands, and raised them to his lips, and Anhyvar did likewise. Even so, it was obviously more than that, and Julia still felt she shouldn't be looking. Then they just stood there—Mirran looking at Anhyvar, and she at him—till the wind came up, and Anhyvar's hair blew across her face, and she had to use both hands to hold it back.

Julia was reminded of Lyssa's long, silver hair, and the autumn leaf that would call her to them. She quickly checked that it was still in her shirt pocket. It was, so she pulled it out—but as the leaf cleared her pocket, the breeze picked up again, and it was twitched from her fingers and twirled away up into the sky.

Julia watched it go with a startled immobility, and almost cried out for Mirran to try and catch it. But

Lyssa had said, "Send it to the wind when you find Anhyvar . . ." And she had found Anhyvar—and Mirran.

She looked over to them, and saw that they were following the leaf's path too. Anhyvar turned to Julia, and said, "You are calling the Rowan Lady—Lyssa?"

"Yes," replied Julia. "At least, I hope I am."

"She has heard," said Anhyvar, looking in the direction the leaf had taken. "She will come."

"How do you . . ." Julia began to ask, when she realized that Anhyvar must know what was going on inside her own memory, or the one she shared with the Ragwitch—but it was all so confusing.

"Don't think too much on it," said Anhyvar, obviously catching Julia's thought from her puzzled frown. "Consider Her memory as a completely different world which we can travel in for a time. Better still, don't think on it at all. Especially now, for I think that it is very much time . . . for us to have a picnic!"

"A *picnic*?" asked Mirran and Julia together, both in tones of disbelief, Mirran's deep voice rumbling under Julia's high one. The wind-swept top of the midden, so recently lit with crackling flames of ice, did not easily inspire thoughts of a picnic.

"Shouldn't we be doing something?" asked Julia. "I mean the Ragwitch could be doing anything right now . . . attacking somewhere, I mean . . ."

She paused as Anhyvar held up her hand and closed her eyes. She concentrated for a few seconds, then opened her eyes again—and stared straight past Julia, as if she were looking at something entirely different. She frowned a little then, and narrowed her eyes as if squinting through frosted glass.

"She is surveying Her latest victory . . ." she said, in the matter-of-fact tone of someone describing the view from a window, "a castle, recently taken. Meepers are reporting to Her . . . they speak of Gwarulch raids to the east . . . oh!"

Her eyes flashed back to Julia, and she stared at her, one hand half raised to her mouth. "Julia, did you know your brother was in this world—in the Kingdom?"

"What!" exclaimed Julia. "Paul? How could he be?"

"I don't know," replied Anhyvar. "But in some way he represents a threat to the Ragwitch—or She thinks he does. She has sent Gwarulch and Meepers to seek him out . . . and slay him."

"No . . ." whispered Julia. "Not Paul . . . he . . . he wouldn't have a chance . . ."

Anhyvar looked out past Julia again, and concentrated. "He has already evaded the Gwarulch twice. And it seems he is now with a strong band of the King's soldiers in the east. The Meeper speaks of the Gwarulch being driven off. So he is safe for the time being."

"Oh, please," exclaimed Julia. "We have to do something soon—I can't let Her kill Paul!"

"Don't worry," said Mirran, catching a look from Anhyvar. "If he is with a strong force he will be safe for quite a time, particularly if it is a long way from Her. And we shall do something . . . but we have to wait for the Rowan Lady—for Lyssa—and I think a picnic is a very fine way to while away the wait."

He proffered an arm to each of them. Anhyvar looped hers through, but Julia still hesitated, till Anhyvar said, "We need Lyssa's advice—and her power—before we can act. But for now, there is a seedcake, lemon sherbet and a summer afternoon waiting just around the corner."

"Where?" asked Julia, looking around at the shells, the red earth, and the windswept sea. The wind was blowing so fiercely that, even with the sun shining, it didn't feel like a summer day.

"This is my memory too," replied Anhyvar. "Or parts of it are. And I remember a little sandy cove, the bright sun shining, and a wicker basket with a broken catch, all full of pies and cakes, and the lemon sherbet in a crystal bottle stoppered with a silver cork . . ."

As Anhyvar spoke, black clouds blotted out the sun. Lightning flickered, and thunder roared. Nervously, Julia took Mirran's arm, and at Anhyvar's word, they began to descend from the midden.

Then the lightning flashed directly overhead, and Julia blinked. The next step she took was on soft golden sand . . . the sky above was the bright blue of a glorious summer day, and a positively huge wicker basket sat atop a blue blanket spread out just above the tide marks. Blinking from the lightning and the sudden sunlight, Julia still noticed that the basket only had one catch, and a silver-corked bottle stuck out of one side.

* * *

Paul shrugged his shoulders back again, trying to get used to the feel of the buff coat that had been cut down to his size—or somewhere near it, anyway. It was very bulky and awkward, and it made Paul feel like a robot from an old film, because he couldn't bend his arms properly—though Aleyne did say that it would get better with wear.

He had a steel helmet too, with a three-barred visor that would never stay up when he wanted it to. It was a very heavy and uncomfortable helmet, but even worse was everyone's insistence that he wear both coat and helmet all the time—because that meant he'd probably need them.

Paul shivered at the thought, and stopped to look out of the tower window, down to the preparations in the courtyard below. The whole place was full of people milling about, but there were two quite different types of bustle. Aleyne's Borderors—regular soldiers who normally patrolled the northern frontier and kept the

North-Creatures out—were very obvious from the blue-striped sleeves of their buff coats, and the glitter of the steel shortbows they wore in special sheaths on their backs, crossed with a quiver of blue-fletched arrows. They moved purposefully, and were generally only told what to do once, and then they did it. The fisherfolk, on the other hand, seemed to be more dashing and less efficient, though Paul expected that it was mainly because they had never had to make ready for battle before. With more than six villages represented, they were a very mixed sight, sporting equipment, armor and weapons even more varied than those of the Donbreye villagers.

Through the crowd, Paul could see Aleyne talking, encouraging, and straightening out problems. He could see Deamus too, looming out of the smoke around the forge where he was beating an old steel cuirass into shape for Oel, who sat nearby with Sevaun, both of them intently cleaning a pile of rusty pike-heads.

The sight of Sevaun working made Paul remember he was supposed to be looking for Quigin, who had organized a gang of spies from rats, magpies and (for nighttime) owls. One of the magpies had flown over a few minutes earlier, calling wildly, before alighting in the tower where Quigin took his reports. So Aleyne had sent Paul to find out what the bird had seen. Remembering this mission, Paul turned back from the window, and started up the stairs again, complaining to himself about the extra weight of coat and helmet.

As expected, Quigin was out on the ramparts of the tower, talking to the magpie. Paul climbed wearily up the last step, and sat in one of the embrasures till Quigin had finished talking and the bird was rewarded with a piece of the burnt bacon left over from breakfast.

"What did the magpie say?" asked Paul, as Quigin straightened up and pushed back the bandanna he'd taken to wearing in place of his hat, now lost forever at the bottom of the sea.

"Good news," smiled Quigin, peering over the ramparts. "Which we should be able to see . . . over there!"

Paul followed Quigin's pointing finger, out beyond the castle to the fields that bordered the forest which in turn bordered the sea. At first he couldn't see anything, then he caught a glimpse of something moving out of the forest—or rather, a whole lot of somethings. They spread out into the field, and a larger shape emerged from the shadow of the trees . . . a much larger shape.

"Are you sure this is good news?" asked Paul doubtfully, shading his eyes to get a better look at whatever it was.

"Yes, of course," replied Quigin. "It's Ethric, and the dogs—and there's Rip and Tear."

"What!" exclaimed Paul. Quigin seemed to be feverish. He was dancing about, pointing to the sky—then Paul saw he was pointing at two cruising shapes which somehow looked rather familiar. They circled closer, and he realized they were very large eagles, with distinctive, wedge-shaped tails.

"Why, they're wedge-tailed eagles!" he said with delight. "Just like the ones at home . . . except maybe bigger . . ."

"Rip and Tear," explained Quigin. "Ethric is the great brindled boar, and the dogs . . . I'll introduce you when they arrive."

"You know them all?" asked Paul. "Where are they from?"

"Didn't I tell you?" asked Quigin. "They're Friends of Master Cagael—my master—and there he is!"

With that, Quigin was off down the steps, almost tripping on the top one and arriving rather too fast at the bottom. Paul looked back to the forest, where a man-sized figure was emerging to walk next to the large creature—presumably Ethric the brindled boar—while the smaller shapes (obviously the dogs) quested back and forth across the fields as they progressed towards Caer Follyn.

Ten minutes later, the outer gates to the castle creaked open, and Quigin was bowled over by five rather large black and brown hounds, who seemed intent on licking him to death in welcome. Then Cagael and Ethric the boar entered more sedately, and the dogs drew back and sat in a line, panting heavily and thumping their tails on the ground in delight.

Quigin got up, and was just going forward to say hello to Cagael, when there was a harsh whistle from overhead, and the two eagles plummeted down to alight onto a peculiar saddle astride Ethric. Even this enormous bristled pig (the size of a small pony) shuddered under their impact. They flapped and hopped till they were comfortable, glared at Quigin with their fierce eyes, and let out two surprisingly gentle cries of welcome.

All around the courtyard, everyone had stopped to watch this imposing entrance, but Aleyne shouted, "Back to work everyone! And welcome, Cagael, Friend of Beasts!"

Cagael pushed back his hat, revealing a round, tanned face under greyish and thinning hair, smiled a smile showing several missing teeth, and said, "Hello to you, Sir Aleyne—and to you, young Quigin. I hope you've been of service, and learnt a thing or two."

"Oh, I have," exclaimed Quigin. "I've been to the Wind Moot, and under the sea . . ."

Cagael smiled again, and said, "You should have learned at least a thing or four! But who's this I see with Leasel?"

Paul, who had fetched Leasel from the kitchen gardens, was soon introduced, and his story told by a combination of Aleyne, Quigin, Paul and, he suspected, Leasel, who exchanged eye-to-eye greetings with Cagael for quite a long time.

Then Aleyne and Cagael went on to speak of the North (Cagael brought news he'd heard from the birds), and Paul was introduced to the animals, much to the enjoyment of the dogs, who were called Ean, Tall, Yither, Wuin and Tan. Which was simply the numbers one to five in the old Chant-Magic language, explained Quigin, but it seemed to suit them. They were of the breed of marmot-hunters from the far south—great runners, hunters and diggers, and clever too. Paul thought they looked like extra-large dingoes with black backs, albeit with a total lack of dingo shyness.

Ethric the boar was another matter. Paul had never seen anything that looked so big and fierce. His tusks were the size of Paul's forearms, and his trotters were shod with steel. Despite all that, he seemed very likeable—his eyes twinkled with a keen intelligence, and he didn't seem dangerous to his friends.

Paul was being formally introduced to Rip and Tear when Aleyne came out onto the steps of the keep, and shouted for silence. When all the noise and bustle in the courtyard stilled, he said, "The Friend of Beasts has brought bad tidings from the north. Caer Calbore has fallen."

A shocked silence met his words, and those who knew the great northern fortress muttered their disbelief at Aleyne's words. But they quietened as Aleyne spoke again.

"The Ragwitch's army is moving south—faster than anyone could have guessed. We must march by tomorrow's dawn, or risk being cut off from the King and the rest of the army. So, my friends—to work!"

All around Paul, people redoubled their pace—fitting armor, fletching arrows, shoeing horses, packing rations and water, and generally preparing for the march. Paul felt the Breath and the Blood in his pocket, and hoped he'd find the Fire Queen or the Earth Lady soon. Aleyne had told him Caer Calbore was the strongest castle in the Kingdom after the Citadel in Yendre itself. Now it had fallen, only the King's army stood between the Ragwitch and the unprotected heartlands of the Kingdom. And against Her Magic, even an army would probably not be enough . . .

* * *

Completely full of food, warm, and rather happy for the first time in ages, Julia was molding the sand under the rug to make a nice snoozing place, when she caught a glimpse of something . . . someone, out of the corner of one eye. Her heart thudded for a second at the thought of Gwarulch, but there was no mistaking the tall figure, with her hair so silver in the sun. As she had promised, Lyssa had answered the call of the wind-blown leaf. Julia ran to her through the wash of the waves, hugged her, and was hugged in return.

"Now, you see it wasn't too hard for you," said Lyssa, as Julia led her by the hand to the rug, where Mirran and Anhyvar sat quietly talking. Both rose as Lyssa approached, and once again went through the formal ceremony of kissing hands. Lyssa didn't seem surprised to see Mirran, only saying, "I wondered what had happened to you all those centuries ago, Sire. Your body and armor were never found, you know. I am glad to see you still sane."

Mirran gave a slight bow, and said, "I was neither sane nor even human for much of the time. I have Julia and your golden wand to thank for a return . . . from the shape and thoughts of a beast. And I thank you for that, Lady, and for all you have done for the Kingdom."

Lyssa smiled, and turned to Anhyvar, taking her by

the hand, "I see you know what the evil you summoned has done, both in your body as North-Queen, and now, as Ragwitch. It has been a long time since we stood together on Alnwere, before the Pool. A very long time, and full of horrors. Do you remember the vision we saw there, and none of us understood it? Or how it would come to pass?"

"Yes," replied Anhyvar. "I remember, and now I understand. I only hope it was not a false seeing, and that I come to it soon."

"What vision was this?" asked Mirran gravely, and Julia added, "Did it show what's going to happen?"

But Anhyvar shook her head, and said, "I cannot speak of it, or it may be altered. Now, my Lady Lyssa, would you care for some refreshment?"

"Water would be nice," said Lyssa. "It is such a strain keeping myself from the tree that is so firmly fixed in your memory."

"Oh—of course," said Anhyvar, rather surprised. "But I only met you in human form once, and as a Rowan, many times."

"Never mind," laughed Lyssa, taking a goblet of water from Anhyvar. "Normally I prefer to be a Rowan. But to the business at hand—we must plan what we can do against the Ragwitch. Perhaps you have had time to gauge your strength against Her, Anhyvar. After all, She is still part of you—or you of Her."

"The evil and pride, augmented and nourished by the Nameless Realm," said Anhyvar, rather remotely, as if she didn't want to talk about it. "And I have little power within, or over Her. I may move around the memory a little—perhaps even take control of the body . . . such as it is . . . for a brief while. But then She would find me and crush me forever—not just put me back to sleep. And to do anything, I would have to move out of this memory to Her main consciousness."

"Or perhaps a part of Her main consciousness She has Herself walled off as a prison for those She absorbs," said Lyssa. "I found it reasonably easy to exist there, though I did not have the power to watch through Her eyes, or to catch Her thoughts."

"You mean the place of the white globe?" asked Julia. Mirran nodded too, to show his familiarity with that prison.

"Yes," said Anhyvar, tracing a pattern in the sand, her forehead creased in thought. "It would be easier to wrest control from there, and harder for Her to fight me. But I will need everyone's strength to help, and even then I fear we could only take control of Her body briefly, and prevent her casting spells."

"That may be enough," said Mirran. "If we can make Her cast Herself into the sea or something . . ." He paused as both Lyssa and Anhyvar shook their heads, red and silver hair flying.

"No, of course," he said wearily. "She has the body of a rag doll—She can't drown . . . but perhaps a fire . . ."

"She's not stuffed with real straw," said Julia. "When She went down into the Namyr Gorge . . . a man threw a flaming torch at Her, and the flames just burnt around Her, and didn't do anything!"

Mirran sighed at this, and massaged the back of his left hand, thinking. Lyssa and Anhyvar were silent, both staring out across the water.

"We have to do something!" burst out Julia, who was thinking of Paul. "Couldn't we make Her fall down a pit or something? Anything!"

"Perhaps," said Lyssa. "Whatever we do, I think we should soon return to the place of the white globe. From that hiding place, we may see our opportunity. Also, the twig-maid fails—and if She realizes that it is not the real Julia, all may be lost."

"Yes," said Anhyvar. "We shall go to the white globe."

She stood, drew the silver star from her dress, and held it up. "Join hands, everyone, and I will take us there."

As she spoke, the star grew until it was a shining doorway against the blue of the sky. They all linked hands, and Anhyvar stepped through, followed by Mirran and Julia, with Lyssa last of all.

17

REDDOW CAIRN

Paul looked back on Caer Follyn with some regret, as the column of Borderors and fisherfolk wound through the gate and onto the inland road. Behind him, Paul knew, lay comfortable beds in warm rooms, and meals on plates, which were eaten sitting at tables. Ahead lay discomfort and danger.

But the prospect of danger seemed lessened by the presence of Aleyne's force, which to Paul's eyes was at least a small army. There were several hundred heavily-armed fisherfolk in the column, and at least a hundred Borderors, with many more Borderors spread out ahead and to the flanks, where they watched for marauding Gwarulch.

Quigin was up ahead too, being asked questions by Cagael, who was also supervising the dogs, who loped well in advance of everyone, to sniff out any hidden North-Creatures.

At the front of the column, resplendent in steel back

and breastplates over a bright buff coat, Aleyne walked beside his horse. A few of the other Borderors had horses too, and one had offered Paul a ride—but he hadn't liked it, finding it almost as much of an effort as walking, and more uncomfortable.

Strangely enough, the prospect of a long day's walk didn't trouble him, even with the pack Aleyne had made up for him, which Aleyne joked was twice the weight of the one he'd left for the Gwarulch in Ornware's Wood. He had a sword now too, or as Aleyne called it, a poniard—a thin, sharply-pointed stabbing weapon. It was strapped to his pack. He'd tried wearing it at his belt, but he kept tripping over it, and it was generally awkward. Paul still hoped he wouldn't have to use it.

He looked back at the castle again, and waved to Sevaun, who was watching from the gatehouse wall. Deamus and Oel were marching with the column, but they'd made Sevaun stay behind with the other children, the wounded and the older folk, along with a very few able-bodied villagers, to keep Caer Follyn safe from roving bands of North-Creatures.

Paul wished that he didn't have to go, but he had an opposite feeling too, a determination to do something about the Ragwitch, a feeling that almost rivalled his desire to stay safe and warm and fed. And he could always think of Julia, and what she must be suffering, if he needed anything to spur him on.

It was a beautiful day for the march, so it was easier to be cheerful about the prospects ahead. Some of the Borderors were whistling; the fisherfolk talked among their ranks, of fish and the sea; and always there was the steady tramp, tramp, tramp of boots on the gravelled road. Above, Rip and Tear circled, sole specks of color in the deep blue sky. It seemed a day when everything could only be happy.

Paul waved at the castle one last time, and ran to get

his place back at the front of the column, where
Deamus and Oel marched at the head of the Donbreye
villagers, their pikes all slanted over their shoulders at
the same angle, steel pike-heads and helmets glinting in
the sun. Paul took up his place at the corner, and fell
into step with them, picking up the rhythm of their talk,
and thinking no more of featherbeds, leak-proof rooms,
or lazing by the fire.

After four days of hard marching, they reached the top
of Sanhow Hill—the easternmost of a chain of hills that
ran towards Caer Calbore from the settled lowlands,
and, therefore, a natural place to stop any south-bound
enemy. Aleyne had expected to find the King's army
there, but there were only a pair of grizzled old farmers
camped atop the hill, their rusty armor and muddy tent
fine camouflage—though not against Cagael's eagles, or
the dogs, who sniffed them out immediately.

They told Aleyne that the rest of the army had
marched on that morning—only a few hours ago. The
remnants of their camp were visible in the valley
below—faintly smoking fires, a broken wagon wheel,
and heaps of raw earth from the digging of fire-pits and
latrines.

"Where are they marching to?" asked Aleyne, shading his face against the harsh midday sun, and looking
out along the row of hills.

"Reddow Cairn," replied one of the farmers. "The
King's Friend of Beasts has swifts . . ."

"Oh, that's Neric," interrupted Quigin. He started to
ask a question, but Aleyne gestured for silence, and the
farmer continued.

"Aye—Neric. His swifts brought news . . . She is
marching with a great host, following the Yanel south.
They're bound to cross the hills at Reddow Cairn."

"A long, low ridge—between two hills . . ." said Aleyne, as if he was trying to remember it.

"Yes," said Cagael, taking it as a question. "There was a battle there many centuries ago between the North-Queen and King Mirran. It was Her first major victory. The cairn that gives the ridge its name was raised in memory of those that fell in the battle."

"How . . . how far away is it?" asked Paul, nervously. He'd felt quite safe until all this talk of Her winning battles as the North-Queen. Now, on this stark hill, he looked down at the lines of soldiers resting down the hillside, weapons close at hand, and the sun bouncing off them and lighting up faces and helmet-tousled hair. They looked like very ordinary men and women, and what Paul had thought was a huge force seemed insignificant among the open hills and the empty camp below.

"Not far," said the farmer, pointing. "Reddow Cairn lies between the next two hills. The ridge itself begins on the far side of that hill, and runs north west to the next one, so you won't see it till you get real close."

Paul shaded his eyes and peered in the direction the farmer pointed. All he could see was a large steep hill, covered in the usual grey-green grass and small trees.

Then Quigin yelped and pointed. "Look—there, on the side of the hill. That must be the King's army!"

Sure enough, on the southwestern side of the hill, they could see a dark column moving around the slope, the sun twinkling on helmets and pike-heads. It was a very long column, twisting and turning as it rose up out of a valley and around the hill. Paul held his breath as he watched, and then let it out with a whoosh of excitement, as there was a sudden, splendid flash of gold amongst the column, and Aleyne said, "That was the Royal Standard. The King is there."

They watched in silence for a few minutes after that,

and Paul felt his courage return with the sight of that imposing column of soldiers. It still hadn't passed, and he was trying to estimate its length, and how many people must be in it, when his thoughts were broken by a harsh whistle, and the sound of beating wings above.

Instinctively, he ducked and felt for his poniard, then relaxed as Tear plummeted down onto Ethric's back. Cagael hurried over, and calmed the madly flapping eagle, before staring into his eyes to find out what he had seen. Seconds later, he turned back toward Reddow Cairn, and said, "Look at the sky! Can you see . . ."

His voice broke off as everyone clearly *could* see—thin black clouds were billowing in from the north towards the hill that the King's army was slowly climbing. Everyone stared, knowing these were no normal clouds, nor really clouds at all. But it was Aleyne who said it.

"Meepers. More Meepers than I have ever seen . . ." He looked for another second, then snapped into activity, shouting down the hill, "To arms! To arms! The Ragwitch attacks! We must be at Reddow Cairn in time for battle!"

Paul shivered as Aleyne shouted, and half-guiltily looked around, to see if anyone else looked as afraid as he was. But Aleyne was leaping onto his horse, Quigin was talked to Tear, and Cagael to Ethric. Only Leasel returned his gaze, and he was relieved to see her ears quivering, as if in fright.

"Don't worry," he whispered to the hare, as he picked up his helmet from the ground. "I'll find the other two Elementals . . . and . . . we'll beat Her for sure . . ."

Leasel's ears stopping quivering, and Paul felt braver as he buckled on his helmet. Tightening the chin-strap, he repeated his words over to himself, and thought of Julia waiting for him to rescue her. I absolutely have to be brave, he told himself. No matter what happens.

* * *

The ring of turf and holly was dry and curling at the edges, and looked almost black in the harsh light of the white globe. Yet as Julia, Lyssa, Mirran and Anhyvar swam toward it, and onto it, both turf and holly regained some of their old life.

Then Lyssa took the golden wand from Julia, planted it in the center of the ring, and sang: a song of lilting, liquid notes, that spoke of summer and cleansing rain without the need of words. As Lyssa sang, Julia felt her skin tingle all along her spine, and golden sparks drifted up the wand, and there was the scent of new green trees. At the end of the song, Lyssa suddenly clapped her hands, and the wand answered with a crack! In an instant, the wand was gone, and in its place, a gold-yellow flame flickered gently, and the turf was once again a pleasant green.

"There," said Lyssa. "We are safe again, at least for a time. Now I shall try to call the twig-maid back from the Ragwitch's senses . . ."

"No need," said Anhyvar, pointing at the white globe. "She is already here."

"Don't look, Julia," said Lyssa, firmly. Julia opened her mouth to ask why, then shut both her mouth and her eyes—for she had caught a glimpse of the twig-maid, feebly swimming back towards the ring of braided holly. A glimpse of herself, somehow twisted and fading, colorless and see-through as an old shirt—the result of being continuously tied to the Ragwitch's evil mind and senses.

Anhyvar took Julia's hand as she felt Mirran shift nervously at her side. Even he, a veteran of many atrocious sights in war, was shocked by what he saw.

Julia felt, rather than saw, the twig-maid arrive and collapse at Lyssa's feet. Then she heard Lyssa sing a brief, sad song, and there was the sound of a harp lamenting. When Julia opened her eyes, there was no sign of her temporary double—only a slight smell of smoke, and the faintest touch of ash upon the turf.

"She served her purpose well," said Lyssa, seeing Julia's stricken face looking at the last spray of smoke wafting up above the yellow flame. "And she was never truly alive."

"I know," whispered Julia, "it's just that—it could have been me . . ."

"But it wasn't," said Lyssa cheerily. "And it won't be. We'll get Her yet—didn't I say so, when there was just the two of us? Look at what you've already done!"

Julia nodded and smiled, grateful that Anhyvar hadn't let go of her hand. Everything certainly did seem more hopeful than in past days—particularly those times when she had been alone, and forced to watch everything through the eyes of the Ragwitch.

That thought reminded her of Paul, and she turned to Anhyvar, and said, "Can you tell what's happening outside? Is Paul all right? She hasn't got him . . . ?"

"No!" said Anhyvar. "Neither She nor Her creatures have your brother. And I think I can do better than tell you what is happening . . . I can show you, through Her eyes. If you wish it."

"I would like to see the Kingdom, and what occurs," said Mirran. "But are you sure it will not draw Her attention to us?"

Anhyvar nodded, and said, "Her thoughts are taken up with the ordering of Her army."

"There is to be a battle?" asked Mirran. He clenched his hands as he spoke, and clicked his nails against each other, obviously agitated, then added, "Who comes against Her?"

"The present King, and all the force he can muster," replied Anhyvar, her eyes looking past Mirran, and out through the blackness beyond. "Her Meepers watch as their army marches from the south—many columns from all over the Kingdom, marching to join the King. They are all coming to a long, low hill . . . the Meepers speak of many banners shining as the sun lowers in the sky . . . the hill is called . . . Reddow Cairn."

"I knew a Reddow Hill," said Mirran quietly, almost to himself. "But in my time, there was no cairn. We fought the North-Queen along the ridge between two hills—it was a fierce and savage battle, the first of many that She won. My brother Asaran fell there, borne down by many Gwarulch. It is a place She knows well . . . an evil omen for the battle to come."

Anhyvar blinked, released Julia's hand, and unpinned her star once again. Holding it to her forehead, she whispered a few words, too soft and strange for Julia to catch, and said, "Close your eyes everyone, be silent—and we shall see what She sees."

Julia obediently shut her eyes, rather too tightly at first, so she saw a sort of tense red light everywhere. Then she relaxed a little, and the red slowly cleared, to be replaced with sunlight. Sound started to filter in, too; the rush of the wind, the snorts and whining of Gwarulch, and the crushing noise of Angarling lumbering nearby. Above all was the voice of the Ragwitch, as Julia had often heard it—through Her own cloth-dulled ears.

It was late afternoon, and the sunlight was harsh and bright, casting long shadows along the ground. The Ragwitch was moving inside a ring of Angarling, the great stones moving faster than Julia had seen before, their irregular, rocking glide finding a new, faster rhythm. They were climbing a wide flat-topped hill of grey-green grass and few trees.

To either side of the Ragwitch, and as far as Julia could see out of the corners of Her eyes, Gwarulch loped along in bands of thirty or forty, each with its chieftain at the head—always a Gwarulch of unusual size and savagery.

There were many Glazed-Folk too, half running in an erratic weave, their red-stained eyes fixed on the ground ahead, tongues hanging out like panting beasts. They carried weapons of all kinds, and howled like the Gwarulch.

Above, dark clouds of Meepers swept the sky, their shadows flitting across the sunlit hill. Every few minutes, a lone Meeper would fly in from ahead, or from one side, and harshly croak its message out to Oroch. He stopped to listen, then ran to catch up with Her again like a spider in a stop-start dash across a kitchen floor.

Julia ran her gaze along this whole vast army, and felt the speed and strength of it, and the terrible sense of purpose and anticipation they all seemed to have. At first she couldn't understand it—then she saw sunlight glint on steel along the ridge above, and the vast roar that could only come from human throats, and suddenly, the top of the hill was lined with human soldiers.

Right in the center of the ridge, a knot of horsemen rode under several great banners, and Julia knew this must be where the King was. She wondered if he was like Mirran, and felt that he must be, to bring his army to fight Her, instead of fleeing or hiding.

On either side of the King's banners, there were masses of pikemen—at this distance looking like upside down wire brushes with every piece of wire moving. They didn't look at all ready for battle, and the Ragwitch picked up speed again, and the Angarling and the whole of Her army likewise. The sound of the rumbling stones and the thudding of Gwarulch feet grew faster, the tempo quickened, and Julia saw that the pikemen were moving too, into ranks six or eight deep, their pikes lowering towards the enemy.

In between the hedgehogs of pikemen, archers appeared and strode forward, and a rain of blue-feathered arrows began to whistle down on the closer Gwarulch, and they became like a line of stumbling drunks with many falling—but still they advanced.

Then the Ragwitch shouted, a shout that filled the whole hill with Her murderous delight, a shout that visibly rocked the human ranks in front. All down the hill, their long shadows quivered and moved, as if even the shadows were fearful of what was to come.

And with the shout, everything suddenly happened at once.

The Gwarulch howled, the Angarling bellowed, and they all began a mad, headlong rush to the top of the hill, a furious charge without any semblance of order. Overhead, the Meepers dived against a storm of arrows, and the hillside was alive with the flash of blue whistling through the air, the thud of arrows striking home, and the screams of Gwarulch or Glazed-Folk.

Everywhere was noise and movement, the screaming and shouting rising above all—and then the great crash came as the two armies collided all along the front of the hill, Gwarulch and Angarling in among the pikes and bowmen in a furious melée.

Through the Ragwitch's eyes, Julia saw the Angarling smash into a wall of pikes, breaking them into matchsticks and useless shards of steel. They ploughed straight on, literally crushing any opposition, and the Gwarulch poured through the gaps, with claws and teeth slicing and gnashing. For a few, fast, furious seconds, Julia saw human faces under helmets, faces shouting and screaming, all trying to hack their way back to the Ragwitch and somehow cut Her down.

But few passed the Angarling, and those who did

were cut down by the huge Gwarulch guard that followed Oroch. The Ragwitch was an unstoppable force as She strode on, straight for the center of the human army, the banners, and the King.

* * *

The noise is the worst part, thought Paul desperately. All the shouting and screams and clash of steel, and the howling of so many Gwarulch. The noise . . . and not knowing who was winning.

Quigin seemed to share his thoughts, and started to say, "I wonder what's . . ." when the noise from the battle suddenly changed—and the enemy sounded louder, more triumphant, and much closer.

For about the tenth time, Paul wished that Aleyne had let him go right up to the battle, instead of making him stay back with the supply wagons. At least he could see what was happening in the battle . . .

They'd seen a little, at the beginning, climbing up the hill towards the rear of the army. But they were soon pressed into service back at the wagons, helping the healers with the constant streams of wounded coming down from the battle's front line.

And always, there was the sound of fighting—the last second of a car crash magnified a hundred times, mixed with the roar of a football crowd and feeding time at the zoo. After a while, Paul could distinguish the sounds of both sides in the tumult, and he knew that the Ragwitch was always getting louder . . . and closer . . . as Her North-Creatures forced their way up the other side of the ridge. The flow of wounded was increasing too— men and women staggering, barely able to walk, or being carried down by others, themselves wounded and often at the point of exhaustion.

Paul took bandages to the healer's tents, and water to the wounded who lay nearby in ever-increasing lines.

He was glad he didn't have to go into the tents where the healers and surgeons were at their work. He'd seen enough outside them, and had been sick early on, before a sort of horrified numbness set in, helped by the constant calls for water or bandages.

He'd seen a few of the Donbreye villagers come in wounded, but no one he particularly knew, for which he was thankful. Most of the wounded could not speak coherently of the battle, though many spoke of the Ragwitch and the Angarling—their faces grey with hurt, or shining with the pallor of the very badly wounded.

Paul was refilling his water bottle at a barrel when there was a sudden lull in the battle noise. He stared up at the ridge, and even as he looked, the noise resumed, even louder than before—and he saw a great line of milling soldiers appear on his side of the ridge, and start downhill—some of them running backwards, or half-turned—a wild helter-skelter mass of scattered figures.

"The pike-wall's broken on the left," said a voice next to Paul, and he turned to see a soldier standing by him. It was one of the Borderors, an old soldier by the look of him, his grizzled hair worn down by long wearing of a helmet, and an old white scar livid across the back of his hand. Now he had a bandage across his forehead, and a great bruise down the side of his face.

"I never thought I'd see North-Creatures get the better of us," he added. "Nothing will stop them now."

Paul looked back up at the ridge. Even in those few short seconds, he could see that there was no hope for that part of the battle. All along the left of the ridge, the King's army was being forced back, and already some had turned to flee.

"There must be something . . . someone can do . . ." cried Paul. "What about the King?"

"The King?" replied the soldier, staring up at the ridge. His eyes scanned the hillside for a moment, scan-

ning the broiling mass of men, beasts and banners, then
settled on a knot of fighting somewhere near the center.
He pointed to it, and Paul caught a glimpse of the
golden banner—the Royal Standard.

"The King's up there," said the soldier quietly. "There's
little chance he'll get away. Little chance for anyone ..."
He gestured at the wounded lying between the wagons,
and added, "Least of all for us. There won't be time to
get away ... particularly with those blood-beaked things
up there. Meepers they're called ..."

He pointed to the sky. Most of the Meepers who had
survived the first attack were keeping their distance,
afraid of anyone who could draw a bow, even the walking wounded. The soldier looked at them for a second,
spat on the ground in disgust, and then spat on his well-
notched blade, preparing it for a pocket whetstone. Paul
noticed his spittle was flecked with blood.

He pushed the stone along the blade a couple of
times, and then said, almost to himself, "It was never a
fair fight anyway, what with their Magic, and Her, and
the Stone Knights. We ... I ... did my best ..."

He frowned, and the whetstone dropped from his
hand, then the sword, and he slowly crumpled onto the
ground. Paul was quick to offer him a drink, but the old
soldier refused.

"Must have got somewhere worse than I thought," he
said to Paul, with a slight grin. " 'Course, they couldn't
have done it without Magic. Gwarulch and Meepers
aren't much normally, 'least when it comes to real fighting ... it's the Stone Knights ... and Magic ..."

He closed his eyes for a second, then looked back up
at Paul, staring and unseeing. "And we haven't got any
Magic any more ... no Magic ... when I was a boy,
there was a Wizard ... lived in a tower ... or was that
a song? And Magic was ... was ..."

His voice trailed off and his eyes closed. Paul

watched him try to grin, but his head lolled off to one side. His breath misted the steel of his cuirass for a second, then it faded, and was not renewed.

Paul stared at him, as if he could see nothing else at all. The noise of the battle, the cries and moans of the wounded, all faded into the background, and the man's voice played over and over in his mind, "Magic . . . and we haven't got any Magic any more . . . no Magic . . ."

Then a voice penetrated his isolation, and he snapped back to find Aleyne standing in front of him—a tired and bloody Aleyne, his breastplate dented, and buff coat torn. He was bleeding from a long cut or Gwarulch scratch down his arm, the blood dripping onto the reins of his white horse, who stood nervously at his side.

"Take my horse to Quigin," he said quickly, before Paul could speak. "I want both of you to ride him out of here. Head south—for Yendre."

"But what about you?" cried Paul. "How are you going to get away?"

"I'm not," said Aleyne, "Or at least not yet. The King and Lady Sasterisk still hold the center of the ridge. I'm going back to help. We have to hold for at least an hour—otherwise no one will get away."

"An hour . . . can you?" asked Paul, shouting, for the noise of fighting was louder and closer. On the ridge, the human forces were constantly being driven back. Paul could make out individual soldiers now, and the Gwarulch biting and ripping among them. As Paul watched, he heard a bellow of inhuman sound, and a great stone battered its way through the melée. The human soldiers fought wildly to get out of its way, but not all were quick enough. Once through the battle-line, the huge stone turned, and crushed back through, spreading death and disarray.

"The Stone Knights of Angarling," said Aleyne grimly. "We cannot stop them. We need rain! Rain to blind the Meepers above, and mud to bog the Stone Knights down."

He looked up at the sky, but it was clear and blue—the only clouds in sight were swarms of Meepers waiting for the army to flee. Paul looked up too, and thought of real clouds—and what they were made of.

"Air and water," he said to himself, thinking back to geography lessons he'd never really listened to. *"Air and water*!" he said again, feeling for his pouch.

Aleyne stared at him, eyes dull with fatigue, suddenly brightening with a spark of comprehension as Paul pulled out the feather of the Breath and the teardrop of the Blood.

"The Breath helped me before," said Paul. "Maybe with both, I can call rainclouds or something. Water and Air!"

"Try!" said Aleyne eagerly. "But do not wait too long. Find Quigin, and tell him to ride with you as soon as the battle-line breaks—if not before. You must not wait then! But I truly hope the Elementals will give us their aid today. And remember—head south, and we shall meet again!"

"Good . . . good luck!" shouted Paul anxiously. He looked at Aleyne's back as the knight trod steadfastly back uphill, heading for the thick of battle, then he turned his attention to the Breath and the Blood. Both seemed to stir in his hands, so he knelt by the side of the old soldier, closed his eyes, and thought as hard as he could of rain.

He remembered a terrific storm he'd been caught in, which had dumped twenty centimeters of rain inside an hour and caused many floods. That was the storm he wanted, and he tried to picture it inside his head, sweeping in to wash the Ragwitch's army down the slope of Reddow Cairn.

Minutes passed, and the sound of fighting grew ever

closer and more threatening, but Paul kept on concentrating. Deep black clouds formed inside his head, complete with the crackle of thunder and the play of lightning across the sky, and he thought the Blood and the Breath were twitching in his closed hands.

More time passed—he didn't know how long—but still he didn't look, seeing and hearing only the storm inside his head. Then thunder crashed all around him, and not just in his mind. Paul's eyes flashed open, and he felt a great shadow roll across his face, and across the wagons and the ridge of Reddow Cairn. The sky was full of black, roiling clouds.

Seconds later, great drops of rain began to fall, punctuating the cries of disbelief from the wounded at this storm which had come from nowhere. But from the top of the ridge, there came a great scream of anger. Looking up, Paul saw a huge, grotesque figure, silhouetted against the lightning-charged sky. It was the Ragwitch, and She was pointing directly at him.

18

JULIA IS SUMMONED/ DANCING WITH FIRE

I am sure it was Paul," said Julia, kneeling down to feel the comforting turf. "I'd recognize him anywhere—even dressed up in a helmet and coat!"

"Whoever it was, he did a fine day's work today!" exclaimed Mirran cheerfully. "That rain! The sight of Angarling bogging down into the mud is one I shall long remember!"

"Yes," said Lyssa quietly. "If it were not for the rain, I fear no one would have escaped."

"Yet that same storm, in saving the King and his army, may well have brought your brother into greater peril," said Anhyvar, who had been staring out into the blackness through the Ragwitch's eyes. "It was Paul, Julia, and She recognized him—and now sends Gwarulch and Meepers to bring him to Her."

"What do you mean?" asked Julia. "He got away—

on a white horse. I saw him! There was another boy on the front ..."

"Yes ... he has escaped the battlefield," said Anhyvar. Her forehead wrinkled in troubled thought, and she took Julia's hands in her own. "He has escaped," she explained, "but in using the Wild Magic he has become a threat to Her. It was the Wild Magic that cast the North-Queen out, and forced Her to take Her current form. She is afraid of that Magic, for it is unpredictable, and strong ... and so, She must see your brother captured or slain. She has sent Oroch and his guard to seek Paul out."

"But if he's got ... Wild Magic ... or whatever it is, can't he beat them?" asked Julia. "I mean, if he can make a storm like that!"

"The Wild Magic isn't something you can get hold of ... or even control," said Lyssa. "It may be summoned, and sometimes dismissed, but what it does in between is anybody's guess."

"Yet it may help Paul," said Anhyvar quickly, seeing Julia's distress. "He certainly summoned the storm ... so he has some bond with the Wild Magic. It may serve him in his need."

"And apart from Magic," added Mirran, "he was riding a very swift horse. He is probably well away by now. And with this rain, the Meepers can't fly, and the Gwarulch can't track."

"That is very true," said Lyssa. "So I am sure Paul will be safe for the time being. You must be brave for him, Julia—and for yourself. For the Ragwitch will certainly call you to Her thoughts soon."

"Oh ..." said Julia, feeling tears starting in the corners of her eyes. "I'd forgotten ... for a little while anyway ... the twig-maid isn't there any more."

"But we will be here," said Anhyvar, giving her a

hug. "And I shall watch and listen, and sometimes I may whisper, to remind you that you are not alone."

"She will probably forget to keep you bound," said Lyssa, "so you will be able to come back here to us . . . if only every now and then."

Julia nodded, and fought back the tears. Then Mirran stood before her, and said, "Her time will come—and we shall be the cause of Her fall. Remember that, and look for our opportunity. She may think She is harming you, and She may delight in doing so, but ultimately the harm will be to Her, by your hand, and ours."

He took her hand, and raised it to his lips, bowing his head. Julia felt a touch of pride, and straightened up, brushing away the starting tears with her other hand.

"I know you will be brave," said Mirran. "And we shall defeat Her."

Anhyvar touched her silver star to Julia's forehead, and it was like the brush of a delightful breeze mixed with the warmth of the summer sun.

"I shall always hear, when you need me," she said. "And we shall see you soon."

Julia nodded, and tried to smile, a smile that turned into a grimace as she felt the white globe pulse, and the pain of the Ragwitch's cold thoughts calling her with Her foul senses.

The others saw it too, and all three quickly hugged her. Lyssa kissed her on the forehead, and didn't say anything—but Julia felt some of Lyssa's calm settle on her, so that she was less sickened by the Ragwitch's call.

"I'll do my best," she said to the three of them, and then before anyone could say anything more, she struck out into the weightless fluid, straight for the white globe— and the evil thoughts and cloying senses of the Ragwitch.

* * *

The white horse stumbled again, and Quigin bent over its neck to peer at the ground in front of them before gently elbowing Paul to wake him up.

"We'll have to walk now," he said, as Paul leaned back in the saddle, and blinked at the darkness about him. "I can't see the ground properly—but I think we're on some sort of trail, going down."

"Uh," said Paul wearily, sliding off the horse after Quigin. He was soaked through, and his sodden coat felt like a sack of sand. Now the excitement of the battle was over, he felt completely exhausted, especially since the fury of the storm had long since given way to the quiet darkness of a cloudy night.

Neither he nor Quigin had any idea where they were. After Paul had seen the Ragwitch point him out, fear had ruled his flight, and Quigin hadn't been much better. But the older boy was characteristically confident of finding somewhere safe to spend the remainder of the night.

"It's definitely a path," he said to Paul, after discussing the matter with the horse. "Going down into a valley. Hold onto the saddle, and we'll walk down."

"Can't we just rest here?" asked Paul, the tiredness heavy in his arms and legs. He was starting to get cold too, and wanted to curl up in the thick blanket that was rolled up across the back of Aleyne's saddle.

"It'll be safer in the valley," replied Quigin, his face just visible in front of Paul. "There will probably even be a house, or a shepherd's hut."

"O.K.," said Paul, reaching up to hang onto a saddlestrap. "Let's go."

They walked in silence then, with Paul counting his footsteps in an effort to keep up the pace. But that reminded him of counting sheep and sleep, so he stopped and just walked without any real thoughts at all, like a thoroughly wound-up clockwork toy.

It wasn't until Quigin suddenly stopped and he ran into his back that Paul realized he'd fallen asleep on his feet. He'd never really believed it was possible to be that tired before. Now he looked around with bleary eyes, and absolutely no memory of how long he'd been walking, or where he'd walked. But they were at the bottom of the hill-path, and in the valley, because the ground was flat.

It was still very dark, but Paul could feel gravel crunching under his feet, and he could see two dim lines on either side, so they were obviously on some sort of road. Quigin seemed to see it clearly, for he started walking again, with Paul stumbling along behind.

Gradually, Paul realized that there was a light ahead, and Quigin was aiming purposefully for that, rather than following the gravelled road. The outline he'd vaguely seen had disappeared, and they were walking on soft ground covered with clumps of grass, and thistles that annoyed Paul into some sort of wakefulness. And there was a small orange glow ahead, comfortable and flickering, like a campfire—very attractive to two sodden boys, who headed for it like single-minded moths, not even thinking of whose campfire it might be, or what might be waiting in the darkness outside the narrow circle of firelight.

But when they finally stood in the flickering light, there was no one anywhere near it, nor any sign of people or North-Creatures. And the fire wasn't a campfire, but a strange mound made of blocks of peat. One of the blocks had slipped away, revealing a core of fire within, and now the whole mound was leaking and sprouting flame. In the increasing light of the fire, Paul saw there were a number of similar mounds nearby, all gently smoking, with only faint glowing lines between the blocks to hint at the fires within.

"Charcoal mounds," said Quigin, tilting his head to watch sparks flying upwards from the broken mound. "At least they were. They must have been left too long. They won't make charcoal if they burn too hot, but they'll make us dry."

"I hope so," said Paul, shivering, and edging closer to the fire. The heat soon made his eyes droop again, but as only the side towards the fire was drying, he had to keep turning to stay comfortable. While Paul turned and steamed, Quigin unsaddled the horse, rubbed it down, cautioned it not to stray too far, then stood next to Paul, companionably turning every few minutes.

They were well on the way to getting dry, when Paul, totally worn-out, turned around one time too many, and staggered straight towards the mound, which was now a roaring bonfire.

Quigin steadied him just in time, and helped him to sit down.

"I think I'll just go to sleep damp," said Paul, yawning so widely he almost swallowed a flying beetle attracted by the fire. "Can I have the blanket?"

"You can have half of it," replied Quigin, also yawning. He looked around at the other mounds and added, "We could get a lot warmer if I open the other . . ."

Paul nodded sleepily, past caring what Quigin planned to do. Quigin does have some fairly silly ideas though, he thought, as he trailed off into the beginnings of sleep.

Despite his tiredness, Paul woke not long after, started out of sleep by the loud bang of something exploding in the fire. Wearily, he raised himself up on one elbow, barely noticing the blanket half under him, or the sleeping form of Quigin, with Leasel tucked in at his side. He hardly noticed because there were a lot of other things to look at—even through the white smoke that was boiling up into the sky.

At least six or seven charcoal mounds were burning fiercely, and Paul felt their heat wash across him like an over-efficient fan heater. They shed a lot of light too—and shadows, that danced and flickered in time with the leaping flames.

Paul watched the dance of the fires, and the capering shadows, and listened to the crack of exploding charcoal, the whoosh of flame, and the more homely breathing of Quigin, who sounded like he'd caught a cold. Heard together, the sounds were like some sort of primitive music, made to the beat of breathing.

Idly, Paul started to tap two twigs together to join in the rhythm of the dancing fires—a small, dishevelled figure in a blanket, tapping steadily under a great pall of smoke in the very center of a ring of seven fires.

The fires grew stronger, and the sweat began to start from Paul's forehead. Still the flames crackled and roared, and his breath grew faster with its rhythm and the heat of the air. Paul tapped on, and when his twigs broke, he began to clap with his hands, the sound sharp and high, even among the crack and snap of the burning charcoal.

Then one fire—the first and nearest to Paul—roared up twice as high again, and split into two raging columns of fire and light. A figure appeared between the columns, arms outstretched, and stepped out of the flames with a flamboyant wave and prancing step.

It was a woman of fire. A tall, very slim woman, in a dress of greenish flames. Her skin glowed with golden heat, and the hair that blazed from her head was of the brightest red. Her eyes were deep with black heat, and when she spoke, white smoke jetted from her nose.

"I," she said, in a voice that whooshed like leaping fire, "I am the Fire Queen!"

Paul stopped clapping, and sat in his blanket, far more wide awake than he felt he wanted to be. A twitch at his side told him that Leasel had woken too, just as Quigin's uninterrupted breathing said the older boy was still asleep.

"Aren't you going to say hello?" asked the Fire Queen, stepping out further from the fire, and setting the grass beneath her feet instantly ablaze.

"Hello," said Paul, hastily extricating himself from the blanket, and standing up. "I mean, good evening, your . . . Ladyship."

"Fireship," said the Lady, blowing on the green flames that jetted from the ends of her fingers. "The correct term of address is Your Fireship."

"Oh," said Paul, watching her green-flamed fingers with nervous eyes. He hadn't forgotten the sudden rage of the Water Lord. "I'm sorry, Your Fireship."

"Apology accepted," replied the Lady. She turned her burning gaze upon Paul, and he stepped back, shielding his face with his arm.

"Now," she said, "Why have you summoned me? With, I might add, some very nice little fires."

"I didn't . . ." Paul started to say, before he realized that in a way, he had summoned her. Or he would have anyway, if he'd known how to. Perhaps he did know how, sort of subconsciously, after his dealings with the other two Elementals.

"I mean," he added hastily, "I was hoping to meet you, Your Fireship. My name is Paul, and . . . I want to ask for some help."

"My help?" asked the Fire Queen languidly. Paul felt the heat of her gaze shift from him, and nearby, a small bush burst into violet flame, and spat out hundreds of silver sparks. "My help? For what?"

"To fight the Ragwitch . . ." Paul began, when the Fire Queen interrupted him.

"Oh, you're *that* Paul!" she said, as if she'd read about him in a newspaper. "Air told me all about you, and your visit to him, and that beastly Water Lord."

"He did?" asked Paul, surprised. "Does that mean you'll help?"

"Not . . . necessarily," said the Queen. Paul peeked a look over his raised arm, and saw that she was smiling. Puffs of different colored smoke came from her nostrils as she added, "What will you do for me?"

Paul opened his mouth to reply, then felt his jaw snick shut as he realized he'd almost said "anything." After all, he couldn't really offer to do some work in her garden, or take the garbage out, or anything like that. But to say "anything" could be really dangerous . . .

He thought about it for a few seconds, while the Fire Queen amused herself turning slow cartwheels through three of the mounds, scattering the coals till they made a sparkling carpet between the remaining four.

"I'll do anything," Paul said suddenly, when the Fire Queen stopped and stood in the middle of the coals. She cocked her head to listen to him, pirouetted with arms outstretched, and then beckoned to him.

"Good," she said. "I want you to dance."

"Dance?" Paul had the fleeting image of himself twirling about, shaking his arms and legs and generally being a disco star. Then, as he saw her beckoning hand, he realized the Fire Queen wanted him to dance with her—dance out on the red-hot coals, with a being of pure fire.

She beckoned again, and Paul hesitated, already imagining the pain of being burnt. He'd dropped a cup of boiling tea on his foot once—that was enough to remember the pain of burns for a lifetime.

The Fire Queen stamped her foot, and sparks leapt into the air, glittering among the puffs of black smoke from her nose. "It isn't polite to keep me waiting!"

"I . . . I can't," whispered Paul. "I'll get burnt."

"Do you think I'd let you burn, when I want you to dance, you foolish boy?" snapped the Fire Queen, advancing regally upon him. "Nothing burns unless I say it can!"

"Oh," said Paul. She was very close now, and he didn't feel the awesome heat he'd felt before—though it was still very, very warm.

"Take my hand. We shall try a little . . . flamenco!"

She extended her hand, and slowly, Paul reached out to take it, as though mesmerized. Green and blue flames ran along the outside of her golden, shimmering hands, and dropped like water to the coals below. Then, her hand closed around Paul's, and he instinctively flinched.

But there was no pain—nor any sensation of heat. The Fire Queen's hand felt strange, almost slippery, but it wasn't hot. And as she glided backwards over the coals, drawing Paul with her, he felt no heat through his boots.

"I don't know how to dance a flamenco," he said, as they stood in the middle of a dance floor of burning coals. "Anyway, don't they dance flamencos alone?"

"Ridiculous! I dance how I like!" cried the Fire Queen, picking up Paul and twirling him through the air as if he were a fraction of his real size and weight. "Flamencos are my dance, and I dance them differently every time!"

She set Paul down, and let Paul's hand drop, then raised both her arms like a conductor. All around, the crack and hiss of the flames became silent, and the coals no longer popped. The Fire Queen gestured once at one mound, then at another, moved her hands in circles through the air, and brought her arms down with the cry, "Begin!"

The remaining mounds instantly exploded into sparks that whistled as they spat in all directions. Smoke snaked in whirlpool columns, creating eerie woodwind sounds. Coals popped and crackled like percussion, and the flames roared like a choir.

The Fire Queen took Paul's hands again in the tumult of the wild music of fire and sound, and began to dance. She leapt and twisted, turned and spun, and Paul followed, his arms stretching to the very edges of their sockets. It was a wild, crazy dance, without form or reason, and driven by an ever-changing rhythm as varied as the flames. Paul felt the music in his head like a mad exhilaration, and abandoned himself to let the Fire Queen twirl and throw him where she would.

Then, quite unexpectedly, there were seven, short, sharp explosions, and everywhere the flames flashed blue. The Fire Queen threw Paul up into the air as the echoes of the explosions died away, up into a cloud of red and yellow sparks that tumbled end over end with him. He saw the world flip and roll in a series of fiery colors, the Fire Queen staring up at him from below, her flaming hair swept back, and mouth open, laughing sparks of every color he'd ever seen.

He fell back down as sparks do, flittering from side to side, and drifting into blackness. The Fire Queen caught him, turned him around, and set him down outside the coals onto the soft, slightly muddy ground. Steam rose from his feet, and once again, without warning, he felt the full effect of the heat.

"A good dance," said the Fire Queen. Behind her, the fires were dying down, and the coals were black and cold at the edges. "Perhaps we shall dance again one day."

She turned, as if to walk back into the heart of the coals, and Paul started out of the dreamy state the dance had left him in.

"Don't go! Please—what about your help? I need . . .

I mean, Your Fireship, I would like to ask for your help against the Ragwitch. To help get my sister back . . ."

"Ah, yes," said the Fire Queen, with a strange, slight smile. "My help, for which you said you'd do anything."

She paused, looking down at Paul. He felt her grow taller, and somehow more remote, and once again, he sheltered behind his arm, half-crouching before the great fiery being that rose above him.

"I danced," he said hesitantly, fearing to offend her. He had suddenly remembered that she hadn't promised anything—she'd only asked him to dance.

Then the heat lessened, and he risked a look. She was still there, a tall, stately figure of fire. But she held a gleaming coal between white-hot thumb and forefinger. She was holding it out to him.

"This," she said, pausing dramatically, "is the Spirit. Do you want it?"

Paul looked at the fiercely glowing coal, at the small wafts of white smoke curling up from it, and nodded. But he didn't hold out his hand.

"Hold out your hand," said the Fire Queen, and then, like a teacher about to deliver six strokes of the cane, "Hold . . . out . . . your . . . hand."

Paul felt the ground was suddenly unsteady, and his hand shook as it moved—just a fraction away from his side. He gulped once, twice—feeling the hot air ripping all the moisture out of his throat. And the Fire Queen just stood there, holding out the glowing coal.

I can't, thought Paul, staring at the gleaming red source of pain. I just can't . . . but at the same time, he saw Gwarulch pouring onto the wharf at Donbreye; Julia shouting for him to leave, as the Ragwitch twined its hand through her hair; Aleyne giving him the white horse, before turning again to battle; the old soldier dying at his feet . . .

Paul shut his eyes, and held out his hand, palm uppermost. For a second, he thought something cool had dropped into his hand, and all was well. Then, he felt the slightest brush of air or smoke, and a searing pain bit into his hand and raced up to his brain, exploding into the worst hurt he'd ever known.

His eyes whipped open, and he stared at his hand, screaming. But the coal he held there was now a gem of brilliant scarlet, and there was no blackened or ruined flesh. And as quickly as the pain had struck, it left, leaving only a dull memory, like the aftereffects of a toothache.

"Things only burn when I decide they do," said the Fire Queen somewhat complacently. She pushed her hands through her hair to comb out the sparks, said, "Goodnight," and vanished. In the second of her disappearance, all the fires went out, and smoke billowed up into the sky.

Trembling, Paul looked back at his hand. The Spirit lay there, its bright glow lighting the ground ahead, and he realized it held all the colors of fire and shimmered and flickered like a flame. Cautiously, he transferred it to his other hand. It was quite cool.

He held it up as a light, and looked at the palm of his right hand. Right in the center there were four tiny flames drawn in the pale lines of scar tissue. He ran his finger over them, and felt the slight ridges of skin—the flames would always be there to remind Paul of his dance.

He looked at the Spirit again, and realized he could hardly stand, let alone see clearly, and stumbled over to Quigin and Leasel. The hare watched him carefully, and touched her soft nose to his palm.

"Thanks," he said sleepily. "But it doesn't hurt . . . not now, anyway."

His last words were mumbled into the blanket, and he fell instantly asleep. By his side, Quigin suddenly stopped snoring, and sat up. He looked around for a moment, sniffed at the smoke, said, "The fire's gone out," to no one in particular, and lay down again. A minute later, he was snoring again, and only the hare was awake, and looking out into the smoke-palled air.

19

WITHIN HER MIND/ RHYSAMARN

Leaden dull limbs, a dry worm-like tongue, the muffled senses . . . and then the vicious, evil pool of the Ragwitch's thoughts—all enveloped Julia once again, stifling her screams.

"Welcome back . . . my child," thought the Ragwitch, as Julia struggled against Her body and feelings. "Am I still so unfamiliar, after all this time?"

"You always will be!" shouted Julia, concentrating her thoughts against Her. At the same time, she felt her own mind adapt to the Ragwitch's senses, and the pain and dizziness lessened.

"You still struggle," hissed the Ragwitch. "And you seem . . . stronger. What has given you strength, Julia? Or *who*?"

A sharp stab of fear ran through Julia, and for a second she thought that Lyssa and the others had been discovered, far too early. Then she caught the Ragwitch's thought—She was thinking of Paul, as She'd seen him from the ridge. Other images followed: Gwarulch rending Paul to pieces, and Oroch tying him up, and a hundred more of Paul being killed, or captured and tortured, or even Glazed . . .

"They're not true!" cried Julia.

"Not yet!" spat the Ragwitch. "But he shall pay for resisting me! As *you* will, Julia. For I have been too patient . . ."

As She spoke to Julia within Her mind, the girl felt a wave of dark and evil thoughts rising up around her, swelling up from every loathsome corner of Her mind and memory. And chief among those memories, and the most threatening and fearful of them, was Her memory of what it was like behind the black door on the day Anhyvar was drawn deep into the Nameless Realm.

Julia had only a second to think of help, to think of Anhyvar, and then the wave was upon her, and she was swamped in evil thoughts, without even the feel of her own body to help her be herself, and not be lost in the Ragwitch.

Everywhere, images of horror and power, arrogance and cruelty, plucked at her vision of herself, drawing every little part of her into the Ragwitch's central thoughts. They offered her part of something monumental—to be a power, to have everything, to take and destroy anything, to feel unchecked rage and hatred, to fulfil any whim of abuse and destruction, to never die . . .

Julia fought back with sunlit days, and books read by the fire, surprises, picnics, mountain walks, friends, parents, faithful pets, Paul . . . anything happy and cheerful that could resist. But she was alone, and she couldn't even remember what she looked like. The evil and hatred were slowly taking her apart.

She almost surrendered—just to give in, to stop the torment, to be lost within Her. But a voice came to her like a golden thread through the darkness, and with it came a vivid picture of herself just as she had been a little time ago, stretched out on a blanket, at their picnic on the sandy beach. And with that picture came Anhyvar's voice, calm and clear, and she said, "You are not alone, Julia, and you are stronger than She can know. She will not prevail against you."

"I know," thought Julia, and suddenly she *did* know, and the darkness broke against her. Julia knew she was real, and looked exactly so, and had friends—even here. And what was the Ragwitch but a hideous over-grown doll full of hate and poison?

With that sharp clear thought, the darkness rolled back, and Julia found herself once again staring out of the corners of the Ragwitch's eyes, as Her thoughts slithered at her, as cold and venomous as serpents.

"Do not think you can resist Me for long, Julia. For there will come a time when I have to spare no thoughts to My enemies—and all shall be turned to you. Your brother too, shall feel a double weight of misery and pain. And you will watch, my Julia. You will watch, and I shall make you enjoy."

Julia did not reply. She saw what had distracted the Ragwitch—a Meeper had landed, and now crept to-wards the Ragwitch, its long snake-like head bowed in submission. It called softly twice, to tell Her it brought news, then cawed out its message in the simple tongue She had taught the creature's ancestors long ago. Julia listened, but couldn't understand, till she caught a thought of the Ragwitch, and noticed Her hand clenched in frustration and rage. The Meeper was reporting that Oroch had lost Paul's trail.

Julia suppressed a cry of triumph, and the Ragwitch struck the Meeper with her open palm, driving it into the ground as punishment for bringing bad news. It looked up at Her, cruel eyes hooded in abject fear, and

listened to Her instructions for Oroch: to keep searching, to use more Meepers, more Gwarulch—to find the
boy, and bring him back to Her . . . preferably alive.

Julia watched the Meeper slink away, and almost felt
sorry for it till she remembered Bevallan, when others
had been in fear of them. She was glad Oroch hadn't re-
ported personally. Some of the Ragwitch's memories of
Oroch had flashed briefly before Julia, and she had
caught a glimpse of the Oroch under the tar-black bandages. Julia didn't want to ever see that again—she had
not forgotten the Ragwitch's threat to him at Bevallan.
Three failures . . . and those bandages would come
off . . .

Then the Ragwitch's harsh voice filtered back
through her ears, and Julia listened to her calling
Gwarulch chieftains by name, harsh, discordant names
that reminded Julia of people clearing their throats and
spitting.

The chieftains came quickly, many of them casting
aside half-eaten morsels or gory bones. Julia had
thought that it was after dusk, but as the Gwarulch approached, she realized it was just before dawn, and the
Gwarulch were breakfasting.

On the ground, it was still just dark, with the pale
pre- dawn light gently relieving the blackness of the
hollows in the ground, the clumps of feasting Gwarulch,
and the standing stones that were the still Angarling.
Above, Meepers flashed into sunlight, their scales glittering as they passed from shadow to meet the morning
sun.

Julia watched the dawning of the day with secret delight. The Ragwitch could feel neither heat nor cold, but
Julia remembered the delightful chill of the pre-dawn,
and then the slow warming, soaking up sun in the crisp,
clean air.

Julia concentrated on that memory while the

Ragwitch ordered Her army to march. Gwarulch listening on the fringes quickly spread the word, and began to gather together their stores of food and assemble near the leaders, while the Glazed-Folk and Angarling, feeling their Mistress' will directly, began to move and shudder. The Meepers circled in the sky, eagerly awaiting the order to head south, to begin the killing and plundering.

But the instructions She gave were otherwise. Julia hadn't really been paying attention, but listened with surprise as the Ragwitch ordered the Meepers and Gwarulch to spare no time for looting or haphazard destruction—but only to move south with all possible speed, to pursue the remnants of the human army, to catch it and to destroy it.

"We will pursue them until at last they face Us," hissed the Ragwitch to Her minions. "And there shall be slaughter and feasting such has not been seen since your far ancestors' time, when I was North-Queen and Ruler of All. Now go! To the south and Destruction!"

* * *

"Sometimes I almost wish you hadn't made it rain, Paul," said Quigin, as he extracted his foot from yet another deep pool of mud. He gazed at it ruefully, and added, "Or at least I wish you could make it stop raining."

Paul didn't answer, because he was busy trying to avoid the mud pool Quigin had trodden in. Unfortunately, the horse (which Quigin said liked the name of Nubbins, though Aleyne called it something quite different), put a great hoof in another one, and splashed Paul all over with mud anyway.

Not that it made much difference, thought Paul, looking down at his sodden, mud-spattered self. It had started raining heavily the morning they had left the charcoal-burner's valley, and showed no signs of letting up, despite Paul's attempts to wish for some sun. So they had suffered the wet for nearly two whole days, with no immediate prospect of being dry or warm.

Even worse than that, they were totally lost. Quigin had met few animals to question, and the bedraggled magpie he'd spoken to that morning could only say that they were heading south, or near enough to it.

Quigin, of course, was optimistic, and felt sure they'd come across a village soon, or a homestead, or a watch-tower . . . but he had admitted to Paul that there was a great swathe of land running between Reddow Cairn and Rhysamarn that was wild and only partly settled. The land they were crossing certainly met that description.

So they walked on, and occasionally rode, but mostly the way was up and down small hills, through heather and stones, or clumps of stunted trees, so they had to lead Nubbins, making for a slow and weary progress. So slow, in fact, that by the third day after finding the Fire Queen, Paul felt that he had sunk to a depth so miserable that he would probably get pneumonia and die. It was still raining, though less heavily, and he had only slept for about three hours, having spent the rest of the night trying to relight a small and pathetic fire.

Quigin had slept most of the night, but Leasel had got up several times to keep Paul company, before going off somewhere just before what passed for dawn on yet another grey, wet, and unpleasant day. Paul had presumed that she had gone for a run or something that hares did, but Quigin was somewhat perturbed when he woke up.

"Leasel just went?" he asked. "She didn't leave a message?"

"I can't talk to her, remember," said Paul rather crossly. "She bounded off in that direction."

"She's been quite good lately," said Quigin, "what with all the emergencies. I suppose now she thinks everything is back to normal, so she can be awful again . . ."

His voice trailed off as an eerie call echoed from somewhere to the north, something like a war-horn being blown by someone short of breath. Both boys jumped, and Paul looked at Quigin, fear showing in his face. That noise wasn't something he'd heard before . . . neither Gwarulch howl nor Meeper scream . . . but something unknown, and therefore, even more frightening.

"That's an animal . . ." said Quigin, calmly. "I think . . ."

The call came again, echoing strangely between the hills. Paul shuddered as it reverberated all around them.

"Whatever it is, I don't want to meet it," he said, trying to pick up Nubbins' saddle.

Quigin didn't answer, but started to stride out of the camp . . . towards whatever was making the noise. With a despairing yelp, Paul dropped the saddle, and made a grab for the older boy—a second too late.

"Quigin! Don't!" shouted Paul, as the awful call sounded again, but the Friend of Beasts plunged into the heather, starting down from the bare hilltop where they had made their camp. Desperately, Paul thought of throwing something at Quigin, but he was already too far away. He hesitated for a moment, then snatched up his poniard, clapped on his helmet, and ran after Quigin, keeping his eye on his friend's sandy mop of hair bobbing through the heather.

Seconds later, Paul lost sight of him, and redoubled his speed, only to come sliding out into another, muddy clearing—and there was Quigin, and the source of the fearsome cry. With its head poked up to the sky, and its long ears pointed back, the creature raised its mouth skyward . . . and brayed.

Paul nearly slid past, forgetting to dig his heels in as relief flooded through him. Then he nearly fell over Leasel, who twitched her nose in amusement, circled around his legs, and shot back into the heather.

"You could have asked it not to bray," said Paul severely to the hare's retreating back. "But I'm glad it's only a donkey."

Seconds later he was patting the donkey's smooth and comforting nose, and ruffling its wire-brush mane. The donkey brayed his name, which Quigin (who had already made the basic introductions) said was approximately translatable as "Hathin." Leasel had heard him far away that morning, and had gone to seek him out. As she said to Quigin, you never knew when a donkey might come in handy.

"Even better," said Quigin, "Hathin knows where we are."

"He does?" said Paul, doubtfully. Hathin didn't look like a terribly smart donkey—he had a very dreamy look in his large brown eyes.

"We're about three leagues northeast of Rhysamarn, apparently," said Quigin, after a brief snort, a bray, and some eye-to-eye communication.

"Rhysamarn!" exclaimed Paul, thinking about Tanboule's red-hot stoves and the cosy interior of his strange house. "Does he know the way exactly?"

Quigin turned to the donkey again, looked into his eyes and did some of the eerie whispering that always made Paul uncomfortable. Hathin brayed twice, nodded his head, and started off, looking back at them after a few meters.

"Wait!" cried Paul, who had found new energy with the prospect of hot food and a roof over his head. "I'll get our things."

"And I'll saddle Nubbins," said Quigin. "But I'll just say thank you to Leasel first, for finding us a guide. Leasel? Leasel! Harrow it! Where has she gone?"

Ten long and weary hours later, Leasel was leading as they stumbled ever upwards into darkness, and Paul was wondering about Hathin's intelligence again. True, the donkey had led them up a mountain, but the only things it seemed to have in common with Rhysamarn were treacherous wet shale and golden heather. At least, Paul presumed it was golden heather, since everything was black and horrible. Certainly, the way they were going seemed totally unfamiliar to Paul. It seemed higher, harder and much further than either of the paths he'd taken before, going up or down.

He stopped again, and prepared to complain to Quigin, but was immediately yanked forward by Nubbins, whose stirrup he was holding onto like a drowning man holds a lifebelt. Reluctant to let this go, Paul shut his mouth, and resumed trudging, using his free hand to push down on his aching calves to ease the strain of climbing.

He was just thinking about really stopping and complaining when the rain stopped instead—quite suddenly—and he felt a light breeze against his face. Looking up, Paul saw the clouds were parting, and the stars were beginning to shine through the last veil of cloud. There was even a sliver of the moon visible, the shadow of the full moon discernible behind it.

Looking back down from the sky to the mountain above them, Paul saw Quigin and the animals silhouetted in the starlight—and down below, like stars fallen on the ground, the twinkle of other lights. Staring out into the darkness, Paul gave a long sigh of relief as he recognized the dark looming shape across from them as the other peak of Rhysamarn, the valley below as the saddle between the peaks, and the fallen stars as the lights from Tanboule's house.

Thirty minutes later they were knocking on the wooden walls with surprising energy, and once again, Paul was calling out, "Hello, Mister Tanboule! It's me, Paul! Can I come in? I mean, can we come in?"

20

THE POTATO HARVEST/ THE RAGWITCH ATTACKS

The last part of that long night passed in what seemed like a few minutes to Paul. He had a hazy recollection of Tanboule's bewhiskered face peering over the side at him, and his cry of, "Come to help with the potato harvest? How kind!" And then a sort of cargo door opening in the side, a plank being let down, and all of them—boys, horse, donkey and hare—trooping up into the cosy, orange-lit interior. After that, everything had fallen into blackness.

When he awoke, Paul found himself comfortably undressed, warm and beautifully dry. He lay beneath a great weight of silky furs that felt so nice he had to wiggle his toes for several minutes just to enjoy the feeling. Then the well-remembered smell of bacon and cabbage cooking summoned him from under the covers and into his clothes (leaving the buff coat and helmet thankfully aside)—which were also dry, and basically cleansed of mud. Not as much as his mother would have thought sufficient, but plenty enough for Paul.

He quickly finished dressing, splashed some water from a nearby bowl on his face, wiped his hands on one of the furs, and climbed up the nearest ladder onto the main deck.

As he expected, Quigin and Tanboule were tucking into great piles of cabbage and bacon and thick slices of bread, with mugs of Tanboule's strange tea. They looked up as Paul emerged, and Tanboule gestured with his fork at a loaded plate sitting on the edge of one of the stoves, and then, more urgently, at a cloth to pick it up with.

Neither he nor Quigin spoke, and Paul felt curiously quiet too. It wasn't until all three of them had finished seconds, and Paul thirds, that Tanboule spoke.

"Well, you seem to have made a tale of your own," he said, fixing Paul with his steady gaze. "Do you think my advice was worth all those cabbages?"

"Umm . . . yes," said Paul. "So far. I still haven't met the Earth Lady though. And I haven't really done anything for Julia . . . I don't even know if she's still all right . . ."

"Hmmm," replied Tanboule mysteriously. He took a gulp of tea, then said (rather smugly), "But I do . . . she is fighting the Ragwitch too . . . in a different way."

"What!" exclaimed Paul, suddenly choking on his tea. "How do you know?"

Tanboule waited for Paul to stop choking, then tapped the side of his long nose with a finger. "The stars see everything, and look deep into everyone below them. One of them saw your sister within Her, and whispered it into the sky. I was listening."

"Oh," said Paul, who wasn't quite sure he understood. "Then she's still O.K.?"

Tanboule looked blank for a second, then he smiled,

and said, "From what little I know, she still exists. More than that, I cannot say."

Paul sat silent, thinking about Julia, and the hideous creature he had seen on the ridge at Reddow Cairn. Somehow, Julia was inside that awful thing . . . the Ragwitch. But even if he could find the Earth Lady, and gain her help, what was he supposed to do then? Really, he thought mournfully, if was just lucky that I thought of using the Breath and the Blood at the battle—they hadn't helped Julia, or really harmed the Ragwitch or anything, just slowed Her and Her army a little, so they could get away.

Tanboule looked at his troubled frown, and pushed another piece of bread over. Paul picked it up absently, ate a mouthful, swallowed, and said, "I don't know what to do! Where do I go now?"

"Are you asking me?" asked Tanboule, leaning back in his chair and rubbing his stomach. "Because if you are, it's a tricky question. Difficult. Worth . . ."

"Do I get some credit for the extra cabbages I planted last time?" interrupted Paul anxiously, as he thought he saw what Tanboule had in mind.

"Worth the harvesting," continued Tanboule, "of at least a third of my potato field. Quigin can do the other third."

"But I haven't asked you anything!" exclaimed Quigin, looking up from his contemplation of a spider.

"No," said Tanboule. "But I am sure you will. Perhaps, for example, you may ask why that particular spider is called a Black Widow."

"I know that," said Paul, before Quigin could ask. "It's because they're black and they eat their husbands."

"Ridiculous!" snorted Tanboule. "They do nothing of the sort. They spin small shawls of black spider-silk across their bodies, thus resembling widows. Look— that one is weaving a shawl now!"

Both Paul and Quigin looked, but the spider scuttled into a crack in the floorboards before they could really see. When they looked up, Tanboule was clearing away the plates.

"Washing up later," he declared. "For we have a great number of potatoes to dig up. And you must tell me more of your story since you left, Paul. I have heard a whisper of it from the stars, a little detail from Quigin, a little more from that redoubtable hare, but I need to know more. Then, I shall try and give you some first-rate advice."

"Good," said Paul, then realizing he sounded ungrateful, "I mean, thanks."

"Anything to get the potatoes in," answered Tanboule. "And if not you, it would be some foolish knight asking questions about love, and not liking the answers anyway."

"I thought . . ." said Paul, thinking of Aleyne, "that those sort of people never got an answer from the Wise . . . they just ran . . . oh . . . into bees or something."

"That's an answer, isn't it?" replied Tanboule, as he opened the hatch above, and let down the rope ladder.

"What more could they want than that?" he continued, his voice fading as he climbed out and down the ladder. "Bee-stings are very educational."

Quigin looked at Paul, and said, "I'm glad we get to dig potatoes for our answer. I like bees, but I hate getting stung."

"Mmmm . . ." said Paul, thinking back to his long afternoon of cabbage planting. "But at least that wouldn't take long, or be hard work."

"Recovering might take . . ." Quigin started to say, as he climbed out after Tanboule. Then his voice changed, and he fairly leapt out of the hatch, exclaiming, "There's a black-shouldered kite! Maybe I met it at the Wind Moot . . . I must . . ."

Paul smiled as his friend's foot caught in the hatch for a moment in his haste to get outside. Then his smile faded, as he thought what else might be in the sky, besides black-shouldered kites. Even on the mountain of the Wise, Paul knew he wasn't safe.

* * *

The man tried to move his head again, but the two Gwarulch that held him forced his eyes back to the Ragwitch, snorting angrily. One made a move to bite at the man's face, but the merest flicker of Her finger stopped the creature in mid-motion, and its jaw snapped shut with an unpleasant, bony click.

Julia felt a shudder in her mind go nowhere, and almost cried out at the frustration of being able to feel, but not do anything. Even moving the Ragwitch's foul body would be an improvement over the endless, unceasing senses that poured into Julia, without her being able to react.

"Where are the King and his army going?" hissed the Ragwitch, lowering Her bloated head so Her shark-toothed mouth loomed inches above the man's head.

"I . . . I . . . I don't know," croaked the man, his eyes staring in fear. "I'm only a farmer normally . . ."

The Ragwitch said nothing, but lowered Her head still more, so Her eyes were staring into the man's, his terrified face filling Her entire field of vision. Julia felt scared too, as she felt dark currents moving within the Ragwitch's mind, forces meshing and joining, obedient to Her will.

Then She touched the man with one puffy finger, and whispered, "But you will tell Me . . . Rornal."

As She spoke his name, Julia felt something flow out of Her, and into the man. His body stiffened, the mus-
~les and veins in his neck stood out like pipes, and his
~s filmed over with a ghastly wash of red. The

Gwarulch on either side of him snickered, and let go—
but he didn't try to escape. He just stood there, the
small muscles in his arms and legs twitching uncontrol-
lably. Julia felt sick, and wished she didn't have to
look—even though she'd seen it before, for the
Ragwitch had Glazed many people now.

The Ragwitch watched silently, drawing back up to
Her full height, even as the man before Her seemed to
be remolded, first arching back, and then bending forward into a bestial crouch. His head rolled to one side,
and he looked at the Ragwitch with tongue lolling, and
eyes devoid of all humanity.

"Now," She said. "Where are the King and his army
going?"

The man's mouth opened wider, and he dribbled a little, before saying, "We . . . m . . . m . . . m . . . arch . . .
to . . . Alnwere."

He almost didn't get the last word out, for his eyes
suddenly cleared and his left hand plucked at the air in
front of him, as if he were trying to grasp somebody's
hand. His fingers closed on the empty air, and he toppled forward, crashing to the ground at the Ragwitch's
feet.

Julia felt surprise ripple through the Ragwitch, and
almost a faint hint of fear. Then, Her thoughts burst in
upon the girl, sticking into her like many sharp pins.

"How did he find such strength? He held out his
hand towards Me—yet should not—he could not . . .
how have you helped him? Who . . ."

Suddenly the thoughts withdrew, and Julia felt a
surge of relief as the pain subsided. Then, like the faint
caress of a cat sliding around an ankle, she felt something touch her mind—and Anhyvar's whisper came to
her:

"I tried to secretly help the man, but She has looked
into Herself, and found that I am free. Brace yourself

for Her attack—and remember, you will soon be with us."

Julia braced herself with the mental equivalent of a long, deep breath, just as She felt the Ragwitch's thoughts returning in a dark, overwhelming tide. But this was no mere test, or cruel playfulness, but a full-scale attack, determined to totally absorb the personality that was Julia.

The first harsh tendrils of Her thought grasped her like an electric shock, and Julia gave a despairing cry as she felt them tear something away, some part of herself. And then more cold tendrils fastened on her, each ripping away something of her essence, stripping Julia of her personality and her will.

Julia fought back with everything good she could remember—everything solid and real and happy—but more and more tendrils came and snatched pieces of her mind, and the memories became black holes she couldn't think around, and there were more and more tendrils, colder and blacker, and more and more holes . . .

In seconds, all that was left of Julia panicked, her defenses collapsed, and she surrendered herself to destruction, as the Ragwitch split her personality into a million fragments, and prepared to digest them into Her central mind.

* * *

Tanboule's potato patch was (to Paul's relief) much smaller than expected. A mere twenty meters square, it lay down the slope of the lesser peak, a strip of dark brown earth, devoid of heather and shale.

Quigin looked at the patch, and whispered to Paul, "Bet there's no potatoes. You couldn't grow them there."

Paul looked at Tanboule's tall figure striding down the mountainside, his arms stretched out like a gawky albatross, and shook his head. He knew that if Tanboule said potatoes, then there would be potatoes.

There were, of course. Hundreds of them, thought Paul gloomily, as he filled yet another sack and dragged it to the edge of the field. Hathin the donkey looked at the sacks, and then at Paul, as if he was hoping Paul would reject his suspicion about who would end up carrying them.

Paul got a new sack from a pile in one corner, and paused to look at Tanboule and Quigin, all hunched over and digging in other quarters of the field. At least it's stopped raining, he thought, looking at the clear blue sky. It was sunny too, and Paul stretched towards the sun, enjoying the heat of it on his face, and the creaking and popping as his backbone straightened out.

He was at full stretch, staring at the sky, when a slight hint of movement touched the corner of his vision somewhere higher up the peak.

Instantly, he was crouching again, and looking up the mountain. Sure enough, there was something moving, something slinking over the crest on all fours. Paul felt his mouth suddenly dry up, and his heart began its now almost familiar beat of fear.

"Gwarulch," said a voice by Paul's ear, and he turned his head to see Tanboule next to him, peering through a long, leather-cased telescope. He shut it with a flick of his wrist, and said with a sniff, "A smaller, slinking sort. A scout for more, no doubt."

Paul gulped, and looked nervously around, then back at Tanboule's kindly face, and his mouth opened and shut without getting out any words. Tanboule raised one eyebrow, but said nothing. Paul watched, aghast, as he walked back to his quarter, and bent over the potatoes again.

"What are you doing?" he exclaimed. "We have to escape!"

Tanboule looked back at him, and nodded sagely. "Of course, Paul, of course. But everything in due time. We have to get the potatoes out first."

"But . . ." Paul began, but Tanboule wasn't listening. Neither was Quigin, Paul noticed. He just kept grubbing up the potatoes. Even Leasel looked away when Paul cast a beseeching glance at her.

Paul looked back up the mountain again, and saw the Gwarulch creeping back up. Reporting to the others, he thought, and memories of Donbreye suddenly flashed into his head—of that first chilling howl, and then the awful rush of the creatures onto the harborside. Or the battle of Reddow Cairn, with thousands of Gwarulch spilling over the ridge . . .

Paul shivered, picked up his trowel, and started digging frantically for potatoes. In a few minutes, he was working in a near frenzy, pulling potatoes out of the ground at twice the speed of Quigin or Tanboule.

"You could hurry up," he said to them in a sulky, half-crying voice. "It's me they want, and if you have to get the potatoes in before we can run away, you could . . . you could . . ."

Savagely, he thrust his trowel into the ground, only to be met by a cry of annoyance—from somewhere, underground. Paul let go of the trowel, and the earth split around it, clods scattering and loose earth blowing away like sand. Then a hand reached out of the hole, a brown wrinkled hand, with the texture of willow bark, and long thin fingers like roots. The hand felt to the left and right, snaked forward, and grabbed Paul's ankle.

He screamed and fell backwards, kicking and straining, trying to loosen the grip of whatever held him. But it wouldn't let go, and another hand burst from the hole and gripped Paul even more tightly than the first.

"Help!" he gasped out, as he felt it pulling him towards the hole, and his feet lost their hold, and slid through the churned up dirt. Quigin started forward, but Tanboule held him back, and the Friend of Beasts didn't even struggle. Paul strained and wept, as he realized the old man was a traitor, and had got at Quigin too.

Then the thing's head burst through the earth, and Paul found new energy to pull away. For whatever it was had a head of stones, all jumbled together, and eyes of cold jewels that sparked in the sun, and hair that seemed to be coils of dirt stuck together. Its teeth were made of black volcanic glass, and it was grinding them noisily.

Paul, in shock, gave one last almighty heave, and the thing leapt from the hole, letting go of Paul, whose head fell back onto the dirt with a loud thud.

The creature towered over him, small clods of dirt raining down from its strange attire, a smock of woven earth in every color, from black through ochre to the white of the whitest sand.

The creature straightened this unusual garment, ran her fingers through her coils of dirt, and said, "Mmmm . . . that's better. Nice of you to give me a hand, dear."

Paul lay silent, staring up at this apparition, that spoke in a warm, comforting voice just like the school librarian (the nice one).

"Oh . . . uh . . . no problem," he muttered, still lying on his back. Then he remembered his manners, and his encounter with the Fire Queen, and hastily got to his feet, brushing off some of the dirt. He had no doubt as to who this was now. "I mean, it was a pleasure, Your Earthship."

"Call me Earth, or E," said the Earth Lady, slapping some more dirt on Paul's head and tenderly smearing a little mud on his ears. She draped a hand across his shoulder, and turned him towards Quigin and Tanboule, who stood silently by.

"And these are your friends, Paul?"

"Yes," said Paul, guiltily, remembering that he had thought Tanboule was a traitor only seconds before. "Tanboule and Quigin . . . and Leasel the hare, and Hathin the donkey and Nubbins the horse."

"Charmed, I'm sure," said Earth, smearing Quigin and Tanboule's hands with mud and leaving a trail of dirt down each of the animal's backs. "What a lovely day for digging potatoes."

"Um, yes," said Paul, as the Earth Lady got down on her knees and started digging potatoes out. Or rather, summoning them out. She just seemed to hold her hand against the surface and potatoes fairly leapt into her palm.

She started to hum a little tune, and soon became totally engrossed in harvesting potatoes. The others watched her for a minute or two, fascinated by the progress of potatoes from all over the patch, just to get in her hand. Then Tanboule looked at Paul, and said (with a significant nod of his head towards the peak), "The sooner they're in, the sooner we go."

"Yes . . . I mean, *yes*!" said Paul, tearing his eyes away from the Earth Lady—the last of the four Elementals—with some difficulty. He wanted to talk to her that second, to ask for her help, before the Gwarulch descended and made it impossible. But she seemed totally intent on the potatoes, and didn't look up at all to give him even the chance of starting a conversation.

So Paul took a deep breath to ease the tension that was building up inside him, and started digging the potatoes again. But even single-mindedly staring at the ground in front of him, and working as fast as he could couldn't distract him or calm him down. He knew that the Gwarulch were there, waiting to attack. And the Earth Lady—possibly the end of his quest—was only two meters away. But maybe he should be patient—the

Elementals he'd met were all strange, powerful and unpredictable. Perhaps harvesting potatoes was something the Earth Lady really liked doing, and if he interrupted, she'd never help him.

Paul let out a little gasp of indecision, fear and apprehension, and looked at Tanboule, hoping that he would tell him what to do. But the wise man wasn't looking, and something told Paul he wouldn't look, that any decisions were up to him.

Then, the multitude of Gwarulch howled in unison, their harsh, drawn-out cries echoing down the mountain, cruel and chilling under the beautiful sky.

Paul's head snapped up, and he dropped his trowel, the howls filling him with fear. There, on the ridge, a line of Gwarulch was spread out, tall shapes silhouetted against the sun. In the middle, a spindly, black-wrapped figure raised its arm—and pointed straight at Paul.

The howls came again, merging into one awful, terrifying shriek of triumph and bloodlust. Then the Gwarulch leapt down the mountainside, eyes and talons glittering in the sun.

And in that same instant, the Earth Lady stood up and threw a clutch of potatoes into a sack, saying, "That's the last of them. Except for one. Come here, Paul."

Paul stood staring at the Gwarulch screaming down towards him, and felt himself move towards the Earth Lady as though he were a puppet. Everything seemed to stretch, and he felt the seconds go by very slowly, marked by the knelling of his heart. His eyes slid over to Quigin and Tanboule, who seemed as still as statues, and then he looked at the Earth Lady.

He thought she was holding a potato out to him, and then he realized it wasn't really a potato, but some sort of strange, yellowish vegetable. It had bulbous extrusions like arms and legs and a head, and two whorls of discolored skin that might be eyes.

"The Body," said the Earth Lady. "A free gift, Paul. You've got them all now—Air, Water, Fire and Earth."

Paul held out his hand, and slowly took the Body from the Earth Lady, almost as if he couldn't believe it was there. He looked at the strange, turnipy-sort of figure, and then up at the Gwarulch raçing towards him, howling and moving with ferocious speed. They were less than eight hundred meters away now—or about a minute and a half, Paul guessed.

"What do I do?" he blurted, his hands shaking as he tried to put the Body in the pouch. It stuck, and he quickly looked down to open it. When he looked back up, the Earth Lady was gone.

"Ride!" shouted Tanboule, seeing Paul's mouth gape in horror. Throwing his telescope away, he picked Paul up and threw him too—onto the back of Nubbins. Quigin jumped up in front, and Nubbins leapt away towards the downward slope. Hathin streaked at his heels, braying in fear at the stench of hunting Gwarulch.

And in the potato field, an old man suddenly disappeared, even as the lead Gwarulch leapt over the piled sacks, eager to kill. They checked their stride, and their piggy eyes slid over the field before they took off again, redoubling their pace in an effort to catch the mounted boys.

Only the black-bandaged figure halted, and then only for a moment. Oroch could smell Sorcery of some unfamiliar kind, and he thought he'd heard the whisper of a human voice . . . a whisper that said something like, "Come to help with the broad beans? Third trellis on the left . . ."

21

THE CHALLENGE/THRUAN

J ulia," said the voices, and then, more urgently, "Julia!"

The girl listened to them dreamily, as she sank further into blackness. The sounds meant something, she thought—but then once again she lost the capacity for thought, and the sounds came again.

"Julia! Julia! Julia!"

She paid more attention this time—became aware that she *could* pay attention—and gained something of the ability to concentrate her sparse thoughts.

Then the singing began. She didn't know what singing was, but something in her responded to it. It was pleasing . . . it drew her up from the total absence of thought. She wanted to understand what it was, why it pleased her . . . Once again she concentrated her thoughts, grasping onto the song that twined around her like a vine. Now she knew it was three people singing, and they were two women and a man.

And she became aware of herself. She was a girl, like
the singing women, but younger. And with that aware-
ness, the song strengthened, became louder, more familiar. And in the middle of it was her name.

"Oh! Oh!" cried Julia, as she felt the tears coursing
down her own soft cheeks, and her own arms and legs
quivering with life, and all her memories rushing back
. . . all the things that made her Julia . . . all the habits,
likes, dislikes, tastes, talents, voice and movement . . .

Hands reached down and lifted her from darkness
into light, and Julia fell sobbing into Lyssa's open arms
as Mirran and Anhyvar stroked her hair, still singing her
name.

Through a veil of Lyssa's hair, Julia saw that she was
back at the ring of braided holly and turf, and the cheerful yellow flame was burning briskly at her side. She
took a deep breath, and stopped crying. As she slowly
quietened and relaxed within Lyssa's embrace, the others stopped singing.

"What happened?" whispered Julia, her mouth so
tangled in Lyssa's silver hair that the words were barely
audible. "I couldn't resist . . . "

"We didn't expect you to," said Lyssa. "We meant to
bring you back before . . ."

"But . . ." whispered Julia, "I was . . . She took me a
. . . apart."

"Yes," said Lyssa. "But Anhyvar was watching—
together we made sure we got you instead of Her."

"How?" asked Julia, leaning back a little to spit out
the hair. Then, in sudden fear, "Can She take me back?"

"No, child!" exclaimed Lyssa, hugging her again.
"Not now—not after we've sung you back together."

"You have been claimed by me," said Anhyvar, smiling. "I hope you prefer that."

"Oh, yes!" said Julia, turning back to smile at

Anhyvar. "And I'm really to stay here with you, and Lyssa, and Mirran?"

"Yes," said Anhyvar, firmly. "But She will try and destroy us all."

"I don't care!" said Julia. "As long as I'm not alone."

"We fight together," said Mirran. "And never have I seen such a formidable gathering of Heroes, Kings and Sorceresses."

Julia looked up at him smiling above her, then looked down, and wriggled her toes in the turf. "Do you mean I'm a hero?"

"Of course," said Mirran, gravely. "You have fought Her many times, and not been defeated. I doubt if anyone else could say that."

"I always wanted to be a hero," said Julia, remembering cosy reading by the fire, or further back, her mother reading to her and Paul, of kings and wizards, dragons and heroes.

"I don't think I want to be one now," she added, thinking of fighting the Ragwitch. "I just want to finish Her off . . . get Paul, and go home."

No one spoke for a second, and Julia felt an unnatural quietness from the others. She looked up from the turf, close into Lyssa's face. Anhyvar and Mirran were standing behind her, their hands loosely entwined, and they both looked very sad.

"Oh, Julia," said Anhyvar softly. "I fear none of us will go home from here. Given great fortune, we may destroy Her. But there is little hope for anything else."

Julia stared at her, and felt Anhyvar's words echo through her. Little hope . . .

"I guess," she said, "I guess . . . I knew all along. But I'm only . . ."

"I know," said Lyssa, gently. "If we could spare you, I would send you ahead of us, to make the great discovery . . . but we need your strength—and there is always

the slightest chance you may be able to escape ...
given some great Magic. And in the end, if we find no
other way, we will all go together. Even if She prevails,
I can make sure She has none of us."

"What do you mean?" asked Julia.

"I cannot promise life," said Lyssa. "But we shall
have a true death—not a lingering existence as small
splinters of Her mind. And if there is a road to travel after life, we shall go together."

"You mean you don't know?" asked Julia. "I mean,
if we're going to ... to die ... won't we go to ...
heaven or somewhere?"

"Heaven?" asked Lyssa, looking searchingly into
Julia's tear-stained face. "Oh—perhaps. No one knows,
my dear."

"Except perhaps the Knights of Drowned Angarling,"
added Anhyvar thoughtfully. "If they ever really died, before they were brought back to be encased in stone."

"But enough of this talk," cried Lyssa, standing up
and pulling Julia up with her. "I am sure that She will
soon try to winkle us out of our hidey-hole. Anhyvar?"

The red-haired Witch nodded, and stared out into the
blackness, her forehead wrinkling in concentration.

"She ..." Anhyvar began, then she cried out, and
held a hand to her mouth, eyes blinking, as the white
globe suddenly pulsed with a savage burst of light,
washing out the yellow glow of the fire. A second later,
a clap of thunder sounded, and the fluid roiled and
eddied around the globe.

Then the Ragwitch's voice came booming—but it
was a voice somehow made up of many Ragwitch
voices, all speaking in unison, and echoing everywhere.

"So! You still defy Us, Anhyvar. Have you forgotten
that once before you were brought beyond the Door—
and can be again! And you, Rowan Lady: we know
your tree at Alnwere, and it shall be uprooted and de-

stroyed! And Mirran—once mewing beast—you shall return to your eternal torment!" The voice faded for a moment, and then returned, diminished to just the hissing, familiar voice of the Ragwitch. "And my little Julia. What strange company you keep. They cannot protect you, Julia. Not from Me . . . not here. You've been a part of Me too long, Julia. You must want to come back to Me . . . to rejoin Me . . . Come back, Julia . . . come . . ."

Julia grimaced, and tried not to listen. But the words were strangely alluring, and their power coursed through her. She found herself pushing at Lyssa, trying to get free, until Anhyvar held up her star, and it flashed blue as the sky.

"Silence!" cried Anhyvar . . . and She fell silent, but only for a moment. Then a hideous cackling, wheezing sort of laugh began to echo all around them. In control of herself once again, Julia crept back into Lyssa's embrace.

"You . . ." cackled the Ragwitch, "challenge Me? *Here*, within My Mind?"

"Yes!" shouted Anhyvar, and her star flashed blue again, with the sound of birds crying to the dawn.

"Yes!" shouted Mirran, drawing a sword of golden flame from the fire, and brandishing it aloft, spitting and crackling, the smell of burning pine cones filling the air.

"Yes!" shouted Lyssa and Julia together, and the golden flame erupted upwards, showering them with sparks like confetti.

There was no answer—save the faint echo of a hissing laugh. But the globe pulsed bright again, and a dark shape began to form inside.

* * *

"Are they still coming?" shrieked Paul into Quigin's ear, as the other boy looked back over both their shoulders, his hands entwined in Nubbins' mane as the horse raced pell-mell down the mountainside, nimbly avoiding rocks and treacherous ground.

"Yes!" shouted Quigin, turning back to get an even firmer grip on Nubbins' mane. In that brief backwards glance, he'd seen the Gwarulch close behind, springing down the mountainside with ferocious speed. They'd stopped howling though, and Quigin hoped their panting, white-frothed tongues meant they were coming to the end of their endurance.

Then Nubbins suddenly faltered, and came to a sliding halt, both Quigin and Paul nearly tumbling over his neck, while Hathin streaked past, still braying in total fear.

Paul was the first to right himself, and he saw why Nubbins had stopped. A man had risen out of the heather in front of them, a tall, strongly-built man with long reddish locks that tumbled out from under his broad-brimmed hat.

Then Quigin managed to sit upright and quieten the nervously pawing horse. He took one look at the man, and slid off, shouting, "Master Thruan! I thought you were dead! Can you cast a Magic spell to hold the Gwarulch off?"

Relief flooded through Paul as he realized this was the Wizard and balloon-maker Quigin had often talked about. He sighed with even more relief when he looked back up, and saw the Gwarulch halted in a long line across the mountain. Obviously Thruan had already stopped them with some sort of spell. Thankfully, Paul slid to the ground, and turned to Thruan and Quigin.

And stopped dead in fright. For Thruan had thrown his head back, and under his hat, his eyes bore the telltale red wash of the Glazed. There was nothing human in his face at all, and he looked at Quigin as if the boy was merely a stone in his path to be removed.

His fist lashed out across Quigin's face, and the Friend of Beasts fell to the heather with only a surprised sort of yelp. Paul saw his friend fall in slow, slow motion, and felt rather than saw, the sudden focus of Thruan back on him. Without any sort of conscious thought, Paul's hand drew the poniard from the scabbard across his back, even as Nubbins leapt forward, steel-clad hooves seeking to crush, and Leasel dashed through the heather to sink her long teeth in the enemy's ankle.

But Glazed as he was, Thruan still had his Magic. With a gesture of thumb and two fingers, he sent the animals reeling to either side of him, to circle dazedly further down the slope.

Paul tried to rush at him then, but the Glazed-Man clenched his fist, and grunted "Berach!," and Paul felt his arm go numb. The poniard fell from his cramped fingers, clattering onto shale. He tried to move his feet, but they were also frozen.

High above, the Gwarulch howled again, and Paul heard the note of victory in their calls, as the red-eyed Thruan advanced upon him, moving with the awful stilted action of the Glazed.

He was muttering as he came, and Paul redoubled his efforts as he caught the words . . . "Bring him to Her . . . the boy . . . bring him . . . send with Meeper . . . She wants him . . . alive . . . or . . ."

He was still muttering when the blue-fletched arrow came whistling up the hill, its steel point like a spark hurtling under the sun. Paul only saw it for an instant in flight, then it transfixed Thruan, and the point was no longer shining.

The Glazed-Man looked at it in surprise, then let out a snarl of animal rage, his lips peeling back to bare his gums. He staggered a little, then his head snapped back to Paul, red eyes open, staring fixedly at his prey. Once again, he started his stop-start, disjointed steps—straight at the boy.

Another arrow whistled towards them, and struck Thruan in one outstretched, grasping arm, slowing him not at all. But with that arrow, the paralysis left Paul, and he dodged away from the Glazed-Man's grasp.

Upslope, the Gwarulch howled and poured down the hill again, to try to gain the boy where Thruan had failed. But a great bristled boar charged uphill ahead of a phalanx of barking hounds, while blue-sleeved archers poured a rain of arrows in an arch over Paul, up into the Gwarulch.

Paul ran, faster than he had ever run before—faster than in Ornware's Wood, so fast his feet seemed to stretch out meters in front of him. Anything, anything to get away from the mumbling, beast-eyed thing that had once been a man.

He could see Quigin's Master Cagael, waving to him now, even as the Borderors ran forward, stopped, fired arrows, and ran forward again. A Borderor was running towards him, waving her sword and shouting something he couldn't hear. Then he did hear it, just as the Glazed-Man above, riddled with arrows, but still burning with obedience to Her, picked up a piece of shale and threw it without even the slightest spell to guide it true.

The Borderor was still shouting "Duck!" when the piece of shale struck Paul in the back of his helmetless head, and he went cartwheeling into the ground. For a second, the mountain whirled around him in a confusion of sky, buff coats, shouting and howls—then everything went totally and utterly black and silent.

Half an hour later, Cagael watched carefully as the soldiers finished rigging a stretcher between the unequally-sized Hathin and Nubbins. Quigin stood at his side, rubbing his jaw with a herb recommended by Cagael to reduce the swelling.

"At least, it works on the dogs," he said to his apprentice with a grin. The grin faded as two of the Borderors carefully put Paul on the stretcher and tied him in. Nubbins bent his head down and tried to look back, but couldn't. Paul's helmet, still tied to the saddle, clanked slightly as the horse straightened up.

"I hope ..." Quigin began, with his troubled eyes resting on Paul, when a shriek above interrupted him, and Tear descended with a great flapping of wings. She hopped a little on the ground, and both Friends of Beasts dropped down on their haunches to gaze into her eyes. They were silent for a moment, then Cagael stood up and went over to the Borderor Lieutenant, who was watching her sentries further up the mountain. She looked up as Cagael approached, and rubbed the callous under her chin, where her helmet-strap had chafed for many years.

"Bad news, Master Cagael?" she asked. "I can imagine no other kind this morning."

Cagael shrugged, and said, "Meepers fly towards us. A band of Gwarulch approaches from the northeast, and another from the east. At least six hundred, all told."

The lieutenant nodded, and said, "We'll move immediately. South. The rest of the army is gathering at Alnwere."

"Mmm ..." murmured Cagael. "There will be healers there, for the boy. He has Magic, Quigin says. Elemental Magic ... perhaps ..."

He looked up at the arrow-pierced body of Thruan, and added, "... and perhaps not. Thruan had Magic too ... even when we were boys ..."

"You knew him?" asked the Borderor Lieutenant

softly. "I did too, you know—though briefly. He tried to save us at the Namyr Gorge."

"Us?" asked Cagael, surprised. "I thought no one escaped . . ."

"Only me. I was sent with a message to Caer Calbore . . . I escaped from there too. Through a sally port with a falconer, when all was lost . . . we fought Glazed-Folk there for the first time. Some of them were my companions from early days . . ."

"Thruan died at the Gorge," said Cagael firmly. He pointed at the body on the ground, and added, "That was a creation of Her."

Aenle didn't answer, but waved the sentries back in, and made a signal for everyone to get ready to move. Cagael had half-turned away when she spoke again.

"I won the prize at Yendre Fair three years running, Master Cageal. Split the wand, even split another arrow once. But that first arrow, uphill in the breeze . . . that was a difficult shot . . . a very difficult shot . . ."

She was silent again for a moment, then shouted at some of the outlying archers to keep their eyes sharp, and for everyone to march hard.

"Alnwere by tomorrow night!" she ordered, and the Borderors nodded tiredly or spat and grimaced, or grinned, each according to their nature.

22

THE WORM/DREAMS AND SHADOWS

T here," said Lyssa, as she braided the last of the
holly leaves into another circle within the first.
"That's the best I can do for the moment."

Anhyvar nodded, but didn't look down. Her eyes
were fixed somewhere out beyond the darkness, where
the white globe pulsed, and the dark shapes within it
took on visible form.

Julia watched the shapes with both fear and fascina-
tion. She couldn't see exactly what was forming there.
Sometimes she thought it was a Gwarulch or Meeper
. . . but it had grown larger . . . and more menacing . . .

Mirran watched the globe with calculating eyes, and
practiced swinging his golden sword, silently cutting
the air, with an economy of movement Julia hadn't
expected—Mirran didn't do any of the grandiose gestures she'd seen in films.

"What do we do when they come out?" Julia asked
Lyssa, when she stood up from her holly leaves.

"Whatever we must!" exclaimed the Rowan Lady. "But to be specific, if we are faced with foes of flesh and blood, we shall fight with Mirran to the fore; if we are attacked with Magic, Anhyvar and I will resist; if the Ragwitch seeks to move us within Her mind, we shall all fight back with the combined strength of our will."

"But what shall I do?" asked Julia. "I mean, besides the last bit, with will."

"You can sing," replied Anhyvar, wiggling her toes into the turf. "That will keep the ring of holly strong—and keep Her power out."

"What shall I sing?" asked Julia. Asking questions and getting things absolutely clear seemed to make the waiting easier. At least it took her mind off the shadowy thing in the globe.

Lyssa seemed to understand, because she took Julia by the hand and sat her down facing their own yellow-gold flame, and sat down beside her.

"It doesn't really matter what you sing. But I'll teach you the proper warding song if you like. It is very old, and very powerful—a good song."

"I'd like to learn it," said Julia. She tried to smile at Lyssa, but it faltered into a sort of gasp, as a horrible cracking noise suddenly came from the direction of the globe.

"Don't look," said Lyssa quickly. "It's only just beginning. There is still time to learn the song."

"O.K.," whispered Julia, flinching as another cracking sound echoed around them. "How does it start?"

"I'll sing the first verse to give you the tune," said Lyssa, and as she spoke, the flame in front of them suddenly shimmered, like a just-plucked string, and a clear high note rose out of it, above the cracking noises from the globe.

Lyssa inclined her head slightly at the flame, and it

played an introduction of flowing, crystal-clear notes. Then Lyssa sang:

> *Rowan to guard, leaf and tree*
> *holly to hide, thee and me*
> *sun-fire and green-tree sing*
> *to ward us here with the ring*
> *Lys*
> *Yrsal*
> *Carral*
> *Rolk*
> *Four runes of ancient folk . . .*

Julia listened, entranced, and the words seemed to flow into her, and relax the tight knot of fear that was building up inside her. There were other verses, and Lyssa sang them while Julia listened, breathing slowly, letting the words and music soothe her. When Lyssa returned to the first verse, Julia joined in and sang as well, the cracking noises and dark shapes momentarily forgotten.

Then, as Lyssa and Julia came back to the first verse again, and the flame shivered out the last, echoing note, there was the loudest crack of all, and the Ragwitch's hissing voice boomed everywhere:

"Let us begin!"

Julia snapped around to look at the globe, but it was gone—in its place floated thousands of glowing shards, slowly spinning out into the fluid. In the middle of this cloud of debris, something was uncoiling, sinuously weaving between the fragments, stretching its lean body out towards the ring of holly. It was like a snake—but not—for its body was easily a meter around, and its head was wide and many-toothed. Vestigial wings fluttered a little way behind its head, and as it stretched, long spikes reared up all along its back. The scales that lined its body were steely grey and blue, but its eyes were a luminous green, and flamed with a malign intelligence.

"A worm," said Mirran bleakly. "Even in my day they were no more than legend. But the old stories described them in some detail."

"I remember them," said Lyssa, slowly, as if reaching far back into a long forgotten past. "There were two, when I was very young—and that was before any stories you may have read, Mirran. They came from the Nameless Realm . . . She must have good memories of that place . . ."

"And welcome to them," interrupted Anhyvar briskly. "I am glad my memories stop at the opening of that awful door. But I have read of these worms—they can be killed."

"A thrust inside the mouth, up into the brain," said Mirran, his eyes watching the uncoiling worm, calculating its speed. "Or so the stories said."

"They spoke true," replied Lyssa.

"Yes—and it must be dispatched soon," said Anhyvar. "We are already at Alnwere Ford, and Her creatures have secured the crossing. She will be there before nightfall, and the Meepers say the King's army is not large. Not after Reddow Cairn."

"Did you hear anything about Paul?" asked Julia anxiously, tearing her eyes away from the worm.

Anhyvar hesitated, then said, "Yes. He was almost taken by Oroch and a Glazed-Wizard—but Borderors interfered, killing the Glazed-One and driving Oroch's band away. He is pursuing them with a larger force— but they were very close to Alnwere."

"And Paul?" asked Julia, sensing something unspoken.

"He was hit by a stone," Anhyvar sighed. "Oroch saw him carried from the field."

"Oh!" cried Julia. "Do you know if . . . is he . . . I mean . . ."

"No, I could not see . . ." Anhyvar began, but Lyssa interrupted her.

"He has arrived at Alnwere," she said. "Alive but unconscious. He is with the Healers, close by my tree. He is in good hands."

Julia started to ask if Lyssa knew any more, but before she could speak, Mirran suddenly pointed with his sword, and said quietly, "It has seen us."

Sure enough, the creature's head was facing them, its eyes intent on the yellow flame. It reared up, its last coils straightening, and started swimming towards them through the fluid, its body wriggling like a sea snake, while its little wings fluttered on its back—a squirmy, silent progress that sent shivers up Julia's spine. It looked about twelve meters long, and its toothy maw was big enough to swallow Julia whole.

"Spears," said Mirran to Anhyvar. "Can you bring us some? Do you remember the boar . . .?"

"The boar spear you broke that day at Caringlass," said Anhyvar, smiling. She reached out into the fluid, and there was a spear in her hand, with a steel crosspiece just behind the head. She handed it to Mirran, then reached out again, and drew forth a bow of dull steel and a quiverful of arrows fletched in the brightest green.

"Yes . . . I remember that hunting party. How could I forget?"

Mirran smiled back at her for a second, but his eyes never really left the approaching worm. It seemed cautious—perhaps the yellow flame was painful to its eyes, thought Julia—because it circled the ring of holly several spear lengths out, like a shark circumnavigating a sinking raft.

Lyssa watched it circle for the second time, then said, "We'd better get something to stick in it, too, Julia."

"I don't think I could carry one of those spears," said Julia doubtfully. "Or use a bow . . . ."

"My spears are very light," replied Lyssa. She reached into the yellow flame, said something under her breath, and pulled out two slender javelins with jagged heads like frozen lightning. She handed one to Julia, and took the other herself.

Julia gripped it eagerly, and practiced a few stabbing motions. The javelin was neither light nor heavy, but seemed just right—good and solid. And it felt safer to have it in her hand, so at least she could do something. She thrust with it again, then moved aside as Anhyvar touched her shoulder.

"Stand aside a little," said the Witch, taking up her bow and shaking her hair to one side. "Let's see what arrows can do in this strange water-air."

Her bowstring twanged, and an arrow sped into the fluid—slower than in air, and more erratic, but it struck the worm full on its armored coils, and bounced off. The worm didn't even seem to notice, but it did tighten its circle, drawing closer to the ring of holly and its defenders.

"The mouth," said Mirran grimly, and he stepped forward to the very edge of the ring, and hefted his spear. Behind him, the other three ranged themselves at the ready, Anhyvar taking another of Lyssa's lightning javelins.

Just as she took it, the worm unwound, and with a shocking burst of speed, it struck!

* * *

One moment, Paul was unconscious—and the next he was awake, his eyes open and staring up into a night sky. Stars twinkled everywhere above him, a great swathe of stars, brighter and clearer than any he'd seen before.

Gradually, he became aware that he was lying on his back on some sort of hill or embankment, judging from the angle and the feel of grass at his neck. For some reason he didn't feel like moving his head to look properly. It was easier just to stare up into the lovely blackness with the march of stars across it, and enjoy the sensation of flying under the sky.

Then Paul heard the breathing next to him: low, soft and regular, and somehow not at all frightening. At first he thought it was some echo of his own breath, but the rhythm was completely different, the breaths longer.

So he raised his head and had a look. The first thing he noticed was just how light it was. There was no moon, but the stars were far, far brighter than any he'd seen before. The next thing was that the grassy slope he was lying on suddenly ended about twelve meters below—and there was nothing beyond and below except for black space and stars. The third thing was that the origin of the breathing was a dog—or rather, a statue of a dog. It looked like a sheep dog carved from petrified wood—as though it had been in the sea for a long, long time.

Paul sat up properly to look at the edge of the hill, and at the dog statue, which was still making breathing sounds. He found it difficult to tell which way was up or down, and a wave of disorientation swept over him. Where were Quigin and Tanboule? Where were the Borderors who had charged up the slope at Rhysamarn? Where was he?

Gingerly, Paul felt the back of his head, and winced as he felt the bruise there. For a second he wondered if that had made him go crazy, but he was pretty certain he'd never think of petrified sheep dogs and a hill that ended in nothing, even if he went completely raving mad. Even more gingerly than he'd felt his bruise, he leaned over and touched the dog—and the breathing stopped.

The dog shimmered, and seemed to become even more petrified, until it was mirror-smooth, with the stars winking and blurring, reflecting on its surface. Then it just got brighter and brighter, and all the star reflections joined together to make one great star, and Paul couldn't look at it. Then, it was gone, and there was a man lying next to Paul. His eyes were closed, and a faint smile curled up the bottom of his smooth, ageless face. Then one eye opened, a pupil swiveled towards Paul, and he sat up, head tilting back to look at the stars.

"Celestial mechanics," he said, indicating the heavens with a gentle sweep of his arm. "What makes the stars wheel their slow, slow way? As we move, and they seem to shift across our sky, they are moving too . . . but oh—so slightly! Even I, since the beginning, have only seen them slip a little way . . . and their elemental selves are so vigorous! Dancing and gossip, forever on the move . . . and yet, they are but the dreams of great incandescent globes. Wonderful, isn't it?"

"Er . . . yes," said Paul hesitantly, somewhat unnerved by this strange man's enthusiasm. "Could you . . . could you tell me where I am, please?"

The man uncrossed his ankles and slowly bent his head back to look at the ground, idly picking up a daisy to chew—from a spot where there hadn't been any daisies a second ago.

"You mean you don't know?" asked the man, in a voice that was younger than it had been. His face was younger too, and his hair, previously silver in the starlight, now reflected glints of yellow.

"I don't think so," replied Paul uneasily. Out of the corner of his eye he could see daisies sprouting and growing up into full flower, everywhere along the hill. It wasn't scary, but it was definitely eerie, and Paul felt the hair on his head sort of rise and get itchy at the back.

"I'll give you a clue," said the man, who now looked about twenty years old (though still with a faint tinge of something ancient). He plucked a piece of colored paper from the air, and unfolded it into the sort of crown you could get from Christmas crackers. It rustled as he put it on. Unlike most cracker crowns, it fit perfectly.

And Paul suddenly remembered things Tanboule had told him, and realized why the place was so strange, and the man stranger still.

"This must be the land of Dreams and Shadows," he said, quite calmly. "And you're the Patchwork King."

"I knew you'd get it eventually," replied the Patchwork King, spitting out the daisy-stalk. "Pah! That tastes terrible! Would you care to join me for a cup of tea? Or coffee?"

"Yes, please," said Paul, frantically trying to remember what Tanboule had told him about the Patchwork King, and whether he was kind and good . . . or horrible . . . or just didn't care . . .

He got up as the Patchwork King leapt to his feet, and nearly walked into a stone wall that hadn't been there an instant before. The King took a huge iron key from his belt, gently moved some tendrils of wild rose, and pushed it into an equally large keyhole. When he turned it, a whole section of the wall pivoted, and sunlight streamed through.

They stepped through into a garden at noon, with Paul sneaking a glance behind him. Sure enough, the stars still gleamed there, despite the sun beating down on this side of the wall.

Paul followed the King through the garden, trying not to stare at the strange plants and oddities that were everywhere: statues, and strange mechanical inventions, wind chimes, and birds that seemed to be made of ice, but which flew and sang in the warm sunlight.

Eventually they came to a tall, impenetrable hedge, and the Patchwork King produced another key, which he touched to the spiky foliage. Nothing happened for a moment, then the hedge stirred and the branches moved apart, till there was a round hole through to the other side.

The Patchwork King bent down and crawled through on all fours. So Paul did likewise, emerging onto cool flagstones. It was nighttime again here—or twilight, Paul thought, as he got up and looked around.

He stood in a courtyard of time candles, all steadily burning, the hours marked in red down their sides. Each said seven, so Paul presumed that was the time. Beyond the candles was a lawn dominated by a huge sundial of rough-carved stone. Beyond that was a small hill, with a ring of broken stones around its crest. A great tree grew from the top of the hill, with wide-spreading branches, and white flowers spilling their petals on everything below.

"I like measuring time," said the Patchwork King, with a wave of his hand that encompassed time candles and sundial. "The problem is, of course, that it is entirely relative to whatever is measuring it."

He looked at Paul, but not as if he expected an answer, and then strode onto the lawn, past the sundial and up to the base of the hill.

"I'm back," he called, as Paul looked around for some house or other likely spot to have tea.

"We've a visitor for tea," he said again, straight at the hill, as if he was talking to someone just in front of him. "Paul—the one we've been expecting."

"You've been expecting me?" asked Paul, surprised again. "How . . ."

His voice trailed off as the hill rumbled, and the ground shook under his feet. With a distant, bass grumble, the hillside split in two, revealing a wood-panelled passage slanting down. It was lined with clocks, and they all began to chime as the Patchwork King took Paul by the shoulder and propelled him forward into the corridor.

The hillside shut behind them, but it wasn't dark— nor exactly light. The twilight from outside just seemed to creep ahead of Paul and the King, as they walked down the creaking passage, the clocks chiming all around. The corridor was extremely long, and Paul counted at least three hundred clocks—but at last, there were no more clocks—just a plain wooden door at the end of the corridor, with a large porcelain doorknob.

"Tea in the kitchen," said the Patchwork King, who looked older again, with lines on his face, and silver in his hair. "Much cosier."

He opened the door to sunlight, which streamed in through three huge round windows, lighting up the white-tiled kitchen that gleamed and smelt of cooking and homeliness. A green-enamelled stove burned merrily in one corner, with a kettle already whistling atop it. And the long table against the windows was loaded with a teapot, cups on saucers, thick white bread and a jar of marmalade.

"Hope you like marmalade," said the Patchwork King. "I can't stand jam."

"I like marmalade," said Paul, and then fearing to lie, he added, "But I think I like jam better."

The Patchwork King nodded, and went to get the kettle. When Paul looked at the table again, there was a tin of strawberry jam next to the marmalade. A tin of his favorite brand of strawberry jam.

"How did you do that?" exclaimed Paul, picking the tin up eagerly. It was so ordinary and familiar he felt like bursting into tears just from holding it. "That's from my world . . . where I come from . . ." He paused for breath, put the tin back down, and said, "If you can get jam from my world . . . your Highness . . . can you send me and my sister back—back from the Ragwitch's world?"

The Patchwork King cocked his head to listen as Paul spoke, but didn't answer. He poured the water into the teapot and turned the pot around a few times.

"Please," said Paul. "You have to send us back. You have to!"

"I have to do nothing," said the Patchwork King, calmly pouring the tea. "I am the custodian of Magic. A watcher, that's all. I only interfere when constrained by Magic."

"Does that mean . . . you won't help?" asked Paul quietly, his sudden, unexpected hope ebbing out of him. Slowly, he undid his pouch and took out the four gifts of the Elementals—the Breath, the Blood, the Spirit and the Body—and put them on the table.

"You can have them if you help," said Paul, not really knowing what he was giving away. "They're very Magic—the Elementals gave them to me."

"I know," said the Patchwork King. "As I said—I watch. But gifts of Magic, or anything else, cannot sway me from my purpose. Here, have a cup of tea."

"Can't you do anything to help?" wailed Paul miserably. "Can't you even send me back to Quigin and the others? I can't just stay here!"

"You'll be going back quite soon," said the Patchwork King. "As soon as a suitable guide comes along."

"Can't I go now?" asked Paul dully. He felt that he had failed, that all his efforts seeking out the Elementals were for nothing, now that the ruler of all Magic had refused to help. Now there was no hope of Julia escaping . . . or Paul himself . . .

"You can go if you like," said the Patchwork King, taking a piece of bread and smearing it with marmalade.

"I presumed you'd want to ask for a spell. That's what people usually come here for. If they know the way."

"A spell?" said Paul slowly, absentmindedly drinking his tea. It tasted strange until he realized it was real tea, not Tanboule's brew.

"China Black," said the Patchwork King, answering Paul's unspoken question. "Yes, I know your mother drinks it."

"A spell," said Paul again, almost to himself. "Could I ask for a spell to send me and Julia home again—is that different from just asking you to do it?"

"Yes," replied the Patchwork King gravely. He had aged again, in those few seconds, and now regarded Paul through old and weary eyes, his face lined and ancient. "Is that what you want? A spell to send you and Julia home?"

Paul automatically went to say "yes," but his mouth hung open, as he suddenly wondered if that was what he wanted. Did he really want to escape to home, when everyone he knew in the other world were struggling for their lives, fighting a losing battle against the Ragwitch? And Tanboule had said Julia was fighting too, inside Her. What would Julia say if he got a spell that took them away without helping?

Paul thought of Quigin, who'd uncomplainingly helped him everywhere, knocked to the ground at Rhysamarn; and Aleyne giving his horse away, and going back up the hill at Reddow Cairn; the fisherfolk of Donbreye, helping him to escape underwater; Tanboule throwing him onto Nubbins; and everything he'd been through with the Elementals. And he remembered when he'd changed from just wanting to get Julia and escape, to wanting to stop the Ragwitch—to stop Her forever.

"Please, Your Highness," he said, taking a deep breath, as all these thoughts and images flashed through his mind, "I want a spell to kill the Ragwitch."

23

THE SPIRE/THE FORGE

Julia screamed as the worm struck at Mirran, staggering him to his knees, his spear clanging harmlessly from the thing's armored nose. Instantly, the worm snapped back for a second strike—but Mirran managed to swing his spear back again, and wedge it in the turf, just in time, the spear shaft bending almost to breaking point as the worm struck again.

"Now!" shouted Anhyvar, and she, Lyssa and Julia all rushed forward and thrust their javelins at the creature. Julia forgot to aim for the mouth, and thrust at an eye instead, moving dangerously close to its maw in her eagerness to hit back.

But the worm merely closed an armored eyelid, and the javelin jarred out of Julia's hands, the vibration sending jabs of pain from hands to elbows. Without even thinking, Julia sprang back, and the worm's retaliatory snap missed her by inches.

In that moment, as its jaws opened to get Julia,

Mirran jumped across from the side, and plunged his boar spear into the roof of its mouth, right up to the crosspiece.

The worm squealed, the first sound it had made—a curiously fragile, high-pitched sound—and whipped back into the fluid, the boar spear hanging from its mouth.

"Quickly, more spears," panted Mirran.

Once again, Anhyvar reached into the darkness and produced a boar spear, and Lyssa gave Julia another lightning-pointed javelin.

"Keep this one as long as you can," she said to Julia. "Every one that goes outside the ring weakens the flame."

"I'll try," replied Julia, keeping a careful eye on the worm. She gripped her new spear more tightly than the first and grimly determined that she'd put it in the thing's mouth.

The worm slowly coiled in on itself, and shook its head back and forth several times, trying to loosen the spear. It seemed little hurt by it—only annoyed.

When it started uncoiling again, Mirran said, "It will strike in a . . ."

He didn't finish as the worm suddenly uncoiled completely, its tail lashing across towards the holly-ring as its head speared in from the other side. Mirran raised his spear to strike back at it, only to have the point skitter off the scales with a noise like fingernails being scraped down a blackboard.

But at the same time, Anhyvar thrust her javelin deep into the corner of the creature's mouth, pulling it back with a vicious twist, accompanied by a spurt of green and oily blood.

Julia and Lyssa thrust at the tail, which probed at them like an octopus's tentacle, seeking to grab something to crush. Every time the tail crossed the border of the holly, golden sparks sprayed from it, and Lyssa and Julia felt a great wash of heat as the warding Magic attacked the tail. But the Magic couldn't stop it, and Lyssa's spears couldn't really penetrate the steely scales—so they could only push it away, as though urgently fending a large boat off a small and fragile jetty.

Wounded, the worm's head withdrew, and the tail slithered back across the turf, trailing sparks. Julia sighed in relief, and looked aside for a second—and the worm's tail suddenly struck back, coiling around her and whipping her off the turf and out into the fluid.

Julia only had time to let out a muffled scream before the coils covered her head and began to squeeze. Desperately, she wedged the spearhead against the coil in front of her face, as the black-scaled body tightened everywhere about her. Kicking with her feet, she managed to get the other end of the spear wedged as well, so it lay diagonally across her body. That made it hesitate, because as it crushed, the javelin broke through the scales, even as the shaft bent into Julia's ribs.

It loosened its coils a little, and through a tiny gap, Julia saw Mirran thrust his boar spear into the top of the creature's mouth, wedge the bottom of the shaft into its lower jaw—and, drawing his golden sword in one swift motion, leap into the very mouth of the worm.

The worm immediately tried to close its mouth, but Mirran pulled the bottom of the first spear in, and wedged it—so both spears held its mouth open. Then, crouched between the two bending, almost crescent-shaped spears, he thrust his sword up into the roof of the worm's mouth with every ounce of strength he possessed.

Green blood burst everywhere, and Julia lost sight of Mirran and everything else, as the tail tightened convulsively, and her spear broke through the scales and went through to the other side. But still the coils tightened.

Julia couldn't breathe, and red spots danced before her eyes, joining together into one great blur of redness.

She had almost blacked out when the coils collapsed around her. Instinctively, she kicked herself free, and pushed out into the fluid. Seconds later, Anhyvar and Lyssa grabbed her, kicked back to the ring of holly, and laid her gasping by the flame.

Mirran was lying there too, his face red and white, like someone who'd just played a very hard game of squash.

"That's the first battle won," he coughed to Julia. "But we were very lucky . . ."

Julia nodded weakly, then groaned as the sudden movement sent pain lancing everywhere through her chest. Bruised ribs, she thought, as the pain subsided into an awful ache. She thought of the worm's great crushing coils, and what could have happened, and started to laugh, in almost hysterical relief.

"What will She do next?" she gasped, in between laughter and groans of pain.

"She's trying to shift us to Her memory," replied Anhyvar, after staring briefly out into the fluid. "The battle has begun at Alnwere, and She can spare little thought for us—so She hopes to remove us to a far corner of Her mind, to be dealt with at Her leisure."

"Look," said Lyssa, helping Julia up to a sitting position. "She has already begun."

Julia looked, but didn't see anything except the familiar fluid, now dark save for the light from the flame. In it, the dead worm still wriggled slowly, amongst the shards of the white globe.

Lyssa pointed, and Julia saw that out beyond the worm, color was creeping in, as well as the vague outline of something—buildings, or the side of a hill. Julia also felt something across her face, but it was so alien to her experience of the fluid that she almost didn't recognize it—a breeze, chill and cold, with the hint of snow or rain.

"Early winter, near the Spire," said Anhyvar, her eyes somehow seeing clearly into that faint tracery in the darkness. "At the time of Her rule, and the place of Her greatest power."

She blinked, and turned to Lyssa, with a look that could almost have been fear.

"Sing!" said Lyssa. "Everybody sing, with all your hearts! If She can remove us to that memory we are lost!"

Julia nodded grimly, and struggled to her feet, clutching her ribs with both arms. She took half a breath, felt the pain explode into her ribs, opened her mouth wide, and took a deep breath.

Lyssa and Anhyvar moved to either side of her, facing out, and she heard Mirran move behind her, also facing out—all of them with their backs to the flame in the middle. Still Julia held her breath, ignoring the stabbing pain in her ribs, and the pounding behind her eyes. The flame played its run of notes, and Julia watched Lyssa from the corners of her eyes, waiting to begin.

Then, at last, when it seemed she could stand it no longer, Lyssa's mouth opened, and Julia let out a great rush of air and sound, and the first word of the warding song burst out into the darkness.

* * *

"A spell to kill the Ragwitch," repeated the Patchwork King, looking at Paul through half-closed, thoughtful eyes. "Are you sure?"

"Yes," said Paul, though his voice trembled. He felt both excited and sort of sick, all at once, as if he'd committed himself to an impossible dare.

"I can give you such a spell," said the King, reaching to spoon marmalade onto his plate, his head coming close to Paul's. He paused after the first spoonful, and stared directly at Paul, his face only inches away.

"But there's one thing you might like to know," he added, still staring.

"What's that?" asked Paul, nervously, wishing he could climb out of his chair and get further away.

The King didn't answer, but starlight twinkled on his face, like the reflected starlight that had shone on the petrified dog. It got brighter and brighter, till once again all the stars merged into one great flash of brilliance.

Paul blinked, holding his eyes shut till the radiance faded. When he opened them again, it wasn't the Patchwork King standing opposite him—it was the Ragwitch.

She loomed above him. Her eyes fixed on his small form, Her hideous mouth gaping. One three-fingered hand reached out to grab him, and She hissed, "You'll have to get this close."

And then She was gone, and the Patchwork King stood in Her place, his hand reaching out across the table. He picked up a piece of bread.

Paul took several quick breaths, and tried to pick up his cup—but his hand shook too much, and the cup fell onto the table, the tea going everywhere. He stared at the pool as it spread, and didn't even move when the hot tea started dripping on his leg.

"*This close . . .*" said the Patchwork King again, from the other side of the table. He took a bite of his bread, and said (with his mouth full), "Do you still want the spell?"

"Yes," said Paul, and then "Yes" again. He moved his leg so that the tea wouldn't drip on it, and looked up at the Patchwork King, noticing that he seemed young again.

"Why did you scare me?"

"I always explain the limitations of Magic," said the

Patchwork King, finishing his bread. As he swallowed, a deep bell sounded, its note echoing through the kitchen, sending vibrations through the table and floor. It was quite loud, but somehow Paul felt that it came from far away.

The Patchwork King listened to it, completely still, till the echoes died away. Then he got up quickly, and said, "Come, we haven't got much time—of your time, that is. I have plenty of mine. But then I can't give you my time, can I?"

"I suppose not," said Paul, bewildered by this sudden activity, and still shaken by the sudden appearance of the Ragwitch—or the shape of Her, anyway. He got up and followed the Patchwork King to yet another newly-appeared door, a solid, plain wood door made from uneven planks.

"Where are we going?"

"To my forge," said the King. As he spoke, he started to shrink, and grow wider across the shoulders. A white beard sprouted from his chin, and a long, drooping moustache sprung out under his nose. "Don't forget to bring the ingredients."

He pointed back at the table. For a second, Paul thought he meant the bread and marmalade. Then he realized he'd left the Elementals' gifts there, the precious objects that he'd even slept with to make sure they were safe. Quickly, he ran back and put them in his pouch.

"Now," said the Patchwork King, who had shrunk and broadened till he was about Paul's height and twice as wide across the shoulders. "The forge!"

He opened the door, and Paul felt a rush of heat against his face, and a sudden flash of memory came to him—of the Fire Queen in her field of burning coals. But the heat here came from a sunken pit in the middle of a rough-hewn cave of stone. A stream ran swiftly through one corner, turning a water wheel, which moved cogs and pulleys that in their turn pumped a huge pair of leather-lunged bellows. Everything clacked and hummed, and the fire whooshed every time the bellows puffed, but it was a surprisingly peaceful noise, complemented by the rushing of the stream.

The Patchwork King crossed to the very edge of the fire-pit, and plucked a long-handled pot out of thin air. It looked very thick and heavy, but he handled it with ease, swinging it with his newly thickened arms. Paul stared at his wide, squat form, back-lit by the leaping flames, and realized he had turned himself into the classic picture of a dwarf.

"I try to look the part," said the Patchwork King, causing Paul to try to blank out his thoughts. He didn't like the idea of anyone being able to see into his mind.

"Now," said the King, ignoring Paul's attempts to think of nothing (which weren't working anyway). "Put the ingredients in the crucible."

He held out the pot, holding it by the very end of its two-meter handle, so Paul didn't have to get too close to the fire-pit.

"You mean the Elementals' gifts?" asked Paul, looking at the fire. "You don't mean to melt them?"

"I will forge them into a spell to give the Ragwitch life," said the Patchwork King. "And beat the spell into a weapon to take that life away."

"I don't understand," said Paul, clutching his precious pouch to his chest. "What do you mean—give her life? And why do you need my gifts?"

The Patchwork King sighed and pulled the crucible back and put it upright so he could lean on it like a staff. He seemed more irritable as a dwarf.

"Questions, questions, questions. No one ever just comes for a spell. They always want conversation as well."

"But I have to know if I'm doing the right thing!" exclaimed Paul. "I have to know!"

"All right! Don't get so excited. I have to make a spell to give the Ragwitch life, to get Her out of that indestructible form and into a human one. Then She can be slain—or banished back into the Nameless Realm, because you can't really kill an essence of evil. But She'll be as good as dead. And I need the gifts the Elementals gave you because they are the Breath, the Blood, the Spirit and the Body—they are true life. Now, can I begin?"

"Yes," whispered Paul. The Patchwork King swung the crucible back again, and Paul dropped the gifts in— one by one. The feather that was the Breath, the teardrop of the Blood, the jewel of the Spirit, and last of all, the root-figure of the Body.

"Yes," whispered Paul again, almost to himself, as the Patchwork King swung the crucible into the flame. "Begin . . ."

Paul didn't know how long he was in the forge with the Patchwork King. Time seemed to slip by strangely, and he fell into a sort of half-dream, where he was somewhere else, and people bent over him, and held a cup to his lips. Once he thought he heard Quigin, and a dog licked him on the nose.

Later, the forge swam into his vision again, and he woke to see the dwarf-figure of the King pouring a molten bar, and hammering, his hammer bouncing from the anvil onto the hot metal. Then he faded away again, into blackness, and true sleep.

Finally, Paul awoke to silence, and sunlight streaming through the windows of the kitchen. The kettle was just whistling, and there was a box of cornflakes and a carton of milk on the table. The Patchwork King was standing by the stove holding a silver coffeepot. He was back to normal size, though possibly taller and thinner than he had been at first, and he seemed middle-aged.

"Help yourself to breakfast," he said, pouring hot water into the coffeepot. "Your guide will be here soon."

"Thanks," said Paul sleepily, straightening up. He seemed to have slept sprawled across the kitchen table, but he didn't feel stiff and sore. He reached across for the cornflakes, then woke up properly, and asked, "Have you finished?"

"Yes," replied the Patchwork King gravely. He put down the pot, reached into the air, and slowly pulled a long, slender spear out from nowhere. It was almost two meters long, and at first seemed entirely made of steel, but it changed color as it moved—and Paul saw within it flashes of fire, and scudding clouds, the blue-black of the deepest sea, and the mottled browns of the earth.

The Patchwork King handed it to him, and Paul realized it wasn't a spear. It was a giant needle, complete with the hole at the end for thread.

"What better instrument to unpick a rag doll," said the Patchwork King distantly, "Woven with the Wild Magic that once cast Her out and made Her assume that form."

"What do I . . . what do I do with it?" asked Paul, as he ran his hand down its length, feeling the alternate currents in it, hot and cold, like fire and water, earth and air.

"It is a weapon, Paul," said the Patchwork King. "Use it like the spear you thought it was."

Paul looked back at the needle-spear, and shuddered as he thought of closing with the Ragwitch, of only being as far away as its slender length. And how would he get that close in the first place?

He was thinking about that when there was a knock on the kitchen door, and the King went to open it, saying, "That will be your guide, Paul. No time for break-fast."

He opened the door, and Paul looked up to see an old woman, tall and slender, with long silver hair. She smiled at him, and the sunlight caught her clear green eyes.

"I am Inyla," she said in a kindly voice that reminded Paul of his grandmother's. "I have come to take you back to Alnwere."

Paul looked down from her eyes, and gripped the needle-spear in both hands. For a second he thought "perhaps it's not too late. I could still get a spell to take us home . . ." then he realized it was too late. The needle- spear was in his hands, and he had to use it.

Suddenly, he thought of Julia, and what killing the Ragwitch meant for her. Paul realized he hadn't actually asked the Patchwork King what would happen.

"What about . . ." he started to say, but when he looked up, the Patchwork King was gone. There was only the old lady, waiting.

"Yes?" she said.

"Oh . . . nothing," replied Paul, looking around, his forehead creased in troubled thought. "I guess it'll be O.K. . . ."

He stood up, and walked around the table to Inyla. She put out her hand, and he took it unhesitatingly, not minding that it made him feel five years old again. Five years old and safe.

"How do we get back?" he asked.

"Just close your eyes," answered Inyla. "Just close your eyes . . . and sleep . . ."

24

THE LAST BATTLE

I t's getting worse," gasped Julia, as they came to a
break in the song, and the flame played its harp-
notes without them. She shivered as a fresh gust of
wind blew across, carrying with it tiny flakes of ice.

All around them, black volcanic glass slowly solidi-
fied into the crater-rim shape of the Terraces surrounding the Ragwitch's Spire. It too, was becoming real, a
dark silhouette looming up through the winter sleet. Despite all their efforts, they were being dragged back to
it—to one of Her most deadly memories: a gathering at
the Spire.

The Gwarulch were there already, still only whispers
of reality that couldn't quite be seen. But they were in-
exorably becoming solid, and the first hints of their awful howling had started to drift past the protective ring
of holly—joining with the sleet-carrying wind to penetrate their haven.

"Can you do anything?" Mirran asked Lyssa, as all

four instinctively drew closer together to gain a little heat from the waning flame.

"We can do what we always planned," replied Lyssa. "Move into Her central mind, and seize control of Her body. But that would only last a few moments, and utterly exhaust us . . . we must not waste the opportunity."

"We may not get any opportunity if we wait too long," said Mirran grimly. "Will the Gwarulch be able to breach the ring of holly?"

"When we are fully in that memory—yes," interrupted Anhyvar, indicating the windswept terraces around them. "But they'll see us well before then. They'll seem half-real to us, and we'll seem half-real to them."

"And half-real is enough to slay us," said Mirran. "I think you had better begin your spells, Anhyvar, Lyssa . . . we must hope we can do something in the few moments we can wrest control from Her."

"Yes," said Anhyvar, staring out beyond the sleet-shrouded Terraces. "There is little time for anyone, now. The battle at Alnwere goes badly. Her creatures have already taken the first two turnings on the road. There is only the top bend now, and after that, the stairway to the Pool, and the fallen stones. They will make their last stand at the top bend."

"I think you are right," sighed Lyssa. "But I wish we could hold out a little longer, for I fear we shall strike too soon."

"We must do as we must," said Anhyvar. "Julia, you and Mirran must keep singing . . . and deal with any Gwarulch that may break the ring. Lyssa and I will prepare the way to Her central mind, and we shall be helpless till that is done."

"What . . . what will happen then?" asked Julia.

"We will be in Her mind, as when you are called to Her. But this time, all four of us will be there, and we shall seize control of Her body—for however long we may."

"But what will we do?" asked Julia again. "I mean, what *can* we do?"

No one answered her, save the Gwarulch, whose ghostly howls faintly overlaid the harping of the flame, and the whining of the wind. Then Anhyvar said, "I do not know. Perhaps we can make Her jump from the hill . . . though that may do little. But we shall try . . ."

Julia looked up at the Witch, and saw the lines of her face set in grim determination, framed by her wildly blowing hair. That look was mirrored in Lyssa's face, and Mirran's too—and Julia realized that her own jaw was clamped, and her forehead wrinkled, just like the others. Whatever happened, they would try . . .

"Before we begin," Lyssa said quietly. "Let me give all of you the gift I promised: the chance of a true death, if we should fail."

She held out a clenched fist, and the others crowded around to stop the wind from blowing away whatever might be inside.

"Take one each," said Lyssa, opening her hand to reveal four shrunken white-green leaves. "Put them on the inside of your wrist."

She took one herself, and showed them how. The leaf stuck there for a moment, then slowly dissolved, leaving only a faint skeleton tracery of itself, etched into the skin, and a bitter, mint-like smell which filled the air.

Without hesitation, the others pressed the leaves to their wrists. It was like an ice-cube, thought Julia, and then like a fingertip tracing lines upon her skin.

"Now," said Lyssa, with the hint of a smile, "You are my blood-sisters . . . and brother. Even as She cannot absorb me, so She cannot absorb you."

"Thank you, my lady," said Mirran bowing deeply. "As one who was a prisoner in Her mind for many centuries, not even knowing who I was, I know the worth of this gift."

Anhyvar said nothing, but kissed Lyssa on both cheeks, and hugged her close. Julia started to say something, but the words choked in her mouth, so she kissed Lyssa too, and hugged her as tightly as she dared, wincing with the pain from her ribs.

"Now," cried Lyssa. "To the end of the Ragwitch!"

* * *

"Now," said Inyla. "Wake up!"

Paul awoke with a guilty start, as if he'd been caught sleeping in class. But he stood in the open, his hair buffeted by a strong wind, and the sun was harsh on his face. Inyla was at his side, and he saw that they were on top of a hill, standing in some sort of sunken pool dug into the top, the stones cracked and dry from the long absence of water.

Huge grey stones lay fallen all around—not unlike the Angarling, save for their color and stillness. Between them grew gnarled, bent-over trees, all leaning the same way as if blown by a great wind. Not very far away, Paul could hear the now-familiar sound of fighting—people fighting the Ragwitch's foul creatures.

"There isn't much time," said Inyla. She pointed at the beginnings of a path leading down from the hilltop. "Take the path, Paul . . . and run!"

As she spoke, she seemed to shrink and draw back from him, and her hand slipped from his grasp. Paul reached for her, but she pointed away, and her body shrank and disappeared into one of the bent-over trees. Still, he heard her voice shivering in the air, "Run!"

Paul only hesitated for a second, then holding the needle-spear above him, he leapt up out of the pool and onto the path. In another second, he was out past the stones and trees, and running, running down the twisting path, towards the sounds of battle.

He saw that down below, the path joined a road cut into the hillside, a broad road, easily wide enough for three or four cars. It went down at an easy slope for several hundred meters, then cut back on itself, forming a hairpin bend, going another few hundred meters before turning back on itself again and zig-zagging down the hill.

There were three such bends, Paul saw, before the road finally leveled out into the valley beyond—and all the fighting was at the third, and topmost bend. A wall of pikemen held back a shrieking mass of Gwarulch and Glazed-Folk—a thin human wall against a seemingly endless column of Her creatures winding up the road. But they seemed to be stopping them, and Paul realized that the road was cut away in front of the pike-wall, leaving a gap too wide for the crushing Angarling to cross. But the Gwarulch and Glazed-Folk would soon fill it with their dead, and then the pike-wall would be forced back by sheer weight of numbers—and the unstoppable Angarling.

Higher up the road, there were more human soldiers, waiting their turn in line, or helping the wounded back from the front. Archers watched the skies, but they fired few arrows, and Paul realized they must have almost run out, for the Meepers were flying closer and closer, without their normal fear.

Then he saw the Ragwitch, looming up out of the massed ranks of Her creatures, a good hundred meters behind the fighting, with a ring of Angarling close around Her. As Paul watched, an arrow sped towards Her, only to falter in midair, and twist into the hillside.

It was an unlucky arrow, for it narrowly missed a Meeper, who pulled up to avoid being shot. Even at a distance, Paul saw that its sudden climb would make it look straight up at him. A second later, he knew it had, for it beat its great wings in sudden energy, and came straight up at him. A boy alone was the sort of target Meepers liked.

Paul stopped looking, and started to run in earnest, keeping the needle-spear at the ready, alert for a shadow leaping across him from below. But the path suddenly turned into steps, and Paul came to them too quickly and almost fell. As he recovered, sharp claws whisked over his head, and a Meeper careened into the hillside. Before it could recover, a startled soldier leapt up from the steps and drove his sword into its leathery neck. It gurgled, tried to snap at him, then fell further down the hill.

The soldier almost fell too, but Paul grabbed him, carefully avoiding the blood-soaked bandage around his thigh.

"Where did you come from?" gasped the soldier, as he dragged himself back upright again, grimacing at the pain in his leg.

"The top," said Paul, pointing as he dashed past. "I have to find Aleyne."

"Who?" shouted the soldier after him, but Paul didn't pause. There were other wounded on the steps, and he was busy avoiding them, and their startled cries and questions.

At the bottom, there were just too many wounded lying around for him to run, and as he slowed, Paul saw that there was a wide cavern under the steps, and there were the healers and surgeons trying to save the wounded as they had at Reddow Cairn. Archers stood guard at the entrance, one firing at a Meeper as it swung too close.

And there was Quigin, leading Hathin up the road, with an injured soldier across the donkey's back. He was holding a bandage to the soldier's side, his sandy head bent as the donkey picked its own way through the rows of wounded soldiers lying on the road.

"Quigin!" exclaimed Paul, leaping over to him. "You're alive!"

"Of course I'm alive!" exclaimed Quigin, but his smile lacked its usual unconcern. "You're the one who was hit on the head! It's lucky you're up—you can help me . . ."

"No . . . no, I can't," said Paul hastily. He held up the needle-spear so its strange patterns glittered and swirled in the sun. "I can't explain now—but I can . . . I can stop the Ragwitch . . . but first I have to find Aleyne."

"He's somewhere down there," replied Quigin. "I saw him with the King, just before we retreated from the Second Bend. Leasel can find him . . . Leasel!"

Both boys looked around, then Paul felt a head butt at his leg, and Leasel was there, her nose twitching. She looked up at Paul, then turned around and started down the road at an easy lope.

"Where is she . . ." Quigin started to say, but Paul was already following her, and the wounded man was slipping from the donkey. Quigin hastened to help him, instantly forgetting everything else.

Paul ran for a hundred meters or so, then slowed again, as Leasel wound her way through the ranks of silent, grim-faced soldiers—men and women who knew this was the last battle of the Kingdom, and that they had already lost . . . all they could hope for would be to take some of Her creatures with them, and to die a true death.

Here and there were soldiers who had marched with Paul from Caer Follyn, and he grabbed them as he passed, and asked for Aleyne, but ran on after Leasel before they could answer. In any case, they shouted after him, and it was always "further down!"—further down, towards the fighting.

Then Paul ducked under a pikeman's arm, and out to
where the road started its bend down and around, to the
pike-wall and the swirling melee. He'd thought the
noise of battle at Reddow Cairn had been terrifying, but
here, closer still, all the clashes and shouts and howls
and screams shook him from his knees up through his
stomach.

But there, under the firmly planted standard waving
golden in the sun, was Aleyne—Aleyne shouting, pointing pikemen in to plug a gap, as the wounded spilled
out from the swirling mass.

Paul rushed to him, and grabbed his arm. For a second Aleyne stared at him, as if he didn't recognize him,
or just couldn't see, then he knelt at his side.

"Paul," he shouted, close to his ear. "What are you
doing here? There's still a chance you can escape . . ."

Paul shook his head, and held up the needle-spear. "I
found out what the Elementals' gifts were for. This can
kill the Ragwitch."

Aleyne stared again, and Paul saw the tremendous
weariness in his eyes. At the same time, he felt the
strength in him, and he held out the needle-spear.

"Take it," he said, suddenly sure that Aleyne would
use it better than he ever could. He didn't really feel
strong enough to stick it in anyone, let alone the
Ragwitch . . .

Gingerly, Aleyne reached out a gauntleted hand, but
even as he touched it, the patterns swirled, and he recoiled, cursing.

"The thing's red-hot! Where did you . . ."

"The Patchwork King gave it to me," said Paul. "I
guess I have to use it. I don't suppose anyone else
can . . ."

"What is this?" asked another voice, and Paul looked
up to see an older man, with a rounded, almost chubby
face, and eyes that might have twinkled in better times.

But he had an air of command about him, and Paul didn't need to see the crown around his helmet to know he was the King.

"This is the boy, sire ... Paul," said Aleyne slowly, as if he were waking from a dream. "He says he can slay the Ragwitch!"

"I fear that is just a fancy, Aleyne," said the King, with a sad smile. "You saw what happened to Sir Harent when he closed."

"The Patchwork King gave me ..." Paul started to say, but a great howling roar from the Gwarulch drowned him out, as the pike-wall buckled and broke, to the booming shouts of the Angarling. The ditch was finally full, and the Stone Knights were attacking.

Hands grabbed at the King, and Paul saw him almost dragged back, soldiers pouring in to form a second wall in front of him. But Aleyne kept a firm grip on Paul.

"Here—put this on," he yelled, picking up a helmet from the ground and handing it to Paul. Then he waved his poleaxe in the air, and Paul saw it was Sir Rellen's, as Aleyne shouted, "To me, Donbreye! To me!"

Paul crouched at Aleyne's side, and tried to lace his helmet one-handed, not wanting to let go of the needle-spear. He fumbled for the laces, then felt gloved hands helping him, and Oel was suddenly kneeling next to him. She smiled, and drew the laces tight under his chin. Then a pair of familiar narrow legs came into sight, and Deamus was there too, dropping an enormous leather jerkin over Paul's head, and pulling it past his helmet. He smiled too, and said something, but it was lost in the roar and clash of fighting.

Then Aleyne was helping him up, and Paul saw that they were a little to one side of the melee, in the center of a tight knot of Donbreye villagers and Borderors. Just then something wet touched the back of his hand, and he flinched, and looked down—but it was only a friendly lick from one of Cagael's dogs, bulky in its armor of studded leather. Cagael was there too, over on the left, with Ethric and the other dogs—and even Quigin, who had just run up. There was no sign of Leasel or Hathin, and Paul hoped they'd had the sense to stay further back.

Paul looked at everyone around him, in the brief second before they joined battle themselves, and felt that it was like a painting he knew very well, with every small fragment of light and color captured forever in his mind.

And there was the enemy, less than fifty meters away. The ring of Angarling, slowly lumbering forward, crushing everything in their path—and in the center of the ring . . . was the Ragwitch.

Paul looked at Her, and felt the fear rising up from his stomach to choke him. Then he thought of Julia, and the Kingdom, and all the dead and wounded, the villages lost . . . and he held the needle-spear aloft, and pointed.

Thunder clapped, and flames burst out of the hillside above the Ragwitch, spreading quickly in the dry grass, white smoke boiling into the sky like the thickest fog. The ground shook . . . once . . . twice . . . and long sections of the road gave way, tumbling Gwarulch to their ruin down the mountainside, and trapping the Angarling deep in holes. Earth and Fire had come to Paul's aid.

Even as the Gwarulch howled, the Angarling boomed and the Meepers screamed above the smoke, Paul pushed forward, and Aleyne with him, both of them shouting, "Charge!"

* * *

"Four runes of anc . . ." Julia sang, and then, "Look out!" as a Gwarulch suddenly loomed out of the darkness, talons ripping across towards Mirran, who met it with a wide sweep of his golden sword, lopping off its head in a flurry of golden sparks.

"They're more than half-real now," said Mirran. "We'll have to stop singing, and . . ."

He stabbed out into the darkness, and a leaping Gwarulch impaled itself on his sword, falling to the turf to be totally consumed in sheets of golden flame.

Julia drew closer to Lyssa and Anhyvar, who stood motionless, eyes closed, next to the flame. Neither had spoken or moved for at least ten minutes, but occasionally they swayed, and their frowns of concentration deepened.

Julia looked at them anxiously, then out into the darkness. The Spire and the Terraces were very solid now, and the wind that howled through was very cold. The Gwarulch could see them now, Julia knew, from the glint of their piggy eyes reflected in the moonlight. All of them were looking in the direction of the flame, and there was a constant stream of new arrivals from the outer Terraces.

"How long will they be?" asked Julia, nodding towards Lyssa and Anhyvar. She knew Mirran wouldn't know, but she had to say something to ease the awful tension inside her.

"I don't know," he answered, smiling confidently back at her. "Not long . . . not long . . ."

Julia tried to smile confidently too, breaking off into a scowl of effort as she thrust her spear at a Gwarulch that sprang towards her. The point razed across its chest, and the creature recoiled, wailing. But Julia shivered as she realized the Gwarulch had touched the turf, and it had hardly flamed at all, and there had been no sparks from her spear. Worse, the moonlight seemed to be getting stronger, and the light within the holly-ring was now only faintly golden.

"How long . . .?" she whispered to herself again, as more and more Gwarulch descended the Terraces, to add more and more staring eyes.

* * *

"Go Paul!" shouted Aleyne as his poleaxe bit through the neck of the huge Gwarulch that had leapt at the boy, and he moved to meet the black-wrapped thing that had pranced behind it, brandishing a jeweled sword. The poleaxe was slow to come free, and he only just managed to parry the creature's first blow, and didn't look across to see if Paul had got through.

Paul had—moving through the gap in the battle-line in a frenzied rush, past the two battling figures, further into the smoke. He was alone now. Everyone else had fallen, or was locked in combat somewhere back along those awful fifty meters. Now there was only the Ragwitch ahead, and the Angarling, sunk to their mighty chests in earth. Paul skirted them, coughing and half-sobbing, and they boomed and shook, but could not get free.

She was waiting in the very center of the sunken ring of stones, a tall ghastly form, shrouded in the smoke. Paul slowed as he saw Her, and lifted the needle-spear, thankful that he couldn't see Her eyes.

She saw him, and hissed, a long, drawn-out hiss of hatred, somehow louder than the noise of battle around them. Her arm rose from Her side, and a black whip of thick and ropy smoke uncoiled from Her three-fingered hand.

"So," She spat. "Paul!"

* * *

The Gwarulch had stopped leaping in, at least for the moment. Mirran was too quick with his sword, as was Julia with her spear of jagged lightning. Now they just circled the ring, snarling, occasionally touching the turf before recoiling in pain.

But the flames grew weaker and weaker, and Mirran's sword no longer sparked, and had lost much of its golden sheen—and the Gwarulch tightened their ring, even daring to step past the braided holly, and onto the outer turf.

Julia stared back at them defiantly, but her hands began to shake as she met their red stare, and saw the glint of their teeth and talons . . . and Lyssa and Anhyvar still weren't moving.

Then, without warning, the flame went out.

Julia screamed, Lyssa and Anhyvar's eyes flashed open, and the Gwarulch sprang, howling, talons and fangs seeking flesh to rend . . . but finding only an empty ring of wilted holly and dying, blackened turf.

* * *

The whip cracked out, and Paul leapt aside, forgetting he could have used the needle-spear to block it. The Ragwitch lumbered forward, still hissing, and now Paul could see Her eyes, black-pupilled and glistening with hatred. She gnashed her shark-teeth and advanced again, and he sprang back, almost tripping on the uneven surface of the road, all broken by the earthquake.

Quicker than he would have thought possible, the Ragwitch's puffy arms brought the lash around again to strike him. Paul parried with the needle-spear, and the lash burst into a stream of water that spilled harmlessly on his chest—and the Ragwitch reared back, staring at Her hand.

Paul gulped, trying to get a breath free from smoke, and found a place on the road with better footing. The Ragwitch backed away too, but Paul didn't try to attack.

"So," hissed the Ragwitch. "You have found some

small Magic . . . something of the earthy sort . . . but it cannot help you, Paul . . . it cannot help you . . ."

Paul shook his head angrily, as if the words were somehow attaching themselves to him, and advanced upon Her again, raising the needle-spear. She laughed, a vicious, rasping laugh, but She moved back—and suddenly, with exhilaration, Paul knew She was afraid.

"Boy," She said, as he edged closer, "I can give you back your sister. Send you back to your world . . . with rewards . . ."

Paul ignored Her, leapt forward, and stabbed. But She surprised him again, jumping away, Her bloated legs leaking straw that fell slowly to the ground. As he turned to stab Her again, one fat three-fingered hand swung around, smashing into his shoulder, sending him sprawling to the ground, the needle-spear rolling away to clank against a rock.

Paul rolled after it, as She stamped with her foot, missing him by centimeters. His hands scrabbled among the dirt clods, and suddenly, the needle-spear was in his hands again, and he swung it around, the point grazing the Ragwitch's arm as She bent to grab him.

She screamed, the high-pitched scream of a car shrieking to a stop, and scuttled back without straightening up, like some ghastly cloth spider. Where the needle-spear had touched, the threads frayed, and straw spilled out of a gaping hole.

Paul got up, and advanced with the needle-spear tucked under his arm like a knight holding a lance. Tears streamed down his face, from smoke and fear and pain, but he blinked them away, and, keeping his gaze on the Ragwitch, slowly advanced.

Then the Ragwitch spoke again, and Her voice was the voice of Julia.

"Slay me," She said, "And your sister . . . your Julia . . . dies with me."

* * *

Julia felt the Ragwitch's cumbersome body first, then the dulled senses . . . and then the pain. It was a feeling so alien to that leathery body that she was disoriented, and found it hard to see or hear. But the Ragwitch's body was all too familiar to her, and soon she was seeing from the greenstone eyes, and listening through the muffled ears.

The others were with her too, she knew. Julia could feel them, feel their separate identities, as though they were all holding hands in the dark. She felt strength flowing between the four of them, building, as they waited their chance.

Then Julia saw Paul, small and pale before the Ragwitch, holding a spear with grim determination, despite the tears streaming down his face. Her heart stammered in fear, and then in hope, as she felt that the Ragwitch was afraid, that this was no ordinary spear, it was something—the impossible something—that could kill Her.

But Paul just stood there, and Julia strained to shout to him, strained to make him use the spear.

Then the Ragwitch spoke, softly, using Julia's voice.

"You can't hurt Me, Paul. Not without hurting your sister. You want Julia to live, don't you Paul? I will give her back to you . . . just throw down your spear . . ."

Slowly, She advanced upon him, and still Paul didn't move. Julia saw the indecision in his eyes.

"Throw it away . . ." hissed the Ragwitch, Her voice breaking out of Julia's and back to Her own. "Throw it away, or your sister dies!"

Paul shuddered, and he lowered the spear a fraction—and in that small gesture, Julia realized that he might not use it, and as she realized it, so did Anhyvar, Lyssa and Mirran.

"Now!" they thought, and all four struck at the Ragwitch's central mind, and She became aware of them . . . a little too late.

Julia suddenly felt something snap, like the elastic in a skirt, and then she was in control of Her body, like she'd just stepped into it from outside. She felt the others around her, like a wall, and beyond them, the Ragwitch, a furious wave of darkness drawing back like the sea, preparing to sweep all before Her. She knew they would only have seconds before it struck.

Without even thinking, Julia rushed forward, raising her arms to pull Paul into her embrace, to hug him . . . and the needle-spear slid effortlessly into the Ragwitch's chest, at the very instant that She broke the four prisoners' will and resumed control of Her body.

* * *

Paul screamed as the needle-spear left his hands, and he fell from the grasp of the Ragwitch. She loomed above him, mouth gaping, and tried to pull the needle-spear out, but Her body started to split along every seam, and straw blew out into the wind, small splinters of greenish yellow, sparkling in the smoke.

Slowly She knelt on the ground, and the crumpled, empty cloth blurred into flesh, and became a woman with long red hair, who hissed and scratched at the needle-spear transfixing her. Then her features blurred, and flickered through several forms: a man's, grim and strong, but smiling in triumph, and then Julia's, her eyes closed as if in restful sleep. Finally, it was the red-haired woman again, but her hands were curled around the needle-spear in acceptance, and her face was calm and kind.

"The vision was true," whispered Anhyvar, and then she smiled at Paul, as if in happy recognition of a friend.

Her eyes closed, and the needle-spear shimmered, the patterns solidifying into four different bands. One, of water, poured away; one, of air, shrieked to the sky like a bird; the fire blazed a trail across to the burning grass; and the earth crumbled onto Anhyvar's body. Body and earth sank into the ground, and there was nothing left, save the silent stones and the fire.

High on the hill above, an ancient rowan cracked, and Paul looked up to see it slowly falling, white flowers tumbling through the air like snowflakes, and the air was briefly filled with the sound of a jangling harp.

Then all was still, save for the sound of fleeing Gwarulch, people shouting, and Aleyne calling, calling Paul's name.

Paul sat and shivered, till a hand touched him on the shoulder, and he looked up to see the Patchwork King, his cracker-crown rustling on his head.

"Come on, Paul," he said. "Time to go home."

EPILOGUE

Paul held the Patchwork King's hand as they walked back through the battlefield, pausing only to dump his helmet. Aleyne was still calling, but he stopped when he saw Paul appear out of the smoke, with the old man at his side.

"She's dead," said Paul. "The Patchwork King is taking me home."

Aleyne nodded, as if this were all quite usual, and laying his poleaxe on the ground, took Paul's other hand.

A little further on, they saw Deamus and Oel, sitting among a group of wounded. Deamus was bandaging Oel's arm, and she had her eyes closed, and mouth set tight against the pain. Deamus looked up at Paul, and said, "There will be a Donbreye again after all . . ."

He touched Paul on the shoulder, and then turned back to his wife. Paul walked on, still in a daze, through a line of exhausted soldiers, who had just slumped where they'd fought, too tired to move. Beyond them, Quigin knelt amidst dead Gwarulch, and Paul saw that Ethric the boar lay dead, and one of the marmot-hunting dogs—and between them lay Cagael the Friend of Beasts.

Quigin looked up as they passed, and Leasel too, from where she sat at his side. He tried to smile, but even he couldn't, and Paul saw that he had been crying.

"If I hadn't found you, Paul," he muttered, "that day in the balloon, this . . . everything . . . would have been for nothing . . ."

"Yes, I guess so . . ." whispered Paul. "I'm going home now, Quigin, but I'll never forget you—or Leasel . . ."

He bent down, and Leasel touched his face with her nose, dark eyes peering into his, lending him some of her serenity.

"I'll never forget you either," said Quigin, hugging him. "Or any of it . . . the Wind Moot, under the sea . . . even today . . ."

Paul hugged him back, then took the Patchwork King's hand again, and Aleyne's, and they walked up the road, past the wounded and exhausted soldiers, and those tending them, past the King and his knights, who bowed as they passed—though to whom, Paul wasn't sure.

Finally, they came to the path to the sunken pool, and the Patchwork King stopped, and looked at Aleyne.

"This is where I leave you, I think, Paul," said Aleyne. "We have come a long way from Awgaer."

"Awgaer," said Paul. "I can say it now . . . I don't know why."

"Perhaps because you've saved it," said Aleyne, quietly. "Goodbye, Paul."

Paul nodded, and hugged Aleyne, his hands barely meeting around the buff coat and cuirass. Aleyne clapped him on the back, and then turned away to go back down to his people.

The Patchwork King started up the steps, and Paul followed blindly. Sick at heart, and weary in both mind and body, he just trudged along, head down, hardly noticing the way. It wasn't until they'd stopped climbing that he noticed they weren't on top of the hill—they were somewhere else.

"Hey!" he said, looking up to see the wide expanse of the sea and the grey spit; and down, to see the broken shells and red earth of the midden under his feet. He felt different too, and realized his clothes had somehow changed back to T-shirt and shorts, his boots to sneakers. And the Patchwork King was gone.

* * *

The picnic basket still needed another catch, Julia saw, and one of the handles looked a bit broken—the side Mirran was carrying.

Then she saw a rock pool, full of small fish, forgot about the picnic basket, and sat down to look. The others kept going up the beach, but fairly slowly. Julia was sure she could catch them up, particularly since Anhyvar and Mirran had the basket to carry, and Lyssa the big silver bottle.

Besides the fish, there was a beautiful shell just sitting on the edge of the pool. Julia picked it up and put it to her ear, and was surprised to hear the whisper of harp strings and muffled drums instead of the roar of the sea.

She turned to race after Lyssa and show her, but the others were already out of sight. Instead, there was an old man in a robe of shifting stars and light, with a paper crown rustling on his head. He smiled, and held out his hand.

* * *

"I'm home . . ." Paul whispered to himself, crouching down to curl up into a tight little ball. "The Ragwitch defeated, the King saved . . . and Julia lost."

Then he felt a touch on his arm, lighter than the Patchwork King's—a familiar touch, followed by a familiar pinch. He leapt to his feet, and there was Julia, looking exactly as normal, except for a mark on her wrist.

"You're safe!" cried Paul happily, throwing his arms around her, and then, in pure brotherly love, punching her on the arm.

"Yes," said Julia. "Thanks to you . . . and Lyssa, and Anhyvar, and Mirran."

"Who?" asked Paul.

"People who helped me," said Julia, sitting down to gaze out at the sea.

"I'm glad there was someone," said Paul, quietly. "I had lots of people to help me. Aleyne and Tanboule, Quigin and Leasel, Deamus, Oel and Sevaun . . . Cagael . . . the Elementals . . ."

"You must have lots to tell," said Julia. "I certainly do. I wonder if we'll remember?"

"If you want to," interrupted the Patchwork King, who seemed to have been there all the time, though Paul knew he hadn't. "I can make you forget, if you wish."

Paul looked at Julia, and both of them thought back over the past few weeks.

"I think I'd like to remember," said Julia slowly, still staring out into the ocean, remembering another sea, and another midden.

"So would I," said Paul, thinking of what he'd said to Quigin.

"As you wish," said the Patchwork King. "You'll forget the worst anyway, and I shall take it from your dreams. Goodbye."

With that, he was gone, and a wind from the sea sprang up, cold against the children's faces. Something fluttered down in the breeze, and caught in Julia's hair. Paul pulled it out, and gave it to her, noticing that the Fire Queen's brand on his palm pulsed twice as he touched it.

"A rowan leaf," said Julia. She smiled, and put it in her top pocket, making sure it wouldn't blow away.

"Come on," said Paul. "I'll race you home."

"No," replied Julia. "Let's just walk. There's plenty of time."